STORM BREAKER

Nisha J. Tuli is a *USA Today* and international bestselling romance author who loves writing slow burns and plenty of yearning.

When she isn't writing or reading, she can be found in the gym or the kitchen (to eat, not to cook) or maybe knitting scarves to survive a Canadian winter. She lives in Manitoba with her husband, their two kids and their fluffy Samoyed.

STORM BREAKER

NISHA J. TULI

MAYHEM
+BOOKS+

PENGUIN MICHAEL JOSEPH

UK | USA | Canada | Ireland | Australia
India | New Zealand | South Africa

Penguin Michael Joseph is part of the Penguin Random House group of companies
whose addresses can be found at global.penguinrandomhouse.com

Penguin Random House UK,
One Embassy Gardens, 8 Viaduct Gardens, London SW11 7BW

penguin.co.uk

Published by Penguin Michael Joseph, part of the Penguin Random House
group of companies, in association with Mayhem Books,
part of Entangled Publishing LLC 2026

001

Edited by Liz Pelletier
Map design by LJ Anderson
Interior organizational chart design and original illustration by Liz Wayant
Interior design by Folio Book Production LLC

Printed and bound in Great Britain by Clays Ltd, Elcograf S.p.A.

The authorized representative in the EEA is Penguin Random House Ireland,
Morrison Chambers, 32 Nassau Street, Dublin D02 YH68

A CIP catalogue record for this book is available from the British Library

HARDBACK ISBN: 978–1–911–75308–7
TRADE PAPERBACK ISBN: 978–1–911–75309–4

Penguin Random House is committed to a sustainable future
for our business, our readers and our planet. This book is made from
Forest Stewardship Council® certified paper

*To everyone who hides in shadows but lives with a spark
burning in their chest bright enough to burn down the world*

Storm Breaker is a pulse-pounding dystopian novel set in a glittering, storm-wrecked Manhattan where the elite rule through legacy—and one forbidden romance could tear it apart. It includes elements regarding death, electrocution, physical and mental abuse, parental abuse, addiction, graphic language, physical violence, hand-to-hand combat, blood, alcohol, trampling via crowd, accidental death, death by falling, parental abandonment, classism, sexism, and sexual situations that are shown on the page. Discussions of murder are also present. Readers who may be sensitive to these elements, please take note, and prepare to enter Amery Academy . . .

THE SOCIETY OF THE SHIELD

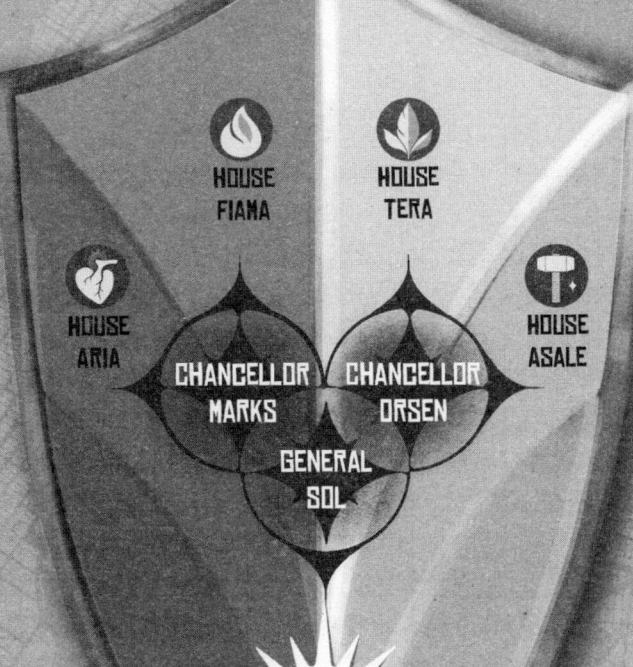

HOUSE FIANA

HOUSE TERA

HOUSE ARIA

HOUSE ASALE

CHANCELLOR MARKS

CHANCELLOR ORSEN

GENERAL SOL

STORM GUARD

TEMPESTADE

Protect

Preserve

Prosper

A Note from The Shield

The Shield proudly welcomes the Class of 3067 to Amery Academy.

Over the next three years, you will be tested—not only for aptitude but for your loyalty, discipline, and resolve. The choices you make at Amery will shape your place within Society and help determine the future stability of New Manhattan.

Whether you pledge to your family's House or earn the right to enter another, know this: each House exists for a reason, and balance depends on those who understand their role within it.

Only the capable will advance. Only the committed will endure.

Protect. Preserve. Prosper.

— The Shield

1

My fiancé smells like feet.

Knox slings an arm around my neck and yanks me closer, causing me to trip. My hands slam into his chest to stop myself from falling, and I inhale another whiff of that sour smell.

I recognize it as the distinct residue of the boiled cabbage stew served in the tunnel markets running below the streets of New Manhattan. He must've paid a visit to the underground today. A shower would have been nice.

Knox doesn't notice my stumble as he lifts his glass and bellows, "To our last night of freedom!"

He's met with a resounding chorus of cheers before he tips his head back and takes a long pull of his drink.

With the wind howling outside, we stand fifty stories up, inside a sprawling apartment owned by Knox's father, Trey Arden. The massive living room is lined with reinforced floor-to-ceiling windows and filled with creamy, ornate furniture and golden tables.

His mother permits only clear liquids, lest anything get stained. I'll never forget the party Knox threw in ninth grade when someone had the bright idea of smuggling in a pilfered bottle of red-tinted cinnamon gin to pass around. The lid hadn't been properly secured and . . . well, I don't think I've ever heard Mrs. Arden scream that loud.

The remnants of that day have long since been cleared away, leaving off-white, brocade-silk-covered walls and crystal chandeliers dangling overhead, casting us in a soft yellow glow.

All the Fiama Society kids from our year are here, dressed in their most sparkling club attire, including short skirts and slashed shirts, showing off taut young bodies and miles of skin. High school is over, and we're headed to university, ready to embark on the next chapter of our lives when we report to Amery Academy first thing tomorrow.

I've been anticipating this day for a very long time.

I watch my best friend, Trinity, across the room take a long gulp of her drink and toss her arms around her boyfriend's neck before they go in for a sloppy kiss. They make out furiously, their bodies pressed together, fueled by the heated charge in the air and a little liquid encouragement.

My chest tightens. I'm not jealous. I'm thrilled Trin found someone who loves her the way Edward does. I want the world for her.

But as Bethany Fawkes sidles over, pressing herself to Knox's other side, my gaze returns to Trinity and Edward, and I can't help but want what they have, too.

Knox's arm tightens around me before he thrusts his cup in my face. "Have a sip, Poet."

I nearly gag on the potent fumes of moonshine brewed by the Hollows, New Manhattan's underground citizens. It's cheap as dirt and packs several punches. No thank you. My preferred poison doesn't taste vaguely of paint thinner.

I knock his hand away as he leans in and presses his open mouth against my temple, almost like he's eating my hair. His hot, stale breath sends a shiver creeping over my scalp. And not in the good way. Those days are long over.

"Stop," I bite out as I attempt to shove out of his headlock.

Knox Arden. New Manhattan's resident fuckboy. My betrothed.

Definitely not by choice.

Finally, I manage to extricate myself from his grasp, sacrificing the band around my ponytail. He's handsome by all measures of the word. High cheekbones. A strong jaw. Tall with a narrow but stacked frame and platinum hair streaked with bright shocks of lilac.

His sleeveless white shirt clings to his chest, and his fair skin is slightly flushed. His black leather boots are heavily scuffed, no doubt purchased from a scavenger. New clothes are easy enough for families like ours to access, but there's a certain cachet in "slumming it" with a rare and expensive scavenger treasure.

"Poet," he whines as I fix my ponytail. Then I spin on my heel to walk away, shoulders set and head high. "Poet, come back! You're being weird."

Weird.

He isn't wrong.

Any time a storm is brewing, I'm definitely weird.

"Ew," Trinity says, catching me as I pass and looping an arm through mine. "I can't believe Bethany's rubbing herself all over him like that. Everyone knows you're getting married after we graduate." She lowers her voice. "Even if you don't want to, *she* doesn't know that."

Her words claw through my chest as we look back at Knox. Bethany is now wrapped around him, his hand creeping up her bare thigh, his mouth pressed to the curve of her offered jaw. Three other girls already surround him, draping themselves like languid pieces of silk. As though his very presence makes their arms and knees go limp.

I try not to blame them. In our House, proximity to the right man means security, and that can be worth everything.

"Want me to kick her ass?" Trinity asks, her freckled white cheeks flushing with anger on my behalf. She's petite and half a head shorter than my average height, but only because she's "towering" in heels. She wears a fitted white dress that clings to her curves and a necklace of sparkling amethyst. Bangs fall over her eyes, and her hair is highlighted with a deep streak of purple, contrasting with her fiery orange locks.

It's the height of Society fashion to dye one's hair with a touch of purple in various hues. General Nyxia Sol started the trend with her midnight-black hair, streaked with a single shock of bright purple down one side. It's also the same shade of the cloud bursts that signal an Empire Storm, named after the color of royalty from the old world.

My own hair is a purple so deep it's nearly black and peppered with brighter streaks of amethyst.

Only mine is natural, a secret I keep to myself.

"Nah," I say, focusing on Knox and his groupies. "He invites it. If anyone needs an ass-kicking, it's *him.*"

"But—"

I raise my hand. "I don't care. Let her have him."

A snort behind me draws our attention to queen-bitches Winter Jenkins and Lacey Turner, both wearing acidic sneers.

"Poor little Poet," Winter says, twirling a lock of her long chestnut hair. "She just *can't* keep the attention of her man."

She thrusts out her lower lip as Lacey dissolves into giggles.

"Don't worry," Winter adds with a wink. "After you're married, I'll see that he's always satisfied."

"Sounds about right," I counter. "The only way to get *someone* to fill that dusty, dried-out hole is to fuck another woman's husband."

Trinity snorts so loud I'm surprised she doesn't blow a nostril. She slaps a hand over her face, trying to contain her laugh. It doesn't work.

Winter's mouth drops open, and Lacey's eyes go wide.

"How dare you!" Winter hisses.

"Get out of my face," I hiss back.

Winter's gaze narrows on mine, but I know from experience that she doesn't have the guts to make a move.

She straightens, huffs, and then takes my suggestion, trying to look dignified as she walks away. Trinity latches onto my arm, gasping for breath. I don't think she notices how hard I'm trembling.

"*Skies*, Poet," she wheezes. "I can't believe you just said that."

I smooth down the front of my sparkly black crop top, trying to conceal my shaking hands. I lift one corner of my mouth in a smile that feels like a grimace. "That actually felt pretty good."

"You're so badass," Trinity says as our attention once again drifts to Knox. Winter and Lacey have now found their way over to him, scattering my short-lived flare of satisfaction.

Edward appears behind Trinity, bearing a fresh drink, and notices the direction of our stares. His straight black hair falls over a pair of dark-brown, angled eyes. He gives me a sympathetic look.

"You deserve better than that," he says so sincerely that my throat tightens.

I roll my shoulders, trying to shake off the fog of Knox's ever-present shadow. "Well, he's what I'm stuck with."

My father is the scion of House Fiama, but leadership is tenuous thanks to infighting between our most powerful families. When Knox and I were born, he formed an alliance with Knox's father to help strengthen his bid for power. It paved the path to his current reign, and thus, our marriage has been a foregone conclusion ever since.

I've made peace with it as much as I can. This is my duty to my city. As members of Society, our union is also part of the greater plan to keep us all safe, fed, and protected from both the threats that surround us and the mistakes of the past.

At least I'll have three years at the academy before I need to face it.

A flash of light catches my eye. I glance out the window as the wind gusts with a powerful blast, tilting the floor beneath us ever so slightly. My palms start to itch, and I scratch them absently.

New Manhattan boasts dozens of Society-owned apartment towers that stretch into the clouds and are prone to swaying in the high winds, but no one bats an eye.

We're used to this.

Another flash, and the sky lights up with a shocking flare of ultraviolet light.

I swallow a gasp as the clouds tumble and roll, swelling in great puffs of lilac and indigo, flashing with hot spots. Soon they'll explode in pulses of galvanic force known as Spark, jagged streaks of energy that spread in every direction, sometimes shattering our protective barriers and killing anyone they touch.

An Empire Storm is coming, and it's coming fast.

As the wind picks up, I shiver.

I can *feel* the storms.

We have two less-common types: Emerald Storms that bring torrential downpours and Blood Storms, which rain down deadly fire.

But Empire Storms pose a constant threat, always on the verge of striking.

My temperature is already climbing, and I continue to scratch my hands and my arms. My exhales turn short as I carefully regulate my shallow breaths.

It feels like I'm coming undone. Like my skin is too tight and starting to split.

This is my curse. A burden. A test of my sanity.

And yet I crave it, too.

I know I shouldn't. I know it makes me a monster.

But it's an addiction waiting to destroy me.

My breaths come faster and sharper, my pulse pounding as the storm outside screams in my ears. Everyone else in the room continues chatting and drinking, unconcerned.

I'm almost positive I'm the only one here affected this way.

When the amethyst clouds start to roll, everyone runs for cover, seeking the relative safety of their homes. Our only true protection is General Nyxia Sol and her army of Storm Breakers, who do their best to shield the city.

But even their methods are fallible, and the storms are often unpredictable.

CRASH.

A window smashes, and everyone screams as we're plunged into the luminescent glow of neon light. A small plasma arc ricochets from the floor, forming a dome, transparent like a soap bubble and filled with jagged sparks of pulsing energy.

It lasts for only a second before it winks out.

Wind gusts into the room, tossing napkins and tugging at hair and clothing. People jump up, drinks spilling as they search for cover, trying to escape a hailstorm of glass, sharp stones, and bits of debris.

I'm shoved to the side with Trinity's arm still linked to mine. We slam into a wall, my elbow connecting with a sharp *crack* that radiates into my shoulder. As we're pushed left and right, I instinctively search for Knox. How close was he standing to the window?

A moment later, I spy him at the far end of the room, brushing splinters off his shirt and shaking out his hair.

My stomach twitches with a conflicted dip because I don't understand how I feel. I don't want to marry him, but I also wouldn't want him to die this way.

I think.

It takes me a moment to register the screams.

Someone else wasn't so lucky.

Through a wall of shifting bodies, I spot someone lying on the floor, their skin charred to a black husk. Smoke curls off them in small puffs of white.

Someone won't be starting at Amery Academy tomorrow.

My stomach turning, I huff out a shaky breath as the clouds flash with more swelling points of light.

If I don't hurry, I might miss it.

The room descends into chaos as people simultaneously try to squeeze closer to the body and also move away. I push through the crowd, sliding between the spaces until I find myself at the door.

I look back. I shouldn't be leaving at a time like this, but someone will deal with it. We have sweepers for these types of incidents, and too many people are already in the way.

After quietly slipping out, I pound up several floors and toss open the door to my parents' penthouse, only to find it empty. They must have gone out to one of their favorite swanky restaurants with their friends. At least I don't have to explain why I'm home already.

I head for my bedroom, still decorated like it was when I was ten years old, with frilly white sheets and pillows and a ruffled canopy. At least I donated the stuffed animals, though I kept my favorite brown bear, Teddy, to sit on my dresser to watch over me.

I just turned nineteen, but he makes me feel safe.

I lock the door behind me and kick off my shoes before tiptoeing carefully across the plush white carpet. Even in my own home, I try never to take up too much space.

Clinging to the window frame, I focus my gaze on the distant spot where I know General Sol will be waiting.

The wind howls, shaking the foundations. I spot a figure scurrying across the plaza far below and press a hand to the glass, urging them to run for cover.

A moment later, another cloudburst illuminates the sky. Lines of energy radiate out, coalescing as they hit the pavement and rebounding into its characteristic plasma arc. It spreads, engulfing the figure in a hailstorm of Spark before they stumble, landing face down on the pavement, dead.

I choke on a quiet sob before looking up to witness General Sol gilded in amethyst light.

She stands atop the Citadel, her long hair tossing in the wind.

She's too far away to make out the details, but I know she's wearing her usual uniform. Fitted black leather from head to toe with tiny buttons running up the sides of her boots and a crisscross tie cinched at her back.

Her darkened silhouette reveals her standing with her arms spread and her face tipped up, as if she's offering herself to the sky. Bursts of Spark slam into her outstretched hands and crackle over her body, briefly illuminating the vibrant streak in her hair.

She is New Manhattan's only official Spark Keeper. Centuries of evolution living in a world plagued by violent electromagnetic forces have immunized people like her to its deadly effects.

More Keepers like her once lived within our borders, but their connection to Spark drove them to madness and violence. They proved too dangerous to exist.

Without General Sol, we would be lost.

Any time the weather turns, she races to her perch, gathering the storm's power to fuel the city's generators.

Another cloud bursts across the sky, but the general is ready. I watch as she gathers the next strike and then touches the dozens of glowing nodes surrounding her in a circle. Lights power on in a distant part of the city that doesn't enjoy the luxury of constant electricity.

Here in one of the House Fiama towers, we receive steady power until the generators run out. But it never takes long before the next storm comes along.

I open the window, bracing myself for a gust of wind.

It tugs at my hair as I lean forward, peering down at the illuminated windows of the Ardens' apartment, but here I'm safely concealed in shadows. Reaching forward, I hold out my hand and stretch my fingers to the sky.

I peer up, waiting, hoping. The wind burns my cheeks and makes my eyes water, but I must be patient.

Then it comes.

Another bright flash sends a burst of Spark careening toward me, almost as if in slow motion.

It strikes my palm, and I attempt another deep breath as my body absorbs the charge. A transparent plasma arc engulfs me as Spark crackles up my arm, circling my shoulders, chest, hips, and legs.

My eyes flutter closed, while electricity rips through my body, cooking my organs, burning my veins, searing my nerves. My mind warps and my teeth rattle, thoughts muddling as I hang on, willing myself through the pain.

I never know how long it takes. Sometimes it feels like hours. Sometimes years.

But no more than a minute or two passes before I can open my eyes. My bones and skin throb. The roots of my hair and the backs of my teeth ache.

The bubble is gone, but I'm still trembling as I look down to admire the purple sparks dancing over my clothing and skin. I approach the mirror on unsteady legs to enjoy the effect. It's like I'm surrounded by dancing fireflies. Like I'm a faerie from another world. It isn't magic, but it *feels* like it.

Twisting left and right, I continue watching the sparks dance up and down my arms and twinkle in my hair. Eventually, my breath evens out. I stop shaking as the effect melts from resonant pulses into the euphoria I crave. I'm floating now.

Every time I do this, it strips a little piece of me.

I can't explain it, but I sense it slowly chipping away at some fundamental part.

It's wrong to embrace this.

But resisting it would be like deciding not to breathe.

I wish I could share this with *someone*. But I can't.

In fact, it will be a few hours before I'm ready to show myself to anyone at all, so I settle back at the window, checking on the sparks every few seconds.

While I wait, I gaze outside to watch our leader and her awesome strength.

The truth is, General Nyxia Sol *isn't* New Manhattan's only living Spark Keeper.

But that's a secret no one can ever know.

2

The next morning, I lie in bed, staring up at my hands, flipping them back and forth. I've returned to normal again, relatively speaking. The storm's charge has ebbed, and I'm no longer glowing with Spark. I *can* extinguish the energy by smothering the points of light with a pinch of my fingers like embers from a fire, but I prefer to let them linger, hanging on to the bliss as long as I can.

Otherwise, they dissipate on their own after a few hours.

The clouds have cleared, and bright light filters through my window. Slowly, I sit up, rolling my shoulders with the phantom sensation of Spark dancing under my skin. It takes a moment to orient myself to the present, as my thoughts remain muddled and fuzzy.

I've discovered that if I go too long without a "hit," I grow anxious and itchy, like my skin is too tight, and I have no choice but to give in to it. But I can never be seen, so I've had to get creative.

My stomach twists. Being at Amery Academy, where I'll be surrounded by people at all hours of the day, will make my secrets harder to keep.

Sitting on the edge of the bed, I stare around my little-girl room, even brighter and frillier in the morning light. I don't know why I've never updated the decor. Maybe a part of me thought I'd never have to grow up if I was always surrounded by my little-girl things.

But as my gaze snags on the Amery uniform hanging in the open closet, I understand everything moves forward whether I want it to or not. Today, I will embark on the next chapter of my life.

It's not like my childhood was anything to cherish anyway.

After heaving myself up, I approach the window and peer at the plaza below. Whoever was blitzed last night was already cleared away by the sweepers after the storm.

Sometimes, we're given a warning, and sometimes, the storm comes from nothing. We're well-protected in our Society apartments thanks to the fully manned Storm Towers strategically placed on the roofs of our neighborhood. However, even that isn't guaranteed, as evidenced by someone's blitzing at the party last night.

More Storm Towers surround the city's perimeter, each one manned by a group of Storm Breakers who have undergone years of intense training. When an Empire Storm hits, they help deflect whatever Spark General Sol can't use for the generators with specialized wands that direct the energy away from the city and into the Towers, which safely ground the charge into the earth.

My phone lights up with an early-morning message from The Shield, our triumvirate government made up of two chancellors and General Sol. Their round emblem features a shield in the center, depicting four different quadrants—one for each House—and is surrounded by the curved, scripted font of New Manhattan's motto: *Protect. Preserve. Prosper.*

Every device in the city is temporarily overridden for exactly seventy-six seconds at precisely eight thirty each day, while we're reminded of the four Houses and their role in maintaining the peace and prosperity of New Manhattan.

Technically, we're supposed to stop whatever we're doing and give the message our full attention, so I sit and dutifully wait for the missive to end, only partly paying attention.

Once it's over, my phone buzzes, and I see a notification from my friend group chat that includes Trinity, Silver Sato, and Hazel Chopra.

I skim through the messages, mostly about who made out with whom last night, until I see one that makes my heart freeze.

HAZEL: *so surreal that Bethany got blitzed*

As more rapid-fire texts fly across the screen, I clutch my phone, staring at it. I think back to the charred body on the floor of Knox's apartment with a shudder. I want to feel bad for her, but a vindictive part of me is struggling to feel much remorse. We grew up together, and yet I can't recall a single time she said something nice to me.

I skim the rest of the texts, but it's just more chatter about Bethany and her faults. I may not care that she's dead, but I won't revel in someone else's pain. Something my father loves to point out as a weakness of mine.

I sigh and flip back to my main list of texts.

There are a few from Knox, wondering where I disappeared to last night and if I want to head to Amery with him soon. I don't bother replying.

Instead, I head into the bathroom and shower quickly before pulling on my dress uniform for the first day of school—fitted black silk pants, high black boots with small buttons running down the sides, and a tailored black jacket with a high collar and flared waist. On the breast is a small crest depicting a flame, marking me as a member of House Fiama. I grab the wide silver ribbon from the hanger and cinch it around my midsection, then tuck my small knife into my boot. Both for protection and the reminder of my brother, who taught me how to use it.

I approach the mirror over the sink, inspecting my light-brown complexion and my midnight-purple hair with its brighter streaks. I was sixteen when my natural black waves began to give way to this puzzling shift. Some instinct told me I had to hide it then, and I've kept this secret from everyone else in my life, too. The fact that so many people dye their hair has made it easy to get away with.

I'm sure it relates to my *other* secret, but I don't entirely understand how.

Gently, I touch the thin, barely visible scar slicing across my cheekbone, courtesy of my father. He has a temper, especially when he's drunk. I was seven years old when he lost a leadership vote to Delta Aziz, and he was dousing his failures in whiskey when I got in his way.

It would be three more years before my father finally won his coveted role as scion, and while the physical scars were healed and mostly erased by a team of doctors, I still wear them like fresh wounds on the inside. He never hit my face again, but that still left the rest of me as fair game.

I swipe on some makeup, covering the evidence of my past, and then some black liner and mascara to highlight the green eyes also inherited from my father. Most of my clothing has already been sent to my dorm room at Amery, and the only thing left to pack is a box with my personal effects.

I toss in my favorite blanket, a few more bits of clothing, skin care, shampoo, other hair stuff, and photos of me with Trinity and my family. I stare at Teddy sitting on my dresser. I can't stand the thought of leaving him behind.

Quickly, I snatch him up and bury him under a sweater, and the tight knot in my chest immediately eases. The last thing I do is put on my necklace that sits on my nightstand. Besides Teddy, it's my most precious possession. A delicate chain dangles with a tiny gold mask encrusted with amethysts. It was an offering from my mom after my father nearly killed me, as if jewelry was supposed to make it better. Nevertheless, I've worn it every day since.

I pick up my box and carry it into the living room, planning to join my parents for breakfast and, more importantly, to make one last-ditch effort to appeal to my father about my future.

My boots squeak on the slick azure tiles as I approach the front door and set my box down for one of our staff to pick up and deliver to Amery soon. I can't believe this is my last day in this place. The entire apartment, decorated in royal blue and silver, with blue silk walls and silver decor, hasn't always felt like a home . . . but still.

I head toward the living room, which is furnished with velvet sofas and marble tables adorned with handwoven blankets crafted by my mother from bits of colorful scrap. The organic designs are entirely at odds with the grandness of the decor, but her art makes her happy. When I round the corner, my parents look up from the long glass table at the far end of the penthouse.

"Poet," my father says, eyeing me up and down as I approach. I can't tell if it's with pride or suspicion. Maybe a little of both. "It's nice to see you in Amery black and silver."

My chin dips in acknowledgment, a silent question sitting on the tip of my tongue. For years, we've argued about my desire to become a Storm Breaker until he shut down the entire conversation with a whispered threat that plagued my thoughts for weeks.

So, I gave up. Temporarily.

I take my usual place next to my mother, settling into the white upholstered chair before our cook-slash-maid bustles out of the kitchen. Cara sets a plate of cheese, cured meat, and a small bowl of fruit in front of me.

Our multistory greenhouses and barns are located at the island's south end in an area once known as Wall Street. Food production and distribution are carefully monitored and controlled by House Tera, another of New Manhattan's four Houses that constitute the upper echelons of Society. Thanks to careful temperature and humidity control, they provide us with animal products, fruits, and vegetables once native to places that no longer exist.

These were things they enjoyed in abundance during the Warming Age, the one where humanity treated their planet like it was there only to serve them, until violent weather and flooding wiped almost every person off the earth.

After Cara pours me a cup of coffee, she hustles back into the kitchen, and I eat in silence alongside my parents.

My father scrolls on his tablet, undoubtedly catching up on the morning news. "Bloody Hollows caused a riot last night," he mumbles to himself. "Third time this month. Might need to recruit some additional Patrols."

House Fiama is responsible for the safety and security of New Manhattan within our borders and manages the city's internal police force, known simply as the Patrol. My father believes that the greatest enemy to Society is "fear." Fear of those who refuse to obey our laws, thinking only of themselves rather than the greater good.

Before my father took over as scion nine years ago, constant rioting and looting nearly turned the city into a boiling pot. But he triumphed where his predecessor failed by implementing dozens of security measures, including strict curfews, increased foot patrols, and security cameras on every corner.

As my father continues reading the news, the groove between his brows deepens. He mutters something about Cameron Jenkins being on his ass while he aggressively sips his coffee.

"Are you all ready? Excited?" my mother, Sariah Graves, asks. Her black hair is pulled into a high half-knot and adorned with a single thick band of indigo, with the rest falling in a tumble of curls. Black kohl rings her eyes, burgundy blush warms her medium-brown skin, and the loose orange dress and gold sandals look effortless on her. As usual, she's stunning.

"Sure," I say as I sip my black coffee. I *am* excited. And nervous. And scared. Toss a dart at a list of emotions, and I'd probably be feeling anything it hits. I can't wait for the parties and the friendships. The fun and even the hard work.

At that, my father looks up from his screen, and I resist the urge to flinch. Grady Graves is a formidable man, whose single look makes my insides turn liquid with apprehension.

"How about a little more enthusiasm?" he asks. His wavy black hair is slicked back from his pale, angular face, offering a clear view of his bright green eyes. He doesn't go in for nonsense like *hair trends*. His words, not mine.

He wears a crisp white button-up and pressed gray slacks. His role as scion is an endless series of duties and tasks that keeps him busy and stressed at least ninety percent of the time.

Maybe if I were allowed to become a Storm Breaker . . .

I think it. I can't bring myself to say it.

So, I flash a toothy smile that has his eyes narrowing.

He keeps his gaze pinned on me as he reaches for his fork and spears a piece of sausage off his plate.

"Poet," he says, and I know that tone. The one where he's about to tell me he's disappointed in me. Or remind me what's expected of me. As if I could ever forget.

He chews the meat, holding my gaze, while I wait until it's my turn to speak.

"I graduated at the top of my class," he eventually says, repeating this mantra for at least the thousandth time. "I was the student leader of House Fiama. They still keep my academic awards in the school's front hall."

I inhale a slow, fortifying breath.

"Yes," I answer, though that's not really an answer at all.

"I expect you to do the Graves name proud," he continues. "You'll only have three years. Three years, and then you'll marry Knox and join the other Society wives. Without a son, it'll be up to you to carry on our family lineage."

My teeth grind as he stares at me. He *had* a son. Someone else to carry on the proud Graves line. My brother, Raine, was twenty-two when a roving band of Solitudes killed him three years ago while he was manning a Storm Tower.

Solitudes live in the uninhabitable wilderness and marshlands known as the Wastes. They're forbidden from entering the city, though they often attempt to breach our borders to steal supplies and sow disharmony. Along with protecting us from Spark, Storm Breakers and the rest of the Storm Guard are also responsible for stopping Solitudes from entering New Manhattan.

My brother was a Breaker, though technically, Raine was my cousin. His mom was my dad's sister, and she fell in love with a Solitude who then killed her, too, leaving my parents to raise her son. But he was my brother in every way that mattered.

I'd like to think my father's reluctance to let me join the Storm Guard is because he's worried I'll meet the same fate as Raine. That might be partly the case, but I know it has far more to do with controlling me.

Raine's departure left a gaping hole in our family that has never healed. I glance at my mother, whose expression remains neutral. Slowly, she turns to me, lays a gentle hand on my wrist, and squeezes.

"Your father only wants what's best for you," she says, and my heart crumples. I wasn't expecting her to stand up for me, but that doesn't mean it's any less disappointing that she never does.

"Dad, if only I could—" I start, but he raises a hand for silence, already anticipating my question.

"Poet," he says, a warning in his voice, causing me to go still. I set a piece of toast back on my plate and shove both hands under my thighs, trying to hide the way they shake. But he misses nothing, and his gaze narrows as a corner of his mouth tugs down in a sneer.

I take a deep breath, then force myself to eat again, trying to pretend that he doesn't scare me. But each bite is like tasting wet cardboard. There's nothing my father hates more than weakness, and I'm always weak around him.

Neither one of us speaks.

For several minutes, the only sounds in the room are my father's fork scraping against his plate and my mother's soft sips of coffee. I chew faster, reminding myself that maybe if I work my ass off and become a good House Fiama pledge, I might even prove to him that I'm meant for life as a Breaker.

Only Society members are eligible to join the Storm Guard, so technically, he can't stop me from enrolling in cadet training. I'll just have to find a way to keep it from him until it's too late to do anything about it.

It's not a great plan, but it's all I have for now.

Satisfied, he gives me a nod and then swipes the screen on his tablet again.

I nibble at a piece of fruit as my gaze wanders out the window. From this high up, I can see for miles. The waterways surrounding our island stretch over flat land, where a maze of boardwalks elevates hundreds of businesses and houses belonging to the city's service workers, known as cogs, who run many of the city's shops or perform jobs like mechanics, maids, cooks, and lower-ranking Patrol members.

I check my watch and excuse myself from the table.

"Trinity will be here to pick me up soon," I announce. My mom looks at me, her big, dark eyes shining with the threat of tears. My parents claimed they were too busy to see me to the academy today, and I'm trying not to let that hurt.

"I'll miss you so much," she says, taking my hand. "Promise me you'll call? And visit us sometimes?"

"Yeah, Mom, of course." I lean down to kiss her on the cheek, catching her familiar scent of honey and mint.

I push my chair in and nod at my father.

"Sir," I say as he offers me another once-over.

"Before you go, remember that I'm counting on you," he says. "And I expect your reputation to remain intact before your wedding. I don't want any *rumors* circulating about you."

My brows furrow as I attempt to parse out his meaning.

"Poet," my father says. "You will keep yourself for Knox."

Keep myself? I almost choke on my tongue as his intentions become clear.

"Excuse me? *He's* the one walking around fucking anything wi—"

A loud crash cuts through my words as my father slams his hand on the table so hard, the glasses rattle. I flinch, and my mother jumps as my heart pounds in my chest. A mug falls over and smashes on the tile with an explosion that echoes through the room like the threat it is.

I see those hands in my nightmares.

Hear the sound of his footsteps in the dark.

"Language," my father bites out with such trembling fury that a lock of his dark hair falls over his eye.

I clench my fists, my nails digging into my palms as I slowly nod.

"Are we understood?" he asks.

No, we're fucking not.

When I was younger, I idolized Knox. I thought he was beautiful and couldn't believe how lucky I was. But as we grew up, he became arrogant and selfish, and he lost my respect. Maybe it happened when he discovered how much he loves his dick.

But I swallow my indignation and say, "Yes."

My father's eyes flash with satisfaction, and a non-zero part of me wants to walk over and punch him in the throat. I glance at my mother, who watches our exchange with wide-eyed worry. I blame her for this, too. If only she would stand up to him.

A knock sounds at the door, and I silently thank Trinity for her impeccable timing.

"Then have a good time," my father says, sitting back and crossing an ankle over his knee. "But not too good."

"Yes, sir," I answer and walk away, reminding myself that soon I'll enjoy some distance from his constant scrutiny.

Soon, I'll be out of here.

Soon, I'll be free of him.

Or so I hope.

Because something in my gut tells me that my father will always find a way to control me, no matter how far I run.

3

I exit Fiama Society Tower A behind Trinity and her parents, Chad and Paris Robins. Mr. Robins works for The Shield, dealing in government security, while Mrs. Robins is a Society wife like my mom.

With them are Edward and his mother, Elena Chu. His dad passed away when we were in middle school, and Mrs. Chu and her son live off what he left behind and the generosity of The Shield and Fiama Society. Once Edward graduates from the academy, he'll be expected to take care of her.

Everyone talks happily as I hike up the collar of my Amery-issued black wool coat, doing my best to forget that I'm the only one who's here alone. Not very successfully.

The nearest gondola dock sits at the front entrance of our building. It's a short ride to our destination at the Central Park Tree Farm's north end. We could have taken the subway, but the tunnels make me claustrophobic. Tight spaces remind me too much of hiding from my father's anger.

Only a handful of solar-powered vehicles remain in New Manhattan, used for emergency services such as fire trucks and sweepers. During the Warming Age, they built too many cars, and their exhaust choked the air to the point that it condensed in the sky and wouldn't clear away. Eventually, it grew so thick and volatile that it morphed into the storm clouds that now plague our world.

Many of the city's roads were converted into canals, so that people and supplies move over the water and are powered by humans instead of engines. Once we learned how to store the unstable energy from plasma storms, Spark became a new form of clean energy that ensures the atmosphere remains free of toxins.

"Still weird to think all of this used to be streets," Trinity says, as if reading my mind, and leans over the dock's railing to peer into the deep channel.

"The canals follow the old glacial low points," Edward says. "It's why they hold water without constant pumping."

Edward has always been fascinated by technology and the mechanics of things and how they work. He's often regaling us with facts about how the city runs. He loves a puzzle.

"That's . . . actually kind of cool," Trinity says while I offer him a smile.

Two arched black gondolas pull up to the dock, gliding silently through the clear blue water. The gondolier grips a long pole used to steer the wide-bottomed boat.

These ornate creations are Society's favored mode of transportation and are modeled after a great city that once existed during the Warming Age. In fact, when the founders of New Manhattan began reconstructing the city, they drew a lot of inspiration from its decor and fashion for our world. I've always wondered if they wanted to bring something beautiful from the past into a place that had been stripped of so much of it.

We hop into the boats—parents in one, teens in the other. The morning is cool, and the air is relatively still, with only a soft breeze tugging at our hair.

The gondolas slip into motion, gliding through the canals that carve their way between districts. We pass beneath narrow bridges and alongside buildings stacked atop the bones of the old city—glass and steel rising from weathered stone, balconies jutting out where windows once faced the street.

Some levels sit half submerged, their darkened doorways just visible beneath the waterline, while above them, life continues as though nothing was ever lost. The city feels layered here, rebuilt rather than repaired, every stretch of canal a reminder of what New Manhattan chose to keep.

I watch it all slide past, curious how much of the ancient unseen world still lingers down there.

As we draw closer to Amery, the scent of the factories beyond wafts toward us. The manufacturing sector falls under the jurisdiction of House Asale and dominates the island's northern end, where everything we rely on is made.

We don't enjoy all the luxuries of the Warming Age, but thanks to Asale's innovations and technology in the use of recycled, scavenged items, we have medicine, computers, phones, tablets, textiles, furniture, household items, and construction materials.

Other items are harder to come by. Precious minerals, for example. Leather is also in high demand. The Central Park Tree Farm is carefully managed, and wood is allocated for housing and vital resources. Thus, paper is precious, and we mostly rely on screens. Most of our entertainment—books, music, and movies—has been preserved from hundreds of years ago.

From this distance, Amery Academy looks a bit like a castle and a skyscraper had a baby, with large windows and iron framing, soaring towers and ornate balconies. Apparently, the architect was inspired by a fantasy book he loved from the Warming Age.

The boats drift through the city, passing dozens of people hurrying to work. A few students we recognize wave as a gust of cold blows through my coat. Pulling my collar up, I stare at the tall spires swaying in the wind.

"Wow, it really is ugly," Trinity says, and Edward and I snort a laugh.

It's not pretty, that's for sure, but I think it has a certain tormented-genius charm.

"They say the architect went loopy," Edward adds. "The storms broke him."

My mouth presses together as I shiver. Pierre Lourde was a Keeper who used his ability to channel Spark into building the academy, turning piles of sand into glass and melting down steel and iron beams at odd angles to suit his brilliant, if a little unconventional, construction.

But constant exposure to the storms warped his mind, making him dangerous and wild. They say he killed thirty innocent people on a rampage before they subdued and then executed him on the spot.

This is why my "gift" must remain a secret.

I'm cursed. Tainted. They refer to people like me as "infected."

Our existence is to be immediately reported to the Extinguishers, lest we become a danger to ourselves or anyone else. General Sol has undergone intense mental training to guard against it. She is the exception to the rule and is deemed a necessary risk so she can protect us all from the deadly cloud bursts.

Every day, I wonder if this is the one where I'll snap. Did Pierre Lourde have any warning? Was it slow and gradual or an instant break? Am I a danger to everyone around me? I've thought about turning myself in a hundred times, but I'm a coward.

I don't *feel* like I'm losing my mind, but would I be able to tell?

It's hard to ignore how *stretched* my thoughts feel after I'm consumed by a blast of Spark. How my mind becomes malleable and porous, my thoughts slipping out, swimming in murky depths.

The sensation never lingers for long, but I *know* it means I'm dangerous, a risk to everyone around me. And I live with the clawing shame that I could end this by confessing my lies.

"Look," I say, hoping to change the subject.

Ahead of us stands a wide arch that runs under Amery Academy and serves as the docking point for the small rafts and gondolas that putter along the waterways. Dozens of people are already milling under the soffit.

Our gondolier brings us to a gentle stop, and I scramble out, followed by Trinity and Edward. Their parents join us a moment later.

"Feels good to be here," Mr. Robins says with a deep breath as he rubs his chest. "Caused a lot of trouble behind these walls. Some of my best years."

"Daaaad," Trinity says as he claps her on the shoulder and grins.

Then he addresses me. "You two look after each other, okay? This place can be really lonely and tough sometimes."

"Of course," I say as Trinity nods. We've always looked out for each other. Nothing will ever change that.

Edward and Trinity exchange a few more parting words, while I scan the courtyard, spotting some familiar faces.

Some unfamiliar ones, as well.

Namely, students from New Manhattan's other three Houses.

When the original members of The Shield first created the Houses three hundred years ago, they did so to help build a world resistant to the mistakes of the past. By making each member of Society responsible for the success and prosperity of their chosen House's duties, they've ensured we'd never fall prey to the greed and hubris that destroyed civilization in the Warming Age.

Where profit and productivity once defined how people lived, we now enjoy a world where our basic needs are met, and Houses Fiama, Aria, Asale, and Tera can prioritize the greater good.

I spot a few students bearing the anatomical heart crests of House Aria on their jackets. They look over, their eyes narrowing.

Aria is responsible for the health of our population, both mental and physical. They're also tasked with ensuring our people's sustainability, since the aftermath of the Warming Age left us with limited space and resources. Thus, they must walk the delicate balance between ensuring everyone has enough to live while also ensuring birth rates don't surpass what the city can reasonably accommodate.

That means Fiama must often work in tandem with Aria, given they're both responsible for keeping everyone safe in their own ways. The result is a struggle for power that causes plenty of strife between our Houses. My father loathes Aria's scion, Surreal Beaufort, a terrifying woman with a mane of dark hair streaked with white. Sometimes I think their feud has gone beyond their work and has become personal.

In the far corner, I spot a small group of teens scanning us with uncertain looks. Though they wear the same Amery black and silver, they aren't quite as polished or enthusiastic. Their hair is free of purple accents, and they all look extremely nervous. Cogs.

Technically, anyone in New Manhattan can attend Amery; however, The Shield only covers tuition for Society kids. But cog families often run profitable businesses and aspire to more.

There are two primary ways to join a House and become a member of Society. The first is to be invited by a scion. The other is to send your child to Amery and hope they can earn a pledge.

I catch the eye of a girl with medium-brown skin and long black hair that falls in soft waves around her shoulders. I offer a little wave to hopefully ease some of her tension. It takes her a moment to realize I'm addressing her, and she returns the tiniest smile.

"Poet," says Mrs. Robins, wrapping me in a hug. "We'll miss you both so much."

"We won't be far," I say, squeezing her tightly as a knot expands in my chest.

"I know, but it won't be the same, will it?"

She's been like a mother to me when my own couldn't be the one I needed. It's not the same as having my parents here, but I suppose it's the next best thing.

After another round of goodbyes, the parents hop into their gondola to return home. A moment later, our friends Silver and Hazel wander over.

Silver is aptly named, with her long platinum hair streaked with deep purple, while Hazel sports a mass of pale lilac curls.

We embrace in a flurry of excited squeals, chattering about our classes and options, upcoming parties, and nights out.

I spot Knox, hovering near the wall, with his arm draped around Winter Jenkins, his posture languid. It's like he's incapable of standing up on his own strength.

I recall my father grumbling about Winter's dad at breakfast. Cameron Jenkins has been attempting to undermine my father ever since he was sworn in as scion, angling for the position himself.

When Knox spots me, he unwinds himself and strides over, his gaze traveling from head to toe. I never understand what he sees when he looks at me.

When we were younger, we were friends. We even liked each other. He would flatter me, telling me I was smart and pretty and that he couldn't wait to marry me.

Apparently, not pretty enough, because I clearly fell short. We were seventeen when we had sex, a decision I've regretted every day.

In my naivete, I thought maybe he'd be loyal to me if I caved to his needs. The very next day, he hooked up with someone else, and I haven't touched him or anyone else that way since.

"Poet," he says, snagging my wrist. I tense up, but if he notices, he doesn't care.

This is another thing I hate about Knox. He doesn't want me but still wants everyone to know I'm his. Despite my apparent shortcomings, I'm still the daughter of one of the most powerful men in New Manhattan. Knox's entire future relies on me, and while that offers a certain kind of value, it isn't worth much.

He tugs me over to his circle of friends, his arm claiming my shoulders as he leans heavily against me like I'm here just to prop him up, both literally and figuratively. I take a calming breath.

"Knox!" exclaims Lacey, flicking her long blond hair over one shoulder. "Will you sit with me at dinner tonight?"

She pouts, stoking the flash of rage that burns in my chest. I'm just a fucking joke to everyone, no better than my mother, forced to endure my father's transgressions with a pained smile plastered to my face.

"Sure thing, baby," he replies and points at her with his finger and thumb cocked. Bile climbs up my throat for a whole slew of reasons.

Lacey beams and then tosses me a dirty look. I remind myself that she can't help how she's acting. Most girls are taught to believe it's better to be like my mother, protected by a powerful man. The reminder only marginally cools my anger.

A bell dings somewhere over our heads, and a door swings open. I scan the shifting tide for Trinity, Silver, and Hazel, but it looks like they didn't follow us over. Not that I blame them.

I'm trapped under Knox's elbow as he propels us into a wide tunnel. We wind through a few corners before we find ourselves in Amery's great main hall.

I've seen pictures, but nothing quite prepares me for the grandness of it all. The floors are shiny wood inlaid with floral and geometric designs, the walls lined with arched windows decorated with metallic gold and silver frames. To top it all off, four massive crystal chandeliers dangle from a domed ceiling covered with mirrors.

I don't have time to truly admire everything because a booming voice shouts, "Everyone! Please line up. Everyone!"

Several men and women in teachers' uniforms shout at us to arrange ourselves in lines marked on the floor. Their attire resembles ours, with black fitted pants and coats, tall black boots, and wide ribbons cinched around their waists, but with gold accents instead of silver.

It takes a few minutes and some jostling to form four groups.

I stand with House Fiama between Knox and Trinity, facing the center of the room. Across from us, House Aria assesses our lines, and the teachers slowly walk past, eyeing us carefully, perhaps deciding who will survive the next three years and who . . . won't.

A glance to my left shows the cog kids have randomly slotted themselves into each House.

That's when the doors open at the room's far end. A hushed murmur ripples through the crowd as a trio of Storm Breakers emerges. They're dressed in their tactical gear that includes fitted black pants and sleeveless vests overlaid with metallic purple harnesses designed to highlight the chiseled strength of their carefully honed bodies.

The two men and one woman also wear sleek, high-tech goggles propped on their foreheads to protect their eyes from flashes of Spark. They proceed down the center of the hall as everyone falls silent.

They're beautiful and intimidating. Absolutely fearless. Slowly, they walk the length of the aisle in their metallic purple combat boots, and I find myself straightening and holding my breath.

I don't care what my father wants; this is why I came to the academy. With my ability to withstand Spark, I could help protect my city, family, and friends. It's all I've ever wanted to do. And maybe if I can prove that I'm useful and good at it, it will give me a bit of freedom from the controlling grip of my father's hand.

As they pass, I recognize Henry, my brother's boyfriend. *Ex*-boyfriend. I haven't seen him since the funeral, when he cried so hard he almost had to be carried away.

He seems older. Harder.

He's also sporting a beard that looks good against his deep-brown skin, and he's buzzed his black curls close to his scalp. I can't help but smile to myself. Raine would have loved this new Henry.

His gaze catches mine for the barest fraction, and his lips press together before he proceeds like he doesn't know me. We were never close, but his dismissal twists a prick of longing deep in my chest.

After the trio leaves the room, everyone bursts into a flurry of excited talk.

Storm Breakers always carry a sort of magnetic pull.

Not only must one be at their physical peak, but they must also be mentally fit. Nothing is more important than the line that protects New Manhattan.

"Please!" comes the same booming voice, trying to settle us down. "Can we please have silence!"

Eventually, everyone quiets before we're introduced to the school's head, Dean Selena Withers, whose piercing blue eyes scan the room. She's a tiny woman with a ramrod-straight posture, her smart black suit contrasting nicely with her fair skin.

My chest tightens as I spot a silver pin with the House Fiama crest on her collar. The dean will be loyal to my father, then, and I make a mental note to stay out of her way.

Next to her stands one of the leaders of The Shield, Chancellor Tennessee Marks, who governs House Aria and House Fiama. He greets us with an amiable smile, his brown eyes crinkling at the corners. He wears a long navy robe over a dark suit, and his brown hair falls in messy tangles around his face.

Thanks to my father's position, Chancellor Marks is a regular fixture for dinner at my parents' apartment, and he's always struck me as a reasonable and fair leader.

Dean Withers begins reciting the academy's rules in a clipped voice.

We have an eleven p.m. curfew. We aren't allowed to leave the premises without permission, except on one Friday night per month, when we're permitted to visit the city until one a.m. No stealing, killing, starting fights, and all the usual things one would expect when a few hundred hormonal young adults are forced to share a building.

While the dean speaks, my palms start to itch, and I scratch them absently. A storm must be brewing. I force myself to hold my hands at the small of my back, all too aware of how many eyes are in this room.

Dean Withers is giving us a rundown of our class timetables when we're interrupted again by the tall double doors at the far end of the hall slamming open. The dean's speech cuts off as everyone looks over to see sunlight pouring into the room, revealing a silhouetted figure.

Someone else has arrived.

Footsteps echo around the space as the stranger enters and then stops a few feet away from where I'm standing. His posture is almost preternaturally still while he stares down the length of the hall. His wavy, chin-length hair is so dark that it almost looks purple as he tips his head.

He wears a fitted black T-shirt and jeans. And a pair of cowboy boots, worn and battered. I've never seen cowboy boots except in movies. A silver piercing glints in the arch of his left eyebrow as his intense gaze sweeps over the room.

High cheekbones. A strong jaw. White skin lightly tanned with a dusting of freckles over the bridge of his nose.

I've always liked freckles.

He looks capable. Confident. Makes Knox seem like a little boy.

Both of his arms reveal a swirl of black tattoos that do nothing to obscure the power coiled beneath his skin. He's huge. Towering over us like some kind of vengeful god.

He looks too different to be Society. A cog, perhaps?

I've seen photos of how people once inked their bodies and pierced them with bits of metal in the Warming Age, but only one group wears those markings now.

Which can only mean . . .

A Solitude.

But he looks nothing like I've ever imagined.

While the storms are the biggest threat to New Manhattan, Solitudes are a close second. A hundred years ago, they organized themselves and invaded the city with rusty, makeshift weapons. They were after our food and supplies and managed to kill thousands of our people before they were finally subdued.

The Solitudes were driven out, except for one concession: they would be allowed to send a handful of children per year to school in New Manhattan so they could escape their old lives and be integrated into our civilized world. It was an attempt to bridge the divide between our people. A show of benevolence from our leaders.

Of course, I've never heard of it actually happening before.

No one in the room seems to breathe as the stranger makes his way down the center aisle, one slow step at a time.

He approaches Chancellor Marks and Dean Withers with the loose gait of a predator who's assured of his kill. I can tell from the stunned looks on their faces that neither of them was expecting him today.

He reaches the front of the room and runs his fingers through his mane of thick hair.

"Sorry I'm late," he says in a deep voice that I swear causes every person in the room to swallow. "I hear this is where I can join the academy."

4

I t takes a few moments for the dean and chancellor to recover from their shock. The rest of us have the luxury of gawking at the Solitude's back while he stares ahead, waiting for them to respond.

Marks is the first to nod, grimace, and then share a loaded look with the dean.

"Of course," Dean Withers says, finally addressing the newcomer. "This is highly . . . We'll have to . . ." She smooths back several strands of coppery hair and tugs on the hem of her suit jacket, trying to compose herself. I'm guessing she's the sort of woman who hates revealing any sign of weakness.

"Please step to the side," she says, waving at the Solitude. "And we'll get your paperwork in order once we complete the room assignments."

The Solitude pauses, his shoulders tensing, almost as if he intends to defy the dean's instructions. From the purse of her lips, I wonder if she's thinking the same. But then he dips his head and walks over to the side of the room, smoothly spinning around to face everyone again before folding his impressive arms over his chest.

Dean Withers clears her throat and shares another look with Chancellor Marks before she addresses us. "Your room assignments can be found on the screens at the end of the hall," she says, gesturing toward a bank of monitors. "Your things should already be waiting for you." After a few last remarks, she dismisses us, and the room breaks into excited chatter.

Through it all, the Solitude stands still, quietly observing. I watch as the dean and chancellor approach him and confer for a moment before they all turn to leave, presumably to complete the "paperwork" the dean mentioned.

Before the Solitude joins them, he glances over a broad shoulder, and our gazes hook ever so briefly. He blinks a pair of hazel eyes as a shiver creeps over my scalp. Will they actually let him stay? Surely he's a risk to every single person in this room. Maybe the dean will offer him a polite handshake and encourage him to return home . . . wherever that might be.

"Poet!" Trinity is tugging on my hand, dragging me to the other end of the hall to find our roommates. We squeal and hug when we see we're bunking together, though our enthusiasm wanes after seeing the other two names on the list. Winter and Lacey are filling out our happy little quad. Great. Silver and Hazel have been assigned to a different room, though at least they'll be together.

Edward is rooming with Knox and his two best friends, Jackson and Sal. He grimaces, and I offer him a "sorry," but he waves me off. I don't think Edward minds them in general, but I understand he's being loyal to me and my feelings. Trin is very lucky to have him.

Two staircases curve in opposite directions at the room's far end, and Trinity, Edward, and I take the left. The corridors of Amery are decorated like the great hall, with gleaming wood floors and ornately decorated walls covered in brocaded silk and gilded molding. Stained glass sconces and marble statues line the walk as we make our way to another staircase.

Trinity says goodbye to Edward before we turn toward the girls' wing. Technically, this is also the House Fiama wing, but we aren't full-fledged Society members yet, only children of the pledged. New Manhattan loves a good ceremony, and we won't be officially welcomed until we pass our initiations and offer allegiance over the next few months.

I glance back to see a group of cogs, including the girl I smiled at outside, following us before they duck into a room across the hall.

Then we enter a massive space with four beds, piled with lace pillows and covered in luxurious white sheets, pushed up against each corner. The walls are covered in white brocade silk, and a crystal chandelier sparkles in the middle, most likely foraged from a fancy hotel or house.

Next to each bed is a white dresser and a wardrobe, while at the foot sits a desk, shelves, and a chair. Our boxes from home wait in neat stacks in our respective corners, and large windows look out onto the Central Park Tree Farm and the distant Wastes beyond.

To the left of the academy stands another tall tower, the Citadel, which houses the government headquarters of The Shield on the upper floors, as well as the Tempestade, the Storm Guard's military operations, in the lower half. If Amery is twisting curves and whimsical details, the Citadel is all straight lines and efficiency. Dozens of wires run out from the roof and the platform where General Sol channels electricity into the city.

I frown as I watch the clouds gather in the sky, swirling and tumbling.

I managed to put aside thoughts of the itching in my hands in the wake of the Solitude's arrival and the excitement of our welcome, but the itching is constant now, burning through my fingers and limbs.

Joining the Storm Guard would mean I could hide in plain sight. I wouldn't have to suppress my need to absorb the storms' energy. As a Breaker, I'd be *expected* to channel small currents of Spark.

At home, I could lock myself in my room and lean out my window, but now I'm surrounded by people for the next eight months.

I can't tell Trinity my secret. If she knew, she'd be obligated to turn me in. I know she wouldn't, but it's safer for both of us this way.

I've heard the rumors of a family who lived below us and hid their child's abilities. The parents were jailed and later executed for deceiving everyone and breaking the law. I'm not sure what really happened to the child, and I'm not sure I want to know.

I know it makes me a terrible person, but my fear outweighs the guilt of keeping this secret.

Someone knocks into my shoulder from behind, forcing me to catch my balance with a step. Winter scowls before she marches to the corner where her boxes sit. Then comes Lacey, flipping her hair like she's trying to relieve a crick in her neck. I can't believe this is who I'm stuck with.

"C'mon," Trinity says, directing me to my corner. "Ignore them."

She stops me before my bed, adorned with Amery's standard-issue sheets. Eventually, we'll decorate and make our spaces our own, but today is a clean slate. A chance to start fresh.

My palms itch intensely, so I press them to my heart to steady my breathing.

In and out, I concentrate on keeping it churning at a normal pace.

"Poet?" comes Trinity's soft voice. "You okay?"

I nod and start unpacking my things. Anything to distract me.

I open the drawers and lay my clothing neatly into their slots. When I come upon Teddy, I check that no one's looking and stuff him in a bottom drawer to keep him out of sight. It's not the same as having him watch over me, but at least I know he's there.

"Let's get some lunch," Winter says to Lacey. She's changed into a more casual version of our school attire—a gray sleeveless tunic with a high collar that falls just past her hips and thick black leggings with bands of silver running up the sides.

The two girls exit the room, but not before tossing another look in my direction. I can hear their mean-spirited giggling from the hall.

As I change into my own casual attire, the clouds thicken, and I resist the prickles biting at the back of my neck. Checking myself in the mirror, I grip my jeweled mask pendant in my fist, trying to focus on something other than my discomfort.

"Poet?" Trinity asks again, softer this time. "What's the matter?"

I inhale a long breath and then turn to face her, plastering on a smile.

"Nothing. Let's go see what's to eat."

She's sitting on the edge of her bed, clutching a pillow to her chest. Inexplicably, her corner is already messy, her clothing strewn about. Her bedroom has always been a disaster, and now that we're sharing a space, this might be the one thing we end up fighting about.

Her gray eyes brim with concern. "You sure?"

Another spike of itchy energy fizzles up my arms, and I scratch my elbows, trying to make it look natural.

"I'm sure," I say. "Let's go find Edward."

She hesitates for another moment and then stands up and crosses the room. Throwing her arms around me, she hugs me tight. It takes me a moment to hug her back.

"What's this about?" I ask. She pulls away and smiles.

"I'm so glad we're doing this together. I love you, Poe."

Tears burn the backs of my eyes. I've waited for this for so long. The distance from my father. Being here with my friends while pursuing my dream of joining the Storm Guard.

"I don't know what I would do without you," I whisper, taking her hand and squeezing.

She grins and does a little hop. "We're going to have the best time."

"We really are," I promise. "Let's go."

As we leave the room, I glance out the window once again. Tingles climb over my scalp, and my chest constricts. I don't know how long I can hide this, but I have no choice.

My life depends on it.

5

We wind through the creamy marble halls of Amery Academy, passing carved statues, polished mirrors, and gilded paintings, many of them salvaged from old museums. A line of students files down a wide, curving staircase, including first-years like us, second-years marked by their green tunics and ribbon accents, and third-years marked by red.

Trinity and I exchange wary looks as a group of massive third-years barrels past us, their conversation loud and intrusive.

A group of Storm Guard cadets.

They wear sleeveless purple shirts that stretch over muscles to reveal defined arms and capable hands, bodies honed for combat and withstanding Spark.

Spark travels most efficiently through blood and muscle versus bone or fat. Thus, Storm Guards strive to be as lean and built as possible, maybe even taking it a bit too far.

"My word," Trinity whispers, clutching my arm.

The men pass in a cloud of cologne and unwavering male confidence.

"Trinity," I say, feigning shock. "You have a boyfriend."

Obviously, I know she loves Edward with all her heart.

She grins and flutters her lashes. "That doesn't mean I can't appreciate the view."

At that, we both cock our heads, staring at the *extremely* tight ass of one of the third-years as he lopes down the stairs.

"View, indeed," I say, and we burst into giggles.

"What's so funny?" Edward asks a moment later.

"Nothing," Trinity says, throwing her arms around his neck. "Just that I love you."

A line forms between his brows, but his hands come to her waist, and he kisses her before they break apart. "Hungry?" he asks us.

"Not really," I say as my skin explodes with another rash of itching. I roll my shoulders as Trinity gives me a worried look. "But I think we're expected to show up."

We join the flow of students and approach a wide arch leading to a massive cafeteria where the delicious smell of home-cooked food fills the air. An aisle runs down the center, and the room is crammed with dozens of long white tables with little stools attached at equal intervals. Unsurprisingly, we've carefully and intentionally divided along perceived Society lines with Fiama, Aria, Asale, and Tera each occupying a corner.

The walls are lined with crisp white tiles, echoing the chatter against the high ceilings.

At the far end of the room hang massive portraits of each current member of The Shield: General Sol, Chancellor Marks, and Chancellor Colt Orsen, like they're watching over us even when they aren't here.

I've only met Chancellor Orsen a handful of times. He's an austere man, with dark hair cut in a precise manner and little humor about him.

I've never met General Sol in person, only seen her at a distance, though my father convenes with her regularly and my parents have dinner at her penthouse occasionally. She never married or had children, despite that being the expectation within Society.

"Poet," Trinity says. "Let's get in line."

I turn my attention away from the portraits and follow my friend to the food counter at the room's far side, where we meet up with Silver and Hazel.

We pass tables full of students wearing second-year green and third-year red, along with others in Storm Guard cadet purple. Some glare and some smirk, enjoying our uncertainty in this new environment.

In the corner, I spot a group of E-squad recruits wearing burgundy, though I think it looks more like dried blood. I shiver as another rash of itching creeps across my scalp.

Extinguishers in training.

The elite force is managed by House Aria, due to the fact that infected Keepers are considered a mental health issue that must be managed and mitigated for the good of everyone. Thus, one of their main responsibilities is to root out Spark Keepers—something they take very seriously.

Their methods are very secretive, but they claim they're just trying to protect infected Keepers from themselves. All anyone knows is that when an Extinguisher comes for someone, they're never seen again.

Hence, I need to do my best to keep my distance from *any* member of Aria.

Thankfully, I've heard they also keep to themselves, and that seems obvious in the way they're hunched together, their heads close, making my skin crawl.

"How's your room?" I ask Silver, who's reaching for a metal cafeteria tray.

"We're with Jade and Apple," she says, naming two other Fiama Society girls we're friendly with.

"Lucky," I say as we both watch Winter and Lacey carrying their food to a table.

"Just ignore them," she says. "They're just scared bullies."

I shrug and then turn my attention back to the counter to study the options. The food at Amery is generally regarded as top-notch. We're all used to the best. I opt for a brie-and-tomato sandwich and some iced tea before I follow my friends to a few empty seats.

"Poet!" a familiar voice bellows as my friends all settle around a table. "Poet!"

I clutch my tray and inhale a deep breath, slowly turning around. I could ignore him, but I know he'll just come and physically retrieve me, and that would be even more humiliating.

"I'd better go."

Trinity gives me a sympathetic look, and Hazel reaches out to squeeze my wrist. They never hold Knox's behavior against me, something I'm endlessly grateful for.

"I'm sorry," I say, walking away.

I drop my tray on the table and glare at Knox, but he doesn't notice or care. Jackson and Sal, his two best friends, sit across from us. They're all talking about their rooms and school and, most importantly, their pledges to House Fiama.

Jackson is a big guy. Broad shoulders, a wide chest, medium-brown skin, and close-cropped hair. He's cocky and a bit intimidating to look at, but he's actually a big softie.

Sal is Jackson's complete opposite, comically so, with pale white skin, wild auburn hair, and a lanky frame. I like him less. His face is a bit too pretty. A fact he uses to treat girls with little respect.

Knox picks up his fork and immediately digs into his pasta Alfredo and fries, stacking everything onto his fork in one enormous bite.

A moment later, another gaggle of his hangers-on crowds around the table. Verity McNichols drops into Sal's lap and grinds her hips before wrapping her arm around the back of his head. They kiss sloppily, with noticeable tongue, oblivious to everyone around them. They've been on-again, off-again fuck buddies for months, but I like her, and I'm worried Sal's just going to break her heart. Or maybe she'll break his. He'd kind of deserve it.

After they pull apart, she sits up and leans across the table, folding her arms.

"Hey, Poet," she says with a grin, her olive skin crinkling around her blue eyes. She shoves two black braids behind her shoulders. "Having fun yet?"

"You could say that," I answer with an eye roll as Knox wraps an arm around my neck and pulls me against him while he basks in the admiration of his "fans." Bile climbs the back of my throat as I'm trapped against his chest. I stiffen, but I don't pull away. I learned long ago it's best if I let him stake his claim first. Knox has the attention span of a goldfish.

Winter has made her way over, glaring at me, and I close my eyes, wishing I could convey how much I'd rather it were *her* being manhandled instead.

Someone tosses a bun in the air, and Knox lurches to catch it, nearly yanking me from my seat.

"Get off," I growl, finally elbowing him in the ribs. "I'm trying to eat."

Knox rolls his eyes but lets his arm fall away as he stabs a fry and stuffs it in his mouth. "Relax," he says, like this is all my fault. "We're here to have fun. You're always so tense."

Thanks to the combination of the storm and my bottomless loathing for Knox, I'm this close to losing my shit. I inhale deeply, trying to center myself and resist the desire to scratch my arms and legs.

My parents think I'm anxious, too, so I spent years with a therapist, learning how to settle my pounding heart and restless limbs. Of course, she couldn't ever know the true source of my distress, so her methods were only partially effective.

I stare around the room, taking in the air of excitement mingling with a dose of apprehension. My gaze slides to Knox, who's pouting as he stuffs more food in his mouth. Why do I feel the need to apologize? He's far too good at acting like a jerk and then convincing me I'm the one who's wrong.

That's when I notice a slight disturbance near the door, several heads turning that way.

The Solitude from earlier stands there in that strange, still way. He's changed into an Amery uniform—a dark-gray T-shirt that stretches over his chest and fitted black pants with silver stripes running up the sides. His cowboy boots have been exchanged for the academy's standard black leather. This close, I can see that his tattoos are actually maps with inked lines of topography and curving arcs representing rivers, lakes, and mountains. For some reason, they make me think of freedom, and I can't help but wonder why he chose them.

The room begins to quiet as more and more people take note of his presence. Knox makes a sound in his throat that's half scoff, half grumble. Verity glances at him and then meets my gaze, her eyebrows rising as if to say, *Get a look at him.*

The Solitude rolls his neck before he heads for the food counter and picks up a tray, whispers following his every move. Knox glares as he stuffs another bundle of noodles into his mouth. He chews slowly, intentionally. Like he's planning something, and I already know it will be painfully senseless.

A moment later, a bullhorn slices through the silence, sending a collective flinch around the room. "Welcome, first-years!" comes a deep male voice from the far end, where several third-years in red and purple are gathered. I recognize the speaker as one of the Storm Guard cadets we saw earlier—the one with the nice ass.

"I'm Devon Carter, student leader of House Fiama!"

The Solitude is forgotten in a chorus of cheers from Fiama's side of the room, along with boos and hisses from the other Houses. Devon gestures to his left, where a woman with a deep-brown complexion is holding another bullhorn. Her platinum hair is streaked with plum and cut to her chin. Her eyes are ringed thickly in black, and if her physique didn't already suggest she's a Storm Guard cadet, her fitted purple tank top would.

"I'm Stevie Daniels, student leader of House Aria!"

Aria begins to cheer, and it's everyone else's turn to heckle their leader while I watch on in silence. Aria tries to drown out the room as they slam their fists on the tables, practically vibrating the ground. The noise does nothing to calm the incessant prickle shifting under my skin.

The student leaders of Houses Asale and Tera, both wearing third-year red, are also introduced to a chorus of boos and chanting. Oscar Cabrera from Asale with his bronzed skin and tousled black hair. And finally, Bellamy Macy from Tera, with his copper complexion and rows of tightly knotted braids.

Stevie waits for the ruckus to settle with a ferocious grin before Devon retakes the floor. "Many of you are used to your cushy little lives," Devon hollers. "Especially Aria, Asale, and Tera."

He winks amid an assault of jeers from the other Houses. A bun smacks him in the chest with a gentle thump, and he narrows his eyes at the first-year who threw it, his expression suggesting he's not about to forget this.

After clearing his throat, he addresses us again. "You're here to prepare for your futures, and the most important part of that is officially pledging your House!"

Now everyone cheers, even if three-quarters of the room do so reluctantly.

Oscar takes over, holding the bullhorn to his mouth. "In the next few months, you will face a series of initiation trials. The first will be one of four choices based on the House you choose to pledge. To continue, you cannot fail your first test.

"After that, you will have two chances to secure your position. The second and third tests are specifically tailored to your skills . . . or, more importantly, your weaknesses. You can't be asked to perform the same test more than once, but this is where we decide if your chosen House wants *you*. The good news is you only have to pass two of the three trials for your desired House, so if you want to change your mind after the first test, because *Asale* is clearly the best House"—everyone either boos or cheers again—"you'll have another chance." He presses a hand to his chest. "Consider it a generous gift from The Shield."

We spend our lives preparing for these tests, undergoing various forms of training: mental, physical, and technical, depending on the mandates of our House. The actual trials change from year to year to keep us on our toes, but the overall point is to push us to our limits. The Shield urges us to carefully consider our pledges, and everyone is given the opportunity to choose the one that best suits their desires.

But House loyalty runs extremely deep, and switching means cutting ties with your existing family and friends in favor of your new life. Newcomers are often regarded with suspicion until they can prove themselves. Thus, most people tend to opt for the familiar and stick with their family's legacy.

Bellamy picks up Oscar's speech. "At the end, your results will determine if you're worthy of joining Tera." He raises a fist, and our side of the room erupts into screams.

"Or Ariiiiiia!" Stevie shouts into her bullhorn, eliciting even more noise.

Devon and Oscar follow suit until the sound reaches a thunderous volume.

Initiation and our final pledges determine the entire course of our lives. Failing to earn a place in Society is a virtual death sentence. A perennial shame heaped onto your family.

It's common for those who fail the pledge to simply . . . disappear.

With New Manhattan's population growing every year, The Shield provides for and protects those who earn it, and everyone is expected to prove their worth. Those who fail are considered failures of the system itself.

My gaze wanders to the back of the room where a group of cog hopefuls all sit, wearing cautious looks. I don't know what happens if they fail. Do they simply go home? Or is their future just as uncertain?

Stevie is still shouting into her bullhorn about upholding the values of Aria and the challenges ahead, before the other three leaders do the same. They introduce the group of people standing at the front as secondary school leaders who will help with the testing, including my cousin Anan Samra from my mother's side, who cheers along with the rest.

He spots me and winks, and it helps settle some of the nervousness tingling in my fingertips. Surrounded by so much happiness and excitement, I feel like my father's lecture this morning was a lifetime ago.

While everyone talks, I study the other sides of the room. Despite The Shield's mandate that we all cooperate, the Houses are extremely competitive and secretive with one another, constantly vying for position. Fiama and Aria are the most powerful Houses and dominate the largest portions of the city. They're constantly battling each other for more territory within our tight borders, which is another reason my father hates Aria so much.

I suppose even when we're provided with everything, there are natural leaders and followers, and our human natures can't be suppressed.

Stevie lifts her bullhorn and shouts a few more insults about the others. I can't help but admire her as the only female student leader. She seems so fearless. I know I'm not supposed to think that about a member of Fiama's greatest rival, but her energy is infectious.

While the others speak, my attention wanders to the Solitude sitting in the corner. He's leaning against the wall behind him, his arms folded as he ignores his food and watches everyone with a detached expression.

I'm surprised the dean allowed him to stay, but the fact that they've issued him a uniform suggests he'll be allowed to pledge if he can pass initiation. Unless this is all a ruse and they're planning to do away with him later?

As if feeling my gaze, his eyes cut to mine, his jaw hardening.

He's so raw and wild and yet . . . magnetic. Not what Solitudes are *supposed* to look like.

I resist the urge to look away, instead meeting his glare with one of my own.

I think about Raine. About his mother, who he never got the chance to know.

Solitudes took them *both* from us.

He looks away, and I realize the itching in my hands has suddenly eased as I return my attention to Devon. The room is chanting, pounding their fists on the tables, the floor vibrating.

"Initiations begin this week!" Devon shouts into the bullhorn. "Be prepared, my little pledglings, because your first test could come at any time, day or night." He scans the faces in the room, the corner of his mouth lifting in an insolent smirk. "And I'm sure I don't have to remind any of you what happens if you fuck this up."

6

I'm in the bathroom brushing my teeth when my phone dings the next morning. Picking it up, I scroll to our group chat to see that Silver and Hazel have been discussing the Solitude at length.

SILVER: *y'all.*

SILVER: *a third year just confirmed*

SILVER: *new guy rolled up here from the fucking Wastes*

HAZEL: *Rook*

TRINITY: *that's his name??*

HAZEL: *weird, right?*

SILVER: *I don't know . . . it's kinda hot*

SILVER: *did you see his arms?*

SILVER: 🔥🔥🙏

TRINITY: *You do not have the hots for a Solitude. And those tattoos! He'd probably eat you after he fucks you*

SILVER: *girl . . . why do you make this so easy for me?*

TRINITY: *Stop it. You're sick.*

SILVER: *and twisted, baby*

HAZEL: *I looked it up. a Solitude hasn't tried to pledge in like ten years, and he didn't last more than a day at Amery*

HAZEL: *"disappeared under mysterious circumstances"*

SILVER: *noo. not before I get to see him shirtless at least*

TRINITY: 😞 *Do you have history this morning too?*

SILVER: *ya*

SILVER: *meet you down there?*

TRINITY: *Me and Poe are almost ready. See you soon.*

I scan the text thread as Trinity finishes in the bathroom, laughing at Silver and thinking about what Hazel said. If the last Solitude only lasted a day, then surely this Rook won't be here much longer. He's a danger to us and everyone within these walls.

Once we're ready, Trinity and I enter the auditorium for our first class of the school year. The massive circular room is already buzzing with chatter as we search for empty seats. Again, we sit divided into our respective Houses.

"Where's Edward?" I ask.

"He overslept. His roommates got creative last night and tied him to the bed with towels," Trinity answers.

I stop and look back. "You mean Knox?"

She shrugs. "Apparently, they were just having fun. Someone rescued him eventually."

I shake my head and spy Knox waving at me, but I pretend not to notice.

"Over here," I say, pointing in the opposite direction, where Silver and Hazel are moving down the row to some empty seats. I notice several cogs scattered around the room, with a few already seated in Fiama's section, and I wonder if that's an indication of where they intend to pledge.

"Oh, looks like someone saved you a seat," Trinity says. I turn around to find her making eye contact with Knox as he gestures me over. When Trinity sees the look on my face, she winces. "Sorry. I wasn't thinking."

I sigh. "Then you're coming with me."

"Okay, I deserve that."

I huff and snag her wrist as a row of students quickly scoots out of our way. I offer them a thank-you as we pass.

"Don't play pranks on Edward," I scold Knox as we approach.

"We were just having fun," he answers with a laugh, echoing Trinity. "He's fine."

Then he winks before turning to Sal and Jackson. I wave at Verity sitting on Jackson's far side, regretting that I said anything. It probably means they'll give Edward an even harder time.

I plop into my seat before Trinity and I start comparing our schedules for this semester.

During first year, we'll take most of the same classes before declaring our majors in second year. Even our futures are determined by our chosen House, with the highest-level jobs falling under their respective jurisdictions. Like most of House Fiama, Trinity's goal is to join the Patrol and become a high-ranking officer, maybe even chief of a large division. Thus, her classes include a focus on the social sciences, physical combat, and leadership.

Knox is opting for a general education that includes a bit of everything from history to finance to ethics, preparing him for his role as House scion. I'm expected to do the same, as per my father's wishes, but obviously, I have other plans.

I've wanted to join the Storm Guard for as long as I can remember, not only because I know it's where I can be most useful, but also because I've never had any desire to join the Patrol. Our welcome package said we could register for cadet training in the dean's office.

The other options open to Society members are positions with The Shield that include communications, border surveillance, and online security.

A few minutes later, a low chorus of excited voices ripples through the crowd. I turn to look back at what has everyone's attention.

The Solitude stands at the door in the same weird, still way as always. He's wearing another version of his Amery black and silver: a fitted black T-shirt, black boots, and pants with silver bands running up the sides.

In the top rows, several girls stare before giggling and whispering to each other. Even Trinity is looking at him with wide-eyed wonder. I get it. He doesn't seem real. Like his edges are a bit smeared because he doesn't really belong here.

Solitudes killed my cousin. My *brother*.

Then *took* Raine's body, so we couldn't even say goodbye.

I've spent many dark moments imagining all the vile things they must have done to him.

So far, Rook has done nothing to dispel the notion that Solitudes are dangerous and to be avoided at all costs. I get the feeling he could happily kill everyone in this room, dust off his hands, and walk out, all while whistling a tune.

Was he a part of the group that killed Raine? They were never caught. He probably isn't old enough, but who knows how things work in the Wastes. Nevertheless, his very presence pries out that jagged piece of my brother I keep locked away, unsealing old wounds that will never really heal.

The Solitude takes a heavy step into the auditorium, joined by a chorus of cruel snickers.

The air has shifted from last night. Everyone was in shock, unsure how to react to his arrival, but people are more confident now. Sure that he doesn't belong here. Whispers follow him as he makes his deliberate way down the stairs. His relaxed shoulders and neutral expression suggest he isn't the least bit affected.

Slowly, his gaze sweeps over us, left and right, almost as if he's judging *us* and not the other way around. He continues down the length of the stairs and stops at the front row, where every seat is occupied.

"Get out," he says to the terrified couple staring up at him.

At first, they don't move. I think he's frozen them to the spot.

He leans in and adds quietly, "I said *move*."

The girl squeaks, and her boyfriend practically tramples her trying to escape. "Sorry," he even mumbles as the Solitude gives him a look that I feel all the way through my chest. When the pair has cleared off, the Solitude—*Rook*—drops into a chair and slings his arm along the back of the second before kicking a foot up on the railing that circles the teaching area.

Everyone stares while they whisper, some horrified and some thrilled, most a combination of both.

Knox scoffs. "Show-off." Then he speaks louder. "Is the scat housetrained?" he asks, using an old slur for Solitudes. I wince, recoiling from his side. "What if he shits on the floor? Who's cleaning that up?"

I watch the back of Rook's head, but he doesn't move. That spurs Knox on as he raises his voice. "His roommates better watch out. He might mistake them for his next meal."

Cannibalism is common lore for Solitudes. It's the kind of story parents tell their kids to keep them in line, and it's one of the grislier scenarios I've concocted for the fate of Raine's body.

"Knox, shut up," I snap. I don't trust Rook for one moment, but Knox is behaving like a monumental dick.

"How'd he even get in here?" Knox continues, ignoring me, of course. "There's no way this animal knows how to read. Can he hold a pen with those paws? Or are they hooves?"

I'm still watching Rook as he slowly turns around to peer at Knox.

I hold my breath, and I swear everyone around me does the same.

Then Rook is standing before I have a chance to blink. He leaps up the rows like he's exempt from the rules of gravity. A few people scream as he reaches Knox. A large fist wraps around his throat as Rook yanks Knox from his chair.

Rook has one foot firmly planted on the seat in front of Knox and the other on the edge of my armrest. He shouldn't be able to balance like that, but he's as steady as a tree rooted to the earth. I find myself frozen, wishing I could escape.

"What was that?" Rook asks, his hazel eyes flashing.

Knox chokes as Rook squeezes his throat, and the room erupts into chaos. People are screaming and running away, but I sit glued to my seat as my gaze jumps between Rook and Knox.

"Say that again," Rook challenges, but Knox just gapes like a fish. Also, he's turning a bit purple. Would Rook kill him? Given the wild look in his eyes, I wouldn't be surprised.

Should I do something? I should do something.

Knox gags as he claws at Rook's hand and wrist, his knees crumpling as he struggles to receive oxygen to his brain.

"Enough," I say, my voice shaking. "Let him go."

Rook's gaze bounces to mine, and I swallow because he's terrifying. His jaw is hard, and his eyes blaze with menace. His head tips ever so slightly. It reminds me of a nature documentary we watched in school about the large felines that once roamed the sub-Saharan grasslands.

"Please," I say so softly, I'm not even sure he can hear it.

But Rook's hand opens, and he tosses a gasping, hacking Knox back into his seat so hard that it tips the entire row. Then Rook cracks his neck and walks back over the seats as everyone in his path leaps to clear the way.

He drops back into his chair in one smooth movement just as the door opens and our professor enters. She's tall, her long brown hair swinging as she walks to the podium in the center. She pauses, scanning us over as though she can sense something just went down, further evidenced by the number of students now scrambling back to their seats.

Knox is clutching his throat and still gasping for breath. I can already see a net of bruises forming on his pale skin.

"Are you okay?" I ask as he shakes his head and continues rocking back and forth. Tears leak from his eyes, and I'd like to say that Knox has learned his lesson, but I know he'll start going even harder for Rook now. If there's anything Knox can't tolerate, it's public humiliation.

"Students!" shouts the professor as I share a wary look with Trinity, who lays a hand on my wrist to check that I'm okay. "Silence! Everyone, take your seats! Silence!"

It takes about twenty seconds for the classroom to settle down. During that time, Edward appears and slides into an open seat near the back. He looks tired, his eyes dull with dark shadows underneath. The brief sympathy I almost felt for Knox quickly evaporates.

"Welcome to Amery Academy," she says, her voice carrying over us via loudspeaker and a small microphone clipped to her collar. She nudges her glasses higher on her nose, drawing my attention to her cheeks. Her complexion is a light mahogany, warm as polished wood, though a faint redness suggests she might be just as nervous as we are on our first day. "I'm Professor McCarthy, and I'm happy to welcome you to your first history class."

I hear a few whispered groans, especially from Jackson and Sal. Knox isn't paying attention. He's staring at the back of Rook's head with his hand still massaging his throat, wearing an icy glare.

"We'll start with the basics," Professor McCarthy is saying now. She picks up a remote and presses a button to dim the lights around us. Another press of a button and a screen illuminates at the front.

"The Warming Age ended in 2587 after a hundred years of war, where the last remaining world superpowers battled over water, land, and food, leading to their eventual downfall and near extinction. Today, we understand that water is our most precious and valuable asset. That we must contain the spread of our population before it overwhelms our resources.

"Never forget, the earth was once littered with the ruins of empires that believed they were eternal; thus, we don't take anything for granted. Thanks to Society and the order we keep, *ours* will be the nation that endures."

She clicks through a series of slides on the screen, detailing the fall of the Warming Age and the years between, when the world was plagued with howling winds and fire. How a group of survivors found one another on the shores of New Manhattan and, by using the remnants of the old world, began to form the last bastion of human civilization.

"Can anyone tell me where General Sol comes from?" McCarthy asks.

A hand shoots up. It's the cog girl I remember from yesterday.

"She was a Hollow," she says. "A scavenger."

McCarthy gives her a pleased smile. "Very good . . . ?"

"Domino," she says as several people in the classroom snicker. "Domino Parsons." A snort of laughter sets off more malicious giggles as her expression crumples. "Most people call me Dom," she adds quietly as McCarthy claps her hands and calls for silence.

I stare at Domino, wishing I could do something, but anything I say will only make things worse. She glances back, and my eye catches hers, only she doesn't smile this time. She turns away and whispers to the girl she's sitting with.

Professor McCarthy is speaking again as she delves further into the story of General Sol, who's always been the most interesting of the three Shield members in my opinion. The chancellors both grew up as Society—Marks in House Aria and Orsen in House Asale—eventually earning their positions as voted by the scions and other high-ranking members of Society. But the general has a much more colorful past.

"General Sol left New Manhattan when she was just sixteen and wandered the Wastes for almost *ten* years," Professor McCarthy says with obvious admiration. "While the land beyond our borders is extremely dangerous due to the storms and the lack of protection, she survived thanks to the immunity she developed."

I scan the room, searching for a hint that those words affect anyone else. Is someone also like me, hiding in plain sight?

"Upon her return, she created a reliable method for capturing galvanic energy using herself as the conduit. While we had ways to siphon electricity before then, none were as consistent or effective. Thus, New Manhattan began to truly flourish.

"Those years also marked the era of the first Spark Keepers to evolve inside New Manhattan. Of course, we all know how dangerous it is to commune with the storms," McCarthy goes on. "Very few have the mental capacity to withstand the madness that drives the infected into acts of depravity sooner or later. In the decade after General Sol's return, the infected were responsible for more deaths than even the war with the Solitudes."

Now my gaze falls on Rook and the back of his head. He sits completely still, like he's either sleeping or absorbing every word. I swear he flinches ever so slightly as McCarthy glances his way.

"Because of that," she continues, "the existence of any infected Keeper must now be reported to the Extinguishers. The ability will often manifest between eight and twelve years of age, though it can reveal itself in much younger children. Parents are responsible for delivering them to New Manhattan's Tempestade, where their mental soundness is put through rigorous tests to determine if they have the capacity to withstand the madness.

"Unfortunately, few ever make it beyond the first round of checks, and for everyone's safety, they must be . . . dealt with."

Her head drops, and she clasps her hands as if taking a moment to honor these lost children.

I shift uncomfortably in my seat.

I was seven when my nanny and I were at the park and a surprise storm caught us.

I was on the swings when she started screaming at me to get off so we could seek cover in one of the nearby shelters. I didn't hear her at first because I was staring up at the swirling clouds as that *feeling* began to take hold. I didn't understand it. All I knew was that something had changed.

Finally, I hopped off the swing and ran across the open space toward her. She was shouting, reaching for me, when I was struck and then engulfed inside a plasma arc. I stumbled and tripped, landing on my stomach.

I remember her wild, frantic screams.

But . . . I wasn't dead.

I looked up at her, and it took a moment to realize I hadn't been blitzed. Our eyes met, and an even greater horror spread over her face.

"Poet," she gasped. "Get over here."

I didn't need any more coaxing. I shoved myself up and ran toward her. She held out her hands and shouted, "Stop!"

I didn't understand until she gestured wildly in my direction. I glanced down to see those purple sparks dancing all over me. When I looked back up, she slowly shook her head.

"You can't tell anyone," she whispered.

My attention returns to Professor McCarthy, still talking about the general.

Of course I never told anyone, and before my nanny left, I'm positive she didn't, either. I don't know why she didn't turn me in, but I'm grateful for it every day.

"While General Sol was lost in the Wastes for so many years, she learned two things. First, how to resist the infection through techniques she developed that she has tried to pass on to others without success.

"And that civilization beyond New Manhattan is extinct. The only things left out there are sprawling miles of dead earth, abandoned cities, and the Solitudes who wander it."

As the professor keeps talking, a door opens at the base of the stairs. A group of men and women wearing black with masquerade-style masks enters on smooth steps.

The professor stops talking and drops her arms. A pinch of annoyance flashes across her face, but she nods and steps back, deferring to the student Society leaders.

I understand this is about to become someone's first initiation.

The eight figures walk to the middle of the room and stand in a line. I resist the urge to duck and hide. That's more likely to draw their attention than anything, and this moment is inevitable.

They all stand with their hands behind their backs, their shadowed gazes slowly assessing us. I wonder what they're thinking. How do they decide who goes first?

Then they break apart, each one claiming a pledge.

They seem more like victims.

One grabs Edward and hauls him up. He searches the room for Trinity, and she stretches a hand toward him. "Be careful!" she shouts.

Another reaches for Domino, and I hold my breath as she's yanked by the arm and taken back through the same doors they came from.

The other six pledges include two members from Aria, one from Tera, one from Asale, and two from Fiama, who I vaguely recognize.

A moment later, one of the masked men returns. He stops in front of Rook, who peers up at him while leaning back in his seat, the picture of cool composure. A latent image of him pledging to Fiama flashes in my thoughts, and I shake it away. There's almost no chance he'll make it past initiation.

The masked man jerks his chin, and slowly, Rook stands up and spreads his hands as if to say, *Okay, so you got me.*

Then the masked man turns and stomps off. Rook waits a second before inhaling a long breath and begins to follow. I watch intently as he glances back, and our eyes catch, my heart tripping over itself.

His gaze narrows before he looks away.

Rook disappears, and I exhale the shaky breath lodged in my chest.

I look over at Trinity, her face pale with worry. "You think he'll make it?" she asks.

I hope not, I think to myself.

It takes me a moment to realize she means Edward, not Rook.

"Of course," I assure her.

I stare at the door as it closes, and a part of me wonders if we'll ever see either of them again.

7

It's the middle of the night, early the following week, when someone shines a flashlight in my face. My eyes peel open, and I squint against the brightness, my heart starting to race.

"Get dressed," comes a muffled voice. I glimpse someone dressed in black, their face obscured by a plain leather masquerade mask.

I guess it's my turn.

My pulse thrashes so fast that my head swims as I sit up. I glance over at Trinity's bed and note it's already empty.

Quickly, I throw off my covers and head to the bathroom, past a sleeping Winter and Lacey, to dress in my casual uniform attire. I come out and throw on my dress coat, securing the buttons and the ribbon around my waist. After I tie up my boots, the mysterious masked person grabs me by the arm and tugs me toward the door.

Outside, two more masked figures stand, their hands clasped behind their backs.

"Follow," one says, then they turn and start walking. I do as they ask while my first chaperone brings up the rear. The lights in the halls are dim, barely illuminating my way. I squint into the shadowed corners as my skin itches. A storm is gathering, and I curse, worried it might throw off my focus.

Of the students who were taken from our history class a week ago, one didn't make it back. Connor O'Tool from House Fiama failed his test and hasn't been heard from since. For now, I try to put it out of my thoughts.

As we march down various halls, I peer at the masked face behind me, but it gives away nothing. Where is Trinity? I'm sure they're forcing me to walk alone to make this more intimidating.

It's working.

We reach the end of a corridor, and one of the figures in front opens a door to an internal stairwell that leads into the dark. We continue marching, our boots echoing against steel. Down, down we go, and I realize we're headed for the tunnels.

Panic shadows the corners of my sight, and I will my fluttering breath to settle. My fear of tight spaces will affect my ability to be my best, too. I take another steadying breath as we circle lower, the stairs transforming from metal to stone.

The smells of the tunnels—stale water and abandoned refuse—drift up to meet us. I cling to the wall for support, carefully placing one foot in front of the other, worried about pitching forward and making a complete ass of myself.

I glance back again, and the masked figure shakes their head in a warning. I swallow a knot and continue the trek into the bowels of New Manhattan. Finally, we reach the lowest level and enter a rounded tunnel, flooded with an inch of water and floating shapeless objects that I try not to think too hard about.

I'm led deeper through the underground, willing myself not to throw up from the pressing sensation of being buried alive. Technically, there are exits everywhere we turn. Ladders lead to the surface, where hatches open into the streets. Except most of them are rusted and don't really look like they'd hold my weight.

Calm down.

I blink and then blink again, trying to adjust to the darkness. A black spot hovers in the corner of my vision, obscuring my surroundings just enough to throw me off-kilter.

We turn a few more corners as the floor dries, revealing crumbled brick and other debris. I listen to the sounds of our footsteps and the echoing drips of water in the distance. After years of living with my father, my hearing is well attuned to sounds that might signal danger.

Finally, we turn another corner to find a circular opening where a massive, heavy door sits open—a vault.

I stop walking, panic clawing up my throat.

Are they planning to lock me in there?

Something pokes me in the back.

"Keep moving," growls the voice behind the mask. I exhale a shaky breath and then step over the threshold into a small room filled with several more masked figures.

Four people stand before me. Three men, bare-chested and wearing black pants, and the other a woman in a sleeveless jumpsuit. I assume this must be the four student leaders of each House.

"Pledge," says one of the male voices. I think it's Devon from Fiama. "You have a choice. To which Society do you seek initiation?"

I scan the silent masks in the room.

"Fiama," I say, hoping no one picks up on the wobble in my tone.

Devon steps to the side, revealing a small pen with a thin, wiry man sitting cross-legged on the floor. "Then your first test is to fight hand to hand with this man who has committed egregious crimes against Society. He has agreed to a combat to the death for a lesser sentence. If you win, you'll move on to the next round. If you lose, your future becomes far more uncertain."

I barely absorb his words; my brain is stuck on "combat to the death." They don't really expect me to *kill* someone, do they? My palms sweat as I study the man. He watches me with a neutral expression, as though a battle for his life is of only passing interest. I can't tell if that means he isn't afraid of me—or if I should be afraid of *him*.

My nostrils flare with indignation. "Was he actually given a choice? What did he do?"

"He hurt innocents," Devon answers, which is really only half an answer. "Our sworn duty as House Fiama is to ensure New Manhattan remains safe and under control. We do that by eliminating those who refuse to follow our laws. Criminals deserve no mercy, thinking only of themselves and not the greater good."

It takes me a moment to process his words. I understand that it's Fiama's duty to keep order within our city, but surely not like *this*?

The atmosphere tenses, and I feel like I'm missing some important detail.

"Who would come up with such a test?" I demand, suddenly furious on the man's behalf.

A pause hangs in the air before Devon slips off his mask, something uncertain passing over his expression. "I mean . . . your father, of course?"

Of course. Every scion devises their House tests, changing things up every year to maintain some level of secrecy. Of course, *my* father would be one to devise a test so barbaric.

I understand he rules with an iron fist. That he's often lauded for how safe he keeps the city. His predecessor failed in his duty, and riots led to countless deaths. I know better than most what kind of man he is, but maybe I never truly understood how far his cruelty stretches.

"I won't do it," I say, lifting my chin. I notice several people in the corner shifting uncomfortably on their feet.

"You have to," Devon counters.

"You said I had a choice. I choose something else."

His brows furrow. "Well . . . technically you do, but . . . you're the scion's daughter."

Of course, he's right. What am I even saying?

I shake my head, tears gathering in the back of my throat. My father would never forgive me if I didn't pledge to House Fiama.

But could I ever forgive myself if I kill this man?

Criminal or not, he's still a human being.

"I don't know if I can. I've never taken a human life," I whisper.

Devon's uncertainty morphs into hardness. "You aren't taking a human life. You're taking a criminal's life." He shifts to his other foot and points at the man trapped inside his cage. "You want to pledge to House Fiama? Then it's time to grow up. This is the only way we protect everything we have."

Those words become a cold dose of realization injected through my veins.

He's being completely serious. They want me to kill someone.

Even when my father isn't in the room, I feel his controlling hand. I run a finger across the scar on my cheek as my stomach lurches. I think I might be sick.

Kill a man or face my father's wrath.

I call up a memory of his fist swinging toward me, then shove the image away.

This test is my *father's* choice. It would *never* be mine. I drop my hand.

"No. I choose a different test."

Devon's gaze shifts to the other three student leaders, who all shrug. "Then which one?" Devon asks.

I consider his question. Now that I've started this, I have no idea what I'm doing. I glance at the man as rage for my father swirls in my gut. This man isn't mindless. I see his burning soul in his eyes. I don't know his story. I don't know who he is. Cog? Hollow? Maybe even Society? It doesn't matter. In the law's eyes, he is only one thing now. A burden.

Shame colors my cheeks on behalf of everyone in this room, including myself. No one here even considers his life to be worth anything now.

The other leaders have removed their masks, and my gaze catches Stevie's. I was already drawn to her confidence, and *nothing* would piss off my dad more than testing for Aria.

My fists clench at my sides. "What's the test for Aria?"

"You run the tower of fire," Stevie immediately says.

I have no idea what she's talking about. "What's that?"

"No," Devon says, lifting a hand. "This isn't choose your own fucking adventure. You pick a House. That's it. No more questions and no more dithering. Fiama or Aria?"

"Aria," I say without hesitation, suddenly sure this is the right choice.

I don't even understand the repercussions and how deep this could ripple.

Obviously, I'm still destined for Fiama, and I'll make it up in the next round. I think of our first day, when they laid out the rules of our initiations. They said we have to pass two of three tests for our chosen House, so I'll just choose Fiama for the others.

I've heard of it happening before. After the first trial, people sometimes change their minds about their desired House. It's part of The Shield's mandate that we all have a say in how we live the rest of our lives. They want people to be sure of their choice. So I can fix this.

My eyes widen as the consequences of this decision truly hit me. If I fail this first test, I'm out. So I *have* to pass tonight. Of course, choosing Aria now means a bigger challenge ahead and no room for error on the next two tests. I might also be resigning myself to something even worse down the road, but I'll have to take that chance.

Devon and Stevie exchange a loaded glance.

"Really?" Stevie asks.

"Really." I try to make it sound more confident than I feel as I take a deep breath and square my shoulders.

"You're *sure*?" Devon asks, giving me one last chance to change my mind.

"Poet," comes another voice to my left. My cousin Anan tears off his mask. "What the fuck are you *doing*?"

When House Fiama finds out I chose Aria's test, there will be consequences.

But it's also at that moment that I realize how trapped I feel.

I'm the property of two men I hate. All my decisions have been made for me.

I don't care if this is the "wrong" choice, and I refuse to kill a man.

Tonight, I'm choosing what I want.

I turn back to Devon and nod.

"I'm sure."

8

A moment later, I'm escorted through another door off to my left, where more masked men and women wait. Without a word, someone grabs my wrist and snaps on a thick plastic bracelet. They press a button, and a red light blinks to life, flashing ominously.

"The tower of fire is a test of stamina," she says. "Think of it like a game of hot and cold. You must reach a predetermined point somewhere nearby." She gestures to the device around my wrist. "That will tell you if you're moving farther or closer to your goal. Red for hot. Blue for cold. Understand?"

I nod slowly. I think so. House Aria members take pride in their physical health, and this sounds like the ultimate challenge to push those limits.

"You have ten minutes," Stevie continues. "And you won't be alone."

"What does that mean?"

Her face stretches into a gleeful smile. "Other members of Aria will be out there tracking you and trying to stop you from reaching the target."

"Stop me how?"

Stevie's grin widens. "They can stop you any way they see fit. We can't make this too easy." She lifts an arm and spins around. "And that's all the time we have for questions."

She strides toward the doorway we entered. "Countdown ready?" she asks the masked figures, who slowly slink out of the room and disappear until it's just Stevie and me. She taps the face of her watch.

"All good?" she asks, pressing a button before a bright red number ten appears on her screen. It's already counting down, the seconds draining away. I suffer through a moment of indecision. What have I done?

"Get set . . . Go!"

My wristband shudders and then beeps before the light blinks more rapidly.

I look at it and then up at Stevie, who's standing with her arms folded.

"Don't just stand there," she says. "Get the fuck out of here."

She steps aside, and I don't wait to be told again, reentering the vault where Devon, Anan, and the other members of Fiama stand at the far wall, watching me, their expressions a worrying mix of anger and bewilderment.

I don't have time to assure them I'm not actually joining Aria. That would be impossible for so many reasons.

Instead, I take off.

The light on my wrist switches to red as I enter the tunnel. I pick left and take a few steps before the light turns blue. Nope. I double back, watching as it flashes red.

Okay, this isn't so bad.

For a minute or so, I wind through the tunnels, ignoring everything around me. The wristband offers just enough light to make out the walls and corners as I weave back and forth until I come to a ladder directing me back to the surface. More blinking as the climb leads me to an elevator with a single glowing button. I press it and ascend before emerging into a dark corridor of Amery I've never seen before.

Sweat is gathering at my hairline, and my breath heaves out in short bursts. It takes me a second to notice movement in the shadows. It's impossible to make anyone out beyond the bright flashing of my light. They can easily see me, but I can't see them.

The scuff of footsteps tells me I'm definitely not alone. I try to calm my breathing, hoping they'll give away their position. Another sound off to my left suggests more than one person is lying in wait.

I take two steps to my left, and the light switches to blue. Two to my right make it turn red. But someone is there. I can make out a large shadow, and then . . . the glint of steel. They have a weapon. My heart pounds faster as I consider my options. I take two more steps, and the light remains red.

So I run, hoping I'm cutting a path between my two attackers. Arms and legs pumping, I sprint with every ounce of speed I can. Something moves off to my right, and I let out a yelp before pain burns in my side.

I grunt and nearly miss a step before I slap a hand over my ribs. Instantly, I feel the telltale stickiness of blood. Someone sliced me open. I'm so shocked that I nearly stop running, but the pounding of footsteps behind me reminds me that I'm fucked if I don't keep moving.

I veer left as my wristband turns blue, the light burning through the darkness. I quickly course correct, breathing a sigh of relief when it flashes red. Another hall and then another, before the light directs me toward an emergency exit.

I burst through the heavy door, but someone is waiting for me.

A slight figure wearing a mask stands at the bottom of the stairwell, blocking my way up. At least I know I'm on the right track.

"Little girl," the figure taunts in a feminine voice. "Time to stop running."

I approach and feint. The woman lurches left as I go right. Somehow, I skirt past her, the wound in my side throbbing as I twist away from her grasp. I make it two steps before something snags my ankle, and I'm going down. I scream as my knee crashes into the metal stair, pain radiating up my thigh and into my hip.

The woman leaps, dropping on top of me. I snag her wrists, squeezing them, trying to stop her from clawing my face. We rock back and forth as the sharp edge of the stair digs into my back, making everything—my ribs, my knee, my spine—hurt.

Thankfully, the woman is smaller than I am. I try to use that to my advantage, rolling us to the side, until she's pinned under me. We bump down a few steps, her spine scraping the edges as a scream tears from her throat.

I release one of her wrists and swing, my fist connecting with her cheek. She howls as her head snaps to the side.

I take the opportunity to jump up, my right leg nearly crumpling under me. Briefly, I wonder if I broke it as I slam into the guardrail, using it for support. My attacker is still recovering from my punch as I try to catch my breath.

We both pause for a moment, and then she's rolling over, pushing herself up. Her mask fell off at some point, and the murder in her eyes matches the blood running down her face.

"Bitch, I'll kill you!" she shouts right before she leaps. I swerve, and then I'm running up the stairs, that red light flashing as I ascend up and up with the woman close on my heels. I make it a few flights before she's on me again, her arms circling my waist as we go down in a heap, collapsing onto a landing between floors.

The metal grate digs into my stomach and thighs as I kick furiously. She snags my ponytail, bending my neck back. I scream and flail, trying to throw her off, but she leans down to circle an arm around my throat, snarling in my ear. I snap my head up, connecting with her nose, the collapse of bone visceral as she screams. I toss her off, then I'm up and running again.

Now I have a head start, and I keep circling up and up as her shouts follow in my wake. I've gained enough ground that she can't catch me as long as I keep moving, so I climb. Thankfully, the red light doesn't waver as I wind higher and higher.

At some point, my attacker must decide it's time to let the next person deal with me, because I don't hear her chasing me anymore. I come to a stop, panting heavily, pressing a hand to my aching flank. I need a moment to breathe, but I'm painfully aware of the invisible ticking clock over my head.

I'm not sure how much time has passed, but my ten minutes must be nearly up.

When my dizziness subsides, I keep climbing. The wound in my side burns, though it doesn't seem to be bleeding too badly. My knee screams with every step, and my legs are starting to feel like jelly.

Finally, I reach another landing before a darker, narrower staircase leads into shadows. I try the door to the left, but immediately my wristband flashes blue. Up it is, then.

I'm not sure how many more stairs I can climb.

After pushing through, I arrive at another door. Heaving it open, I step outside. I'm on the roof of Amery Academy. The view is dizzying. I can see the factories, greenhouses, and barns; the miles of flats; and the wild, sprawling Wastes beyond stretching across the horizon.

I'm not afraid of heights, but I sway on my feet.

The wind is fierce, battering against me, and I cling to a wall for balance. The storm has picked up, and though I'd temporarily forgotten about the vague itching in my hands, distracted by my test, now tingles dance over my skin. The clouds tumble, flashing with glowing purple hot spots before discharging in the distance. I wish I could reach out and absorb that energy. Channel the agonizing pain ripping through my body before sinking into the bliss that always comes after.

It would give me the courage I need right now.

But that isn't an option.

Another flash of light reveals a body lying at the far end of the roof, smoke curling off the surface of charred skin.

Like everyone, I run for cover when the storms arrive because I harbor the same fear we all do—that I will be struck. But my worry isn't that I'll die.

It's what they'll see when I survive.

A shadowed figure emerges on the far side of the roof. I prepare myself for another fight when a masked Stevie steps into the light.

"Not bad, kiddo," she says, folding her muscled arms and cocking her head.

I have absolutely no chance of surviving her one-on-one, and I almost choke on a sob. This is it. I made the foolish choice to piss off my father, and now I'll fail and be cast out of Society. My life is over.

Stevie confidently crosses the roof without a shred of fear. She stops near the edge to my right and peers down before gesturing me over. Still clinging to the wall, I force myself to release it with aching hands, and then, with my arms out, I slowly approach on careful steps, like I'm balancing on a thin wire dangling over iron spikes.

And I haven't even found the edge yet.

When I reach Stevie, she shakes her head and points up to a nearby pole, where a long wooden beam stretches across the gap between Amery and the Citadel to a second pole on the far side. In theory, the other building isn't that far away, but it might as well be a thousand miles. Several figures are gathered on the opposite side, obscured by the darkness. Waiting for me.

A piece of rope is attached to the middle of the beam, and Stevie grabs the end and holds it out to me.

"Tie this around your waist and get ready to jump!"

I do as she asks before she hands me another coil of rope with a hook at one end.

"What do I do with this?" I ask, and she shrugs.

"Figure it out."

I look at the rope, then at her, and then at the line of people in the distance.

She's got to be kidding me.

Stevie rips off her mask, and for some reason, that makes me feel better.

Like I'm not here all alone. "You can still give up," she screams into the wind. "But if you walk away now, it's *all* over."

She's right, and I don't believe her anyway. The look on her face suggests she'd push me off the edge as soon as she'd let me walk away.

"No shame. Fiama kids aren't usually cut out for this shit."

Her confident smirk stirs something inside me—a feeling I'd long buried after my own father took away all sense of safety and freedom in my life. I made a rash choice in picking Aria over my own House for one night, but as I stand up here with the world sprawling at my feet, I feel a kind of freedom I've never experienced before.

I forget about my surroundings. I forget my craving to absorb the energy cracking in the air and peer across the divide.

I see my father's face and recall his scolding before I left home. I've tried to distance myself from his awful words, but they return with the force of a gut punch.

You will keep yourself for Knox.

Three years. And you will join the Society wives.

I've spent my whole life trying to please him. Trying to mold myself into the image of who he's always wanted me to be. Choosing Aria's test is the first truly rebellious thing I've ever done, and fuck does it feel good.

I shake my head to indicate I'm not changing my mind.

Stevie grins as the wind whips her hair, and a purple flash highlights the contours of her nose and cheeks. "Then have at it! Stand on the X. And make sure to swing straight."

I accept her offering and shuffle near the spot she indicated. I look down, and the world tilts. The wind buffers against my back, and I spread my stance. I grip my tether with one hand and hang the coil of rope off my shoulder, still wondering what I'm supposed to do with it.

"Let's go!" Stevie shouts. "You have one minute left!"

This is my moment.

The one where I decide.

I could choose to walk away from it all.

But without a House, I can't join the Storm Guard, and *that* is the only thing I've ever really wanted.

I hold my breath. Count to three.

Don't look down. Don't look back.
I back up a few steps.
Then I'm hurtling toward the edge.
And I jump.

9

The wind whistles in my ears, and my stomach climbs into my throat as I swing out from the edge, willing myself toward the far side. The rope digs into my stomach as I drop sharply, my hand burning against it as the wind is knocked out of me. I cling to my tether while kicking against nothing as I swing up.

Laughter. The masked figures on top of the Citadel are laughing, because they already know what I've just come to understand: the rope isn't long enough. Panic claws up my throat as I reach the zenith of the path and then swing away.

What in the Skies is this? What do they want?

The rope sways back, topping out toward a cackling Stevie. "Looking good!" she shouts, clearly enjoying herself while I dangle uselessly, probably looking like a fool.

Then I remember the second rope and the hook.

Quickly, I unwind it, allowing the end to drop. They've given me plenty of length, and as my tether swings back toward the Citadel, I fling the hook, hoping it'll catch the edge of the building.

It hits the stone, bouncing off and nearly tugging the rope from my grasp.

I try a few more times without success. This is impossible.

That's when I notice the flashing light on my wristband. As I swing toward the far side, the light turns blue.

Wait. Am I not on the right path?

Another swing back and the light flips to red before turning blue as I swing toward Stevie again. Red at the bottom of the arc. Blue on the edges.

I'm not supposed to reach the other side; I'm supposed to go *down*. *Shit. Shit. Shit.*

I make another pass as more laughter follows in my wake. They understand what I've just realized. But if I fall, what happens? Will something catch me?

I consider my options and look up. The beam. There's nothing else to use the hook with. This must be it.

Instinct guides me as I fling the hook up. It snags on the beam, and I almost cry with relief. The other end hangs down, several feet longer than my tether. I'm slowing, losing momentum as the arcs grow shorter.

I'm running out of time.

I gather the free end of the rope and tie it around my waist before I go fishing for the knife tucked into my boot. Then I quickly saw through the first rope. I try not to think too hard about what will happen. How much is this going to hurt?

The first rope gives, and I plummet, a scream tearing from my throat as I drop before the second rope stops me with a jerk. I cry out as it digs into my ribs, and I'm dangling again, the knife somehow still clutched in my hand.

Now what?

That's when I spot the net far below. *Skies.* I need to let myself fall.

"Ten seconds!" Stevie shouts from above, her voice carrying on the breeze.

Can I do this? I have no choice. Quickly, I saw at my tether, the fibers slowly giving way, strand by excruciating strand.

I focus, willing clarity into my mind.

I empty it of every thought.

Inhale a deep breath just as the rope breaks.

I plummet, a scream ripping from my throat. I'm moving too fast to feel my limbs. My throat burns as I drop down, down, down.

The wind jostles me left and right. I try to slow myself, but obviously, nothing I do makes any difference. I'm at the mercy of gravity and acceleration and the gusting winds.

The earth races up toward me, and I wonder if I've just made a huge fucking mistake.

How bad could being married to Knox be?

I imagine our lives sometime in the not-too-distant future. Me at home alone, probably drinking to numb the pain, wondering who he's fucking tonight—

SLAM.

I hit the net with a jolt. It feels like I've landed face-first on concrete.

It slaps my stomach and hips and thighs. My hands burn, my wrists tangling with the net.

Thank Skies.

But it's not over yet. I bounce up, flying into the air with my arms and legs kicking and spinning. It takes a few more rebounds before I finally come to a stop. I roll onto my back, peering at the sky as another flash of light paints the world in amethyst. I'm not sure I can move. A green light blinks in my periphery, revealing my cheerfully glowing wristband.

I made it. Somehow, I made it.

Someone shakes the net. "Get off!" they shout.

With great difficulty, I heave myself up, as every muscle and joint screams with pain.

My head spins, and I stare between my hands, willing it to stop. The ground is mere feet away. I was this close to splattering against the earth.

Finally, I look up to find a trio of masked Society members. They tear off their coverings and stare at me, eyes narrowing.

"Let's *go*," one of them shouts. I grab my knife that's also lying on the net and crawl across. From the corner of my eye, I see something that nearly has me hurling up breakfast, lunch, and dinner. A mangled body. Or what's left of it. Someone who missed the net.

My mouth opens on a soft exhale as I turn my attention back and scramble over the edge. Hopping down, I wince at the ache in my knees and the burn in my side. My stomach is bruised, and my ribs feel like they've been beaten with hammers. The two men and one woman watch me, their eyes brimming with suspicion.

I am not one of them. I was just knifed, attacked, and then threw myself off a fucking building to pass their test, but I do not belong in House Aria.

"Hi," I say with a small wave, instantly feeling ridiculous. I quickly tuck my hand behind my back. The man on the far left gestures with his chin toward a door where more members of Aria guard the entrance.

It's then that it all really sinks in.

I'm in enemy territory. I've crossed their lines, and I have no way to defend myself. I can hold my own in a fair fight. We're all given lessons in defense from a young age to protect ourselves from potential Solitude attacks. My brother took it a step further when he did his best to prepare me for everything life might throw my way.

But I'm completely outnumbered here. Surrounded by people who make it a point to hunt down those like me. I clutch my knife tighter in my hand as bright clouds tumble overhead, reminding me of what I am.

But I can't let them see my fear.

With my head held high, I march toward the entrance. When I reach the door, three enormous men tower over me, surrounding me in a circle, all dressed in the bloodred shirts marking them as E-squad recruits. They don't say anything; they just stare me down. My hands itch as bright clouds tumble overhead, reminding me of what I am. A monster. A freak. A danger to them all.

If they knew, they'd happily tear me to pieces.

"Excuse me," I say, trying to make it sound confident, but it comes out a little squeaky and breathless. I size up the beast standing directly before me, bending my neck to meet his beady blue eyes.

I swallow thickly, but I'm not fooling anyone.

"Brick, let her through," comes a voice off to my side. I don't dare look at the source of my rescue. I just stare at Brick like I'm not about to pee my pants. They hate me, and they don't even know what I am.

He's expressionless, a blank wall with his squared-off features. What an apt name.

He cocks his head and finally steps aside. I hesitate for only a second before I walk past, trying to keep an even pace. More Aria Society kids line the hallway, each one eyeing me with varying degrees of everything from curiosity to unconcealed hostility.

More bloodred shirts. More people who would hunt me to the ends of the earth.

The only thing I know for sure is that not one of them wants me here. Not now, not ever.

At least it's overshadowing the itching in my hands from the storm.

I kind of forgot to consider just how unwelcome I'd be here.

As I make my way down the hall, their ire burns up the back of my neck. I feel their hatred and their distrust. The absolute certainty that if I try to pledge to Aria, they will eat me alive.

Finally, I reach the end of the hall, which deposits me in the same grand space we all stood in when we arrived. My chest expands with relief, though I don't know why. It's not like I'm any safer here.

I look back to find everyone still watching me with resentment. They all know who my father is. I am an interloper among their ranks.

I can practically feel the target stamped on my back, as if I had handed them the bucket of bright red paint myself.

What have I just done?

10

I wake up frazzled and agitated. The storm never broke yesterday, leaving me desperate for a dose of Spark that never filled the air. Every muscle in my body aches like I've been clenching them for hours. Maybe I have. I didn't sleep much after I returned to my room sometime in the middle of the night.

Between the itching from the storm and the adrenaline in my veins, I could barely lie still. I tossed and turned while Winter and Lacey snored softly from their corners. I kept thinking about what I did. I *intentionally* tested for Aria just to piss off my father. He's going to lose his shit. Skies, I wonder if there's any chance he won't find out. Probably wishful thinking.

I slap a hand over my face and groan.

All my anxiousness is compounded by the fact that Trinity's bed remains empty.

I check the cut on my side that I bandaged up last night using the first aid kit I found in the bathroom. Thankfully, it was shallow, but my torso is covered in bruises from the ropes. Then I quickly shower and change before heading for the cafeteria and filling my tray, while trying to avoid everyone's stares.

I'm sure I'm not imagining the way they're all looking and whispering behind their hands, suggesting the news is already making its way through Amery's halls. I silently curse. I *knew* I couldn't keep this a secret for long, but I was hoping I'd have at least a day or two before everyone found out. I wonder if my father already knows.

Our phones all ding with The Shield's early-morning pledge, and everyone grows quiet, listening to the emotionless female voice reminding us of our duty to New Manhattan and our Houses. My cheeks warm at the pointed reminder of what I did last night, as I feel every eye in the room fall on me. When it's over, I stare at my tray, willing myself not to cry. I don't deserve the luxury of tears. I did this to myself.

After it's over, I search for a spot to sit. Deciding I don't want anyone's company, I find an empty seat, dropping my tray on the table. I grab my fork and am listlessly picking at my food when a hand cinches my wrist.

I freeze, peering up at Knox, who's staring me down with a grim expression that can't mean anything good.

"We need to talk," he says, pulling me up from my seat and dragging me through the crowd. *"Now."*

"Knox!" I shout as I stumble over my feet, his hand squeezing hard enough to make me wince. We exit the cafeteria, and Knox looks left and right before pulling us into a narrow corridor and pressing me against the wall.

"What did you do last night?" he asks, leaning in and getting in my face, causing my pulse to jump. "Do you have any idea how stupid you've made me look?"

I grit my jaw, realizing he isn't worried about *me*; he's just worried about himself.

I have no explanation for him. And even if I did, the words sit lodged in my throat. I'm hyperaware of his touch. Of the lack of space between us and the unyielding wall against my back. My breath grows shallow, my gaze darting past him, searching for an escape.

"Poet," he says, leaning close enough for me to inhale the nauseating scents of hot sauce and eggs and coffee on his breath. "Explain yourself."

I open my mouth, hoping for something, *anything* I can say to soothe him. But my throat is still too tight. Knox must finally realize the effect he's having on me, because he steps back, rolling his eyes.

"You ran the tower of fire."

"I did," I say, voice measured.

"Why the *fuck* did you do that?"

"I couldn't kill that man," I say, finding my voice now that I have the space to breathe. My heart still skitters in my chest, but I'm familiar enough with the feeling to ignore it.

He blinks and straightens, backing into the other wall with a thump.

"You couldn't kill him," he says dully, like that's the most ridiculous thing he's ever heard. "He's just a fucking criminal. Who cares?"

"I do!" I shout back. "That isn't justice!"

"Keep your voice down," he says, looking past the hall where a few stragglers are clearly trying to eavesdrop. "Get the fuck out of here," he tells them, and they scurry away before he rounds on me again.

"It's fine," I say, ducking past him and ignoring the tightness in my chest, knowing that *Knox* apparently has no qualms about killing another human being. He really will make the perfect leader of House Fiama someday. "I'll make it up on the next tests."

Knox inhales a long breath and pinches the bridge of his nose. I note the vein pulsing in his forehead, deriving a grim sort of satisfaction from knowing I'm the source.

"If they'll even allow that," he says, as something desperate flashes across his expression.

"They will. They said I had to pass two out of three. Other people have switched after the first test." My voice is small.

"Our entire futures are riding on this, Poet. I can't marry a member of *Aria*, and I certainly can't lead House Fiama with one as my wife."

Not our futures, *his*.

Again, I nod silently as he tugs a hand through his hair. "I thought you'd be fine on your own, but you're staying in my sight from now on," he adds. "I'll walk you to class, and you'll wait for me to pick you up. Meals are with me, and you're only alone when you're asleep. Got it?"

No. No no no. I open my mouth to protest, but he rushes toward me, caging me in.

"I'm serious, Poet. You could fuck up everything."

Another bell rings in the hall, and now we're late for class.

"Knox, I have to go," I say with a shaky breath.

I attempt to slide out from under his arm, where his hand is pressed to the wall, my body squeezed against his. I hold my breath, trying to create some distance. I don't want to touch him, and I certainly don't want him following me around everywhere I go. This wasn't the plan. I was supposed to get a break. Some space from him *and* my father.

His jaw clenches, and a flash of rage passes through his eyes. In moments like these, he reminds me of my father so much that I find it hard to breathe.

So I manage to step away, adjust my bag on my shoulder, and consult my school app for my classroom location before I leave without saying a word. A moment later, I hear Knox following close behind.

"I don't need a babysitter," I say, still looking at my screen. "I can't get into any trouble during class."

He scoffs as he trails me to the lab, where I have my first biology class this morning. We reach the partly open door, and I whirl around to face him.

"I'm here, okay? See, no trouble."

He narrows his eyes as the professor's baritone floats out the door.

"You'll wait here after class until I pick you up," Knox says.

"Absolutely not. I'll go straight to my room. You're not following me everywhere."

"Poet—"

The door to the classroom swings open, and a professor stands in the doorway bearing the crest of House Asale on his chest. He's taller than Knox and fills out his Amery uniform with a solid frame. Dark hair falls over his eyes, and one might consider him handsome in a classical way if he didn't have the meanest sneer on his face.

"Are you supposed to be in this class?" he asks. "Or are you planning to stand out here interrupting my entire lecture?"

"Just her," Knox says, gesturing to me.

"And where are you supposed to be?" the professor asks Knox, looking down his nose.

Knox shrugs. "Another class."

"Then I suggest you make your way there, given that you are already late."

Knox rolls his eyes and addresses me. "Wait. Here," he repeats before walking off.

The professor pauses before he steps aside and gestures for me to enter.

"Sorry," I mumble as I pass. Everyone watches as the professor picks up a ledger from his desk.

"Can I presume you are Poet Graves?" he asks with that same condescending tone.

"Yes, sir," I say.

"I don't tolerate tardiness in my classes," he answers. "Being a scion's daughter does not grant you special privileges in *this* room."

"Sorry," I repeat. "It won't happen again."

"See that it does not. Now take a seat. There's an empty one at the back."

The room is divided into a series of tables, each with two stools. They're all filled except for the last seat in the corner. My hands tighten on the strap of my bag when my gaze meets Rook's. Of course he's the only one without a partner.

I nod and make my way over, sliding onto the stool and studiously avoiding eye contact.

Rook snorts as I open my bag, pull out my tablet, and face the front.

During it all, everyone watches me, some more obviously than others.

Because I was late? Because they heard me arguing with Knox in the hall? Because I'm sitting with a Solitude? Or because I chose Aria last night? There shouldn't be so many reasons for me to be the center of attention.

"Now that everyone is here," the professor says, "perhaps we can begin. *Again?*"

I'm going to *kill* Knox for this. Though making me late is the least of his crimes.

"As I was saying, I'm Dr. Sellers," he starts with a braggy air as he lists a bunch of titles and accolades with acronyms I've never heard of.

Through it all, I can *feel* Rook at my side. Sometimes I think he's watching me and sometimes just studying the room. What I do see are the people constantly glancing our way, focusing on me first, then on Rook as though we have anything to do with each other.

I inch away in my seat, trying to make it look like I'm simply adjusting my position, but the stool isn't very big, and my butt slips off the edge. I catch myself just before I fall, and I'm sure no one would notice at any other time, but there's way too much attention on me now to get away with it.

My cheeks heat as I push myself back up, doing everything I can to avoid eye contact with Rook. But another soft snort from his direction tells me he knows exactly what just happened.

Dr. Sellers is still droning on, loving the sound of his voice, and I try to tune him in. I don't want to miss anything. Biology is understandably a big part of Storm Guard training, as it's vital to understand how substances in the body react to the Spark generated by cloud bursts.

"Physiological changes from electrical stimulation include increased blood flow and effects on the peripheral circulation. Varying doses and durations of Spark result in alternating responses . . ." Dr. Sellers is saying now.

"In front of you are several specimens of cell clusters that have been exposed to varying amounts and intensities of galvanic energy. Today, you'll take a look and note their differences and similarities."

He continues to discuss the research he expects and the report we must write with our . . . partner. At that announcement, I go still. Group projects have never been my forte, but an essay coauthored with a Solitude?

My gaze slides to Rook, only to find him tapping away on his tablet. I study the curvature of his profile. His straight nose and strong chin. The piercing in his brow. The bit of scruff on his jaw.

He's clearly not like anyone here, but he's not at all what I expected. There's no denying that he's actually kind of . . .

He looks up and catches me staring.

My cheeks burn with fire. I was about to indulge in a thought I should not be entertaining. It isn't treasonous to admire a Solitude's appearance, I think, but it would definitely get me on some kind of list or something.

I quickly look away, inspecting him from the corner of my eye as he scrolls up his screen.

Can he read? I admonish myself immediately for the thought. I shouldn't make assumptions. But everything I know about Solitudes suggests school and learning aren't high on their list of priorities.

Rook is attending this class, though, so that must mean something.

Skies, what is wrong with me? Why am I wondering any of this?

Dr. Sellers finishes his instructions, then pings our devices with a summary of our assignment. He heads over to a table at the side of the room and starts passing out microscope slides. Placing the small box on our bench, he looks down at me, and his gaze jumps between me and Rook.

"Will this be a problem?" he asks. He's clearly addressing me. Despite my tardiness, forcing me to work with a Solitude still gives him pause.

Rook sits with his bent knees spread and his big hands on his thighs. I notice they're covered in little scars that match the ones laddering up his arms. They're nice arms. Thick with corded muscle and the lightest dusting of hair. I get a closer look at his tattoos and the varying sinuous lines denoting water and mountains, along with little stars joined by thin lines.

Why am I thinking about his *arms* now?

When I look up, our eyes meet, and I can't decide what I read in his expression.

Is this a problem? Every part of me says yes. He's a Solitude. Even sitting next to him is probably dangerous. But then something flickers across his expression. There for the barest moment and then gone. Something that speaks to a deeper nature under the wildness of his exterior.

I'm sure it's nothing. Just because he's kind of pretty doesn't mean anything.

"If it is, you can take a zero," says Dr. Sellers, and my head whips around. "I'm sorry?"

"Your choices are to do the assignment with your partner or take a zero." Wow, that escalated quickly.

He's giving me an out, but he's still mad about earlier.

Obviously, I can't take a zero. Storm Guards don't get zeros on assignments. *Poet Graves* doesn't get zeros on assignments.

Again, I glance at Rook. He gets no say in this, I suppose.

"It won't be a problem," I answer, and Dr. Sellers dips his chin, the corner of his mouth tipping into a smug smile. I've been punished for disrespecting his classroom schedule, and the world is right again.

"Excellent," he says before he walks away, leaving me alone with Rook and his unsettling presence.

Everyone dives into their work, and slowly, I swivel in my seat to assess Rook.

He's sitting perfectly still as he returns the favor, perusing me up and down.

"I can read," he says, his gaze holding mine. I can't help but notice that his eyes are the green of forest leaves in the center, melting into golden brown around the edges. "And write."

I blink at the unexpectedness of the comment. "What?"

"I know that's what you were thinking," he says, his voice low, his tone devoid of emotion. "I can help with the assignment."

"I didn't think you couldn't," I say primly, lying through my teeth. I drag the microscope toward me and pick up the first slide. "I expect you to pull your weight."

I'm rewarded with another derisive snort while I adjust the knobs, bringing the slide into focus.

"And you can stop with that," I snap. "I will not be *snorted* at every three seconds. Use your words if you have something to say."

He raises one eyebrow as he regards me with cool composure. Then he leans in, just a little bit, causing the air to compress in my windpipe. I swallow it down like a brick. "And who's gonna stop me, Princess?"

My eyes narrow. "Don't call me that."

"No? Isn't that what you are? Royalty in this little world?"

I press my mouth together, annoyed by his words for some reason I can't figure out.

"Shut up," I say, my cheeks heating with embarrassment, knowing that was the weakest comeback ever.

Though Rook doesn't snort, I can *feel* the laugh he's holding in at my expense.

"We have work to do," I say, trying to move past it, as I begin taking notes about the damaged cells in my viewfinder. Over the next thirty minutes, we don't say much to each other, only exchange terse requests to pass the next slide and pose questions about what we're looking at. I'm careful not to touch him as we exchange items back and forth. I wonder if he notices.

Only once does his hand brush mine. It's the softest touch, but every hair on the back of my neck rises to attention. I quickly snatch the slide away, while he continues like he hasn't noticed anything.

Rook understands the assignment with ease. I don't think Solitudes have schools, but someone taught him these things. Throughout it all, I feel his assessment, weighted with unspoken words. The side of my neck goes hot. It's like he's waiting for me to freak out or start screaming or react in some irrational way.

Our classmates remain focused on their work, though I can feel them sneaking looks at Rook and me. We're a spectacle for so many reasons.

My foot bounces on the rung of my stool as I watch the clock's minute hand counting down the hour. My knee is still sore, my ribs hurt, and the hard stool is starting to make my wound ache. My bandages are holding, but I should really get someone to look at my cut.

"You'll be free of me soon," Rook says in a low voice, catching the direction of my stare. "At least until our next class. I suppose you might have to be seen with me to finish our essay."

I toss him a look that I hope conveys the plunging depths of my irritation when someone new enters the room. She walks over to converse with Dr. Sellers before their gazes fall on me. Oh great, what now?

"Miss Graves," Dr. Sellers says. "Apparently, you have a . . . visitor."

"Who?" I ask, already collecting my things, thrilled for a chance to escape.

"It seems . . . it's your father."

I stop moving, my stomach dropping to my feet. Every eye in the room lands on me as my neck flushes with heat.

My father.

There's only one possible reason he's here, and this is going to hurt.

11

*S*hit. *Shit. Shit.*

Lead pellets sink through my chest as I follow the messenger's instructions to the dean's office. I see my feet, hear the thud of my leather boots against the tiled corridor. But it's like my body belongs to somebody else.

I don't even have it in me to be nervous.

In fact, I feel almost nothing at all.

It seems like it takes forever and no time at all before I find myself in front of an ornate set of carved doors. The left sits slightly ajar, and I take that as an invitation to enter.

Inside, I find a room decorated with plush cream rugs and walls dressed in white silk. Ivory wood desks and cabinets fill the space, along with a reception desk where a woman sits clicking away on her keyboard.

At my entrance, she looks up and blinks. "Can I help you?" she asks in a crisp voice.

"I'm here to see . . . Dean Withers." My voice cracks as a concerned line forms between her eyes. "I'm Poet Graves."

My cheeks heat as she gives me a pitying look. "Oh. Of course." She pushes herself up from her desk, rolling her chair back.

Everyone else in the office studies me with open curiosity. I recognize that I will feel self-conscious about this later, but their scrutiny slides away as I focus on what awaits me. It is a bittersweet reprieve.

At the edge of the reception desk sits a tablet with an invitation for those interested in Storm Guard training to sign up for the cadet program. I've been hesitating for the past week, worried that my father will find out.

My fingers itch to pick up the stylus, but he sits on the other side of one of these doors, and I have no doubt he's already angrier with me than he's ever been in his life.

"This way," the receptionist says, waving me over. I glance one more time at the tablet, then follow her down a hall toward another grand door. She raps sharply on the surface before swinging it open.

The dean sits at another desk made of creamy white wood, only this one is three times the size of any in the reception area. Inlaid with frescoes along the back and sides, the top is painted with a stunning array of watercolor flowers.

Across from her is a set of chairs in which two people currently sit.

My parents.

"Hi," I say. "Mom, Dad, what are you doing here?" I force the inflection in my voice, as if I don't know exactly why they've come. I fool no one.

My parents share a meaningful look before my father turns toward Dean Withers. She presses her hands to the surface of her desk and stands.

"I'm sorry we haven't had the chance to meet formally yet," she says to me. "I've heard so much about you from your father."

I blink. Has she?

The question is enough to pull me out of my fog, and my thoughts snap into focus.

"However, you have more pressing matters to deal with today. Hopefully, we can get to know each other better at some point."

She rounds her desk and reaches for my mother. "Sariah, it was so good to see you."

My mother nods stiffly and allows the dean to clasp her hands in hers, but there's no warmth in it. Dean Withers purses her lips at my mom's obvious dismissal. It throws me off. I've never known my mother to be rude to anyone.

"Grady," the dean says to my father. "Sorry we couldn't talk any longer, but I must be off. Feel free to use my office for as long as you need."

My father offers her a warm smile and takes her hand before kissing the back of it. "It's always a pleasure, Selena."

Her cheeks blush a soft pink before she pulls her hand back.

I'm not surprised. I've met this charming man before. *This* is the scion of House Fiama. *This* is not my father. I catch the flash of annoyance that flits over my mother's face. What on earth is going on here?

"Poet," the dean says to me with a dip of her chin, and then she walks out.

"You know each other?" I ask, stalling for a moment.

"We've been friends for many years," my father says evasively, and I again catch my mother's pinched expression. Is Dean Withers one of my father's . . . dalliances? Surely he wouldn't be so *obvious* right in front of his wife?

The door closes behind the dean, leaving me alone with my parents. The weight in my stomach intensifies. It's a feeling I'm all too familiar with. Dread.

When I turn back to my father, all pretense of affability is gone. In its place is the man I know and fear.

"Poet," he says in that voice. The one I know so well. "Care to explain what happened last night?"

He says it calmly, almost frighteningly so, but I don't miss the pulsing vein in his temple. My entire body trembles, so I clasp my hands in front of me and hope he doesn't notice.

I open my mouth, then close it. Everyone wants an answer from me, but I don't have one. I just acted on instinct. It felt like the right thing to do.

"I can't," I say, and his jaw hardens.

"Do you have any idea what you've done?" His voice shifts. Becomes cold and deadly. Scary. "Do you know how foolish I look right now? The sharks are circling, waiting for me to make one wrong move, and then my daughter, my only child, walks into Amery and makes a mockery of me!"

His voice pitches up until he's shouting loud enough that I'm sure every word is carrying beyond these walls. He's a towering pillar of fury, his face flushed, his eyes wild. His fist curls at his side, and I wonder if he plans to use it.

I take a step back. It's instinctive, but we all notice it.

I don't know what to say to calm him down. An apology won't fix anything. What I did was unforgivable; I know that. He's right, and I've humiliated him. I enjoyed a brief moment of satisfaction by defying him, but I took it too far.

Unlike Knox, this isn't just about him. I am *his* daughter and therefore an extension of his leadership. I didn't just betray my father last night; I betrayed everyone in Fiama.

"Answer me!" he shouts. "Why did you do this?"

Tears burn the backs of my eyes as I shake my head. I will not let them fall.

"I'm sorry," I gasp. "I'll fix it. I still have more tests. I'll fix it. I promise."

"Trey is beside himself," my father says. "He's threatening to end our alliance and bond Knox to the Jenkins girl." He continues on, shouting about the Ardens and our marriage. About everything he stands to lose if Knox marries someone else. I feel myself shrinking under the weight of his ire. My father might be the scion of House Fiama, but only if he has the support of Society's highest ranks. Many people might believe he's currently the best thing for the city's safety. But that doesn't mean others don't want his power. That they don't think they could do the job even better.

Jenkins. As in Winter, my roommate and nemesis. Someone who would give anything to take my place. She has no idea how much I wish she could.

I shake my head and focus on my father. I nod along, trying to absorb every word of his anger. My attention slips to my mother, her back straight, her gaze darting between my father and me. Our eyes meet for the briefest second, anguish and despair flashing over her expression.

I know she's sorry about everything, but she's also never tried to stop it.

And it's silly to hope. What could she possibly do?

"Poet, are you listening to me?" my father shouts, and I nod immediately. I *am* listening. I *feel* every word imprinted onto my skin.

"I'll fix it," I vow again. "I swear to you I'll fix it. Everything will be fine."

My father huffs out a long breath. His eyes are bright with rage, and that lock of dark hair has fallen over his eyes. He shoves it back and peers at me like he's trying to parse out the delicate pieces of me he wants to break.

"You had *better* fix this," he says in a low voice. "So help me—"

I raise a hand. "I will pledge to Fiama. You have my word."

Finally, his shoulders drop. "I'm counting on you," he says, and I nod, again suppressing the urge to cry.

"I know you are," I answer. "I *know*. I won't let you down."

"Without your brother—"

"Please don't," I whisper as the first tear slips down my cheek. I can't bear to hear anything about Raine right now. He pledged to Fiama without question. He did everything that was expected of him, and then he was taken from us. It isn't fair.

My father grinds his jaw, his eyes flashing before he huffs out a long breath. "Fine. The only reason I expect to be called to Amery again is to oversee your pledge to Fiama in two months."

"Of course," I say. He nods and turns to my mother, who stands up from her chair and smooths down the front of her dress. Why did she even come if she wasn't planning to say a word?

"I miss you," I say to her, and she rushes over to hug me. I wrap my arms around her and bury my face into the crook of her shoulder. I inhale deeply, savoring the smell of her perfume as she rubs the back of my head.

"Is everyone being kind? Are you okay?" she asks. That feels like a loaded question, and I can't bring myself to burden her with the truth.

"Yeah, everything's fine," I lie, feeling the tension loosen in her body. We hug for another few seconds before my father clears his throat.

"Sariah, we should go. We're due for lunch with the general in twenty minutes."

My mother pulls away and wipes the corner of her eye. She takes my hand and searches my face before giving me a watery smile. "Take care of yourself," she says before she turns and scurries out the door.

When she's gone, I look up at my father, who offers me a scrutinizing look.

"Don't fuck this up. You won't like what happens then," he says before turning and leaving, too.

After the door slams, I count to fifty before I'm strong enough to move. My hands shake, and my breath hiccups in shallow gasps. The various aches and pains in my body throb with the echoes of my conversation and the stress slowly crushing me under its weight.

My only consolation is that the storms are quiet today.

When I'm sure my parents must be gone, I look around the room, wondering why I've been left alone in the dean's office. But small red lights buried into the ceiling remind me I'm being watched.

As I enter the reception area, several pairs of eyes find me. The woman who helped me earlier offers me a sympathetic look. Obviously, they all heard every word. They aren't Society, so I assume all they see when they look at me is a spoiled rich girl, and they aren't wrong. I am exactly that.

When I backed down from killing someone in the name of the city's protection, I further proved my uselessness.

Why am I the only one who couldn't do it? Am I just . . . weak?

Nevertheless, the receptionist's expression is kind, and that nearly breaks me.

With my fists clenched, I pass through the desks, and again my gaze snags on the tablet for Storm Guard registration. I stop in front of it with my fingers twitching.

I let my family down today. My entire House. My father is rightfully angry with me.

But a quiet, selfish voice whispers in my head that my family hasn't ever done much for me. I've been beaten and cowed into submission. Forced to marry a man I hate.

But I've also had a roof over my head and a full belly my entire life. I think of Rook. I could have been a Solitude, cobbling scraps together simply to exist.

The smart thing would be to walk out of here, pledge to Fiama, graduate on the path my father set for me, then marry Knox.

I can make myself do at least one of those things, but there's one I will never be able to live with.

My father is already furious, so what's another transgression?

I pick up the stylus from the holder, gripping it tightly enough to make my knuckles blanch. I feel the receptionist's eyes on me as I tap the screen. I stare at the blank lines and the names already listed, most of which I don't recognize.

Except one.

Rook Athira

His strangely artistic script is scrawled three lines up, and I don't know why that confirms my decision.

Before I can think twice, I scribble my name on the next blank line.

Really, what could my father do that he hasn't already threatened?

12

After leaving the office, I keep my head down and shuffle through the halls. News travels fast in our circles, and I'm sure everyone already knows the scion of House Fiama was here. My only hope is that being sequestered away in Dean Withers's office means they didn't hear every word of my scolding.

I continue in the same vein through all my classes for the rest of the morning, saying very little and dreaming of a moment to myself when I don't have to answer to anyone or be perceived at all. When I return to my dorm room, Trinity still hasn't appeared, and now I'm officially worried.

Winter and Lacey both eye me from where they lounge on their beds before lunch. I recall what my father said about Trey Arden allying with Winter's father instead, and I can't help but feel a twinge of excitement at the prospect. But then I wonder if my father would need me at all if Knox married someone else.

"What are you staring at, Freak?" Winter asks, breaking through my inner monologue. She and Knox really would deserve each other.

"Have you seen Trinity?" I ask, pointing to her empty corner. Winter pulls a face of disgust.

"No," she answers before returning to scrolling on her phone. I need to find Edward. I turn on my heel and head for his wing, ascending the staircase to find a hall similar to ours, bearing the distinct and ripe odor of teenage boys.

My nose wrinkles as I search for Edward's room.

Unfortunately, that room also belongs to Knox.

After knocking, I enter to find him, Sal, and Jackson tossing a football among them. They've already overturned a chair and a lamp, the bulb lying smashed on the floor waiting for someone else to clean it up. I somehow doubt a single one of them has ever made their own bed in their entire life.

"Poet, where were you after class?" Knox asks. He sounds annoyed more than anything, but it doesn't stop him from catching the ball and passing it off to Sal. "I told you to wait."

"My father was here," I answer, and his eyes widen. "He wanted to speak with me."

"Oh, about the . . . thing?" Sal asks, wincing.

"Shut up," Jackson says. "Leave her alone."

"Was just asking." Sal pouts, and Jackson rolls his eyes.

"I'm looking for Edward," I say. "Have you seen him?"

Their gazes ping to his empty corner as if they've completely forgotten he lives with them.

"No?" Sal says, scratching his head.

"No?" I ask.

"I mean, I've seen him . . . I just can't remember when."

I sigh as my phone buzzes in my back pocket, and I reach for it. "Useless."

A breath of relief expels from my chest when I see that it's Edward, but that relief is short-lived.

EDWARD: *Trin*

EDWARD: *Eighth-floor balcony*

EDWARD: *Now*

The hairs on the back of my neck stand up as I scan his messages.
I read them once and then again.
That's when I start running.

. . .

bolt through the hallways, hopping on an elevator. After asking for directions, I find the balcony Edward mentioned. My blood runs cold at the sight of Trinity on the floor, leaning against the railing, her body limp.

"What's going on?" I ask, rushing over and dropping to my knees. "Trinity!"

She looks up, and then she throws her arms around me, sobbing into my shoulder.

"Poet," she gasps. She's shaking and crying so hard that she can barely breathe, wet, choking sobs hiccupping from her throat. I hug her so tightly that it feels like her ribs might crack, but she clings to me as the wind whips around us.

After a few moments, she ever so slowly stops trembling. Edward watches us, a guarded wariness in his eyes. When Trinity finally catches her breath, she pulls away, and I grip her by the shoulders.

"Trinity, what happened?" I ask.

She slumps against the railing.

"I tried to fight him," she says, clearly referring to the man she was asked to battle with. Plenty of people have passed their Fiama initiation by now, which means several people have died. I stop. Not died. They were murdered. Taken and caged and then used as an example. No matter their crimes, this *can't* be what justice truly looks like.

My stomach churns, bile threatening to climb up my throat.

"But he was too strong. I tripped, and then he was on me . . ." She chokes on another sob. "I fought him off as long as I could, *any* way I could."

She looks so defeated, but she's also too pale with sweaty curls of red hair clinging to her temples. A warning fires in my head.

"But you passed, Trin," I say, trying to soothe her. "It's over. Only one trial left. You can do this."

"I didn't *pass*," she moans. "I couldn't kill him . . . but he couldn't kill me, either. They called it a tie. So, by the rules of initiation, they're letting me try again, but I have to finish *both* of the next tests. This one didn't count."

It's not an ideal outcome, but it isn't hopeless. Really, we're sort of in the same situation. My gaze holds hers, tears trickling down her cheeks, eyes wide in desperation.

"Trin, is something else the matter?" I scan her from head to toe as she reaches up and pulls away the lapel of her coat, revealing a long, festering wound slashed across her collarbone. I'm no expert, but it's already oozing and looks infected.

"Skies!" I say, sitting up and holding out my hands without touching her, worried I'll make it worse. "We have to get that looked at immediately."

"What's the point?" she asks, tears filling her eyes. "I'm about to be cast from Society. I'd rather be dead. Anything is better than this *humiliation*."

She inhales a shuddering breath, her eyes sliding closed as her head lists to the side. I think she might be on the verge of passing out.

"Trinity," Edward says, shaking her gently.

He stares up at me, his hair falling in his eyes, as if I have any idea how to fix this.

"Does anyone know?" Trinity asks, her voice hoarse and cracking.

When I don't answer, her eyes open.

"I'm not sure," I say.

Even within Society, there are hierarchies, and the Robinses aren't a family with much significance. It means Trinity has always enjoyed the luxury of flying under the radar, and her every move doesn't incite a flurry of gossip. Nevertheless, failing to pledge is a stain on anyone's family.

This is really what Amery is all about . . . deciding who is worthy of Society's resources and who is not. That *we're* all just a liability, and like a diseased plant, we're pruned to keep the entire vine from dying.

I always knew this on some level, but witnessing Trinity's desperation, having just felt my father's wrath, the truth lances me through the chest.

My mouth presses together in frustration as I wonder about the utter futility of this system. What's the point of it all? I shake my head. These aren't thoughts I should be having. We're reminded every single morning of the point. Without it, order inside New Manhattan would break down. *Everyone's* lives would be in jeopardy, from Society to cogs to Hollows.

"No," I say firmly. "We're getting you to the med wing." I gesture to Edward, who moves like he's working through hardened concrete.

"Help her up," I say, trying not to snap at him. He's obviously in shock.

Trinity's head lolls again, her consciousness ebbing, and I'm going to *kill* whoever let her walk out of her test injured like this. But this is what Society does. They take care of their own until you're not.

But Trinity's still Society, and I refuse to let anyone be done with her yet.

Between Edward and me, we drag her down the hall, doing our best to keep her head protected. She keeps blacking out, her entire weight sagging against us. She's always hated how short she is, but I'm finding myself grateful that she's so tiny.

"When did you find her?" I quietly ask Edward.

"About an hour ago," he answers. "She'd passed out against the railing."

I think about where I was an hour ago. Being scolded by my father while Trinity needed me.

"I woke her up, and she just started screaming and crying," he continues, nearly on the verge of tears himself. His voice cracks, and he shakes his head. "Thank Skies you showed up when you did. I couldn't get her to listen."

I swallow thickly against the burning sensation in the back of my throat.

"The elevator is this way," I say. I'm pretty sure the med wing is on the third level, a few floors down. Trinity sags against me, nearly knocking me over. "Lift her legs."

As we attempt to pick her up, a familiar face rounds the corner, and I resist the urge to groan.

Rook.

He stops and watches with a blank expression, his gaze roaming over me and then Trinity, a dark eyebrow arching.

"What are you staring at?" I snarl. I'm really not in the mood for anyone's bullshit.

"Do you need help?" he asks, throwing me off.

He's huge and could probably carry Trinity one-handed. She's passed out cold, which only makes her heavier. Maybe we do need help. I stumble against her weight, and Rook is beside me in a flash. He catches me by the arm, steadying me with a firm grasp, and my stomach flutters with a weird little dip.

Before I can examine that thought, he scoops Trinity into his arms and starts walking away.

Edward and I stare at his back and then at each other. He shakes his head as if wondering why he didn't think of doing that. I chase after Rook, who's already halfway down the hall.

"Thank you," I say as I catch up. His only answer is a grunt as we reach the elevator and file into the tight space. I jab the button, and the doors slide shut while I watch Rook from the corner of my eye.

We quickly arrive at the med wing, turning down a narrow corridor toward the entrance. I knock on the door, and it takes a moment for it to pop open to reveal a woman with mahogany hair and light-brown skin in scrubs.

She looks at Trinity, draped in Rook's arms, before her gaze falls on him. Her eyes narrow, and I can read everything in her expression. But she has the wrong idea.

"She's hurt," I say. "It happened during her trial."

I shove past Rook and gesture toward the nearest empty bed. He handles Trinity carefully, like an antique porcelain doll, settling her gently on the narrow mattress.

The medic's mouth snaps shut, and she follows us across the room.

"Excuse me," she says before Rook steps out of the way. Edward and I move to the far side as the medic cuts Trinity's jacket open, revealing the oozing wound.

"This is infected," she says. None of us reply. Obviously.

The medic looks up, and I notice her name tag reads Dr. Perez.

"What happened?" she asks as she starts gathering supplies, laying everything on a wheeled tray she drags to Trinity's bedside.

I shake my head. "We don't know exactly. She just said she was knocked down."

Perez flattens her lips in disapproval and begins to assess Trinity. "I'll ask you to step outside." Her tone is firm but polite. "Once she's stable, you can see your friend."

Someone takes my arm and begins to maneuver me away as a few more medics file into the room. I can't take my eyes off Trinity's pale face. Her eyelids flutter, and I want to stay, but I'm hustled into the hall, where I stand between Edward and Rook. A moment later, the door slams in our faces.

"Is she going to be okay?" I ask Edward in a whisper.

He runs a hand over his mouth and down his chin before sagging against the wall, then sliding to the floor. He looks miserable. "I don't know, but I'm not going anywhere."

Right. Yes, good. Me neither.

Finally, I turn to Rook.

"Thank you," I say, hating that it sounds like a mixture of suspicion and surprise instead of the gratitude he deserves.

He must pick up on my tone because his gaze darkens. Then he scoffs—a sound I'm becoming far too familiar with—before brushing past me and heading down the narrow hallway, disappearing without a word.

I should go after him and offer an apology and a proper thank-you, but I'm suddenly too tired to stand. Between running the tower of fire, Knox, and my father, it feels like I'm wearing a lifetime of stress chiseled into every bone.

And now I'm terrified for my best friend's life.

Instead, I sink down next to Edward, straining to hear what's happening on the other side of the door. All I catch are the muffled beeps of medical equipment interspersed by prolonged stretches of silence.

Edward hardly blinks, like his entire life depends on keeping the door in sight.

"She'll be okay," I whisper, trying to believe it. Even if she comes out of this alive, she needs to be well enough to pass the next two tests.

Edward and I lean together, and a sob escapes my throat as the weight of everything cracks me open. Tears spill down my cheeks as I try to drag air into my lungs. Edward shifts, his arm coming around my shoulders.

"I love her so much," he whispers, his body trembling.

"I know. I do, too."

Then we both fall silent.

All I can think about is how much it will break me if I lose one of the most important people in my life.

13

I jolt awake as a door opens nearby. The sensation is disorienting, and it takes me several seconds to remember where I am. My neck cracks as I lift my head off Edward's shoulder. He's leaning against me, snoring softly.

Dr. Perez hovers over us as I wipe a spot of drool from the corner of my mouth, inadvertently shaking Edward awake.

"Trinity," he breathes, his legs shooting straight out.

"It was close, but she's stable for now," the doctor says. "The infection had already entered her bloodstream, but I have her on a strong dose of antibiotics. I cleaned the wound and stitched her up. We can deal with the scar when she's feeling better, but she'll need to remain in the med wing for a week or so. Just until I can be sure the infection has cleared."

Edward nods and shoves himself up, using the wall for support. I follow him into the room, where we find Trinity sleeping peacefully in a bed in a far corner. The lights sit low, and she's loaded up with various tubes and monitors, which pump and hiss softly.

"I gave her something for the pain," Dr. Perez says. "It'll probably be a few hours before she wakes up." She walks to the other side of the bed and lays a hand on Trinity's wrist, testing her pulse before making a note on her chart.

"What time is it?" I ask.

"About three in the morning," the doctor answers. "You should probably get some sleep. Classes will start up for the day soon."

She clucks sympathetically as Edward shakes his head. "I want to be here when she wakes up."

The doctor tips her head. "I can give you a note to get you out of class for a day, but that's as long as I can extend it."

"Thank you," he says.

"Me too?" I ask, and she nods.

"But why don't you take shifts? One of you should sleep. You can't stay up all night and all day."

"You go," Edward says to me. "I want to sit with her for a bit. Get something to eat and a few hours of sleep, and then I'll trade off with you."

I'm about to protest, but I watch as he takes Trinity's hand and gently strokes the back before pressing her fingers to his mouth. I think of the doctor's words just now. *It was close.* We almost lost Trin, and I sense he needs a moment alone with her.

It occurs to me that he must've passed his initiation test. I have difficulty picturing Edward killing anyone, but he must've done it. I've always thought he'd be better suited to House Asale with his love of technology and building things. But maybe he felt like he had no choice. He has his mom to take care of. Without him, she'd have no one.

I remember everyone in that vault looking at me, willing me to choose that man's death. The flash of anger in their eyes when I didn't. Maybe this is a part of my father's plan. Making us all complicit in this violent act normalizes the brutality.

"Sure, I'll be back in a few hours to relieve you," I say before making my way to my dorm room through blissfully quiet halls. Mercifully, I make it back without being spotted and ease open the door. The curtains are drawn, revealing the sun starting to rise over the horizon.

Maybe on purpose.

Maybe so I'd immediately see what they've done.

My breath hitches as I take in my destroyed corner of the room. My bedsheets have been ripped, the pillows shredded, and the furniture broken. In bright red letters on the wall, someone has painted "traitor" and then finished the job by staining my sheets with handprints. My wardrobe hangs open, most of my uniforms torn and ruined. I stare at the mess, sucking in deep breaths and willing myself not to cry.

Winter and Lacey sleep peacefully in their beds. Did they do this? Or did they watch someone else violate my space?

Trinity's corner remains untouched, and that's because she might have faltered on her test, but *I'm* the traitor.

A tear slips down my cheek, and I wipe it away with the back of my hand. I can't stay here tonight.

I find a blanket that's mostly intact and dig up some soft leggings and a T-shirt. Then I remember Teddy. I slide open the drawer and almost weep in relief when I find him lying untouched under a pile of my sweaters.

I hug him close, pressing my nose into his head as I cling to the shreds of myself.

When I enter the hall, I'm surprised to find Domino with her arms crossed, leaning against her doorway.

"You okay?" she asks.

"What are you doing up?" I respond as I tiptoe over.

"I don't sleep well," she answers. "I heard what happened to your friend and heard them doing *that*." She gestures to my room. "I'm sorry."

I shake my head and wipe my nose with a shrug. "It's not your fault. Besides, I'm probably the one who's wrong here."

Domino considers my answer before continuing. "I heard you coming back and wondered if you might need somewhere to sleep tonight."

The softness in her voice unlocks a rusty latch in my chest. There's a guardedness about her posture, but I'm also unaccustomed to the kindness in her tone.

"Yeah, I'll find a bed."

My first instinct is to head to Knox's room, since Edward's bed is empty, but the thought fills me with deep revulsion. He'll definitely get the wrong idea, and I really should stop running to Knox every time I need something.

"We have an extra bed," Domino says, waving a hand. "You're welcome to it."

I stare at her and then at the door like she's a shining beacon in the middle of a foggy night.

"You sure?"

"Yeah, why wouldn't I be?"

"Because I'm . . . and you're . . ." She arches a brow in what I can only describe as a challenging look, daring me to finish that sentence. "Because that doesn't matter and thank you. I'd be grateful for somewhere to sleep."

"I'm Domino," she says, holding out a hand.

"Poet," I say, shaking it. She smirks and opens the door before gesturing me inside.

"Oh, I *know* your name. Welcome to your bed, at least for tonight."

14

I awaken to the sound of banging, bolting upright, instantly alert. I scan the room. Light streams in from the windows. What time is it? It takes me several seconds to remember where I am, and a few more to calm my galloping heart. Domino's room. She offered me their extra bed last night.

"Where is she?" I hear someone's muffled demand through the walls. *Knox.*

I sit up, and the clock tells me it's almost noon. I rub a hand down my face, feeling like I've been hit by a brick wall. Domino and her roommates left, probably hours ago, to head for class, and I slept through the entire thing.

Knox is still shouting, and I haul myself out of bed, gathering the clothes I tossed on the floor last night and throwing open the door.

"Knox," I yell. "What are you doing?"

He whirls on me. "Where have you been?"

"I slept in here last night."

"Why?"

I brush past him and punch the keypad outside my door.

"Why aren't you in your bed, and why weren't you in class this morning?"

We both enter my dorm room and come to a halt. The damage is even worse in the stark light of day. The angry red letters seem to hover off the wall like they've been hammered in place with rusty nails.

Traitor.

I'm a traitor to everything my House represents. I rejected their test and effectively spat in the face of our duty. The weight of my choice seeps through my skin like poison. I am the House scion's daughter, and it is *my* responsibility to uphold its values. I didn't just betray my father; I betrayed everyone in Fiama.

"What the fuck?" Knox asks, his expression a mixture of astonishment and anger. "Who did this?"

"How should I know?" I answer, dumping my clothes into the hamper and fumbling through my ruined things for something salvageable to wear. It seems they didn't touch most of my dressier outfits. Instead, my school stuff seems to have been the target. My pants are all stained with paint splatters, but they'll have to do. I rescue a clean sweater from the drawer where I've been keeping Teddy.

I return him to the pile, not bothering to hide him. Knox knows all about my attachment to my old toy, and I don't think even he's a big enough dick to give me a hard time about it right now.

I head for the bathroom to change. Looking down at myself, I uselessly wipe away a splash of red. I throw some water on my face and run a brush through my hair before tying it up in a loose ponytail.

When I return to the room, Knox is pacing back and forth on his phone. "Get someone to clean this up," he's demanding with authority and barely contained rage. "This is a mess. She needs new uniforms, too. I'll kill whoever did this."

He seems genuinely pissed, and I can't decide if it's on my behalf or if this is about something else. I'll never understand this strange need to "protect" me while also disrespecting me at every turn. But I suppose it's no different than my parents.

While Knox rages on the line, I hunt down my phone, finding it at the bottom of my bag where I tossed it last night. I need to head back to the med wing. Hopefully, Trin's awake and feeling better.

"Where are you going?" Knox asks as he disconnects from the line. "Someone is coming to clean this up."

He waves a hand, and I nod. "Thank you for taking care of that," I say, truly meaning it. I don't know how I'd deal with this otherwise. "I'm going to see Trinity now."

I head for the door. He sidesteps in front of me, blocking my exit.

"What are you doing?" I ask.

"Poet, you can't be seen with her anymore. They had to rescue her from that fight—it's embarrassing. Your image is tarnished enough, and you need to cut her off."

I inhale a fortifying breath. "My *image*? Trinity almost died. I'm not worried about my image."

Knox backs up and leans against the door, effectively barricading me in the room. "What did your father want yesterday?"

"The same thing you do," I say wryly. "But I've promised to fix this."

"Why did you do it?" he asks.

"I told you. I couldn't kill that man."

A muscle in his jaw ticks, and his arms tense where they're folded over his chest.

"Trinity is my best friend," I say in a low voice. "You cannot stop me from seeing her. I've put up with a lot of your shit, Knox, but this is where I draw the line. If you keep me from her, any chance we have for happiness is over. I'll never forgive you for this."

His mouth presses together, but he must understand how serious I am because he says, "Fine. Go. But you're having dinner with me and my boys tonight."

When I open my mouth to argue, he shakes his head.

"I know things have been . . . distant between us this past year, but you're my fiancée. We need to present a united front. Your best friend is about to be kicked out of Society, and your position protects you from some of the fallout, but you're also on thin ice. People need to see that we're solid."

I stare at him for several silent seconds. It's the most articulate thing I've heard him say, possibly ever. He almost sounds like the leader he's intended to be.

"Understood," I say. "But I'm not waiting for you after every class. I can find my way around school without a babysitter."

"Then you're eating all your meals with me," he counters.

"Fine," I say. "I can live with that."

We've never engaged in this type of negotiation before. It's the first time in a long while that I feel like maybe I could make this work. Skies, I must need more sleep because that's preposterous. I will find a way to escape him without blowing up my family, but at least for now, I can find peace in this arrangement.

"Then say hi to Trinity," he answers, his lip curling in derision. The bitterness in his words crashes me back to reality, reminding me of every invisible scar he's scored under my skin.

"Sure," I bite out. "I'll do that."

I wait for him to move. Slowly, he steps aside, and I glare at him before wrenching open the door and stopping. "I have no idea why you're like this," I say. "Sometimes I think you could be so much better, but then you have to go and become the worst version of yourself."

Something flashes over his expression. Maybe a tiny moment of comprehension. Or maybe I'm just seeing what I want.

Before he can reply, I slam the door behind me.

A real partner would have asked to join me—not to watch over me but to offer support.

A caring fiancé would make sure my *best friend* is okay.

One moment of possessive reasonableness doesn't wipe away the years of hurt Knox Arden has caused.

What was I just thinking? We could *never* make it work.

And yet, unless I can find a way out of my engagement, someday I'll have no choice but to live with it.

15

On my way down to the med wing, my phone pings.

SILVER: *poet, where the fuck are you girl??*

SILVER: *where's trin???*

ME: *i'm here. on my way to see her.*

HAZEL: *is she okay??? we heard what happened*

SILVER: *ppl are saying she passed out in the hall*

SILVER: *is she ok???*

ME: *I think so. they're taking good care of her.*

HAZEL: *can we come?*

ME: *i'll let u know*

SILVER: *keep us posted?*

ME: *ofc*

SILVER: *and did I hear the solitude helped??*

ME: *yea, rook carried her to med after she passed out*

SILVER: *gorgeous and gallant. what did I tell u*

HAZEL: *stop it, or I'll tell Trin you're horny for a Solitude while shes in the hospital*

SILVER: *she'd understand*

I snort out a laugh and round the corner to the medical center to be greeted by a shocking sight.

Rook stands across from the door. At first, he continues staring ahead, a foot pressed to the wall and his arms folded, doing nothing to stop me from objectifying the swell of his shoulders. Or his biceps.

His hair hangs a little in his eyes, slightly messy, like he just rolled out of bed. I wonder what he wears at night and then quickly dismiss that inappropriate thought.

My pace slows as I approach.

He turns his head with a hard look that makes my stomach tighten, heat gathering around my navel. Also inappropriate.

"What are you doing here?" I ask, too high, too sharp, trying to cover up how flustered he makes me. It sounds like another accusation. Fuck, why can't I speak to him like a normal person?

"They wouldn't let me in," he answers. "I wanted to see how she was doing."

He glares at the door as if he might burn holes through it.

"Who wouldn't?" I ask.

"Them." He jerks his chin, and I understand what's happened. Rook is a Solitude, and though technically he's allowed to walk these halls, he also isn't welcome here.

"I'm sorry," I whisper on a reflexive instinct, earning me another sharp look.

Then I knock on the door and wait. It opens a moment later to reveal Dr. Perez and a second doctor I haven't met before.

"I'm here to see Trinity," I say. She nods and steps aside.

I turn to Rook. "Come on, then."

Dr. Perez blocks his entrance before addressing me. "He shouldn't be in here," she says. "It was an emergency last night, but I don't want him in my ER." A quiver of fear simmers in her eyes, churned up by some old bottomless hurt. She lost someone to the Solitudes. So many people in this city have been victims of their ruthless violence. I get it.

"He helped my friend," I say softly. "He's a student at this school, just like any of us. What if he got hurt? You'd be obligated to help him. It isn't right to keep him out."

I can't believe I'm defending him, but it also doesn't feel right to deny him access.

Dr. Perez hesitates. I can tell she still wants to refuse, but after a moment, she steps aside.

Rook saunters through the door, peering down at her, towering a good head taller over her slight frame. He stops and glares, and I note the hardness of the doctor's swallow. I resist the urge to sigh and roll my eyes. I see his side, too. He's within his rights to be angry about this treatment, but he's also really not helping his case.

"Stop it," I tell him, and his dark glare falls on me, pulling up another conflicted flutter in the pit of my stomach. I can't figure out what to do with my hands, so I clench them, trying not to reveal how much he affects me.

He smirks because I am clearly not a very good actress, then crosses the room to where Trinity lies in her bed.

"Poet," she says quietly when she spots me.

"Trin!" I gasp, running over and leaning down to gently hug her. She's all bandaged up and wearing a blue hospital gown. Her hair is tied back into a high ponytail, and dark circles ring her eyes.

"Oof," she says with a wince.

"Sorry," I say, releasing her. "I'm so happy you're awake."

"Sort of," she says, touching her head. "Still pretty woozy. They have me on some strong painkillers and all these antibiotics."

I sink down on the edge of her bed.

"I was so scared," I say, taking her hand.

Her expression crumples. I know what she's thinking. Soon enough, she'll have to face what happened during initiation. She can hide in this room until she's healed, but she can't stay here forever.

"Do you want to talk about it?" I ask. Her lips press into a grim line, suggesting she never wants to think about it again. That's when her gaze falls behind me, landing on Rook.

"Uh? Hi?" Trinity asks, her gaze widening. "How long have I been out?"

"Rook helped carry you when you fainted," I supply. "He wanted to check that you were okay."

"Oh," she says. "Well, thank you. I appreciate it."

"You're welcome," he says before dipping at the waist in a slight bow. "I'm glad to see you're physically on the mend, at least."

His gaze pings to me and lingers for a heartbeat before he turns on his heel and walks away. I watch him pass Dr. Perez, who eyes him like he might pounce. He stops and stares at her again—I presume to shake her nerves up a little. Maybe she kind of deserves it.

Then he walks out and disappears.

I frown at the empty doorway before focusing on Trinity, who's studying me with an inscrutable look I can't interpret.

Her shoulders relax a little, and she asks, "How was your initiation? I never got the chance to ask."

I exhale a sharp breath, and then I tell her what I did.

"You tested for Aria?" she says slowly when I'm finished speaking.

"Yes, but I'm fixing it." I feel like I've been saying that an awful lot.

"Why did you do that?" she asks, her eyes wide.

"I couldn't *kill* a man," I answer, a little more sharply than I intend.

Trinity flinches, and I huff out a breath, recognizing the judgment in my outburst. Tests are still ongoing, but I've yet to hear of anyone else from Fiama who refused. Maybe that's to be expected when most of my House wants to join the Patrol. Briefly, I wonder if Fiama's initiation has always been this violent or if this is my father's doing.

Regardless, Trinity tried.

Even if she lost, she had every intention of killing that man.

That truth sits between us for a moment until she finally asks, "What did your father say?"

"He threatened me, of course, and said the Ardens would ally with the Jenkinses instead if I don't fix this. My family could lose everything . . ."

Something passes over her expression, there for a moment and then gone before she shakes her head. "I'm proud of you," she says, and I blink.

"You are?"

"Yes. You made a decision for yourself. I know it wasn't easy, and people are mad, but you stood up for yourself. I haven't seen you do that in a really long time."

I'm too stunned to speak for a moment.

"You really think so?" I finally ask, and she nods. "Everyone hates me, and I thought maybe you also—"

She shakes her head. "No. Don't do that. Nothing could ever come between us."

"Thanks," I whisper, realizing how much I needed to hear those words.

We both fall silent, listening to the soft beep and hiss of the machines.

Trinity bites her bottom lip, rolling it back and forth.

"What will you do for the next test?" she asks carefully.

"I'll make sure I qualify for Fiama," I say. "I can't . . . I can't do anything else. I promised my father and Knox. Besides, I've always known this was my fate."

Trinity nods. "If you think that's best."

"What . . . about . . ." I let the question hang between us.

"What about me?" she finishes. "I don't know. I suppose I'll get out of this bed and see if I can't kick the second test's ass."

I smile at her. "What an unbeatable pair we make."

Trinity pulls a wry face as the door opens, and Edward enters. He's freshly showered, damp hair hanging in his eyes. He walks over to plant a long kiss on Trinity's forehead.

"How are you?" he asks, and she blinks heavily as her head hits the pillow. It's clear she's starting to fade. While Edward fusses, I ask the doctor to look at the cut I sustained during the tower of fire. She assures me that it's healing nicely. After applying some fresh bandages, she shoos me out, but Edward refuses to budge.

So I say goodbye to give them some space, only to find Rook waiting at the end of the hall.

I hesitate for a moment and then make my way over.

I narrow my eyes, trying not to notice how well he fills out his T-shirt.

"Why are you waiting here?" I ask.

"I'm not waiting. I'm standing."

"Here? In the middle of the hall?"

He shrugs his wide shoulders and looks around. "The light is good here."

"For what?"

"Standing?" He raises one brow as if it were obvious.

I huff out an annoyed breath, but he *is* kind of right. Sunlight gilds the arch of his pierced brow and the curve of his cheekbone, highlighting the smattering of freckles bridging his nose. His eyes, which appear green and gold most of the time, reflect with bright flecks of copper. Skies, he's beautiful.

His head tips as if he's reading my mind. "Can I help you with something?"

His voice is low, dark, an arrow straight to my chest, sending shivers climbing over my scalp.

"How long are you planning to stand here?" I ask, my tone wobblier than I'd like.

He shrugs again. "For as long as I want."

"Okay, well, I'm going to get something to eat."

He pushes himself off the wall so that we're inches apart, then towers over me as he licks the corner of his mouth. My gaze tracks the movement, zeroing in on it as I catch a breath of his scent. Crisp and fresh. Green grass and apples, I think.

He's so close, I can feel warmth radiating off him.

"You don't need to clear your schedule with *me*, sweetheart," he says in that voice that works its way into the seams of my shaky equilibrium.

"I wasn't, I—" I sputter, then cut myself off. "I *know* that."

"Then enjoy your lunch," he says.

"Enjoy your . . . *standing*."

"Will do."

I hate that I'm such a messy tangle while he remains entirely unaffected.

By me. By anything at all.

So the only thing I can do is glare before I walk away. I refuse to let him see how much he rattles me.

When he starts whistling, I peer over my shoulder to find him casually leaning against the wall with his arms folded while he stares up at seemingly nothing.

I take one last look and then force myself to turn away.

It's only a moment later that I realize I'm smiling.

Why does that scare me so much?

16

I manage to spend the weekend avoiding Knox, sequestered with Trinity and Edward in the med wing, where we do our best to cheer her up without much success. It's also a reprieve from the constant looks and questions about my own botched initiation. Silver and Hazel come to visit, and though they try to act normal for her sake, I can tell they're uncomfortable. I understand why. They're worried for Trin, of course, but being associated with either of us risks their reputation with Fiama now. It's our friendship up against their family legacy . . . Still, I won't pretend that it doesn't hurt.

But I must eat eventually, and Knox finds me in the cafeteria on Monday at lunch. He drops into the seat next to me without being asked. "Why am I hearing rumors that you're hanging out with the scat?"

"I'm not hanging out with him," I say. "And don't use that word. It's vile. He happened to be nearby when Trinity fainted, and he carried her to the med wing. He was actually really helpful."

I recall my conversation with Rook when I found him outside the med wing the other day. He claimed he was just *standing* there, but I can't shake the feeling that he was waiting for me. Which is ridiculous. Why would he do that?

"You let him *touch* her?" Knox asks with obvious horror.

I give him a disgusted look. "What do you care? You didn't even ask if she's okay. Or me, for that matter."

Knox rolls his eyes, picking up his fork and shoveling potato salad into his mouth as Jackson and Sal sit across from us with their lunch trays.

"Hi," Jackson says, his gaze darting between us.

"What?" I ask.

"Nothing," he says, raising his hands in surrender.

"You clearly have something to say."

He shrugs as he picks up his mug and sips his coffee. "You sure give us a lot to talk about these days."

"Jackson," Knox says, a warning in his tone.

"I'm not trying to give her a hard time. Poet, I'm not. I'm just worried about you."

Sometimes Jackson is very good at sticking his foot in his mouth, but his heart is in the right place.

"I'm okay," I say.

He gives me a knowing look before he glares at Knox.

We're interrupted by the arrival of Winter and Lacey, both of whom I've been avoiding like the plague. Knox made good on his word to have my room cleaned up and new uniforms delivered. I also suspect he said something to the girls, because they've gone from openly hostile to pretending I don't exist at all, which is perfect. I welcome that. Hopefully, we can keep this up for the next three years.

Winter sits down on the other side of Knox, while Lacey plops down beside Jackson and immediately starts giggling and tossing her hair. Jackson focuses on his food, mostly silent, and I watch them, realizing what's going on. Jackson is totally clueless that Lacey is into him. Unlike Sal, who'll go down on any girl who gives him the time of day, Jackson has always been a bit more reserved when it comes to women. And it's not for lack of options. He's got that quiet, broody thing going on that makes him seem a little mysterious.

He really isn't, but the vibes are immaculate.

I'm not sure whether I should encourage Lacey's attraction, so she has something to focus on beyond hating me, or if Jackson is way too good for her and deserves someone better.

The conversation continues as I pick at my food, realizing I don't have much of an appetite. I scan the cafeteria, noticing Rook near the counter, holding his tray between his large hands. As if feeling my attention, he glances over, and my chest squeezes with a foreign sensation that feels like a very bad decision. I quickly look away to meet Knox's narrowed eyes, as though he's trying very hard to put something together.

Rook is now shuffling his way between the tables, searching for an empty seat.

I should never have looked over, because Knox clearly noticed and is now focused on Rook. Though the bruises on Knox's neck have faded since the day Rook humiliated him, Knox has clearly been plotting his revenge. He has a look in his eye that suggests the time has come. So I do my best to distract him. Something tells me that Knox can try, but he'll lose to Rook every time.

"What's on your schedule this morning?" I ask, tugging on Knox's wrist, but he ignores me as he continues staring at Rook.

I brace myself because I know that look far too well. I've played witness to it since we were six years old. He's definitely plotting something.

Something reckless.

As Rook passes, Knox sticks his foot out. It all happens in a flash. Rook smoothly steps over it and spins around, his fist cocked. It connects with Knox's face with a crack. Knox's head whips back, and he tips over, scattering plates and glasses of juice everywhere.

A general rush of shouts and screams accompanies dishes clinking and people leaping up from their seats to avoid the mess.

"Shit," I hiss under my breath as Knox groans and flops onto the table. Blood oozes from his nose, dripping down his face and pooling under his chin.

Rook leans over and hauls Knox up by the back of his shirt before pulling him close. "Didn't learn your lesson last time?" Rook snarls in his ear. "Fuck off and leave me alone."

Then he shoves Knox away. Knox slides off the seat, landing on the floor. Through it all, I can't seem to move. Why am I always next to Knox whenever this happens?

Also, why was that kind of hot? It wasn't. Skies, I need therapy.

Rook wipes his nose with the back of his hand, glaring at me and everyone else.

Inexplicably, his tray is still balanced in his other hand. Even the glass of water remains upright, and I swear he didn't spill a drop. Okay, that *is* kind of hot.

He continues his way down to the end of the table, where he slams into his seat, picks up a bun, and tears into it with his teeth.

While he stares ahead, chewing slowly, I think he's trying to make it seem like he doesn't care, but I suspect this all bothers him more than he's letting on. Understandably. A part of me wants to go over and apologize, but I don't think either of us wants the attention that would draw. It's better for Rook if I keep my distance.

Knox is such an ass. Did he really think he'd trip him like some dumb high school movie from the Warming Age?

"I think he passed out," Sal says, hovering over Knox. His left eye is already swelling, and blood continues to drip down his face.

Jackson sighs and plants his hands on his hips. "Great. Now he'll never shut up about this."

17

It feels like it takes forever, but our third week at Amery finally comes to an end. That Friday night, I stretch my legs across my bed as I lean against the headboard, my tablet opened to a book that I'm not really reading.

Trinity *should* be leaving the med wing soon, and I can't wait.

No one knows when the student leaders plan to start the next round of initiations, and the waiting is wearing on my nerves. As far as I'm aware, no one else from Fiama tested for another Society. From our House, two people failed, and one person died. Only Trinity's first challenge resulted in a draw. I know she feels humiliated, but I still think it could have been worse. At least she's still alive.

Part of me is eager to get the next part over with so I can redeem myself and pretend none of this ever happened. Of course, another part is worried I could die trying or be asked to do something even worse. I'm not sure what I'll do then. I refuse to hurt anyone; I don't care who they are.

Rook obviously passed his first test, since he's still here, but no one can seem to agree on which House he opted for. I consider what it might be like to pledge the same House. When he first arrived, I was terrified of the prospect, but maybe things have shifted. Of course, once Knox takes over as scion, he'll probably make Rook's life a nightmare. Plus, despite everything I know about Solitudes, I can't picture Rook hurting someone willingly.

Wherever he ends up, I can't help but notice the way my heart flutters and my stomach drops every time I think about him. Something I should definitely keep to myself.

A knock comes at the door, and Lacey walks over to open it, tossing me a glare. Several people tumble into the room, and from the volume of their voices, the pungent smell, and their general pink-cheeked dishevelment, they're clearly already stewed in Hollow moonshine.

The newcomers make their way to the other side of the room, draping themselves across Winter's and Lacey's beds. Verity and Sal stumble over to Trinity's empty corner, making out as Sal rolls on top of her, practically dry humping her in front of everyone.

"Um, hello," I say, raising my voice. They ignore me. Or maybe they just can't hear me over the sound of Verity's moans and Sal's sad little hip thrusts. "Hey! Could you not . . . do that there?"

Finally, they pull apart and glare. Verity and I have always been friendly with each other, but everything's changed now.

"Trin is still in the med wing, and I'd like to keep her corner clean," I add, knowing I'm being irrationally territorial, but this is *her* space. I spent last night tidying it up now that Dr. Perez has given her the all clear, but Trinity claims she's still not feeling well enough to move.

I know she's avoiding everyone, and I understand her desire to hide.

But she can't stay there forever.

"She's no longer Society." Verity sniffs. "Who cares?"

"She still is," I say, trying to keep my voice steady. "And *I* care."

"Fine," Verity says with a huff before the couple scoots off the bed, joining their friends to the sound of derisive laughter, definitely at my expense.

I try to ignore it, hoping they'll all leave soon. Picking up my tablet, I flip through a few pages, searching for something to occupy me, when there's a ding on my phone.

SILVER: *sogno tonight. u coming, poet?*

Sogno is a multistory club themed like a dreamscape, with fluffy clouds and bartenders and waiters dressed in practically nothing but white feathered wings.

Its notoriety is legendary, and we're barred from entry when we're younger. Trinity and I have been waiting for this moment for years. I can't go without her—it wouldn't be right. Plus, I'm not really in the mood for partying.

ME: *i think i'll stay in, but thanks. i'm a bit tired*

SILVER: *waiting for trin?*

ME: *yea*

I wait for her to convince me to come. To voice some word of protest. I know it isn't fair to hope, but Silver has been keeping her distance since my initiation.

While I understand it, it also hurts.

ME: *have fun*

A long silence follows, and I imagine Hazel and Silver discussing their reply. When it comes, my heart sinks.

SILVER: *thanks!*

SILVER: *u too*

And that's it. At least for tonight, I suppose.

Another knock comes at the door, and I quietly groan as another group enters. I recognize several faces, and a few try to catch my eye before remembering they're supposed to be shunning me.

I focus on my screen until a shadow falls over me and someone collapses onto the foot of my bed. Knox drapes himself across my feet, and Jackson stands above me with one hand on his hip and the other planted on the wall.

Jackson offers me a brown glass bottle of Hollow moonshine, and I shake my head.

"Come with us," Knox says, a touch too loudly. "We're heading to Sogno."

"You're in a better mood," I say, catching the scent of liquor on his breath. The bandage from Rook's punch is gone, and only a bit of bruising remains around his eye.

"It's the weekend," he says. "I'm getting wasted. I'll deal with that little fuck later."

His eyes darken, and I regret reminding him about his beef with Rook. I've seen very little of him for the past week. He missed biology class yesterday, and I actually do need to speak with him about our assignment that's due on Monday.

"I don't want to go anywhere," I say. "I'm too tired." May as well use the same excuse.

"Boring," Sal calls out as he ambles over, making a loud snoring sound as he grabs the bottle from Jackson.

"You guys have fun," I say. "I'd really rather just stay in."

Knox studies me for several long seconds, and I think he's about to argue.

"If that's what you want," he says with an arched brow.

"That's what I want."

Again, he pauses as if he has more to say but changes his mind. "Next time?"

I shrug. "Sure. Maybe. We'll see."

"She's so enthusiastic, isn't she?" Sal says in a dry tone. "It's like we're threatening to rip out her toenails."

A momentary flare of guilt burns in my gut. It's kind of nice they seem to care more than my so-called friends, but I still don't want to go without Trinity.

"It's not you," I say, hoping to appease him.

"We're so handsome, too," Jackson says with a pout as he tips the bottle into his mouth, and I can't help the twitch of my smile.

Knox stuffs his hands in his pockets and gives me an *are you sure?* look.

"Next time," I say with a bit more confidence. "Okay?"

"Okay," he says, which seems to please all three of them. I shouldn't be so grateful they're talking to me, but after Silver and Hazel's dismissal, I can't help it. Being with Knox offers a kind of currency that protects me despite my status as a social pariah, but I'm also a mouse befriending a lion.

Knox gestures to his friends, and they leave while Winter and Lacey continue entertaining. I'm attempting to lose myself in my book when a harsh crackle zips down my spine. I inhale sharply as it spreads to my fingers and toes, making them tingle. The threatening storm is starting to build, flashes of lilac streaking across the sky every few minutes. I stare out the window with my knees tucked up, watching the clouds tumble.

They're moving fast, and I'm not sure I can withstand their pull tonight. It's been too long since I absorbed a cloud burst, and my plans to stay in my room go up in smoke as another buzz flashes in my temples. At the very least, I need to hide. I'm not sure I can conceal my discomfort tonight.

Trying to go unnoticed, I slide off the bed and grab my bag, intending to head to the library. At the last moment, I snag my coat, just in case, and quietly slip into the hall.

Music pounds from the various dorm rooms, and a door opens to my left, a group of kids stumbling out. I wait a few seconds for them to leave first, hoping to avoid any more awkward interactions tonight, then hang a left at the bottom of the stairs as another tingle spreads along my back. I don't think I can ride this out in the library after all. I need relief. I need to touch Spark.

I consider my options. I could go to the roof, but what if someone sees me up there?

A balcony? No. They're too exposed and open.

What I need is to get out of the city, where no one can find me.

I've done it before, when I was desperate. I know a spot where I'm invisible on the city's outskirts.

Another loud group appears at the end of the hall, and I freeze as Domino emerges with her cog friends. I consider bolting, but she calls my name.

"Poet!" She grins as she approaches. "This is my friend Journey." She gestures to a pretty brunette sidling up next to her.

"Nice to meet you," I say.

"You're the one they're all talking about," Journey says, perusing me with an unflinching look. "What's it like being rich and powerful? Or maybe you're less powerful now? People are mad, but they also seem to kind of fear and respect you. I guess it's confusing, right?"

I don't think she breathes even once as I find myself slowly backing away. Not from *her* as much as this list of questions that makes my stomach hurt. The last thing I want to talk about is what it's like to be hated by everyone you know.

"Journey," Domino says, an air of impatience in her tone. "You're doing that thing again."

"Oh yeah," Journey says with a wince. "Sorry."

"We're headed to Sogno," Domino says, perhaps to cover for her friend's gaffe. "What about you?"

I'm still wearing my uniform, clearly not dressed for a night out. She looks behind me as though she expects a group of friends to materialize.

"No," I answer. "I've got some homework to do. Have fun."

Then, before they can invite me to come—not that I should expect them to—I walk off. A moment later, I stop and turn around. "Thanks again for giving me a place to sleep the other night."

Domino nods. "Sure, anytime. It's always empty if you need it again." Her friend smiles in agreement, loosening a tight knot in my chest. It's a small act of kindness, but I appreciate it more than they know.

Without saying anything else, I turn again and head toward the library. It's Friday night, so I'm not surprised to find it empty. "Library" is probably too strong a word to represent what this room is. I've seen pictures of what libraries used to look like in the Warming Age, when they still printed books. With everything digitized, libraries are now just large screens suspended above tables with chairs at which to work and study, where everyone is expected to speak in a hushed voice.

A security guard sits in a chair near the door, his feet planted wide and his hands clasping the armrests as he nods off. I'm searching for a quiet corner when someone steps out from behind a large screen, nearly knocking me over.

Rook clutches a tablet in his hand. He's dressed casually in the same jeans and cowboy boots he was wearing when he first arrived. My gaze zeroes in on his feet.

"Where did you get those?" I ask. He looks down and then back up.

"A scavenger," he says with a shrug.

"You have scavengers in the Wastes?"

It *feels* like a ridiculous question the moment it's out of my mouth, and his smirk confirms it.

"Yeah. In fact, they bring us the really good stuff before they head to the city." He taps his heel on the edge of a table leg as if to demonstrate that fact. It's hard to argue, since I've never seen anything like them before, except in pictures from the past.

"What else do you have?" I ask, reluctantly curious about his world. His brow arches, and he props his hip on the table with his arms folded.

"We have everything," he answers confidently.

"That's not what they tell us."

He huffs out a derisive laugh. "I'm aware."

"Then why did you come here?"

He narrows his eyes. "Curious today, aren't we?"

"Yes," I answer, refusing to take his bait.

"Fine," he says, running his fingers through his hair, his forearm flexing in a way that is a bit too distracting for my taste. "We don't have *everything*. No school like this or your Houses. And survival's much harder."

I glance at the tablet clutched in his hand.

"But you can read."

"I can read."

"Is that . . . common?"

He hesitates as though he doesn't want to answer.

"Most people can manage the basics," he says. "But they're also focused on other priorities."

I nod. It's not completely surprising to hear.

"I finished our biology assignment," he says, flipping the screen around. He swipes a finger up, showing me the completed essay. I eye him with suspicion and scan it, impressed by his analysis.

"If you don't have school, where did you learn all this?"

"I didn't say we don't have school. I said we don't have one like this."

My gaze meets his. "Why did you finish it? You've been missing classes."

"I've been avoiding your boyfriend." His tone suggests it isn't because he's scared of Knox but rather annoyed about having to teach him yet another lesson about respect.

"He's not my boyfriend." The words are out before I can stop them.

A line of confusion forms between Rook's brows before it smooths away. Thankfully, before I can do something I'll regret like reach out and touch it. "Oh yeah?" I'm not sure why that seems to amuse him.

"Yeah." I don't elaborate, but I want to clarify that I *don't* belong to Knox.

"Okay, if you say so. And I finished it because I thought it would be easier that way."

He leaves the thought hanging.

Easier for me or for him?

"I don't want to take credit for your work."

He huffs out a snort. "It's not a big deal. You can owe me one."

I raise a brow. "That doesn't exactly put me at ease."

"Well, it's done. So, unless you want to redo it for absolutely no reason, you'll just have to accept it."

"Next time, I'll do the work."

"Will there be a *next time*? So eager to work with me again?" The corner of his mouth crooks up in a cocky smile, and it's all I can do not to wring his neck.

"You know what I mean—"

A sizzle scrapes up my back, buzzing under my skin with such force that my heart skips a beat. I slap a palm to my chest and retreat a few steps as Rook reaches out.

"You okay?" he asks, his big hand wrapping around my arm to help steady me. It does nothing to calm the acceleration of my heart.

But I can't answer.

I need to get out of here immediately.

Without another word, I turn on my heel and walk away.

"Hey!" Rook calls. "Where're you going? Are you okay?"

I don't look back as I duck out of the library and run.

18

Another sizzle of energy crackles across my skin as I burst out of the room.

The storm is drawing closer, and I need a place to touch it.

I hear Rook call after me, but I don't want him to notice anything suspicious.

He'd turn me in to the Extinguishers in a flash.

I skirt through the halls, keeping my pace measured just in case.

As soon as I spot a swirl of clouds through a window, my decision is made.

I drop my bag behind a statue to conceal it, planning to retrieve it later. Then I button up my coat, jog to the door near the front . . . and make my way outside.

With my collar up and head down, I brace against the wind. The streets have emptied, save a few brave—or possibly naive—souls. The canals are closed due to the high winds, but it's better to take the tunnels regardless. The train is faster, and I'm too obvious out here. Too exposed.

I take a deep breath and veer right, heading for the nearest subway entrance. Even down here, hundreds of security cameras are mounted everywhere, so I pull up my hood and shrink into its shadows.

The city maintains a vast network of industrial-size pumps to keep the tunnels dry and free from the water that surrounds us. There isn't enough room for the Hollows to live aboveground, so this ensures they have somewhere to go.

As I scramble down the stairs, I enter the crush, immediately feeling confined. A glance to my right shows a wall lined with stands selling various scavenged items, along with moonshine and other provisions.

Bright caged lights set in the walls cast everything into harsh shadows, and flickering screens mounted to the corners play The Shield's messages on a loop, reminding everyone of our duties and obligations to the city.

I check my phone, confirming I still have several hours before curfew hits—more than enough time to make it back. I push through the turnstile and then wait on the platform, where I find a mixture of cogs and Hollows. I also spot the occasional Society member, including some kids from Amery, who I assume must all be headed to Sogno.

Ducking my head, I move away, hoping they won't spot me.

It doesn't take long before I hear rumbling in the distance. The effect of the gathering storm is less pronounced underground, but more tingling ripples over my skin, forcing me to rub the back of my neck and then my hands. A hot spark erupts at my nape, and I spin around. It almost feels like I'm being watched.

I shake off the sensation as the train comes barreling toward us and hisses to a stop.

I clamor in with the masses, finding a corner to stand in. Then fold my arms and try to make myself inconspicuous despite the itching in my fingers.

But I still can't shake the feeling that someone is watching me.

I chalk it up to anxiety and the gathering energy that always makes me a little anxious when I've gone too long without absorbing a hit of Spark.

We careen through the Hollows' underground city, past markets and squares, where hundreds of people make their homes. I spot a scavenger swap, where tables are piled high with clothing and various bits of kitchen equipment and decor.

The train empties the closer we get to the end of the line, which finishes in the factory district, where House Asale maintains control. It turns out to be the busiest station of all, suggesting a shift must have just ended. I slip out among the scramble of bodies, thankful for their cover.

When I'm free, I pound up the stairs, racing against the storm. If it hasn't already started, it's only a matter of minutes, and I don't want to miss it.

Hot spots flash across the sky in splashes of ultraviolet light, vibrating in my bones as I scurry along the train platform and down the stairs at the end. With my arms folded and my head down, I walk quickly, winding past warehouses and factories.

Two massive Storm Towers stand in the distance. If I squint, I imagine I can see the Breakers staggered on their various platforms. What I *can* see are the glowing purple Spark wands they each hold in a hand. About two feet long and an inch in diameter, the wands are made of shatterproof glass and filled with a core of pure galvanic energy that attracts bursts of Spark. A special rubberized handle at one end helps tamp down the effects of flowing electricity, helping to protect the Breakers from being blitzed.

I head for a tear in the chain-link fence, where the terrain has made it impossible to place a tower, before slipping through.

We accidentally discovered this spot a few years ago when Knox and his friends got it into their heads to explore the Wastes. Those flat, stretching miles have always held a sort of tepid fascination for all of us.

I also think Knox wanted to show off.

Thus, Knox, Sal, and Jackson dragged me and a few others along with the theory that we were more protected in a group.

It didn't take long to find the nearly invisible break in the metal, almost as if someone had come before us. It was a million-to-one discovery that's proven useful to me more than once.

That night, we didn't make it to the Wastes.

The ruined portion of Old Manhattan beyond was so dark that a few people got freaked out and wouldn't stop crying. So we aborted the mission and slunk back home.

I never forgot about it, though, and so I came back alone a few weeks later to uncover what became a refuge.

Another flash follows me past a bombed-out building, crumbling from neglect.

That same wary prickle I felt earlier touches the back of my neck, and I stop, peering over my shoulder to find nothing but shadows.

Bending down, I retrieve the knife tucked in my boot, gripping it in my hand, just in case. I refused to kill that man for the sake of the initiation, but I have zero hesitation about defending myself. Keeping one ear peeled for anything unusual, I pick my way over rocks and debris, a few stacks of bricks where buildings once stood. My destination is a towering wall of massive flat rocks piled about a hundred feet up.

From my reading about the Wastes, I've learned these were left behind during the floods that wiped out the people of the Warming Age. Inhaling a deep breath, I pick up my pace, losing myself in their tall shadows. I stick close to the rocks as I make my way to the tunnel I know leads to the other side.

When I spot it, I exhale the breath trapped in my chest and head down the path. I'm sure it's man-made. It's too straight to be natural. I often think about who might have carved this and wonder if they were in a similar situation to mine.

I emerge on the other side, and from here, it feels like I'm the only person in the world. The city sits behind me, shielded by the rock at my back.

The wall curves gently to my left and right, spreading out in a subtle arch, almost like an embrace. In the center sits a single large rock, a few feet high, and I scramble onto it, staring into the darkness.

The clouds obscure everything, including the moon, making the surrounding details hard to parse out. In the distance, hot spots flash, illuminating the world around me with temporary bursts of light. For some reason, I'm reminded of Rook, and for the first time, I really consider the sprawling world stretching into the distance.

How far away did he live? Did he cross these miles alone? Was he scared? Does he miss his home? Everything I've ever learned about Solitudes suggests that whatever place he left was a wretched half-life, but maybe he has people who love him and he was forced to leave them behind.

A small crash overhead tells me the storm is moving closer, and I tip my face up, watching the sky. My limbs tremble as I stand, arms spread and feet wide, bracing myself against the wind.

Another crackle sends a shiver across my scalp, and I call to the Spark, willing it to find me. It always does when I give it the chance. It's like it knows me and seeks me out. It seems silly to say out loud, but I can't shake the sensation that it understands who I am.

Another brilliant flash bursts across the horizon, an explosion lighting up the sky. The Spark coalesces, slamming into my chest. Instantly, a plasma arc swells, encasing me inside its thin, transparent walls as bolts of energy sizzle against my skin.

Pain.

It rips into me, chewing through my lungs and heart and brain, forcing me to my knees, and I shudder at the onslaught. At the all-consuming, drowning need. I quake in a sort of stupor as it rolls through my limbs and spreads to my fingers and toes.

My hands and knees strike rock, fingers digging into stone as I cling to the shreds of myself. The hairs on my arms rise as I tear apart, my lungs expanding, contracting, filling with lead.

Seconds pass. Minutes. Entire lifetimes, maybe.

I lose myself in the moment, tumbling through time and space. Tiny flickers flash in the corners of my vision as Spark buzzes down my limbs and dances along my spine. Static crackles in the air, snapping in my ears.

I feel my hair lifting, swirling around me like my own personal whirlwind.

I want to scream. I want to cry. But I also want to sing.

Then it ends, the plasma arc winking out.

I stare at the ground, panting as the pain morphs into euphoria, like I've been dipped into a hot bath after coming in from the cold.

Slowly, I open my eyes and sit back on my heels to study my hands, flipping them back and forth to watch purple sparks dance over my skin.

Here in the darkness, I'm like a beacon, reflecting the power of my world.

My mind bends in on itself, and for a moment, everything turns to dust. I shake my head, waiting for the empty spaces in my brain to fill. I know this is wrong. I feel it in the way my thoughts warp and twist, suggesting a mind teetering on the edge of control.

The air around me pulses like a beating heart, and I hum to the resonance that's become my own personal melody. It's always strongest when I'm out here, away from the noise and bustle of the city. I roll my neck and twist my head back and forth as I shake my arms and hands.

Slowly, I look around, inhaling deep breaths as the wind tosses my hair and clothing. I almost feel like I could flap my arms and take off into the sky.

And then . . . movement at the base of the rocks catches my eye.

A shadow melting into darker shadows.

I blink and blink again, then it's gone.

The air in my chest twists, grows claws.

I'm almost positive someone was just standing there.

19

Someone saw me. Someone is out here with me. Are they already headed to the Extinguishers to report what they saw?

"Hey!" I shout. "Who's there?"

As if they'd ever reveal themselves.

My earlier euphoria is doused under an icy shock of reality. This was reckless and impulsive. I've gotten away with it before, but perhaps I've grown too confident.

My gaze focuses on the tunnel entrance, lost in the distance of the craggy shadows. Maybe I just imagined it, and my stretched mind is playing tricks on me. Who would be out here? And if they were planning to accuse me of something, surely they would have done so?

I check the time and realize I need to get moving if I want to make it back to Amery before curfew. With a huff, I pinch at my hair and clothing, snuffing out the remaining sparks, like I'm flipping a switch. I wish I could bask for hours in the sensation of this energy moving across my skin, but there's no more time.

I jump down from my perch, cross to the far side of the rock wall, and enter the ruins, my gaze checking left and right.

Still, I can't shake the sensation of a presence creeping up the back of my neck.

I move quickly, guided by the lights of the storm, attempting to cast off the lingering sensation of my mind folding itself in half.

When I reach the train station, I inhale deeply, trying to calm my racing heart. I hop onto a waiting car just as it lurches to life and lumbers into the heart of the city, muttering a quiet curse to myself when we stop at the station nearest to Sogno. I should have anticipated this.

About a dozen House Fiama kids are making a scene on the platform, where other passengers have formed a ring of distance around them. I pray they opt for a different car, but the doors slide open, and they stumble in, their chatter cranked to full volume.

The group laughs and giggles as they shove into one another, not the least bit aware of the people around them. I tuck farther into my corner and pull my hood up, keeping my eyes averted.

On the other side of the platform, a night market is crammed with people sorting through piles of clothing. I notice the Patrol doling out rations of drybars to Hollows. The packaged bars are condensed with nutrients and intended as a filling substitute when fresh food is scarce.

I stare out the window at the faces, my gaze snagging on a woman who sits against the wall, dressed in gray and black clothing, her knees tucked up and her head tipped back.

There's something familiar about her that I can't put my finger on.

My eyes narrow as I study her intently, trying to decide if she's real or just a product of my post-storm confusion. But I don't get the chance to examine her further as the train starts to move and picks up speed, once again hurtling us closer to Amery.

After a few minutes, raised voices and shouts signal that a fight has broken out in the middle of the car. I stretch onto my tiptoes to see what's happening. The train slides to another stop, and a mass of people spills onto the platform, clashing with the group that's already waiting.

At the center of the mess is an Aria kid fighting with a Hollow.

I recognize Todd Henly and a Hollow about our age. The latter is lean and wiry, while Todd has a firm, athletic frame.

The Aria kids have formed a barrier around them, chanting and shouting, egging Todd on.

Todd and the Hollow clash, wrestling as they wrap their arms around each other's waists. The train won't move due to a gridlock of bodies jamming the door.

I can't look away as the boys scrabble and fight, their faces turning red. Todd lifts the Hollow and slams him onto his back, to a chorus of cheers, before raising his arms and spinning in a circle of triumph. More and more people gather at the edges as they catch wind of what's happening.

The wiry boy lies on the ground, winded and gasping for breath, while Todd celebrates his victory before taunting him again.

But the Hollow isn't afraid. I see it in the determined set of his jaw. He rolls over onto his hands and knees, struggling to his feet, then sprints, ramming into a surprised Todd, knocking him back. They go tumbling together, punches wailing, as they slam into a door on the other side of the car.

Suddenly, the door where Todd and the Hollow are still struggling hisses open. Someone must have pulled the emergency release. Todd and the Hollow go tumbling off the edge, landing on the tracks. The crowd condenses, some following the fight onto the tracks while others push their way toward the platform in the other direction.

I'm shoved left and right, squeezed into my corner. I need to move.

That's when a hand closes around my wrist. I shake it off, but it holds me firmly and pulls me against a warm, hard body.

"You need to get out of here," someone says in my ear.

A voice I recognize immediately.

Rook.

Where did *he* come from?

I'm too surprised to reply as he shoves through the crowd, dragging me behind him. He's much bigger and taller and divides the seething bodies in a way I couldn't on my own.

The mass is frantic now. We're jostled left and right, and someone screams in terror as several more people are knocked onto the tracks.

Somehow, we make it off the train and across the platform, though not without several elbows to my ribs, a few knocks to the head, and my pinkie toe taking the brunt of someone's errant heel.

Still, it's a small price to pay as Rook drags me to the stairs and up the first few steps.

From here, I can see the tracks and the people trying to climb back up, but there's no room. A woman scrambles over the edge but is kicked back without anyone realizing it. She screams as she hits the tracks and tries again, along with the dozens of others who crawl over one another like frightened ants.

"We need to help them!" I call out.

Rook nods but doesn't break his stride as we shove up the crowded steps. "We can't do anything from here," he argues. "We need to alert the Patrol."

I watch as Todd winds his arm and punches the Hollow in the jaw. The boy goes flying and lands on his back, his neck snapping and his head hitting the side of the raised track. I stop climbing with a gasp, my hand covering my face.

"Come on!" Rook hisses. He tugs on my arm, and we continue up.

The ground begins to rumble, signaling an oncoming train from the opposite direction.

"Skies," I whisper. Everyone on the tracks is about to be crushed.

But Rook is right. We need to get help. He doesn't let up his vise grip on my arm as we continue our climb. I can't look as a high-pitched horn squeals in warning, the train barreling into the station.

My eyes squeeze shut, and I look away as we ascend, step by agonizing step.

The *screams.*

They shatter the air against a backdrop of screeching brakes, crushed bodies, and the crowd's frantic shouts.

Rook tugs on me again, and I focus on pushing up and up.

When we finally reach the top of the stairs, we burst onto the street crowded with people.

The screams float up, dousing us in the horror of death.

But they've become distant and muted, and I can't seem to get enough air in my lungs.

I notice several Patrols already arriving, and I watch as Rook quickly fills them in on what just happened. After they disappear into the station, Rook continues dragging me away from the chaos as I stumble after him, until we finally reach a quiet plaza.

He eases me onto a bench, and I bend over, putting my head between my knees as nausea swirls in my gut, threatening to bring everything up.

I lose the battle with my stomach.

Spying a garbage can, I leap up and hurl everything into it. A gentle hand gathers my hair, holding it back while I grip the edges of the bin. My necklace is hanging out of my shirt, the mask dangling and the amethysts winking in the light as I picture the people trapped on the tracks. My snot mingles with my tears until I'm spitting up bile and my knees have turned to rubber.

I'll hear those screams for the rest of my life.

Finally, I stop, breathing heavily as Rook releases his grip on my hair and lets it settle over my shoulder. He backs away a step and stuffs his hands into his pockets. Wiping the corner of my mouth, I stand up and quickly braid my hair into a single plait to keep it out of my face. Then I tuck my necklace back into my shirt.

I cling to the edge of the garbage can for several more seconds as the wail of sirens fills the air, and another wave of nausea makes me dizzy. An ambulance barrels past, red lights reflecting off the plaza's dark stone.

I sniff and swipe my nose with the back of my sleeve.

"Thank you," I whisper to Rook. He nods, then points to the bench, where we both settle side by side. Propping my elbows on my knees, I drop my head, waiting for the last of the nausea to fade. Rook sits quietly next to me, and we don't say anything for several long minutes. I listen to the sounds of chaos in the distance as my vision blurs, a familiar numbness seeping through my limbs as I try to imagine myself somewhere else.

I picture the Patrol subduing the crowds. The ambulances picking up the injured. I wonder what became of everyone. The Fiama kids and the Hollow that Todd probably killed. I wonder if anyone from Amery was hurt, and I wonder if maybe they deserved it a little bit.

Then I shake my head, trying to cast off that equally horrible thought.

Finally, my breathing slows, and I return to the earth, no longer floating inside my body. The effects of touching the storm still linger, making the events of the last half hour feel somewhat distant, almost fuzzy around the edges. But not enough to soften the terror of what I just witnessed.

My gaze slides to Rook, who stares at the fountain with a dent between his brows.

"Are you okay?" he asks, not looking at me. I shake my head, though I'm not sure if he can see it.

"Not really."

"Yeah," he answers, inhaling a deep breath, his head tipping forward, hair falling around his face.

"What were you doing on the train?" I ask.

Slowly, he looks over. "What were *you* doing on the train? Weren't you at Sogno like everyone else?"

My gaze shifts to the ground. "I left early," I say.

"Is that so?" he asks, and I'm sure he can tell I'm lying. His tone definitely suggests he doesn't believe me, which annoys me for some reason.

"Yes," I answer sharply, looking up again. "Why else would I have been on the train?"

He shrugs. "No other reason, of course, but you ran out of the library pretty fast?"

Then he straightens, his shoulder brushing mine as he sits back on the bench. His gaze flicks to me briefly before darting away. I notice he didn't answer my initial question, so I don't reply to his, returning the favor.

"We should head back. It's almost curfew, and the last thing you need is to be caught out late," he says.

I make a sound of indignation. "The last thing *I* need?"

He arches an eyebrow, and I can't help but admire how annoyingly good it makes him look. It pisses me off, but his smug derision digs in like a splinter, giving me something tangible to focus on.

"According to everyone, you've gotten yourself into some trouble lately," he says.

I scoff. "I did nothing wrong."

He doesn't reply, and I get the sense he's allowing me to fill the silence. I desperately want to ask about his own initiation, but I hold my tongue. I'm shocked the gossip mill hasn't dug up more information, but then my usual source of news is Silver, and she's not really talking to me.

I don't want him to think there's anything I find compelling about him. I shouldn't even be talking to him. If my father found out I've been . . . not friendly exactly, but that I've even spoken to a Solitude, he'd lose his shit.

A siren's wail punctuates the relative silence, which becomes Rook's cue to stand. I follow him up, and we face each other as he peers down at me, searching my face. I'm too shocked to move when he reaches out and touches my jaw, a thumb sweeping over the curve of my cheek.

My breath hitches as he shifts closer, and I swear his eyes grow darker.

Is he planning to kiss me? I lean in, pulled like I'm a distant planet dragged into his orbit.

My lips part, my mouth dry.

"You have a scratch," he says, his voice hoarse, strained. I think he's trembling. I'm just not sure why. Another swipe of his thumb, and then he pulls his hand away. Quickly. I blink, realizing I've misread the entire situation while noticing the drop of blood on his finger before he wipes it on his pants. "But I think you'll live."

I nod, heart in my throat, stomach hanging somewhere around my ankles. Skies, I'm such a fool. I remember my breath smells like vomit anyway. Probably for the best.

"Let's go." He gestures for me to start walking, and we head down the street, weaving through the crowds, our hands and arms occasionally brushing by accident. Every time his skin touches mine, my breath hitches.

Luckily, that last subway stop isn't too far from school, and we get back just as other students are returning from their night out. Their general air of merriment suggests they haven't heard about the accident yet.

Rook ducks his head and slips through the spaces as several people greet me, asking what happened when they notice the scratch on my face. I don't get the chance to say anything as he disappears around the corner, leaving me on my own.

He just saved my life. Held my hair back while I puked into a trash can.

Touched my cheek with such careful tenderness . . . and now I don't even warrant a nod good night.

I hate that it bothers me so much.

20

The following week at Amery is somber.

Everyone's been shaken by the tunnel incident, and most weren't even there to witness the worst of it. Three kids from Amery died, including Todd. They shut down the entire train network for forty-eight hours to investigate the matter, but I'm not sure what they'll find.

At night, I lie awake, hearing the sound of the train cars screeching into the station.

And then come the screams. The *screams*.

They play on a loop, echoing in the recesses of my darkest thoughts.

In my mind's eye, I see Todd and that poor Hollow tumbling off the tracks.

The families of the dead students arrived at school a few days ago. I was passing through the main hall as Dean Withers greeted them. They stood together with their heads bowed as she offered them condolences.

They took the bodies to be cremated, and I couldn't stay to watch. I found a quiet corner of the library where no one could see me, and I sat curled up in a ball in one of the plush leather chairs until I stopped shaking.

Now, it's the middle of the night, and I lie awake, blinking up at the ceiling.

Another storm is brewing in the distance, and combined with my nightmares, I haven't slept much in days. Despite playing witness to that tragedy, it's a good thing I took time to escape the city to absorb the cloud burst that night. I'd be crawling right out of my skin otherwise.

Giving up on yet another night of sleep, I toss off the covers and pull on some comfortable clothing, wincing at the ache in my limbs. I've been avoiding everyone except for Trinity. She's the only one I could talk to about any of this. I did leave out the part about Rook, worried she might freak out.

For the last few days, she's been complaining of dizzy spells and bouts of nausea. But I've known her long enough to know when she's lying, and she's faking it to hide in her hospital bed and avoid her inevitable confrontation with House Fiama.

In a lucky but grim twist of fate, the tunnel incident bought her some time while school officials dealt with the fallout. But Dr. Perez told me they're discharging her today, and she can't avoid it any longer.

I slip through the halls quietly. Days ago, Dr. Perez gave Edward and me the entrance code, knowing we like to visit her at all hours.

I enter the dimly lit room. It's peaceful here. Quiet. I can see why Trinity doesn't want to leave.

I pad over to where she lies sleeping, her chest rising and falling softly, and drop into the bedside chair, propping an elbow on the armrest before leaning my head on my hand.

I watch her, finding calm in the rhythmic pulse of her steady breathing. Within a long list of worries, the main thought that's been itching at the back of my mind is actually Rook. And not because I nearly made a complete fool of myself when he touched my face.

Why was he on the same train? How did he find me so quickly, and how did I fail to notice him? My focus was on the House Fiama kids making such a commotion, so maybe he was also hooded and I overlooked him.

I can't help but recall that shadow by the rocks after I absorbed Spark.

Did he follow me? And if so, what did he see? And why?

"Poe?" comes a soft voice that stirs me from my thoughts. Trinity blinks up at me heavily. "You okay?"

"Yeah," I say, sitting up. "Just couldn't sleep, and I thought I'd come check on you."

"Still having nightmares?" she asks, and I nod.

"A little bit." We're quiet for a moment before I reach out and take her hand. "You have to leave today."

She presses her mouth together. "I know. I'm scared. Are they . . . talking about me?"

"Not really," I say, and I think I catch a flash of annoyance in her eyes, but that can't be right. "Honestly, everyone's so distracted by the train incident. I think it's the best time for you to return. We'll attend the memorial this afternoon, and you can hold your head high. Who cares what they all think?"

"I do," she grumbles petulantly, and I huff out a laugh.

Of course she does. We all do. We're literally raised to care what Society thinks. It's ingrained in us from before we can even talk.

"Well, maybe it's time for us to care a little less," I answer softly, and her surprised expression jumps to mine.

"What are you saying?" she asks.

I shrug and tuck up a knee under my chin. "I don't know. I'm tired. It's been a long few weeks."

"You can say that again," she answers before sitting up. "Remember when we were little, and we'd hide under the covers when the storms came?" Her voice takes on a dreamy quality. "They always made you so nervous."

They did, but I don't elaborate on why, though I have no doubt she's always suspected something.

"And your nanny would bring us cookies and hot chocolate, and she'd sing to us, and I don't know, it would make me feel better, too."

The corner of my mouth tips up in a soft smile.

"Of course I remember."

"Those times were so much . . . simpler."

I suppose it's easy to think of them that way. By then, I had a secret that could get me killed and a father who nearly did so with his temper. I'm not sure "simple" is the right word, but she's having a moment, and I don't correct her.

"Sometimes Raine would try to scare us by hiding under the bed," I add, and she laughs.

"What a jackass," she snorts before her eyes spread. "Sorry. I didn't mean . . ."

"It's okay." I wave her off. There was a time when I could barely hear his name spoken aloud and certainly didn't want to be reminded of his shortcomings, but time has eased that ache, tamping it from sharp and bright to dull and chafing. I consider it progress.

"He *was* such a jackass when he did that. Among many other things."

Her shoulders ease as she laughs softly before we both fall silent again.

Trinity blinks, and I watch as she wipes a tear from the corner of her eye. "What am I going to do, Poet? I don't know if I'm strong enough to pass the next two tests. What if this is it for me?"

I'm not sure how to answer her.

"I'll be there with you no matter what," I say. "And I don't care if you aren't Society. You and I are friends forever."

I watch as tears fill her eyes, and she holds her hand out to mine.

We clasp our fingers together, and she squeezes them hard.

I stare at our hands, thinking of the days when we'd run around the playground or walk down the hallways at school, confident that we were safe.

"I'm not sure it will be that simple," she says, and I look up.

"We'll figure it out," I say. "They can't keep us apart."

21

It's raining when Trinity returns to our dorm room later that afternoon. Despite the regularity of the storms, it doesn't rain often in New Manhattan—something due to the air pressure and currents I don't really understand.

Thankfully, Lacey and Winter have already left for the memorial, so Trinity has a bit more time before she's forced to confront an audience.

She still wears a bandage across her collarbone, and I help her into her high-necked jacket to cover it up. Once she's in her dress uniform, she steps back to assess her reflection.

"You look great," I assure her, and she shakes her head.

"I'm such an embarrassment."

"Don't say that," I counter sharply. "Is it really such a bad thing that you didn't take someone's life?"

"Poet." She whips around to face me, her eyes wide like I've suggested something disgusting. "What's gotten into you lately? Stop *saying* things like that—you'll be in even more trouble than you already are. And stop acting like you aren't in as much shit as I am. You tested for *House Aria*. You're a traitor as far as everyone in Fiama is concerned."

"Everyone?" I ask as her accusation slices deep.

"That's . . . No . . . Poet . . ." She trails off and rubs her face with her hands. "I didn't mean it like that. I don't think you're a traitor. What I think is we've both fucked up in the most spectacular but different ways, and we both have targets on our backs."

"Fine," I say. "I'm heading to the memorial. Are you coming, or are you planning to hide forever? Not sure you want to be seen with a traitor."

It's a low blow, but I'm not feeling very charitable after her hurtful words.

"Don't be like that," Trinity says. "I'm sorry. You know that's not how I meant it."

I exhale a long breath. "We're both on edge," I answer, but it feels rather noncommittal.

I'm not ready to forgive her yet.

"I'll come," Trinity says, though I can sense her wariness. "I guess I'd better get this over with. Edward is waiting for me."

At least she has Edward. Sometimes I wonder, if it came down to the two of us, who she would pick. Boyfriends will come and go, but friends are forever, right? Except they're madly in love and will probably get married, and I really don't know what it will be like to settle into our lives and attend Society parties, all while knowing *she* loves her husband, and I'm stuck with Knox.

How long will I be able to pretend before my own unhappiness comes between us?

"Then we should go," I answer, crossing the room and digging through my closet. I throw on my coat and button it up before we head into the hall and down to the courtyard teeming with people.

Edward finds us immediately. He takes Trinity's hand and gives her a firm look. He's with her, too, and she collapses against him as they hug. His gaze meets mine, and he nods quickly in thanks for taking care of her.

No one has noticed us, and by silent agreement, we hang at the back of the crowd to ensure it stays that way. I spot Knox with his friends and duck behind Edward. I've been avoiding Knox as much as possible, while he blows up my phone with demands to see him that I ignore.

In the center of the square stands a raised platform with a podium and a microphone, both covered by a tent. A light drizzle falls from the sky as the clouds begin to take on an emerald hue.

Several teachers mill about the front under a canopy protecting them from the weather.

A moment later, a door opens in the side of the building, and two figures emerge.

Dean Withers and . . . and General Sol.

A soft murmur ripples through the crowd as she walks out surrounded by six members of her Circle Guard, the people trained at an elite level as her personal shield and who travel with her everywhere.

They wear sleek white uniforms made of some kind of shiny material that protects against assaults and carry stunners powered by Spark that can be set to incapacitate or kill.

The two women trot up the steps as the general's Guard spreads out around the stage.

The dean and the general are a study in contrasts. Dean Withers is delicate and small—almost like a bird—with her auburn hair and a fluttery white dress under a swingy white wool coat. General Sol towers a good foot taller, dressed head to toe in black leather that molds to a body that has clearly seen countless hours of training.

As her keen gaze slips over the crowd, I get the sense she's aware of every single person in the plaza and knows exactly who we all are.

Dean Withers approaches the microphone as a light drizzle coats everyone without the luxury of a tent.

"Welcome," she says. "I'm sorry we find ourselves together under such . . . tragic circumstances. The loss of a student is one I always take personally, and to lose three so suddenly, so violently, is a knife straight through my heart."

To illustrate her point, she flattens a hand to her chest and closes her eyes as she inhales a breath so shuddering, it rattles through the speakers. I can't help but think the entire thing is a performance. After all, people have died from their initiations in this very building, and no one seemed to bat an eye.

She continues speaking for a few more minutes, sharing some nice details about each student who's gone. Given they were all third-years, I didn't know much about them.

That Hollow was so young, and I wonder who he was taken from. Is there anyone to mourn him now? Does he get a nice ceremony with a member of The Shield in attendance? What about the other people who died on the tracks? I'm pretty sure I know the answer.

When the dean is finished, the rain is falling harder, pelting us softly while she remains dry under the tent alongside the general. I shiver as a cool breeze seeps through my jacket. Dean Withers gestures to General Sol, who stands with her hands clasped behind her back, her posture straight.

Her long hair tosses in the breeze, but only just enough to make her look impressive but not disheveled. She approaches the microphone, and that renews everyone's interest. As she clears her throat and begins to speak, I sense how everyone leans forward ever so slightly.

She's a magnet, and we're helpless to resist her pull.

"Thank you for taking the time to come out this morning. Dean Withers invited me here to speak with you on behalf of The Shield. Chancellors Marks and Orsen send their sincerest regrets that they couldn't be in attendance as well," she says. Her voice is strong. Confident. Nothing wavers in her tone. "I know you're hurting deeply after this tragedy. I, too, feel this loss personally. I know you all, even if you don't think I do. I know your parents, and I consider each of you one of my own."

I notice many people sharing looks. Unlike Dean Withers, General Sol's words feel genuine. Real. Like they were taken from the heart.

"It is and has always been The Shield's duty to protect the citizens of New Manhattan from every threat, whether from the outside *or* inside." She pauses dramatically, and her meaning is clear. We were all children when the worst of the riots were happening before my father took over as scion, but we remember some of the details well enough. This incident is a reminder never to forget what could happen again.

"Thanks to our four Houses, we keep order in our world," she continues. "House Fiama, House Aria, House Asale, and House Tera are the pillars on which our safety rests. Without their vigilant efforts, we would be no better than animals, scrounging for food and fighting over scraps."

Several nods go around the plaza.

"It's more important than ever to uphold the values of Society set forth by the original members of The Shield all those years ago. Many of you will go on from Amery to become the very same leaders who will aid us in this charge. The very same people will sit atop these towers and ensure our small nation's ongoing success."

She raises her arms to encompass our surroundings and the city stretching in every direction. "You are New Manhattan's future, and I need each one of you to stay safe. To remember where you come from and that no matter which House you represent, in the end, we are all family."

General Sol smiles at a few quiet grumbles, likely reading everyone's reaction to that.

"As you make your way in the world, you'll understand that while your House is important, the greater good is equally so. When you graduate, no matter your path, you will work for the betterment of New Manhattan as a whole. I look forward to getting to know many of you over the next few years. Please stay safe. Stay careful. And most of all, never forget that inside the city, you are free from the maladies that plagued the old world. You have food. You have clothing and shelter, and most of all, you have The Shield to protect you."

She presses a hand to her chest and utters, "Protect. Preserve. Prosper."

Everyone repeats her words before a chorus of applause turns into a few cheers and shouts. The dean returns to the mic and says a few more words as I stare about the courtyard. Rook is leaning against a pillar on the far end, his hands stuffed in his front pockets and one ankle crossed over the other. I haven't seen him since he rescued me from the train that night. I still owe him a thank-you, but it seems like he's forgotten about the incident. And me.

It's then that I notice how many people are peering over their shoulders, casting surreptitious glances around the plaza. For once, they aren't directed at Rook, but rather at me, Trinity, and Edward. It seems we've finally been noticed. Trinity realizes it, too, because her brow furrows with concern, and she takes a step back.

"We should go," Edward says, taking Trinity's hand.

The dean is still speaking as he tugs Trinity away, but Dean Withers waves and calls to the back of the crowd, stilling them both.

"Excuse me," she says, tapping the mic. "You haven't been dismissed."

That's when every pair of eyes in the courtyard turns to find *us*. Dean Withers holds a hand over her brow to see more clearly, and it takes only a moment before a soft "ah" can be heard through the microphone.

At the general's quizzical look, the dean covers the mic and leans to whisper something in her ear. The two women confer for several seconds before the general returns her focus to the crowd, her gaze sliding over everyone before it finds me.

Then she speaks into the microphone again.

"Poet Graves," she says as my cheeks heat and my stomach flips, every eye in the courtyard homing in on me. "I'd like to speak with you in private."

22

Within minutes, I find myself alone in the courtyard with an increasingly heavy drizzle of rain matting my hair. Once the general made her wishes clear, everyone quickly had somewhere else to be. I can't even be mad that Trinity and Edward ditched me immediately.

Even the dean left me on my own, and isn't that some kind of breach of student-school protocol?

General Sol hops down from the stage, oblivious to the rain, while her Circle Guard waits a few paces back. She's even more intimidating up close. She has several inches on me, and I have to stare up to meet her gaze. In her early sixties, she has fine lines hugging her eyes and mouth.

I don't think she means to, but the way she assesses me makes me feel like a bug.

"I hear there was some trouble with your first initiation test," she says.

"Yes, General Sol," I say.

"I've known your father a long time, and I've heard a lot about you. What happened?"

"Things . . ." I'm not sure how to explain it.

Why is it so hard to tell her that I couldn't kill a human being for no reason?

"I had a momentary lapse of judgment," I finally say.

She considers my answer, her gaze searching my face. "I hope I don't have to tell you how important your position in House Fiama is," she says. "You won't be at Amery long, and The Shield is expecting support from you and Knox. New Manhattan cannot maintain peace without cooperation from the Houses."

I nod. Of course, I know. It sometimes feels like it's the only thing I know.

"The grip on our safety is tenuous," she continues, and I blink in surprise. "The Solitudes are growing bolder, more vicious. They're infiltrating the city almost nightly." When she senses my confusion, she tips her head. "The news is kept quiet. We don't need anyone to panic."

"I see?" I say, wishing I sounded more confident.

I don't understand why she's telling me all this.

"But the threats within our borders are just as worrisome, if not more so. Your father does an admirable job of keeping them in check, but tensions in the city are escalating, as we saw from last week's incident. A shift in Fiama's leadership wouldn't benefit any of us."

She pauses, letting those words sink in as I gauge her meaning. If I don't marry Knox, then it might threaten my father's position. If he's ousted as scion, it might lead to the same turmoil we faced in the past. The Shield might rule us, but they have limited control over who the Houses choose as their scions.

"But a House is also responsible for all its pledged members," she continues. "Society must act with the dignity of the position they've been afforded, not brawl in the tunnels and lead people to question the tenets that keep our world stable."

I nod slowly.

"I'm telling you all this because Knox Arden is young and has a lot of growing to do. I believe he will make a great leader someday, but he'll need . . . corralling. Someone with a cooler head and level thinking to help guide him. I know from speaking with your father that you are smart and dependable. You are the anchor Knox needs."

Her words settle around me like an iron straitjacket. Not only am I being forced into this marriage, but I'm also now responsible for Knox's behavior. None of it surprises me, but that doesn't mean it's any easier to swallow.

"Is that everything?" I ask, realizing it comes out more impertinent than I'd like. I brace for backlash, but the general's lip curls up in a half smile.

"You have spirit. You'll do just fine, Poet Graves. I'm counting on you."

Then she steps back and assesses me up and down.

"There *is* one other thing," she adds. "It has nothing to do with all this, but increasing numbers of the infected are being reported to the

Extinguishers. They've been gathering them up before they can do any harm, but the numbers are unprecedented. The most shocking thing is just how quickly they're becoming mentally unstable. Most show up already violent and difficult to control, and the rest aren't far behind."

She pauses and stares at me, and the back of my head flames with heat and nerves.

"Please pass along the message to your classmates, so they can immediately report any signs of the infected in their midst."

"Okay," I say, trying to keep my voice even.

"And remind anyone that if they're caught hiding either their own ability or someone else's, their punishments will be . . . unpleasant."

I can barely breathe around the balloon swelling in my chest. Somehow, I manage an affirmative response that appears to satisfy her well enough.

"Until we meet again, Poet Graves," she says with a bow before spinning on her heel and walking away.

A shiver races down my spine at her words.

I've always lived in fear, wondering when and if my secret will be discovered.

Why does that moment suddenly feel so much more inevitable?

23

For several minutes, I stand perfectly still, trying to calm the racing of my heart. That entire conversation was . . . upsetting. Does she suspect anything? Surely, if she did, I'd already be in the hands of the Extinguishers, preparing for whatever horrible things they do to people like me. I'm sure it was just an overall warning. I hope.

The wind kicks up, the drizzle turning to heavier rain as a burst of verdant light flashes across the sky, signaling the start of an Emerald Storm. The main difference between these and Empire Storms is that the cloud bursts don't send energy hurtling to the earth. Only the rain. They also happen much less often.

New Manhattan is surrounded by water, most of it brackish and purified by massive underwater tanks, so while it's clean, it's not always the freshest.

Emerald Storms bring with them something else—water that is clear as crystal and tastes almost sweet. Apparently, it's what drinking water was like before they poisoned so much of it during the Warming Age.

Thus, the water is collected and used by The Shield and Society. It's sold in green glass bottles at high-end grocery stores behind doors with little alarm bells. It's actually become valuable, and the cisterns are closely guarded, since many people believe Emerald Water brings good luck. Collecting it for yourself is illegal, though many people do it regardless.

Thankfully, these storms don't affect me in the same way.

As the rain falls harder, I make my way toward the building and enter to find the hallway empty save the dean, who's clearly been waiting for me.

"Everything okay?" she asks, wringing her hands. "The general is . . . happy?"

I'm not sure how to answer that, so I settle on something neutral.

"Fine. It was fine," I say, and her shoulders relax.

"Okay, good. That's good. I was worried she was angry."

"Well, she isn't happy with me," I say as my phone dings with a notification, and it's a reflex to pull it from my pocket. I keep hoping Silver and Hazel will reach out. Or maybe my parents. Instead, I find something that surprises me.

It's a message from the Tempestade. Storm Guard cadet training starts today, and *I'm* invited. The dean makes a sound of disapproval, and I peer up to find her looking at my screen.

"What is it?" I ask.

"I wanted to talk to you about this as well. You've applied for the cadet program," she says. "I was under the impression you were expected to pursue a general degree."

My jaw clenches as I stuff the phone back into my pocket. "That's what my father would prefer, yes."

"I see," she says. "Scion Graves donates a lot of money to our institution." She raises her hands as if to encompass our surroundings.

"And?" I ask, already understanding where she's going with this.

"And I'd hate to lose your parents' generosity."

I huff a sound of derision. "I'm sure." I shake my head. "But I was accepted by the Storm Guard, and training starts in twenty minutes. Are you planning to stop me?"

She seems to consider that. "Technically, who the Storm Guard selects is outside my purview, and I cannot keep you from entering training." I'm about to open my mouth when she raises a finger. "But I could . . . tell your father. He would have some sway."

I should have anticipated this. My father's fingerprint, his influence, his presence are a part of everything, whether he's in the room or not. Plus, I already sensed that he had some history with Dean Withers.

"I want to be a Storm Breaker," I say, my throat knotting with the fear that this will be taken away before it even begins. "It's the only thing I've ever wanted to do."

She gives me a sympathetic look. "Because of your brother."

I blink. I mean, partly, I want to honor Raine's memory, but my desire is so much bigger than that.

"Yes," I say, because I suspect that's what she wants to hear. "But I want to protect the city, too. This is my home, and I want to be a part of defending it."

Her expression softens, but the uncertain flicker in her eyes tells me I haven't won her over yet.

"When I graduate, Knox and I will marry and inherit our trust funds." Her eyes widen. "And I could see it in my heart to be extremely generous toward the dean who allowed me this opportunity and didn't go running to my father."

I let the words hang between us. I have zero clue if I'd have the power to do this. I'm pretty sure our money will be controlled by my husband, but I only need *her* to believe it.

"He'll find out eventually," she says, and I nod.

"I know, but I'll deal with that day when it comes. For now, I'm asking for some discretion."

She considers my proposal, so I drive the knife in deeper. "Once I'm gone, my father will have no more children to send to Amery, and his charitable interests might move elsewhere. I, on the other hand, will owe you a debt that lasts at least as long as your career."

That does it. She straightens and nods.

"We have an agreement," she says. "But when your father shows up, I will say you went against my orders and that I had nothing to do with this."

"Heard. And understood," I say.

As if my father will care when she's the one responsible for me, but I'll keep that to myself.

"Then get going," she replies. "You don't want to be late."

24

I hurry through the hallways, glancing at my phone as it dings with another notification. My heart lifts when I see it's our group chat.

SILVER: *what did the general want???*

HAZEL: *everyone's talking about it. what happened?*

SILVER: *what about you, trin?*

SILVER: *feeling better?*

A moment later, my heart nose-dives in the other direction. I miss my friends so much, but what would I tell them? I can't assume anything I say will remain a secret between us. A young woman's place in Society is always precarious, and the inside track on two of the school's most talked-about students is a form of social capital. I don't know if they'd use it, but Amery is changing us all.

I tuck my phone away without answering and quickly head toward my destination, putting Silver and Hazel out of my mind.

I turn the corner to find a Storm Guard standing by a set of tall metal doors banded with iron and bolts controlled with an electronic panel. He's huge, his bulging arms revealed by his sleeveless black jumpsuit and metallic purple harness running across his shoulders and chest. He dips his chin in welcome.

"Name?" he asks.

"Poet Graves," I say as his head snaps up.

"Raine's sister."

I nod, my throat tightening.

The man says nothing, just tips me a nod that feels like a gesture of respect before he presses a finger on the control panel.

The doors hiss open, and he waves me inside. I slip in to find a massive room, the ceiling stretching overhead. It's filled with a row of beds, each surrounded by glass walls, next to various machines and instruments. It almost looks like a hospital, though I doubt we'll be healing anyone here today.

About two dozen other students have already arrived, and my gaze immediately finds Rook leaning against the wall at the far end of the room, his hair hanging in his eyes and his arms folded across his chest.

I receive cool looks from a handful of House Fiama members, but no one I know very well. Only my closest friends are aware that my father wouldn't approve of my presence in this room, so there's no reason for anyone here to tell him.

Most of the students come from House Aria, and they're *all* eyeing me up and down. The rest are a small mix from Asale and Tera.

Then I spy Domino with her chatty cog friend, Journey, standing at the edge. They smile at me, and I wave, relieved to see some welcoming faces. I desperately need allies. Maybe even friends?

Finally, I turn to the front of the room, where three Storm Guards stand, including Henry, Raine's ex-boyfriend. I didn't realize he'd become an instructor.

Behind them is a sight that sends chills down my spine. Two Extinguishers, marked by their bloodred uniforms, similar to the Storm Guard but with black leather harnesses.

Why are they here?

Several others have noticed them, and most people seem just as uncomfortable with their presence. I suspect it's because both men are terrifying with their hard expressions and weapons, and not because they're all hiding a secret, too.

Henry steps forward and clasps his big hands behind his back. He doesn't utter a word for the class to fall silent. He simply watches us until we're all focused on him with rapt attention.

"Welcome," he says in a clipped voice. "You are the only ones brave enough to attempt initiation into the Storm Guard. Congratulations on this first step."

It sounds like a compliment, but it feels more like a warning. And I don't think I'm the only one who feels that way, thanks to the nervous glances darting around the room.

"I am Lieutenant Henry Crawford, level-four Breaker." He gestures to his left and right. "With me are Brooklyn Lee and Chandler Pierce, both level-three Breakers."

Brooklyn is lean and tall while Chandler is built like a tree. They both nod at Henry's introduction. "The three of us will be leading you through all aspects of cadet training over the next few months. And that starts with these."

He gestures to the beds on the far side of the room. "Life as a Storm Guard means standing out on the towers, where you will often be exposed to Spark. Some of you simply won't be cut out for Guard life due to your inherent vulnerability. Some will have high natural resistance, while others will have none at all. Your first test, then, is to determine which. Those of you with low tolerance to Spark will have the opportunity to join other divisions in the Tempestade, such as the research and development team, intelligence, or training, among other things."

A ripple of worried comments circles through the room as Henry raises a hand.

"Every role in the Tempestade is important and vital to the protection of New Manhattan. Failure to qualify for the Storm Guard isn't a failure at all, but a new opportunity."

I can tell no one believes that, and neither do I, but this is one area where I'm sure I'll be fine.

"Those with a natural tolerance will go on to cadet training," Henry continues, "and there you'll be exposed to small charges under close supervision as your resistance slowly builds over the next few months and throughout your careers."

A hand rises. I recognize Melyssa from House Fiama.

"Will it hurt?" she asks.

Henry nods. "Absolutely." Well, I guess there's no sugarcoating it. "And it might kill a few of you. We almost always lose at least one."

A collective intake of heightened breath echoes around the room.

"However, it's a necessary casualty. Only the strongest can stand out on those towers."

Melyssa nods, though her pallor has turned ashen, much like most of the faces in the room.

"And of course . . ." A smile curves one corner of Henry's mouth. "Those of you who demonstrate the *highest* tolerance to Spark, who are the *strongest* and finish at the *top* of your class"—he spreads his arms wide to include Brooklyn and Chandler—"will be invited to join our most elite force and train to become Storm Breakers."

Everyone erupts into excited whispers at that. A flare of warmth spreads through my chest as I consider the prospect.

"If you're accepted into the Breaker program, you'll learn how to use a Spark wand. As I'm sure many of you know, this device is constructed with a core of galvanic energy, and it will be your job to catch and neutralize Spark. Make no mistake, if you miss, you'll be hit. This is why we can only accept the best."

More nervous whispers circle around the room.

Skies, this is so *badass*.

"Once your wand is hit, you'll transfer the energy it collects into your respective Storm Tower so that it can be grounded into the earth, thus helping to protect the people of the city. It isn't foolproof, but it's the best defense we have."

There is no higher honor in the Storm Guard, and this has been my goal for as long as I can remember. I was burdened with the secret of what I am when I was seven years old, but I can use it to do something good. Stand on those towers and shield the people I love. Be more than just Knox's *wife*.

"First, you must build up your muscle mass," Henry continues. "That means long hours in the gym and specialized nutrition to optimize performance and tissue growth. Early mornings and late nights, in addition to your regular class load."

He pauses as if waiting for an objection. When none comes, he continues.

"And finally, though your main role is to protect the city from storms, your position on the outskirts exposes you to the dangers of what lives out there." He gestures to some vague spot in the distance. "We are under the constant threat of attack from those beyond our borders—those who want to come and take what you have for themselves. You must learn to protect yourselves, too. That means combat training. Hand-to-hand with an arsenal of weapons. Your work in the gym will help."

He pauses again, letting those words sink in. If any of this is meant to deter me, it's only making me want to join more than ever.

"Your training will also include simulations inside a controlled environment, intended to re-create what it's like being caught in a storm."

He goes on to speak about a few more exercises we can expect, and my stomach tightens with a mixture of nerves and anticipation.

"Finally, once you've completed first-year training, you'll be tested," Henry says. "A final trial will challenge everything you learn in here." He thumbs behind him. "If you pass, you'll be admitted into the second-year cadet program."

He stops talking while we all wait silently. "Any questions?"

I have about a million, but I bite my tongue. I don't think he wants to be peppered with my worries and fears. There will be time later.

Nervous whispers fill the room as several people in lab coats arrive, all holding tablets.

"I'm Dr. Eze," says a woman with ebony skin and long black braids woven with strands of purple. Her lapel is pinned with the crest of House Aria. "As Lieutenant Crawford shared, we'll start by testing your resistance and tolerance against a dose of Spark. The level of your resistance is a part of the same evolutionary process that creates Keepers. However, it stalls out in ninety-nine percent of the population before they reach any meaningful level of immunity."

More looks are shared around the room, and my gaze snags on Rook's. He's watching me with a set of arched brows and a knowing look, but I can't tell what he *knows*.

I think again of that shape I saw in the shadows, trying to remember its exact size and weight. Was it large enough to be Rook? It was so quick, and the dim light and my momentary disorientation might have been deceiving me.

"The electrical currents you experience today won't be exactly the same as those you might experience during an Empire Storm," the doctor continues. "Since we cannot simulate the galvanic energy inside cloud bursts as they happen, we've developed the best approximation of them. Though it's not perfect, it will help you build up your resistance over time, and our extensive studies have shown that it's nearly as good as the real thing."

A hand goes up. A student from House Tera. "What about . . . Will it make us . . ." She trails off.

"Go mad?" someone else asks. "Being exposed to Spark?"

"No," Dr. Eze assures. "As I said, this isn't real Spark, and even if it were, the tolerance required for Guard duty is orders of magnitude removed from what Keepers can survive. It would kill you long before you could channel enough Spark for it to affect your mind."

That answer seems to ease several people's worries.

"Anything else?" Henry asks.

"Why are *they* here?" someone asks. It's Rook, and he's watching the two Extinguishers who've remained silent during this entire exchange.

For the first time, Henry seems nervous. "Ah . . . there have been increasing reports of infected Keepers being captured in the city over the last few months. As a result, we'll all be seeing more of the Extinguishers in our daily lives so they can identify risks as soon as possible."

He doesn't have to finish the thought. Most people don't know if they're infected unless they've been accidentally hit by Spark. They're often the most dangerous type of Keeper, walking through life, unaware of how close they are to snapping. The Extinguishers are here to watch over us and arrest us if one of us is revealed.

I recall General Sol's warning less than an hour ago, and suddenly, I don't feel very well. Sweat breaks out on my forehead, and my stomach knots up. I knew joining the Storm Guard might mean exposure, but I've spent years reading everything I could get my hands on about the training process.

I already know most of what Dr. Eze just told us. That until we're standing on those Storm Towers, we'll never be exposed to real Spark. Years ago, I even "borrowed" one of Raine's Spark wands and tested it out. Thankfully, I reacted exactly the same way any normal Breaker would.

It's a risk that I'm willing to take.

After all, I've always felt like I'm living on borrowed time.

However, I didn't factor the Extinguishers into any of my calculations.

Why are more people being reported lately? I have no sense of the total number of Keepers arrested each year because those details are kept a secret. How many people are living in fear every day of their lives? Is it more than I think?

Then Henry cracks the barest smile. I try to find reassurance in it as I'm quietly freaking out.

"Don't worry, you'll get the hang of it. It's not all as scary as it sounds, but you must bring your best every moment of every day."

He's met with another wall of silence before gesturing to a woman who's just appeared through a door. "Then let's get started."

A few are selected to begin, while the rest of us wait, and panic swirls in my chest.

Rook is one of the first to be chosen, and as usual, he looks relaxed and confident.

I watch as he lies down on a bed that's covered in a clean white sheet. Dr. Eze then attaches a series of electrodes to his forehead, arms, and hands.

The Extinguishers march up and down the aisle, peering into the various glassed-in rooms. Their heavy boots seem to echo through the atmosphere, and my limbs start trembling as my heart beats in my throat. I try not to look too closely at them, hoping I don't draw their attention. How will this affect me, and how will they know what I am? Do I walk out? Refuse their test? Surely if I do so now, they'll know I'm hiding something.

I chew on the corner of my lip, my heart pounding in my chest.

The dark-haired one looks over, and it takes every ounce of restraint I possess to keep my posture loose, like I have nothing to worry about. He pauses, his gaze sweeping over me as I turn to meet his eyes. I blink and look away, staring at my feet, hoping this is how anyone would act. Let him think I'm just intimidated, not scared for my fucking life.

A moment later, he keeps walking, making his way down the line before stopping at Rook's bed to watch. I hear him speaking to Dr. Eze. Something about Rook being a Solitude. Rook's eyes flash; he's clearly not a fan of being talked about like he isn't there, but he keeps his mouth shut.

Someone knocks into my shoulder, momentarily distracting me from the spiral of my thoughts. Domino says, "I gotta confess, I wasn't expecting to find you here."

I don't really look at her as I answer, "Why not?"

She holds up her hands and shrugs. "Aren't you engaged to that blond guy? Knox?"

I inhale a deep breath at the reminder, then let it out. "What of it?"

"Nothing, sorry," she says, perhaps sensing she's stuffed her foot in her mouth. "I just thought you'd be destined for . . ."

"Life as a Society wife?" I ask, and she winces.

"Sorry. I shouldn't have assumed."

I shrug as I watch Rook and Dr. Eze on the other side of the glass. "I can understand why you might have thought that."

I turn to Domino, wanting to assure her I'm not upset, but she just smiles. "Well, I think it's badass."

I can't help but smile back. "You're pretty badass, too."

She barks out a laugh. "If I last more than five minutes, maybe."

I try to play along and chuckle, but I'm once again focused on Rook and the Extinguisher, who appears to have taken a special interest in him. The tests are starting, and we both watch as everyone's bodies twitch from the currents now running through their systems.

It doesn't take long before a guy at the far end starts howling in pain as he thrashes in his bed so hard, he kicks a doctor in the face and knocks the nodes off his skin. He flips off the bed, lands on his knees, and hurls up the contents of his stomach, vomit coating the floor and his hands.

"Oh no," Domino says, covering her mouth and looking away. "I can't watch people throw up." She puts her head down and crosses the room, facing the wall as she waits for the cleaning crew that's just arrived to remove the guy, the puke, and the now-unconscious doctor. Well, this is going great.

Thankfully, the others appear to be faring better. They lie on their beds with a determined set to their jaws, perhaps willing themselves to survive this.

Once again, I watch Rook.

He's clearly feeling the charges, evidenced by the pained look on his face. His hands have balled into fists, a vein is pulsing in his temple, and he's shifting a little where he lies.

The dark-haired Extinguisher is watching Rook intently. Does he see something to give him pause? Or is it just because Rook's a Solitude?

Another person starts screaming and begging to be let go.

The tests end, and thankfully, no one else throws up, no one dies, and only one unconscious person has to be carried out on a stretcher.

Most notably, no one is arrested.

They're all given a few minutes to rest before, one by one, they peel themselves up and stagger into the main area. Everyone looks a little punch-drunk and wobbly, with their hair standing on end, their pupils blown, and their limbs twitching.

Rook runs his hands through his hair, the crackle of static snapping around him. He seems fine, and the Extinguishers are now focused on the next group approaching the beds.

Dr. Eze consults her tablet. "Poet Graves? You're up."

25

It takes only a few minutes to get settled in the same bed Rook just vacated. It's still warm from his body, where his scent lingers. Fresh grass. Green apples. I shake my head, trying to dislodge wayward thoughts of what it might be like to get closer to it.

"I'm going to attach these," Dr. Eze says, bringing me back to reality as she peels the stickers off a new set of nodes and affixes them to my skin. Then she turns to the beeping machine next to her, adjusts a few knobs, and presses some buttons.

"We'll start slowly," she assures me with a warm smile. Through it all, I'm excruciatingly aware of the Extinguishers and their stunners nearby. What kind of monster chooses to join them? Who delights in hunting down innocent people to be delivered to some nefarious fate?

But I acknowledge they might be necessary.

That I'm not innocent, and that *I* could be the monster, not them.

My heart is pounding through my chest as Dr. Eze lays a gentle hand on my shoulder. "Just lie back and breathe," she tells me. "Nothing to worry about."

Sure. Easy for her to say. Even if I weren't terrified of being discovered, the fact that someone left the room unconscious a few minutes ago would worry anyone.

Then she slowly cranks a dial as the machine whirs to life.

I feel it instantly. Electricity runs under my skin and through my bones like little muted rivers. It's different from Spark, just like she claimed. There's no all-consuming pain threatening to rip me apart. It burns just a little, and

I wince at the slight discomfort, but this is nothing. I must make a sound because her gaze flicks to me before returning to the screen.

"You're doing great," she assures. "A little more."

She twists the knob another notch before the pulse kicks up. I can't quite describe the sensation. It's like I've been wrapped in cotton and held against an electric fence. It isn't pleasant, but it isn't the bittersweet agony I'm accustomed to.

A presence appears at the glass wall separating me from the rest of the room. The dark-haired Extinguisher is watching me intently now. I wish I knew what he was looking for. Can he see it? Or is it Dr. Eze who'll be able to tell?

My palms turn sweaty as we continue in the same vein for what feels like several minutes. I try to mimic the same discomfort I witnessed in everyone else, hoping it appears like I'm being affected the same way. I wince and squeeze my fists. Close my eyes and inhale deep breaths.

Pulses thrum through my body, almost like I've been filled with dense slabs of foam. It's heavy and light at the same time.

The Extinguisher moves around the glass and approaches the bed, stopping at my feet. From here I can read his name tag. Lieutenant Dire. How fitting. My vision smears as my breathing turns short. Why is he coming over? Did he do that with anyone else? Suddenly, I can't remember a single thing that happened in the last ten minutes.

He tucks his hands into the straps of his harness and squints at the dials on the machine. Dr. Eze turns to face him, allowing him to study the monitors with her mouth pressed together. Even in my increasingly panicked state, I get the sense she isn't a fan of his scrutiny.

"All good?" he asks.

I stop breathing. Black spots form in my eyes. I squirm on the table, torn between ripping off the nodes to run away and lying here perfectly still, hoping that somehow, I'll escape this. Dire taps the glass on one of the dials, and I flinch, almost like he's threatened to backhand me.

"All good," Dr. Eze says, her voice cheerful. Cool and calm. It takes me a moment to process her words. Dire doesn't move, his eyes narrowing further.

A scream tears through the room, and we all turn to look. Someone is thrashing wildly in the next bed. Points of light flash over their skin as they scream and scream in agony. I recognize a guy from House Fiama. Jacen. Suddenly, he stops, his limbs going limp, his head lolling to the side. Puffs of black smoke curl off his skin, now turned a sickly shade of gray.

Lieutenant Dire quickly rushes over as doctors gather around the dead student.

"Skies," I whisper.

Dr. Eze reaches down and squeezes my wrist, and I start breathing again. Lieutenant Dire's focus has moved away from me, and air floods my lungs as my vision returns to normal. I exhale and then inhale several times before wiping my forehead.

The doctor looks down at me, and something flickers across her face, an expression like a question lifting in her gaze. A quick brightening of her eyes and then the press of her mouth at the corners. It feels like an unspoken message.

Does she know? Can she tell what I am? Did she just lie to the Extinguisher? The only thing worse than being a Spark Keeper is lying to protect one. Why would she do that for me?

We break eye contact, and she flips off the machine. The pulses take a few seconds to dissipate, leaving only a slight trembling in my limbs. They're already carrying Jacen's body away. Henry told us we always lose one.

"It's okay," Dr. Eze says with a reassuring smile, but the knot of worry is permanently buried in my chest. If she suspected something, I'd already be in handcuffs. Right? "Take your time getting up. You'll be a little wobbly for the next hour or so."

Slowly, I sit up and swing my feet to the floor, staring at the tiles as I wait for my head to stop swimming. My heart flutters like it's been shocked several times; I'm starting to understand why Storm Breakers have limited lifespans.

"You did well with that level of charge," Dr. Eze says, her tone business-like. "We can start there again next time and likely maintain that strength. It's not about hammering it in; it's about building up a tolerance, but I can tell you already have a natural immunity."

I look up quickly and meet her gaze. She holds it and arches a brow ever so slightly. Is she trying to tell me she knows? And that she won't report me? I'm probably imagining things.

Someone opens the door to our enclosure, pulling our gazes apart.

"Ready for the next round, Doctor?" an assistant asks, and she nods.

I'm struck by how quickly we're just moving on from Jacen. Like it never even happened.

"Just give Poet a moment, and then you can send in the next cadet."

The doctor begins typing something into her tablet. I wish I could see if it's about me and, more importantly, what she's saying. I'm still aware of the Extinguishers watching. I can't risk asking.

I've been delaying for too long because she looks over with a furrow between her brows. "Is there anything else I can help you with?"

"No." I shake my head. "Thank you."

She returns to her work, and I enter the main area. I don't feel quite like myself. The false charges pulsing under my skin are a foreign invader, throwing off my balance.

Plus, watching Jacen die is completely fucking with my head.

"You look a bit pale," comes a deep voice. It's Henry, and he's giving me a concerned look.

"I don't feel great," I admit.

"That's normal at the beginning," he says. "Makes most people a bit nauseous. The good news is you've passed the first hurdle and can start training. But for now, you're free to leave and lie down."

Right. I'd almost completely forgotten that's why I was here at all. I lay a hand against my stomach and nod. "Okay, thanks. I think I'll do that."

I spot Domino now in the examination room. She sits on her bed and gives me a little wave. The image of Jacen's skin curling with smoke flashes before my eyes, and I watch until I'm assured she's okay handling the current.

"Henry," I say, turning toward him. "How are you doing?"

He takes a deep breath, running a hand over his closely shorn curls. "I'm fine, Poet."

He gives nothing away. It's been three years. How much does he miss my brother? I want to ask him what he's been up to. Has he found someone new? Is he in love again? I hope so. He deserves to be happy.

"You should come by the penthouse for dinner sometime," I say. "My mom would love to see you."

His brows draw together. "Would she?"

The question is pointed, and it's then that I understand I probably knew very little about their relationship. I only saw the brother I loved and the man he brought home. Did my parents disapprove? Henry is pledged to House Fiama but isn't from a family of particular influence. I suspect that mattered to my father.

"I'm sorry," I say, even if I'm not entirely sure what I'm apologizing for.

Henry blows out a long sigh that seems to sit heavy in his chest. "Maybe you and I could have lunch sometime and catch up?"

I give him a weak smile. "I'd love that."

"Great, now go get some rest."

With a nod, I make my way into the hall and toward my room on shaky legs.

Every once in a while, my world tilts, and I have to stop to catch my breath.

"Poet?" comes Knox's voice.

Damn, I've been doing such a good job avoiding him lately.

"Are you okay? Where have you been? I've been looking for you. Why do you keep ignoring my texts?"

It's too many questions for my clouded thoughts. I bypass them all as I keep walking, trying to appear steadier than I feel.

He shuffles beside me, easily keeping up, before grabbing me by the elbow. I bristle at the contact.

"What's wrong?"

"Nothing, I'm just not feeling well. I'm going to lie down."

"Where were you? Where'd you go after the memorial? What did General Sol want from you?"

More questions. Things I don't want to answer.

"Can we talk about this later?"

I dismiss him, but he isn't to be deterred.

I try to pull my arm away. His grip only tightens, and that finally sets me off.

"Let go of me!" I bite out. He doesn't. "I was where I was. It's none of your damn business."

"I'm responsible for you—"

"No, you aren't yet, actually."

"If your father hears of this, he won't be happy."

"Knox, I don't give a fuck."

"What has gotten into you lately?" he hisses, dragging me close and getting into my face. His hot breath toasts my skin, and it takes everything in me to settle the familiar sense of nausea swirling in my gut.

"Let go!" I try to wrench myself free of his hold, but his grip is bruising.

"Is there a problem here?" comes a third voice, cutting through our argument like a poison-tipped arrow. Knox goes still and swivels his head to Rook, who leans across the hall with his arms folded and one ankle over the other.

"Nothing that has anything to do with you, scat." Knox sneers.

"Stop calling him that!" I snap, furious that Knox would use such a foul word to describe *any* human being, regardless of who he is. "What is wrong with you?"

"You're defending him?" he snaps right back. "Solitudes killed Raine, or have you forgotten? How do you think your brother would feel knowing you were siding with one of these animals?"

"I know who killed Raine," I say, trembling with fury. "You don't have to remind me. But Raine was a Storm Guard, and he knew the risks."

My voice cracks, and warmth slips down my cheeks. I don't know exactly what I'm crying for. So many things threaten to spin out of my control—General Sol, my father, the Extinguishers—and I'm on the verge of breaking in half.

"You should probably let go of her." Again, it's Rook, his focus zeroed in on where Knox still has me in a firm grip. I wince as his hand tightens further, and Rook's eyes darken. *"Now."*

"This is none of your fucking business," Knox replies, his body shaking with fury, his face turning mottled.

Rook pushes himself off the wall and approaches so he's standing right before us. His sharp gaze meets mine before traveling down my arm and back up again, and I get the strangest sense that he's trying to tell me something. He circles a broad shoulder, almost like he's preparing to throw a punch. He's a few inches taller than Knox, definitely bigger and more built. The threat is clear. "I'm not going to ask you again. Let. Go. Of. Her."

The tone in his voice vibrates with bottomless menace, and Knox's confidence falters for a second before he recovers. "Who's gonna stop me?"

I've gone still, watching this exchange, wondering why Rook is coming to my defense.

Rook takes another step, leans in, obviously using his height to his advantage. "I will."

Finally, Knox's grip loosens ever so slightly. I seize the moment, mirroring the motion Rook just showed me, as I circle my arm, and Knox's hold breaks.

Rook noticed that I'd frozen.

His silent suggestion just reminded me that I'm *not* helpless.

I scramble back, trying to put some distance between Knox and me, and swear I catch a flash of pride in Rook's eyes. A heartbeat later, he has Knox pinned to the wall, his forearm braced against Knox's throat.

"Apologize," Rook says.

I rub my skin, now tender and bruised. I'll have to wear long sleeves tomorrow. It's the first time Knox has ever physically restrained me, and it sets off a whole new set of alarms. Ones that sound far too much like my father.

"You can't—" Knox attempts to choke out, but Rook presses harder, cutting off his air.

"Why must we keep doing this?" Rook asks. "How many times do I have to humiliate you before you fucking get it? *Apologize*."

Knox scoffs, his feet scrambling as he tries to gain some leverage against the wall, but Rook is iron, and he isn't going anywhere.

"Sorry," he mumbles to me. There's no sincerity in it, but the point has been made.

"If I ever see you touch her like that again, we'll do this until you learn a fucking lesson."

Then he releases Knox, who quickly steps away, creating some distance. "You'll pay for this, sc—" He breaks off, his jaw clenching as if it's causing him physical pain not to degrade Rook with vile names. Maybe he's finally scared. Good.

"I doubt it," Rook says. He waits, his hands stuffed back into his pockets.

Knox glances between us. "You can move along now," he says, clearly trying to maintain some control over the situation. "We aren't done here, and this doesn't concern you."

Rook shrugs and tips against the wall. "I don't think so. I like standing here."

Despite everything, he appears perfectly at ease, his shoulders loose and his expression blank.

I recall our conversation outside the med wing and him *standing* in the hall. I don't know if it's an intentional move to make me laugh, but suddenly, a snort blasts out of me.

Knox looks more confused than ever.

I swear that Rook is also clamping down on a smile, and something about that touches some secret place deep in my chest.

"What's going on?" Knox demands, his gaze darting between us. "What's *funny*?"

His expression turns suspicious. He's probably jumping to several conclusions that aren't even remotely true.

I roll my eyes. "Nothing. Absolutely nothing is going on. We *are* done here, though. I'm tired, and I'm going to lie down. Don't follow me. Run to your dad. Run to mine. I don't fucking care. But you don't own me, and I don't answer to you. At least not yet."

And hopefully not ever.

Then I turn on my heel, leaving them both behind.

26

The fight with Knox follows me for the next few days. Everyone heard us yelling, and it's humiliating. Maybe even more so with Rook playing witness to the entire exchange. I don't understand why he came to my rescue, but I do appreciate it all the same.

I stand in front of the bathroom mirror, examining the mottled purple bruises Knox left on my arm, and then tug down the sleeve of my shirt to keep them hidden.

The last thing I need is a conversation about this with anyone. I know I shouldn't just brush it aside, but it was a onetime thing, and . . . I sigh. Even I can hear how ridiculous I sound.

I don't know what to do, though. Who would I even tell? My father certainly won't care, and right now, he's the only one who could save me from this future.

Then I make my way down to the cafeteria, where I'm headed off by my friends.

"Poet!" Silver says, wrapping her arms around me and drawing me into a hug. "We've barely heard from you lately."

"How are you doing?" Hazel asks, her gaze sharp but kind.

"I'm fine," I answer a bit warily. We haven't talked because *I* haven't been answering their texts, but *they've* been avoiding me in public.

"We heard what happened with Knox. And General Sol? I couldn't believe it when she called you aside. What an honor," Silver says, looping her arm through mine. "What did she want to talk about?"

My heart sinks. My instincts were correct—she's fishing for gossip.

"Nothing important," I answer, pulling my arm from hers. "Speaking of Knox, I'm late for lunch."

"You two are doing well?" Hazel asks, blinking her dark eyes framed by long lashes.

"Sure," I say. "See you later."

I toss a wave over my shoulder and hurry away, not in the mood for interrogation or discussing how Knox and I are *doing*.

He's been even more clingy since our argument. I think it's part of his desire to prove to everyone we're fine and he has things under control. After all, if he can't control me, his helpless little fiancée, how can he be expected to rule our House?

And because of that, I can't keep my secret about cadet training for very long.

A few minutes later, we're standing in the lunch line when the attendant spies me. "Poet Graves?" she asks, and I nod before she turns around and deposits a tray on the counter. It's a large plate laden with chicken, veggies, and pasta. "This is for you."

"What's that?" Knox asks, his eyes narrowing. "Why are you getting a special meal?"

"No reason," I say, scooping up the tray after a quick thank-you. Knox fills up his plate and follows me through the dining hall. I scan the room, noting a group of second-years chatting by the door. Then I spy Jackson and Sal at a table toward the back. I'd prefer to eat alone, but I know Knox will make a fuss, so I resign myself to his presence.

"What aren't you telling me *now*?" Knox accuses as we sit across from Jackson and Sal.

I pick up my fork and dig into some noodles, stuffing them into my mouth.

"I just . . ."

"That's a cadet meal," Jackson says, peering up at me. He doesn't say it with any judgment—just a question and maybe a touch of concern. The big blabbermouth.

"A cadet meal? Poet, tell me you didn't," Knox says. "Tell me you did not sign up."

I sigh and twirl my fork through the noodles. "So what if I did?"

"Are you serious right now? You don't think you're already in enough trouble?"

I shrug and take another bite. "Isn't that precisely why I shouldn't care? It's not like I can make my dad any angrier."

Sal scoffs from across the table. "I think you're underestimating Scion Graves."

I frown, knowing he's probably right.

"Poet—" Knox says, and I put up a hand.

"I don't want to hear it. I'm doing this. I'll keep up with all my other classes like I'm expected to. If I flunk out of training, then so be it; I'll finish my general degree like my father wants."

"And if you don't flunk out?"

I understand he means the question to be a worst-case scenario, but I can't help savoring a tiny thrill of satisfaction knowing he thinks I *could* finish.

"Then . . . we'll cross that bridge when we get there."

Knox glares at me, his jaw tight. I can see the thoughts running through his head, trying to decide how to change my mind.

"Please," I say, hoping to appeal to some sense of his decency. I know it's in there somewhere. I used to love him, and even if it wasn't in a romantic way, we were friends. That little boy who wanted to protect me from my father all those years ago has to be *somewhere* in there. "Just let me do this. I'm not hurting anyone. I need to try."

"To what end?" he asks, and I try not to flinch. To what end, indeed. I can never actually be a Breaker, according to him and my father, but again, I keep all thoughts of defiance to myself.

"To prove to myself I can do this." I pause and inhale a deep breath. "And for Raine."

It's a dirty trick. A low blow to use my brother's name in this way. But I know Raine would be rooting for me. I know he would approve.

Jackson makes an *aww* sound, and his lower lip thrusts out. "How can you say no to that?" he asks, and I think Jackson just became my favorite person in the entire universe.

"He's right," Sal adds. "Look at her. She just wants to honor her brother's memory."

I can't believe they're defending me. I hold my breath, afraid of sidelining whatever careful momentum they're building on my behalf. Who would have thought Jackson and Sal would become my advocates?

"It's not like she's really going to make it past first year anyway," Sal adds, and my temporary admiration deflates. He digs into his food, clearly oblivious to the fact that he's just insulted me, but I let it go, because Knox appears to be considering his friends' arguments.

Sure, why listen to me about my own life?

Obviously his friends' opinions should take precedence.

"Fine," Knox says, and I blow out a tense breath. "But we keep this between us. If Grady or my father find out . . ."

"Trust me, I have no intention of telling either of them," I say, wondering when the hell Knox started calling my dad by his first name.

He presses his mouth together and then attacks his plate without another word. I think I've won this round, and I hate myself for being grateful to him, but I guess this is what I've been reduced to.

Still, I'll take it.

As I pick up my fork, I notice Trinity on the far side of the cafeteria. She's sitting across the table from a girl with dark-brown hair, wearing the burgundy shirt of an E-squad recruit. Trin is leaning in while the girl talks, and I frown, wondering what they're doing together.

"How was your second initiation last night?" Knox asks Sal across the table, turning my attention toward them.

"Fine," he says as he looks away.

"You passed?"

"Of course I fucking passed," Sal says. "What do you take me for?"

"What did you have to do?" Jackson asks.

"You know I can't tell you that," Sal answers.

He's right. No one is allowed to disclose the details of their second and third initiations, but that doesn't mean everyone follows that rule.

"Tell us," Knox says, digging for more. The second test is designed to expose your weaknesses and fears. What is Knox afraid of?

"No, fuck off," Sal practically snarls, and it's obvious Knox is touching a nerve. They've been friends forever and have always been loyal, but Knox is very competitive.

Sal constantly rises to Knox's bait, while Jackson tends to ignore them both when they get this way.

After that, it seems none of us feels much like talking, so we all move on to eating quietly, surrounded by cafeteria noise. Trinity has left, and I don't see the girl she was talking to anymore. I stare around the room, my gaze lingering on Stevie and the members of House Aria as I consider the upcoming rounds of initiation.

What will my next test be? They can't ask me to repeat the same test, so they can't make me fight anyone again. But they could still ask me to hurt someone. If I refused, I'd be without a House. I close my eyes at the thought, wondering if I could bring myself to do it. I'd be cut off from everyone and everything I know.

I could consider Asale or Tera, but I have no clue what kinds of tests they give. It could be something equally bad. Or be something I know absolutely nothing about. What if Asale asked me to design a tool or code a computer program? I'd fail before I even started.

After all, the point of pledging is to prove your worth. That you deserve to be a part of Society. And as Stevie told me the night I ran the tower of fire: they can't make it too easy.

Suddenly, my lunch sours in my stomach, and I drop my fork with a clatter.

"I gotta go." I stand up from the table, and without waiting for a response, I leave and head to my room to grab my things. I have my first gym session today, and I'm eager to get there early.

Fifteen minutes later, I walk into the gym to the sound of music blasting through high-set speakers, the low murmur of conversation, and the clink and clang of weights. I inhale the smell of rubber and sweat, weirdly thrilled to be participating in mandated exercise.

Quickly, I scurry to change into my gym attire—purple shorts and a long-sleeved top—before I go to meet my trainer.

I notice a few other people from cadet training, including Rook, who's talking to Brooklyn, one of the Storm Breakers from our first day of cadet training.

Rook's gaze finds me briefly before it flicks away, and I try to ignore the weird emptiness his brush-off leaves in my chest. We haven't spoken since he defended me against Knox, and it seems I owe him yet another thank-you for his help.

"Poet," comes a voice to my left, and I breathe a sigh of relief at the sight of Henry. "I'll be your trainer today."

It's so good to see him, and I offer him the first genuine smile I've felt in a while.

Over the next hour, I follow Henry's instructions as he leads me through a series of exercises to help build muscle and strength. It feels amazing to empty my mind and lose myself in the movements as sweat pours down my forehead. This is exactly what I need. Something to distract me from everything going on.

Throughout my training, I remain aware of Rook on the near side of the room. Brooklyn puts him through his paces, and our eyes meet once or twice. Every time he glances my way, my stomach does this little dip that it really shouldn't. I'm helpless to control it.

Knox assumed something about Rook and me the other day, and while I dismissed it, the truth is, I do feel *something* when I'm around him. I know it's wrong. Nothing could ever happen between us.

I might not want to marry Knox, but Society depends on a man like my father ruling House Fiama. I recall my conversation with General Sol. That a change in leadership wouldn't benefit any of us.

If he loses his position, it could create instability, and all those terrible things could happen again.

I can't be the reason people suffer.

I'd accepted my duty to my city and Society, but I never thought about how it would feel to find something, or *someone*, I could never have.

I let out a sigh. Does it really matter? The way Rook looks straight through me every time our glances meet suggests my misplaced interest is entirely one-sided anyway.

Stop feeling sorry for yourself, Poet. Control the things you can.

I can't have everything I want, but I *can* become a Breaker. I grit my jaw and force my rubbery arms to complete another ten reps for Henry.

"Great job!" he says and helps guide the weight back to the rack. "Now, let's work on your quads."

I smile back and move into the next exercise.

Finally, the hour is up, and Henry leaves me with a schedule of what to work on for the next week. Weight training is four days a week, with another two days of cardio and one rest day, with stretching or yoga every day. This is a lot, but I'm determined to keep up.

After a quick shower in the locker room, I'm off to history, finishing the day with an hour of math. By the time I return to my room, I'm so exhausted I can barely move.

I open the door to find Trinity alone, tapping away on her phone while she lies on her bed.

"Hi," I say. "How are you? What have you been up to today? I saw you talking to someone earlier."

She looks at me, and I can tell from her bloodshot eyes that she's been crying.

"What happened?" I ask, my questions forgotten as I cross the room and sit on the edge of the bed.

She shakes her head and shows me the messages on her phone. They're from her parents. They aren't cruel, but they aren't particularly encouraging, either.

"They said I needed to pass my next two tests or . . ."

Tears roll down her cheeks as she clutches the device to her chest.

"Or what?" I'm genuinely curious what they plan to do. Mr. and Mrs. Robins have always been kind to me. They're fair and reasonable, even when Trinity and I were causing trouble.

"They'll disown me," Trinity says. "My sister will become an only child."

I sit with those words.

"I don't get it," I say.

"What?"

"How can our parents raise us for our whole lives, then just . . . reject us because of this? Why are we all so convinced this is the only way?"

"Poet, what are you saying? Of course this is the way. Without Society we become like they did in the Warming Age, with no order, no discipline, leading us down a path to destruction."

I chew on my lip as I stare out the window. The skies have been quiet this week, which has been a relief, but I sense another storm brewing in the distance.

"Yeah, I know that's what we're all taught."

I push up from Trinity's bed and walk to the window, noting a distant flash of lavender on the horizon. Thankfully, it's recent enough since I absorbed my last dose of Spark that I'll be able to weather this one inside.

"Poet?" Trinity asks, and I turn around. "What am I gonna do if I fail?"

She stares at me with watery gray eyes, and her sincerity guts me. She has no clue what comes next, but neither do I. I wish I could give her the answers she seeks. I wish we could return to the old days when we were two little girls worried about clothes and parties and not much else.

But those days are over. Our innocence was stripped away the moment we were asked to kill a man with our bare hands.

"I don't know, Trin. I don't know."

27

The next two weeks pass in a blur of classes and cadet training. I'm up with the sun daily, working out in the gym before any of my room-mates rise, and meeting with Dr. Eze and her team for more tests and conditioning after classes.

I'm adapting quickly to the charge, and she praises my ability. I wonder if this rapid acclimatization is related to being a Keeper, but as far as I can tell, the doctor doesn't appear to notice anything different about me.

Winter and Lacey continue to act like Trinity and I don't exist, and we haven't heard much from Silver or Hazel, so I bury my head in schoolwork. When she isn't with me, Trin spends most of her free time with Edward. I wish we had more time together, but my schedule is beyond intense right now.

I've noticed some positive changes, though. She's smiling again and says she's feeling better about her future. I'm relieved she's coming out of her funk, and I'm determined to find time for us to have a real chat about it soon.

As the days pass, more and more people are pulled aside for their next rounds of initiation. The morning after his second test, Knox appears with a black eye and numerous scrapes on his arms, legs, and face. But to no one's surprise, he passed with flying colors.

I dread to think what he was asked to do.

Through it all, I exist in a state of constant nervousness, waiting for my turn to arrive. Trinity and I share a quiet moment almost every night, anticipating the inevitable. Our tests will change both our lives, one way or another. I can't help but bring up Rook, probably a bit too much. Trinity *must* notice my ill-advised fascination with him, but she doesn't call attention to it.

Another week later, I'm on my way to class when a group of masked figures steps into my path and surrounds me.

I don't even have it in me to be scared; I'm just relieved we're getting this over with. I can't live with the uncertainty any longer.

My only reservation is the storm that's been brewing on the city's northern horizon all afternoon. I'm long past due to absorb a cloud burst, meaning I've been itchy and restless and not as focused as I'd like.

"Come with us," a mask to my left says, and then we're walking. I wonder if we're returning to the tunnels.

But instead of going down, we exit out through the main doors and around a corner to arrive at the gated entrance of the Central Park Tree Farm. During the day, it's open to the public to enjoy as one of the many green spaces curated throughout the city.

Unlike the others, this one is carefully monitored and guarded, and harming the trees in any way is a crime punishable with severe consequences. This park represents the sum total of the usable construction wood left in the world. Trees in the Wastes are sparse and spindly, made of wood too soft to do much with.

My escort leads me through the gates, where another masked person stands to admit us. Under a canopy of leaves, I'm led down a path lined with softly glowing lanterns anchored into the earth. They're rarely lit at night to conserve energy, but they must have received special permission tonight. Lucky me.

I hear the soft clicks and whirs of insects and the hoot of an owl in the distance. Without much wildlife left in the world, the city's green spaces are carefully curated with flowers and shrubs to foster stable ecosystems, offering sustenance and a suitable environment for a handful of species necessary for us to sustain life. Bees and butterflies, especially.

I've always loved looking at images from the Warming Age of huge wild animals with fur and stripes and spots. Giant white bears that lived on ice floes and birds with massive tails shimmering in a variety of colors.

The sounds from the city grow muted as we weave deeper into the gardens. Finally, we come to a stop inside a stone plaza with a fountain supporting three statues of The Shield. General Sol is wearing her Storm

Guard uniform, one foot propped up, her face cast skyward, a hand reaching toward the clouds. Chancellor Marks wears a long robe and holds a tablet, his finger raised and his mouth open as though he's mid-speech, and Chancellor Orsen wears a three-piece suit with his hands in his pockets as he stares into the middle distance.

In front of the fountain stand two more masked figures who wait for me to approach. I scratch at the back of my neck as the clouds tumble overhead.

"Poet Graves," says the left voice, who I recognize as Devon. "Welcome to your second initiation test."

"Normally, you'd be given the option to either stay with your first test's House or switch to another," comes the other mask. This one is Stevie.

"I choose House Fiama," I say quickly. It's where I belong. And from the way Stevie keeps looking at me, she agrees and doesn't want me, either.

Devon raises a hand. "Not so fast. As Stevie said, *normally* that's how it would be. But we've been asked to do things a little differently for you."

"Asked by who?"

"Our instructions came from The Shield," Devon says.

"Okay . . ." I trail off, my heart starting to accelerate as it pounds in my ears. Why won't they let me choose now? What's about to happen? I scan our surroundings, hoping for a clue.

"We've hidden two people in this park," Devon says, sweeping out an arm. "They're both in situations that will kill them. One is a person who's been accused of several crimes . . ."

"And one is a Keeper," Stevie finishes for him.

My eyes widen, and I start to feel sick. Oh Skies, I might *be* sick.

"You have a decision to make," Devon says. "You can only save one. Your choice will determine whether you can pledge to Fiama or Aria."

Fuck me.

They've planned this perfectly, haven't they? I didn't want to kill that man last time, so they're allowing me to save one. But by doing so, someone else still has to die.

A Keeper.

Someone just like me. Someone who was caught or turned in, maybe by someone they trusted. While *I* stand here, clinging to my own secrets and deciding whether *they* live or die.

"Won't the Extinguishers just kill the Keeper anyway?" I ask.

"Not if you can save them," Stevie says. "Sometimes, Keepers are offered the option of being exiled from New Manhattan and living in the Wastes, as long as they promise never to return. This Keeper has asked to leave the city."

"Really?"

She nods. I had no idea this was an option for Keepers. Obviously, living in the Wastes would be incredibly hard, but at least you'd still be alive, though maybe not for long.

"What about the other accused of crimes?" I ask. "What happens if I save them?"

"They get to return home," Devon says. "They'll have fulfilled the conditions of their sentencing. It'll be like nothing happened."

Hardly, but I don't say that out loud.

"What if I can't save *either* of them?" My voice comes out scratchy and tight.

Stevie cocks her masked head. "Then in *your* case, we would have to bid you adieu from Society. This is your last and only chance."

I nod because I suppose I expected that. They've already altered the rules for me, likely due to a million strings pulled by my father. So why not another? None of it helps the shivers of panic spreading over my scalp.

A prickle works its way up my back, reminding me of the oncoming storm. I scratch again as I briefly worry about exposure to Spark. But then I remember General Sol uses her channeled electricity to power a barrier that protects the trees from errant strikes. As if on cue, a large net flickers to life overhead, crisscrossing with lines of purple light.

We all look up as everything is painted with a soft amethyst glow.

I try to tamp down the restlessness in my limbs as I roll my neck and focus on the task at hand.

"You have ten minutes," Devon says, gesturing toward two paths through the trees about a hundred feet apart. "The left leads you to the criminal and House Aria; the one on the right, toward the Keeper and House Fiama. Understand?"

Unfortunately, I do. If I save the accused, the Keeper dies, which suits Aria and their Extinguishers just fine. If I save the Keeper, the accused dies, and it's one less person for Fiama to deal with.

"Rescue your prize and deliver them to the front gates to pledge," Devon finishes.

My mind starts racing. Did these instructions really come from The Shield? Or did my father set this up as a true test of my loyalty? How can I possibly make this choice?

Bile rises in my throat. Ten minutes. That's practically nothing. When I thought I'd found a loophole in refusing Fiama's first test, I was only buying time. Of course, I knew none of this would be easy.

"What if I choose neither?" I ask, trying to find another way to save all of us from this fate. "I'll test for Tera. Or Asale."

Stevie's eyebrows shoot up. She clearly wasn't expecting me to say that.

I wasn't, either, but that was before I was dragged into this fucking forest.

Devon shakes his head. "I'm sorry, but that is no longer open to you. These are your only two options."

His expression is almost sympathetic. I know then that my father is responsible for all of this. He's always thought me weak. Too emotional. Too *soft*. When I refused to fight that man, I revealed just how much. He wants to push me, force me to make a hard choice. He wants to make me just like him.

I shake my head as tears burn in my eyes.

Skies, I can't do this. I can't make this choice.

I only have one other option. One I never thought I'd have to face.

"I won't pledge to either," I say. It comes out quiet, my breath tight. I'll lose everything. My family. My friends. But at least I won't be a murderer.

Devon and Stevie exchange an uncertain glance. I see something in their expressions. My father isn't the only one who thinks I'm weak now. I'm starting to realize that almost everyone here is already at least a little bit like him.

Devon sighs and turns back to me. "We can't force you to compete, but we were told that if you tried to walk away, they'll both die anyway."

"What! Why?" I cry out.

His expression hardens, that brief moment of uncertainty gone. "Because you don't have that luxury. You are the daughter of the scion, and . . ." He shakes his head and scoffs. "Do you know how many people would *kill* to be in your place? And you're treating it like it's some kind of burden?"

I exhale a sharp breath like I've been kicked in the chest. Of course. He's like everyone else. He sees my rejection as a rejection of everything he stands for.

"You have no choice," he finishes. "Now quit stalling and prepare yourself."

He nods to Stevie, who unfolds her arms from where she's been standing, watching our entire exchange. My gaze meets hers, and she tips her head as something flickers behind her eyes.

"Ready?" she asks.

Not at all, but I nod anyway, spreading my stance.

Ten minutes.

I face off toward each path, imagining the two people somewhere in the shadows. How far away are they?

The park is huge. It could easily take me ten minutes just to reach them.

Quickly, I set the timer on my watch, waiting for the signal.

Stevie calls out, "Ready, get set—"

A terrified scream pierces the silence off to my left, and I don't wait for her to finish before I start running.

28

It sounded like it came from close by, and I maintain the possibly foolish hope my "prizes" aren't hidden too deep in the trees.

I don't even remember which direction I went.

It wasn't a conscious choice to save one or the other.

I just heard the scream and reacted.

"Where are you?" I shout. Another cry has me veering left, crashing through bushes until I emerge into a small clearing and quickly happen upon a man inside a wooden cage suspended from a rope stretching between two massive trees.

I try to remember which way I went. Left. That means this is the accused person.

House Aria.

I don't have time to consider the implications of that right now. I just need to save him.

The cage swings back and forth over a large pile of rocks.

I let out a long sigh. Maybe this isn't so bad?

But then the cage suddenly rises a few inches, and my gaze follows the rope up to see that it's attached to a mechanical crank that's slowly lifting the man toward the sparking purple net of General Sol's protective tree barrier.

My stomach sinks. If the cage reaches the top, the man will be dead.

He spots me and falls to his knees as he grips the bars and presses his face between them.

"Help me!" he shouts.

I scan the area, spotting an axe leaning against a tree.

I assume that's for me.

I waste no time running over and grabbing it.

The pile of rocks under the cage offers a few feet of elevation, but they're uneven, and the highest point is barely wide enough for me to stand.

"Move away," I shout and swing the axe with as much force as possible, trying to keep my balance.

The edge bites into the wood with a sharp *crack* that vibrates down my arm with a painful jolt. The cage sways but continues to lift a little higher.

I tug the axe free to find a generous split in the wood, but it isn't large enough to break the cage open.

"Again!" I scream, not waiting for his reply. With less than a few feet left between him and the Spark barrier, he's this close to being blitzed.

I swing the axe with a grunt, but I miss, and the momentum causes me to slip off the rocks, my knees slamming to the forest floor, the axe tumbling from my hands.

"Fuck!" I shout, grabbing the handle again and climbing back to the peak. "Hold on!"

This time, I prepare myself with the axe gripped in both hands, and I spread my stance as much as I can on the uneven surface. When the cage comes for the downswing, I leap, lifting the axe and swinging with everything I have.

It connects, shattering the bottom of the cage.

I slip as the axe falls from my hands, and I go tumbling. The man screams, but he follows me down, and we both roll to the bottom.

I find myself on the ground breathing heavily, alive, but I think I hit my head.

Blood drips in my eyes, and I definitely banged my knee.

Then I check my watch. Three and a half minutes have passed. I can't waste any more time.

I struggle to my feet and grab the man's arm.

"Come on!" I say, tugging on his wrist. "We have to go. If you want to live, we have to *go*. They'll kill you!"

My voice reaches a feverish shriek that finally rouses him enough to push himself up. He staggers to his feet, and I grab his forearm and tug him back to the path, shoving him in front of me as he continues to stagger.

I'm not gentle. We don't have time for that.

"Run!" I scream. "Snap out of it! You *have* to run!"

I shove him again, and he trips over his feet, just barely catching himself.

"Come on!" I shout, shaking his arm, pulling him along, practically dragging him through the dirt.

"This way," I say, directing him down the same path I came.

I cross the threshold where Devon, Stevie, and the rest of my masked escort awaits. They watch as the man falls to his knees while I bend over, trying to catch my breath.

"You'll let him go?" I ask, looking up at Devon. "I saved him. You said you'd let him go."

His masked face stares down at me for one long second.

"Tell me you'll let him go!" I shout.

After another moment, he quickly jerks his chin before he looks over at Stevie.

Then she pulls off her mask.

"Congratula—" she says, but I stand up, turn around, and start running again.

29

"**H**ey!" Devon shouts. "Where are you going?"

I ignore him and keep running. I'm saving them both.

There was never any other choice.

I check my watch.

I have about five and a half minutes left.

I veer down the right path to find another clearing. Ahead of me, a small wooden platform swings below a high tree branch suspended by long, braided ropes. On it kneels a woman with her wrists and ankles bound in iron cuffs.

Below her, a pit dug into the earth stretches along the platform's path.

It's filled with sharp iron spikes. *Fuck.*

The platform acts like a pendulum, arcing through the air, but instead of losing momentum, it appears to be gaining speed as it tops out at a higher point with each pass due to some kind of mechanism attached to the tree branch.

The platform swings while the woman clings to one of the ropes. As the platform reaches its zenith, she screams as she lifts, her chained legs dangling midair like dead weights.

My heart climbs in my throat as she's suspended in nothing for less than a second, and the platform drops, swinging the opposite way, directly over that pit filled with spikes.

With her ankles and wrists bound, she has very little mobility or strength to hang on. If she falls, it's over.

Think, think, think.

I scan the area, searching for another helpful tool. But there's nothing.

What are my options here? All I have is my small knife tucked in my boot. I pull it out and approach the platform as it arcs to the bottom of its trajectory, but it's moving too fast for me to catch it.

The platform reaches its full height, nearly inverting itself.

The woman screams again as she clings to the rope, and her body twists wildly in the air. What do they want?

Maybe I was never intended to save her at all. Maybe this was just about the choice itself. I wouldn't put anything past my father at this point. Well, fuck that. He will not turn me into the same monster he is today.

My jaw hardens as the platform swings over the pit again. Another scream as the woman is suspended for even longer before the platform narrowly catches her.

Finally, an idea forms.

I tuck my knife away and then run back, giving me some distance. With my hands loose at my sides, I watch the platform as it slowly careens toward the ground.

Maybe if I knock the platform with enough force, I can alter its trajectory enough to clear it of the spikes.

The platform drops as I gauge the distance.

It's coming down as I count the seconds it takes for it to make a pass. Twenty seconds. Ten. Five.

I run. With my arms and legs pumping, I gather speed, jumping as I meet the path of the arc.

My hands slam against the edge of the platform, and I grip it. Using every muscle in my core, I swing my legs forward with every ounce of strength I can summon.

Now I'm moving with the platform. My breath sticks in my throat as I pass over the spikes with barely a breath. As the path continues back, my grip slips, one hand falling away while I use the other to cling on, my fingers digging into the wood.

Now I'm dangling over a pit of fucking iron spikes.

No, no, no. I do *not* die like this.

I throw my free hand up, snatching the edge with both hands again—thank you, daily strength training at the crack of dawn.

When I look down, my heart stops. I think I did it. Whether it was the impact or just my dangling weight, the platform's trajectory has shifted enough that I can jump down without getting skewered.

With a deep breath, I let go.

My feet hit the ground, and I roll to my side, rocks digging into my ribs. But I survived.

Throughout it all, the woman never takes her eyes off me, but it's clear that she's frozen. Petrified with terror.

"You have to jump, too!" I scream. "When it's at the top! Into the bushes! You have to jump!"

It's a long drop, but I just survived it. Of course, she can't use her hands or feet to protect herself, but this is her best chance. I could try to break her fall, but that might just kill us both.

"Jump!" I scream, my voice cracking. Finally, the woman moves. Almost as if in slow motion, she hurls herself off, just before the platform reaches its peak again.

I whisper softly to myself, hoping, *hoping* she survives.

She hits the bushes, then the ground with a dull thud and rolls.

I have only a fraction of a second to feel relief before I'm up and running.

The woman is alive. A little worse for wear but alive. I sigh as I search for some way to open her cuffs, but they're bound with a heavy lock.

"We have to get up," I croak. "We have to make it to the gate."

I don't even know if that's true.

I've already broken the game's rules.

I don't know if they'll let any of this slide, but something tells me we still have to cross the finish line to have a chance of coming out of this unscathed.

A quick glance at my watch tells me we have less than a minute. "Hold on," I say, not giving her a chance to protest. Thankfully, she's small and slight. I bend down and sling her over my shoulders. Adrenaline is pumping through my veins, and it feels like she weighs almost nothing.

I stagger back to the path and struggle toward the fountain. I pick up my pace, running as fast as I can with the woman bouncing on my shoulders.

The fountain appears before us like a lifeline.

I check my watch.

Ten seconds.

The time ticks down as the masked faces grow closer.

The woman is crying, shouting. She's getting heavier, and I list to the side, nearly losing my balance. Somehow, I save us both from falling, then I'm running again.

Just a few seconds left.

My watch buzzes as I trip past the finish line, roughly setting the woman down as her weight crashes into me, and we both stumble.

I stagger for several steps, tripping over my feet before landing face down on the pavement with a smack.

30

No one helps me up.

It takes a few seconds before I push onto my knees and sit back while Devon and Stevie, now maskless, stare down at me, clearly confused about what to do. Behind them stand the others in a circle.

"What the fuck was that?" Devon asks, gesturing toward the trees.

I lurch up onto a throbbing knee and look around.

The accused man is gone. "Where's the person I saved?"

"He returned home. Like I said," Devon says. *Good.*

The Keeper kneels on the ground, eyeing the circle of masked people.

"Uncuff her," I demand. "Let her go."

Stevie huffs and gestures to a pair of Extinguishers who must've arrived at some point. I recognize Lieutenant Dire from my first day of cadet training. He leans down and unlocks her ankles and then uses her wrist restraints to pull her to her feet.

"She gets to leave the city now?" I ask, my voice shaky, suddenly reminded of the itching spreading through my arms and legs. "That was the deal."

Dire rounds on me and pins me with a dark look, his gaze scanning me from head to toe. I swallow thickly, resisting the urge to scratch. The last thing I need is any more of his attention.

"Yes," Stevie says, answering for him. "Get her out of here."

The Extinguishers drag the woman away as I watch her back, hoping she finds a better life beyond the city's borders. That's probably wishful thinking, though. Still, maybe at least this gives her a fighting chance.

Now all the attention returns to me as I force myself to my feet. I don't know what I did, but my knee hurts and my ankle throbs and I can feel my hair sticking to my forehead. I try to clear the strands away, but my fingers come away coated in blood.

I think I'm mostly fine. Physically, anyway.

I wipe the blood on my pants and wait for my sentencing.

Devon shakes his head and runs a hand through his hair.

"What the fuck do we do now?" he asks Stevie.

"I don't know. Kick her out?"

I make a sound of protest that has them both turning my way.

"Have something to say?" Stevie asks.

"You said I'd only be kicked out if I didn't save them."

"Yes, but then you saved them both!" Devon says, throwing up his hands.

"Sorry?" I say, though obviously, I'm not sorry. How could they ask me to make this choice?

Devon huffs out a sound of frustration and paces away, again tugging on his hair.

"Let's go inside," Stevie says. "We can talk this over."

"You've entered cadet training?" Devon asks me, and I blink.

"Yes."

"And you know that if we kick you out of Society, you can no longer train?"

"Yes." I swallow my pride and my dignity. "Please. I want to be a Breaker more than anything."

Something imperceptibly softens in her expression before she gestures to everyone around the circle. "Let's go."

Devon and Stevie take up the front of the line, and I limp behind them, surrounded by my group of masked escorts. Someone moves in beside me, revealing my cousin Anan.

"What were you thinking?" he asks in a furious whisper.

"Can we not?" I really don't want to discuss this with him or anyone. No one can convince me I did the wrong thing tonight.

He shakes his head, and we continue in silence, returning to the school and turning a corner. Then we climb several flights of stairs. My knee throbs during the entire climb before we level off at a wide marbled hall.

Several mirrors hang down its length, and a domed ceiling curves overhead, painted with blue skies and white clouds.

A door stands at the end, and we approach it before Devon and Stevie stop. "Wait here," Devon says to me, and then everyone disappears inside before they close it behind them, leaving me alone on the other side.

I don't know what to expect. What will they do with me now?

A few students pass, tossing me curious looks as I sink onto a marble bench near the door. It's then that I remember I have blood on my face, and I stand up again, approaching a mirror.

I'm a mess. I look around for a bathroom, but I need to be here when Devon and Stevie come for me. I think I've caused enough trouble for one night.

I give up and return to the bench, favoring my sore knee. My ankle feels a bit better, at least. With my elbows planted on my thighs, I drop my head in my hands and wait. Ten minutes pass, then fifteen. The itching from the storm eases as it moves off, and I sit back in relief.

Another half an hour later, and I'm getting restless.

My phone dings, so I pull it out. It's Trinity, and she's looking for me. I text her my location, then go back to waiting, staring at the door, my hands, and finally the floor.

"Poe!" Trinity calls from the end of the hall. She's out of breath, her cheeks flushed, a cut marring her eyebrow. "I've been looking for you for hours!"

"What happened?" I ask as she drops onto the seat next to me. "You're hurt."

She swallows hard and shakes her head, still trying to catch her breath. "I took my third test this afternoon."

She's smiling, seems okay. My heart lifts with hope. "And?"

She breaks into a grin. "I passed."

"Trin!" I shout, throwing my arms around her. "I'm so happy to hear that."

"Thank you," she says.

"But didn't you have to finish *two* more?"

She nods. "I completed the second test a few days ago. I didn't want to say anything until I had good news."

"Well, that's great. Congratulations," I say.

"But there's something you should know." She pulls away, her expression serious. "I didn't take House Fiama's tests."

I shake my head. "What?"

"I tested for House Aria."

"I'm not following."

She exhales a sigh and twists her fingers. "I thought it was hopeless," she says. "But I got friendly with some students from Aria. They offered me a deal to pledge to their House instead."

I shake my head again. "I'm still not following."

"I'm becoming an Extinguisher," she says proudly. "They're seeking recruits and said they'd help me pass my tests if I agreed to sign up."

"An Extinguisher?" I say, my voice hollow. "But . . . why?"

"Fiama was done with me, Poe. Devon told me I had almost no chance." Her eyes fill with tears. "I had to do it."

"But your family will still disown you!"

"I know, but it's still better than the alternative," she says. "At least I'm still Society."

"Yes, but you'll be . . ." I can't even bring myself to say it. My best friend wants to join the monsters who hunt down and kill people.

People like me.

"What's the problem?" she asks. "I fixed this! We can both join Aria together. It's perfect!"

I sit back. "Trin, I'm not joining Aria. What makes you think that?"

"Your first test . . ." she says. "You tested for House Aria!"

"I know, but that was a mistake. I have to join Fiama. You know that."

Some of her enthusiasm wanes when she realizes I'm serious.

"Trin, you didn't really think—"

"What happened to you?" comes another voice. It's Knox. His eyes widen as they scan me up and down.

"I had my second test," I answer. I make eye contact with Trinity, who's possibly just noticing the blood even though I'm pretty sure it's hard to miss.

Knox steps closer, hovering over me. "What happened?"

I sit up and lean against the wall. "You know I can't talk about it."

He wouldn't understand why I did it anyway.

"Poet, did you pass House Fiama's test?"

I sense Trinity waiting for my answer, too.

She really thought she'd figured out a perfect solution to her problems.

I've never been so grateful that we aren't supposed to disclose what happens during our initiations.

When I refuse to answer, Knox sits down on my other side. "Poet, we'll be married in a few years; you can tell me. I'll find out soon enough anyway."

I sigh and pinch the bridge of my nose, which makes the cut across my forehead ache.

"Wait, what are you doing out here if you just did your test?" he asks next.

Now his expression turns to suspicion as he puts two and two together.

I press my mouth together. "Waiting for Devon and Stevie."

"Why?"

My gaze shifts away, and I'm sure I couldn't look guiltier if I tried. Knox grabs my chin and directs my face toward him.

"What are they doing?" he demands. "Why are you waiting for them?"

I wrench my face from his hold. "No reason."

"Poet . . ."

"They had to discuss my results."

The words slip out, and I regret them the instant they're out of my mouth.

Knox's eyes flash, and he snarls, "For fuck's sake, what *happened*—"

The door to the room opens, rescuing me from his questioning. Several people file out, their masks clutched in their hands.

"They'll see you now," Anan says. I can't tell from his tone how much trouble I'm in. Regardless, I leap up, grateful for the chance to dodge Knox and Trinity.

I don't look back, sliding past Anan and entering the room.

Devon and Stevie stand in the center of a salon decorated entirely in emerald and gold.

"Close the door," Devon says, and I turn around to do as he says, then stare at the floor before I will myself to face them again.

"Approach," Devon says, and I clutch my hands as I take a few careful steps across the plush rug with my heart pounding in my temples.

"You really made this hard for us tonight," Devon says.

I don't reply. I don't think he's expecting me to.

"But we've discussed it with Chancellor Marks and General Sol."

He glances at Stevie, and she continues. "Your test concludes with this—what do *you* choose, Poet Graves: House Fiama, the House of your heritage, the House run by your father, or House Aria, the House you were never intended for?"

I blink, caught completely off guard.

Despite their assurances that it's my choice, I wasn't really expecting anyone to ask me what I wanted.

"You're letting me choose? I'm not being kicked out?"

Devon sighs and shakes his head. "Apparently. Those are our orders. Your brother was a good guy, and he spoke so highly of you. I'm not sure why you're doing this, but I also know you aren't reckless, and you might have your . . . reasons."

His gaze flicks to the doorway, where I presume Knox is still waiting, and I wonder if he understands.

"Plus, the general doesn't want to prevent you from joining the Storm Guard," he says. "Technically, you did what we asked—we never said you couldn't save them both."

"Truthfully, we never thought anyone would do that," Stevie says, scanning me from head to toe with what might be a touch of admiration.

I inhale a deep breath.

They're letting me choose.

I can't decide if this is a gift or a minefield because, whatever my choice, I can't blame anyone but myself.

A lot of things cycle through my thoughts.

My father and his warnings, first and foremost. Of how he threatened me in Dean Withers's office.

He could lose everything if I do this.

If I don't pledge to Fiama, Knox will marry Winter Jenkins instead.

I understand he meant it as a threat, but presented with this choice, it becomes a lifeline. A chance to escape.

Winter *wants* him.

For whatever reason.

And my father's ambitions have never been my responsibility.

Maybe if he'd asked me even once. Maybe if he'd cared at all about what I wanted.

He's always claimed he's the only man for the job as Fiama's scion. The only one who has the stomach to do what it takes to keep us protected. But I've seen what he's truly capable of now, and maybe Fiama would actually be better off in someone else's hands.

I think of Trinity, my best friend who's defended me and protected me for so long. She's been with me through everything. I think of the look on her face just now when she thought she'd figured out a possible future where she could be happy despite her mistakes.

She really thought we'd switch Houses together.

And maybe it's my turn to protect her for a change.

I think of Knox sitting outside, believing he has a right to know everything about me, and how I had to *negotiate* with him to remain in cadet training, like a prisoner.

He wants to control me and every aspect of my life.

My entire existence will become a series of compromises for my freedom. I've always understood that I'd move from the crush of my father's hand to becoming another man's property. A few weeks ago, I thought there was no avoiding it.

But a door to freedom has just cracked open, allowing in a sliver of light.

And I think about how cadet training makes me feel alive. Like I'm a part of something, and how, for once, I made a choice solely for me.

I can't let them take all of that away.

If I become Mrs. Knox Arden in three years, that's all I'll ever be.

My eyes meet Devon's, and they widen ever so slightly.

He doesn't understand it completely, but he understands something.

I look at Stevie, and she watches me with her head tipped, her expression brimming with curiosity, like I'm an animal tethered to a pole and she can't tell what I'll do next.

She also doesn't get it, but maybe someday she will.

"House Aria," I say, lifting my chin.

Those two damning words ring between us, cementing my destiny . . . and probably my demise.

31

The silence in the room aches.

Devon and Stevie exchange a look, and then Devon speaks. "Poet, are you sure?"

No. Yes. I don't know.

"I'm . . . sure," I say, hoping I sound more confident than I feel. Probably not.

Devon shakes his head and rubs a hand along the back of his neck.

"You said I had a choice, and this is what I choose."

I'm making a mistake. I'll tear my family apart. This will put me so much closer to the Extinguishers and their scrutiny. But . . . Trinity needs me, and it might be what I need to get me away from Knox once and for all.

"Is this actually about Knox?" Devon asks, almost like he's reading my mind. "Because you can't throw everything away just to piss off your dad. I get that it feels good right now, but you need to think of your future."

Is that what I'm doing?

But I don't want to piss my dad off. That *would* be a trivial thing to do.

What I want is a voice in my own life.

This choice will only make my life harder in so many ways. I don't know why it matters so much to Devon, but I'm over worrying about how my choices affect the men in my life.

He's not even *in* my life. Why does he care at all?

I turn to Stevie, who's watching the entire exchange silently.

"Will House Aria have me?" I ask, and she studies me.

"I admit, I wasn't thrilled with the idea," she says. "These tests are supposed to be a clear and easy choice, but watching you save them both . . ."

She scans me up and down with an obvious sort of approval.

"Makes you far more interesting than I first thought. Why did you do it?"

"It . . . seemed like the right thing to do."

Stevie nods. "I can't make them like you. You understand you are the daughter of a rival House's scion, yes? No one will trust you. They'll all think you're a spy or intent on some form of sabotage."

I huff out a short breath. "Do *you* think I'm a spy?"

Stevie wrinkles her nose and folds her arms. "I don't think you're a spy. I think . . ." She shakes her head. "Well, it doesn't matter what I think. No one will stop you if you want to pledge to House Aria."

"But you should be the one to tell your father," Devon says.

Right. Of course.

"What about Trinity?" I ask. "She just told me she's also pledging to Aria."

Stevie sighs. "Yeah. Another thing I'll need to deal with." She shakes her head. "Tonight has definitely shaken things up. Is that why you did this? Because of your friend?"

I shrug. "Partly."

Stevie appraises me with another look. "Then she's lucky to have you."

"Will everyone hate me?" I ask Devon.

He arches a brow. "What else would you expect?"

I sigh. "This is all so stupid and arbitrary."

I feel them both go still.

"I'd keep that thought to yourself," Devon says with an edge to his voice.

"Yeah. Sorry." I rub my face.

"You'll need to switch dorms," Stevie says. "We can do it tomorrow."

"That's it, then?" I ask.

"That's it," Stevie says. "The pledge ceremony is in a few weeks, and then you'll be one of us."

She grimaces, and I almost have to laugh.

"I'm not so bad once you get to know me," I say hopefully, and she gives me a searching look.

"I think you're about to become a giant pain in my ass," she says, and this time I do laugh.

Possibly.

Probably.

House Aria. I'd never really considered it until a few minutes ago.

This might be my chance to escape.

Maybe.

Or I might actually be building myself an even smaller cage.

"Okay, you can go then," Stevie says. "Welcome . . . I guess."

With that resounding endorsement, I leave the room to find Knox pacing outside. He stops when he sees me, and suddenly, the implications of my decision become a roundhouse kick to the chest. "Well? What happened?" he asks.

Trinity waits beside him with an expectant look on her face.

My mouth opens, but I can't make the words come out.

He must read it in my features because his eyes widen. "Poet, tell me you're pledging to House Fiama. Tell me!"

I shake my head, tears pressing the backs of my eyes. "I have to go," I manage to choke out, then I turn and start walking. When I sense Knox behind me, I stop and spin around. "Don't follow me. I need to be alone for a minute."

For some reason, he listens. He's probably in shock.

I take the opportunity to flee, walking as quickly as I can.

"Poet!" he calls. "Come back!"

But I can't.

My decision has been made.

Now it's time to face the consequences.

32

It takes me an hour to stop shaking. I pace up and down various empty halls, searching for a quiet corner to freak out.

Finally, I find myself inside an atrium filled with plants and flowers, buzzing with bees and butterflies. This must be where second- and third-year biology classes take place.

Mercifully, it's empty and silent, except for the gentle trickle of water from a few small fountains decorating the space. I inhale the humid air and the earthy scent of soil mixed with the fresh smell of flowers. This is exactly what I needed.

I approach a window and peer out, noting we're high above the ground. New Manhattan stretches before me, twinkling with lights. I notice a few sections where the power has gone out, leaving everyone in the dark until the next storm arrives and General Sol siphons more Spark.

Fiama Society Tower A stands far in the distance, high above the world like a reminder and maybe an accusation. I have to tell my father what happened. Despite everything, he deserves to hear this from me.

I pull out my phone and stare at the screen, thumb hovering over his name. I don't think I've ever been this nervous in my life.

I inhale a deep breath.

Then I chicken out and text my mother first.

I just made her life harder, too.

Maybe it was selfish of me, but she also refused to protect me. She never said a word against my marriage to Knox or supported my desire to join the Storm Guard.

And though my father would have steamrolled over her objections, the effort would have been noticed and appreciated.

ME: *I need to talk to you.*

MOM: *What is it? Everything okay?*

I look around the space, ensuring I'm alone before switching to video call mode. My mother answers almost immediately, her worried face filling the screen.

"Baby?" she asks, her dark eyebrows drawing together. "What happened?"

I inhale a deep breath, willing strength into my body. There's no point in dragging this out.

"I completed my second test," I say. "And I'm pledging to House Aria."

She goes completely still.

Doesn't blink. Doesn't breathe for several long seconds. If I couldn't see her sitting right in front of me, I'd swear she passed out.

"Mom?" I prompt when the silence stretches too long. "Say something."

Her mouth opens and then closes. Opens again.

Finally, she speaks, and the sound is raw. Filled with grief. Like someone died. Maybe me. "I'm not sure what you want me to say."

I drag a hand through my ponytail, my entire body trembling.

"I'm wondering . . . how . . . how do we tell Dad?"

"*We?*" she asks.

In that moment, I sense something snap between us in that single harshly flung syllable. A thin, fraying thread I didn't realize I was still holding.

She exhales sharply. "Your father will hit the roof. The one *I* currently live under while you're off having fun. There is no 'we' here." Her eyes harden. "Why are you calling me with this? Were you hoping I'd do it for you?"

The words land like a slap.

I don't know why I thought—just once—she might stand up for me instead of supporting him. I've built this version of her in my mind for years, but she's never really been that person at all.

"How could you do this to me?" she asks, her voice a whisper. "He will . . . I don't even know what he'll do. You have to fix this. Go back and ask them for another try."

I peer out the window, scanning the lilac-hued clouds as they dissipate across the sky. "I can't," I say quietly. "It's done."

"Your wedding," she blurts, as if the idea has only just occurred to her. "What will Trey and Molly *say*?"

I press a hand to my chest. It feels hollow. Scooped out.

"I don't want to marry Knox." The words hang there, bare and exposed. I've never said them out loud. Not like this. "He is *just* like Dad."

Her eyebrows draw together. "Poet, what do you mean?"

My eyes narrow, but I don't hesitate. "You know *exactly* what I mean."

Every raised hand. Every flinch. Every silent meal.

Each bruised moment settles between us.

She doesn't deny it.

She doesn't say anything at all.

I swallow. "Mom, I wanted to tell Dad before he heard it another way. I thought you might be able to help." My voice falters. "I shouldn't have assumed that. I'll just call him."

"No," she says.

I blink. "What?"

"I said no." Her tone snaps tight. "I'll take care of it."

"But—"

"I said I'll take care of it. I know you think I'm helpless, but I *do* know how to talk to him."

"Mom, what are you—"

She disconnects the call before I can ask any more questions.

What did she just mean? Relief balloons in my chest that I may get out of being the one to share the news. I'm nothing but a coward.

But then I worry about my mother and how he might react. She seemed sure she knew how to talk to him, though. If she really knows, why hasn't she ever done it before?

Maybe she has?

I slump against the window and watch the city's lights from my perch. I'm unsure how long I'm sitting there before realizing how late it is.

Slowly, I stand, surprised that my legs hold me up.

With another look around the atrium, I open the door before I head for my room, where I'll spend my last night in the company of House Fiama.

33

I return to find my room empty.

I text Trinity because we really need to talk more about what happened. Then I clean up the blood on my face and do my best to patch myself up before changing into my PJs.

As I slide under the covers, my knee throbs. I banged it up pretty good today, and it might cause me some trouble during my workout tomorrow, but I'll push through it.

When Lacey and Winter return, I pretend I'm asleep so I don't have to talk to anyone. As much as I fear moving into House Aria, I also can't wait to put some distance between us.

I assume Trinity must have gone to find Edward, and I wonder what her plans are now. Dating across Societies isn't wholly unprecedented, though it is rare, and a marriage requires both sides of the relationship to cede to the same House.

As I wait for her to return, I drift in and out, trapped in a state of perpetual anxiousness. I toss and turn, replaying the conversation with my mother in my head.

I'll never forget that look on her face when I broke whatever was between us forever.

Eventually, I must cave to exhaustion because when I blink my eyes open, slivers of early-morning light filter around the edges of the curtains. It feels like I've been kicked and dropped and twisted through a vise.

My watch tells me it's way too early to be awake, but I doubt I'll be able to sleep anymore. I roll over and look across the room to find Trinity fast asleep, snoring softly. It's her last night in this room, too, and in spite of everything, I'm relieved we're doing this together.

My knee aches as I get up and limp to the bathroom for a shower. When I emerge, Trinity is dressed and sitting on the edge of her bed, running her palms over her thighs.

"Hi," she whispers, aware of Lacey and Winter still asleep.

"Hey," I say. "We should talk."

"Maybe not here?" She nods toward our roommates. "I need to meet Stevie before breakfast to receive my new room assignment."

I exhale a short breath. "Same."

She blinks, and it takes her a moment to process my words. "Poet, did you really—"

"Not here," I reply, again gesturing to Winter and Lacey. "Let's go somewhere else."

She nods and stuffs a few things into a backpack while I dress and do the same.

My things will be moved later, but for now, I grab a few essentials to get me through the day.

We both exit quietly, saying little as we head toward the library. It's mostly empty, so we find a corner where we won't be overheard.

"Tell me everything that happened," Trinity says. I recount the events of my night—how I was given two choices and when I chose both . . . or neither, depending on how you look at it, they left it up to me.

"But why?" Trinity asks. "Why did you choose Aria?"

I sigh, shake my head. "Partly for me. Partly for you."

Tears form in Trinity's eyes. She wipes them with the back of her hand. "You shouldn't have done that."

I shrug. "I'd do anything for you, Trin. You know that. And now I won't have to marry Knox. I hope he's happy with Winter."

A line forms between her brows. "But your father—"

"I've ruined my family," I say hoarsely. "I know."

I tell her about the awful conversation with my mother.

"But they started this. They left me no choice." I try to say it firmly, like I really believe it. They wouldn't listen to me, but what if I've overreacted? Maybe things would have been fine with Knox. I think about the bruises he left on my arm, reminding myself that despite the consequences, the alternative was so much worse.

Trinity nods, and we're both silent for a moment.

"You aren't serious about joining E-squad," I say, my voice low. "That was just to get you into Aria, right?"

"No," she says, confusion passing over her expression. "I want to join them."

"But why?"

"I'm no longer Fiama, and I need to do something."

"But don't you want to do something . . . good?" My voice turns a little too loud, and she frowns.

"I *am* doing something good. I'll be protecting everyone from the dangers of infected Keepers."

I shake my head. "Don't you think what they do is kind of terrible—"

My words cut off as a small group of people enter the library. They wear the dark-red shirts of E-squad recruits, and they're eyeing Trinity and me.

"Of course not," Trinity says. "They play a vital role in our Society. A vital role in *our* new House."

The reminder is a cold dose of water. I've willingly joined the people whose duty it is to deal with people like me. Now I'm living among them, circling a little closer to possible exposure. I might be sick.

I pull my water bottle from my bag and take a long sip, trying to settle my stomach. I have to talk her out of this. Somehow. She's so much better than those brutes.

I tense up as the E-squad recruits approach, then stop breathing when they stop at our table. A woman stands in front of two men. I recognize her as the same person I saw Trinity talking to not that long ago. I'd completely forgotten until now. She's tall, lean, with sharp features. Her tank top reveals her sleek arm muscles.

"Robins," she says with a grin. "We heard you passed last night."

Trinity nods eagerly. "By the skin of my teeth."

I wonder what Trinity was asked to do.

The girl claps her on the shoulder. "You'll be rooming with my girls and me," she says. "C'mon. I'll take you there now."

"Really?" Trinity asks, her eyes widening like she's won some kind of prize. "Thank you!"

"Of course," the girl says, her gaze flicking to me while I try not to flinch.

"Oh, sorry!" Trinity says. "This is Ruby. And that's Brick and Axel." I remember Brick from when he tried to intimidate me after my first test. He doesn't look any less like a blank wall in the bright light of daytime. "This is my best friend, Poet Graves."

Ruby folds her arms and cocks a hip. "We know who she is," she confirms. "I hear you're joining Aria, too." She doesn't say it with any kind of pride, only suspicion. But great, the news is already spreading. I shouldn't be surprised.

Two people switching Houses in one night? That's news worthy of a wildfire.

"Yeah, speaking of which," I say. "I need to go meet Stevie."

All three E-squad recruits are creeping me out, and I don't like being anywhere near them.

"I guess you're good?" I ask Trinity uncertainly. She can't really want to leave with them. I thought we'd share a room. Isn't that part of the reason I chose to join Aria?

"Yeah, I'll catch up with you later."

"Sure," I say. I hate this. I grab my bag and stand as Ruby and the others fill the vacated seats. I toss out a quick goodbye, but Trinity is already deep in conversation with her new friends and doesn't respond.

So I head for the main hall, where I find Stevie casually leaning against a pillar, dressed in Storm Guard purple.

"Wasn't sure you'd show up," she says, eyeing me up and down.

"Yeah, well, I did consider running away to the Wastes."

That earns me a laugh.

"Talked to your dad?" Stevie asks.

"Yeah," I answer. "To my mom, at least."

Stevie winces. "How did that go?"

"About as well as you can expect."

She studies me, probably wondering what in the Skies is wrong with me. *Same, Stevie. Same.*

"Did the E-squad find your friend? They're supposed to show her to her room."

"Yeah," I say. "They did. Will she . . . be okay?"

Stevie cocks her head. "Why wouldn't she be?"

"I don't know. They seem . . . intense."

She laughs, and I get the sense she doesn't entirely disagree.

"She's one of them now. They hold tight to their people."

That sounds ominous.

I look around the almost-empty hall. "Should we get going? I need to have breakfast and head to class."

"We're just waiting for one more," Stevie replies, when footsteps echo behind me.

I turn around to find Rook sauntering toward us. I should have known. He's dressed in first-year gray—a T-shirt and black pants with his standard-issue boots. Dark colors really work on him.

He approaches with his usual stoic expression in place. His arrival makes my heart flutter against my rib cage, and I order it to behave. But of course it doesn't listen.

If he's surprised to discover that I've left Fiama, he doesn't show it.

"Morning," he says, doing that thing he does, running a hand through his hair. I'm staring for a second too long, and he arches a brow before I tear my gaze away.

"Just how many people joined Aria yesterday?" I ask, and Stevie huffs out a laugh.

"There's a handful of you," she answers. "But you two are definitely the most interesting." She pushes herself off the pillar. "Come along, little pledglings."

We head up the staircase curving around the other end of the hall, and I shake off the sensation that I'm crossing a threshold into hell.

This is just another set of dorm rooms; get a grip.

Having Rook trailing behind me with his sure, confident steps actually makes me feel a little better.

Halfway up, Stevie pauses and looks back at me, searching my face. I'd say she looked concerned if I didn't know any better. She opens her mouth and then closes it before turning and continuing up the steps.

The Aria wing contrasts directly with Fiama's, doing nothing to dispel the notion that I've entered enemy territory. Instead of creams and golds, Aria is adorned with black silk walls in ornate brocade and embellished with iron and silver. The effect is just as elegant but darker and more sinister.

It's louder, too. Thumping music pounds behind doorways even at this early hour, and the air is charged with something electric.

Stevie leads us down a hall and throws open a door. My new room is just like my previous one, except for the color scheme and the presence of two of my new roommates lounging on their beds.

"Silla and Cece, meet Poet," Stevie says.

I think she's trying to welcome me in her own aloof way, but as she cautioned, I can join House Aria but she can't make any of them accept me. Silla and Cece are obviously less than delighted to meet me.

"Hi," I say weakly, clinging to the strap of my backpack, but neither of them replies.

"That's your bed," Stevie says. "Another new pledge took that one a few days ago."

A moment later, a familiar face appears from the bathroom.

"Domino!" I exclaim, suddenly intensely grateful to see her.

"Hey," she says with a grin. Silla and Cece ignore her.

"You two know each other?" Stevie asks, flicking a finger between us.

"Kind of," I answer, and she nods like that satisfies her.

"Then stick together, because you'll need it. Good luck."

She nods at Silla and Cece, who give her a deferential bow of their heads. "I'll see you all around. Try not to kill each other."

With that declaration, she gestures for Rook to follow.

He pushes off the doorway as our eyes meet for a brief second. He scans me up and down, and I think he wants to say something but then changes his mind before turning to follow Stevie.

I face Silla and Cece, who are busy on their phones. That's fine. This is hardly any different from my old roommates.

I actually have far more pressing things to worry about.

Trinity to start. Her desire to join E-squad.

And my father.

He *must* know by now.

"Everything okay?" Domino asks, and I turn around.

"Yeah, you?"

She nods and can't seem to contain her smile. "My parents are thrilled I'm joining Society."

A snort from the other side of the room blasts through her excitement, causing Domino's smile to falter.

"Oh, shut up," I say, and Silla rolls her eyes.

"I'm so happy to hear that," I say, trying to muster some enthusiasm.

There's a certain kind of irony in the fact that I've just fucked up my entire life, but Domino gets a real shot at something better. It's a grim slap of reality and a reminder of the privileges I've been afforded . . . and possibly just threw away.

"I can't believe we're stuck with the losers and outcasts," Cece says loudly, speaking to Silla.

"We're accepting new members," I say without missing a beat. "We meet on alternate Wednesdays. You'll fit right in."

My phone dings, and I see it's a text from Edward, asking me to meet with him.

Cece scoffs, and I stuff my phone into my pocket. "I gotta go."

I find Edward near the cafeteria. He looks terrible. His skin is pale and clammy, and his hair hangs limp in his eyes.

"Edward?" I ask, alarmed by his state. "What's wrong?"

"Have you seen Trinity this morning?" he asks.

"Yes, about an hour ago."

"She broke up with me last night," he says.

Wait, what? Well, that explains his appearance.

"Why?" I ask. "What happened?"

"She found me after her test," he says. "Said she was pledging to Aria and joining the E-squad. She said there was no future for us."

I huff out a breath and lean against the wall.

"I'm so sorry," I say. This is so unlike Trinity. What is she doing?

"You have to talk to her. Maybe she can still pledge to Fiama. This can't be the end for us."

"Edward, I don't think she can do that. She's made her choice. She seems pretty happy with it, too."

"Why would she do this?" he asks, tears brimming in his gaze. "We love each other."

I shake my head, wishing I had an answer. They *don't* really have a future together. Breaching House lines will make things even more difficult, but I thought Trinity loved Edward. Would she really give him up so easily?

Watching him makes my stomach hurt, like it's been filled with cement.

"Let's go," I say, throwing an arm around his shoulders. We're accumulating an audience, and I drag him away, searching for a spot where he can have his breakdown in private.

I force him a few stumbling steps along a corridor and then duck us into an empty room. He slides to the floor and tucks up his knees, laying his head across his arms. I settle in front of him, bending a leg under me and giving him a moment.

I want to cry, too, but one of us needs to keep it together. It feels like my best friend changed overnight, and I wonder if this is my fault. Maybe I wasn't paying close enough attention.

"Have you talked to her parents?" I ask. I wonder if they've been in contact with her. Did they notice something that I missed?

"They're not answering my calls," he says, wiping his nose with the palm of his hand. I press my mouth together. I've known the Robinses for years; I can't believe they'd just abandon Trinity.

"I'll try calling them," I say. "Maybe they'll talk to me."

"Why would they talk to *you*?" Edward asks, his tone sharp. "You're *Aria* now. Just like *her*. Did you plan this together? Did she do this *for* you?"

I try not to flinch at the harshness in his words. "It's complicated."

"What about your father?" Edward asks. "Could he help her? Get her back into Fiama?"

Edward isn't thinking straight. He's lobbing suggestions that have no basis in reality.

"I don't think I can. As you just reminded me . . ."

His eyes darken. "Right."

"Yeah," I say, again swimming in the foggy repercussions of my reckless decision. Would my father have listened to me anyway?

"Well, that's just great," Edward adds. "What the fuck, Poet? I hope you understand what you've done."

It's an unfair statement, but he's hurting, so I let it slide. He pushes himself up and gives me a dark look before turning and stalking off with his shoulders hunched.

I stare after him in surprise. Edward's always been so kind and mellow. I'll give him some time and then try to talk to him again.

I message Trinity, telling her what's just happened, but she doesn't respond.

My stomach rumbles, reminding me it's been a while since I've eaten. Not since lunch yesterday.

I check the time. The cafeteria will be full by now. Do I skip meals forever?

But I'll have to confront everyone at some point.

I'm a pariah. An outcast.

Technically, I'm still Society, but I don't think that will matter much to anyone in that room.

Time to get this over with.

34

It's almost laughable the way everyone stops talking when I walk into the crowded cafeteria a minute later.

Silence fills the room with the barest clink of cutlery against plates and bowls. I clear my throat and lift my chin. I will not be shamed or cowed.

A set of heavy footsteps fills the silence, and I feel a presence behind me.

I don't even need to look to know who it is.

I recognize his scent.

It's earthy and grounding. Reminds me of sunshine on a rare clear day.

The thought is disconcerting.

I shouldn't *know* his smell. Be able to parse out the notes and subtle qualities. But I don't examine it further; I'm just grateful I'm not standing here alone anymore. I shift my weight and look up to find Rook standing beside me, staring at everyone staring at us.

"So, do you ever get used to this?" I whisper, and he snorts. The sound is so incongruous that I almost laugh. We must both look like we're losing our minds.

"Eat your breakfast," he practically growls to the room. "Don't you all have better things to do than worry about us?"

He brushes past me and heads over to the food line, ignoring everyone's scrutiny with an indifference I can't help but admire. I take his cue and follow, causing the room to break out of stasis as the chatter resumes.

We both move along the counter, separated by a few bodies. When I've collected my plate, I look up to find him sitting at a table near the wall on the Aria side of the cafeteria.

As I survey the room, my gaze meets Knox's. We gauge each other, and

I look at the empty seat where I'd normally eat. Knox's expression is hard to read, but we both know I can't sit on the Fiama side anymore. Not that I think he still wants me there.

I remind myself that this was the plan. To distance myself.

I tear my eyes away and head toward Rook.

Everyone is still staring as I set my tray down across from him.

He looks up and arches a brow. "Oh, you want to sit with *me* now?" he asks. "Your friends don't want you anymore, so I'm finally good enough?"

I flinch, the words a slap delivered to tender flesh. My eyes swim as I quickly snatch my tray back.

"I'm . . . I'm . . . I thought . . ."

"What? We'd be outcasts together?"

He's absolutely right. What was I thinking? That somehow, we were on the same team now? I've done nothing but be horrible to him, and Knox has been even worse.

"I'm sorry," I mumble.

I turn to leave, but he touches my wrist, fingers gently closing around it. His hand is warm, his skin a little rough, and my entire body grows hot.

"Sit," he says, his voice low and gruff, like he's mad about the invitation but is offering it nonetheless.

"It's okay, I'll—"

"Sit," he says, more firmly this time. He releases my wrist, and I watch him wipe a palm on his thigh. I press my mouth together, then sink into the seat across from him again, inhaling sharply as his knee brushes mine.

He jerks away, and I shake out my napkin and lay it over my thighs, trying not to be hurt by how little he wants to touch me.

"Thank you," I say, and he looks up, peering at me like he's trying to figure something out.

He grunts in reply and then attacks his food like it's personally wronged him.

While we eat, I pull out my phone, checking for the millionth time for something from my parents.

If my dad would just yell at me, we could get this done and move on. I know our relationship is over, but I hope to make amends with my mom, at least. I scroll through the series of unanswered texts I've sent, realizing the worst part is not knowing.

"Waiting for an important message?" Rook asks in a low voice that has me glancing over. "From lover boy, perhaps? But wait, he's sitting right there, isn't he?"

He says it with such disdain that my eyes narrow. "Not sure how that's any of your business."

"You made it my business when you started yelling at him near my standing spot."

I lean in, narrowing my eyes. "Then perhaps you should find a *new* standing spot."

"I've tried," he says dryly before tearing into a piece of toast. "Somehow, you keep finding me."

I'm about to retort when someone asks, "Mind if we join you?"

Domino stands with Journey, her chatty cog friend.

"Sure," I say as they sit beside Rook and me.

"I guess we're all the new Aria outcasts?" Domino asks, though she doesn't seem that upset about it. I guess she's already spent her first couple of months at Amery on the outside looking in.

"Does seem that way," I say.

"I'm Journey," she says to Rook and holds out her hand, but he just stares at it and then continues eating.

I notice Journey's chestnut hair is sporting a streak of purple, and Domino's braid has acquired some plum-hued highlights. They're both settling into this new way of life. "Nice hair," I say.

Journey smiles and gives her head a little shake. "Thought we should try to fit in."

"Yours is amazing," Domino says. "How often do you have to get it done?"

I run a hand through my purple locks. "Thanks, and every few weeks, I guess."

"You need to give us your stylist's name," Journey says. Then she leans forward in a conspiratorial hunch. "Tell me, what's it like being the scion's daughter?"

Her eyes sparkle with curiosity. I blink at the abrupt change in topic and decide I don't feel like pretending today. "Sometimes it really fucking sucks," I answer, and her expression falls.

"But you're the main character. *Everyone* knows who you are!"

I grimace, but Journey doesn't pick up on my discomfort.

"I promise that isn't always a good thing. It's hard to wear the weight of people's expectations."

Her forehead creases, and I sense she doesn't like my answer.

"Well, *I* think it would be nice to be that important," she says, picking up her fork and digging into her eggs, but then I understand. "Fame" is a strange thing. Those who have it usually want to escape it, and those who covet it can't imagine why anyone would want anything else.

"When you're a cog, no one thinks you're important," she says. "Must be nice to matter. That's all I'm saying."

I nod along with her because I also see her point, but this conversation is officially making me uncomfortable.

"How are you settling in?" Rook asks Domino as he turns toward her. "Your family must be very proud of you."

His gaze flicks to mine for the briefest second, and I get the sense he changed the conversation on my behalf. But why would he? He probably thinks the same as Journey.

"They're pretty happy," she says with a grin. "We knew it was a long shot, but I've always wanted to join the Storm Guard."

Journey gives him a quizzical look. "What about yours? Do you have a family?"

Rook's mouth presses together, and I can't help but lean forward, hoping for the answer. Rook is such a closed book. A mystery worthy of ancient burial sites.

Who is he? Why is he here?

"I have a family," he says evenly. "There are six of us. I'm the oldest, with two brothers and one sister."

"Oh," Journey says, her eyes widening. "I've heard about this. Solitudes have a lot . . ." She lowers her voice. "Of babies. Like . . . a lot."

The implication of her statement is clear—Solitudes can't control themselves like the animals we all claim they are.

Rook's jaw ticks, and something passes behind his eyes. With a glare, he stands up, grabs his tray, and walks off without saying a word. We watch as he all but tosses it on the collection counter, dishes and utensils rattling, and then stalks out of the room.

Journey's eyes spread wide. "What did I say?"

I shake my head and then stand up and leave.

"I should probably go, too," I say to Domino and Journey.

After depositing my tray with only slightly less fanfare, I beeline for the door.

I have about fifteen minutes before class, and I pull out my phone again to check for something from my parents or maybe Trinity.

Nothing.

I consider calling my mom but decide to give her a few more days. To do what? Calm down? Calm my father down? Stop hating me for everything I've done?

What if he was so angry that he hurt her?

My stomach twists with a bottomless pit of worry.

So I dial someone I'm hoping can help.

35

She picks up on the second ring, her voice brimming with worry. "Poet? Is that you?"

"Mrs. Arden," I say, trying to keep the shake out of my voice.

"What is it? Is Knox okay?"

"Yeah, he's fine," I assure her. "That's not why I'm calling."

I hesitate.

"Poet. Are *you* okay?" The sympathy in her voice tells me she's already heard everything, and it loosens the ball wedged firmly in my throat.

"I'm sorry to call," I whisper. "I just . . . I need you to check on my mom. We had a fight and—" I choke on my words as tears threaten to spill.

"Sweetheart," she says. "It's okay. Calm down. I spoke with her this morning—she's fine, I promise. I mean . . . she isn't *fine* . . . but she's not . . . Your father . . ."

She trails off. No one likes to say it out loud, but the Ardens know all our secrets. The day my father left me with the scars they couldn't fully wipe away, it was the Ardens who Raine and I ran to. He was barely bigger than I was, but he did his best to carry me to their front door, where I passed out.

Trey went to look for my mother, who had also been caught in my father's path of anger. The Ardens called for a doctor, and we spent weeks living with them while we healed. Knox would sit in bed next to me, and we'd watch movies and eat snacks until we both fell asleep with the TV screen flickering.

Strangely enough, those nights are some of my best memories.

I was half asleep more than once when I heard my mother and Mrs.

Arden talking in low, serious voices. Even then, I understood my mother needed to leave my father, but she wasn't brave enough.

There aren't many avenues in New Manhattan for a woman like my mother.

She attended Amery but never used her education, and at her age, the job prospects were almost nothing. Her choices were to ignore my father's abuse or be left with nothing, which might have meant life as a cog or, even worse, a Hollow.

In my less charitable moments, I think she stayed mostly for herself, but I know she did it for Raine and me, too.

"Okay," I say to Mrs. Arden with a relieved sigh. "Thank you for checking on her."

"Of course . . ." She hesitates, and I can feel the words hanging between us on the other side of the line. "If there's anything I can do . . ."

This situation couldn't be more complicated if I tried.

I joined Aria to escape *her* son. I don't know Molly Arden's true opinion on our engagement, other than she's always seemed as enthused about it as everyone else.

Does she know who her son became? Does she care?

"I'm sorry if I've hurt your family or Knox—" I start to say, but she interrupts.

"You do what's best for *you*, Poet," she says, her voice firm. "You hear me?"

My chin trembles as a combination of grief and gratitude squeezes my chest.

"Okay," I manage. "I'll be . . . I gotta go to class."

"Call me if you need anything." It's an empty sentiment. There isn't anything she can do for me anymore, but she's always been kind, and it's clearly an impulse.

"Can you . . . tell my mom I'd like to hear from her? I know she's upset, but . . ."

I touch the necklace against my collarbone, flipping the jeweled mask between my fingers, thinking of the woman who tried to raise me.

After another awkward pause, Mrs. Arden answers. "Of course. I'll let her know."

"Thanks." Then I hang up and tuck the phone into my pocket, my heart beating so fast that it's making me lightheaded. I want to go lie down, but spending time in my dorm room doesn't sound any more calming. I think of the atrium I found last night, but classes are starting soon.

I lean against the wall with my forehead pressed against it, waiting for my pulse to steady.

The bell rings, and I straighten up.

I should look for Edward and see if he's okay. I should find Trinity.

I should get someone to look at my knee, which is throbbing painfully and seems to be getting worse.

But I don't do any of that.

When I'm ready, I inhale a deep breath and limp to class, deciding to deal with all of it later.

36

Over the next two weeks, I keep my head down and my focus on my schoolwork.

Dr. Perez confirmed a tear in the ligament of my knee and prescribed a dose of painkillers. She showed me how to wrap it up and keep it protected at night, then ordered me to take it easy. Henry even altered my training schedule to focus more on upper-body work while my leg heals.

Trinity is also busy training with E-squad. It sounds a lot like cadet training if I'm being honest, but with the added bonus of learning how to torment other people.

Anytime I'm with Trin, her new friends tend to show up, almost as if they're watching her, and I make myself scarce. They creep me out. And frighten me.

Sometimes I wonder if I'll be scared of Trinity one day, too.

Edward isn't faring well, either. He's miserable without Trinity. I'm still upset by the way he spoke to me, but I try to remember we're not always the best version of ourselves when we're hurting.

I've also managed to avoid Knox, though he's been desperately trying to corner me into talking. I've become a ghost, appearing in class just as the starting bell rings and then sneaking out the second it's over.

My mom isn't answering any of my texts, and I still haven't heard from my father. The silence is the worst part.

Have they already forgotten me completely? Was I so unimportant?

Or is this some sick part of my punishment? Is my father plotting something that I can't even fathom?

Trinity said her parents aren't talking to her, either. Intrinsically, I understood what House lines meant and that they were the standard by which we all existed, but I refuse to believe they're more important than a family's love. Maybe I'm just being naive.

Through it all, I can't stop an incessant itching from working its way under my skin. During an Empire Storm last night, the need to absorb the cloud bursts became a living thing beating against my ribs. I clutched the blanket and stared at the ceiling while my roommates slept silently.

I don't know how much longer I can hold out.

The bright spot in my week was an email informing us about a special cadet training session happening this afternoon. Domino, Journey, and I arrive at the training facility after lunch, their excitement infectious, and for the first time in weeks, I allow myself to cast off my worries and focus on what's in store for us.

However, when I spot the same two Extinguishers from our first day of training standing in the corner, a prickle of fear works its way up the back of my neck. They're here to watch us again.

"Welcome to a special exercise we have planned for you," Henry says. "Today, you'll enter the contained training simulation for the first time to test your endurance and agility, and to get a feel for what to expect when you're manning the Storm Towers."

He steps aside for Dr. Eze, who's clutching her tablet with a huge smile.

"And we have wonderful news," she says. "Something extra special. For years now, Tempestade scientists have been hard at work trying to contain the specific electric charge derived from Empire Storms in order to facilitate enhanced training for current and future Breakers like yourselves."

She says these words with pride, but something prickles up the back of my neck.

"Until now, only General Sol has been able to 'capture' the plasma energy of Spark in a usable way, but our scientists have recently had a breakthrough. They've only been able to isolate a small charge," she continues, "and most of it will be reserved for current Guard training until a reliable replication method can be achieved. But . . ." She smiles bigger. "I managed to convince them to give us a small dose for each of you today."

She's acting as though this is the greatest news she's ever shared. Her enthusiasm causes everyone to start smiling and talking at once.

"What if we get hit?" Domino asks, accompanied by several nods around the room. "Won't we . . ."

Dr. Eze raises a hand. "There are some risks, yes," she answers. "But I assure you, the charge is too small to cause a blitz. If you're hit, you'll be temporarily incapacitated. If that happens, we have doctors standing by to transport you to the med wing immediately."

The room's initial enthusiasm has dimmed somewhat in the face of this information. That's when my gaze meets Rook's across the room to find his permanent frown is etched a little deeper.

We've basically avoided each other since the incident in the cafeteria, but he holds my gaze steady now, and I feel warmth creeping up my cheeks. I look away.

"Cadets," Henry says, his deep voice cutting through the din. "This is what you signed up for. When you're out on that tower, it's you and the storm with nothing in between. This is a breakthrough in the fight against one of our worst enemies, and we must embrace this new challenge. Anyone wishing to abstain from the simulation today is welcome to sit out." He lifts a hand toward the door. "But you will not be welcome back. The Storm Guard has no room for cowards."

His words are harsh, meant to either embolden or break us. I consider leaving. The risk of being discovered sits heavily in my chest. Uncomfortable silence is accompanied by the shuffling of feet and averted eyes as we consider our choices.

A woman near the front—a tall brunette from House Fiama—looks up, scans the room, and then walks toward the door. The Extinguishers move to intercept her. She stops and stares up at them.

"Come with us," they say.

"What are they doing?" Domino whispers.

I shake my head. I'm not sure, but I have my suspicions. She's drawn their attention by deciding to leave.

I swallow nervously.

If I enter that room and I'm hit and absorb Spark, then I'm exposing myself to the truth and potential incarceration. Or possibly death, because let's be real, no one seems to escape the Extinguishers. I think of the woman from my test who was exiled to the Wastes. A part of me wonders if I was being lied to that night. Even if she did leave, how long could she survive out there all alone? Either way, it's a grim fate.

But I also can't walk away. Not only because I have to do this but because I don't want to stamp an even larger target on my back. Either option is a risk, but at least I have a chance if I choose the simulator.

One of the Extinguishers leaves with the brunette, and we all watch the door close behind her with an ominous thud.

"Anyone else?" Henry asks.

No one moves.

"Then we'll begin."

37

The simulation room is a massive underground cube carved from the earth with high ceilings and walls lined with some kind of rubberized substance covered with projected grids. It's at least three stories tall and several hundred yards wide.

Dr. Eze informs us that the walls and floor are intended to absorb electricity and help minimize damage to our internal organs if we're hit.

Reassuring for everyone else, I guess.

They've re-created a miniature city with twenty-foot-tall buildings, along with walls and tunnels that can serve as hiding places and obstacles. Along one side is a metal platform lined with a bunch of screens and dials accessible by a set of metal stairs, all set behind a plane of protective glass.

"This exercise will last for about ten minutes," Dr. Eze says through a microphone from the elevated perch with Henry at her side. Lieutenant Dire stands next to him with his hands behind his back. "Today, it will be just us, but as we continue training, we'll be joined by higher-ranking Tempestade officials. They'll want to assess your abilities and decide which battalions you'll join once you graduate."

She adjusts some knobs on the panels lining the platform, her expression bright with excitement. "I'm very eager to see how this will play out."

We're divided into two teams, and the objective is for everyone on our side to tap the far wall while our opponents attempt to stop us. Simple enough, but the task will be made more difficult by the addition of random Spark attacks.

"If you're struck, you're encouraged to continue as long as you're able,"

Henry says, also speaking into the microphone. "After all, when you're out in the field, stopping isn't an option. If you're unable to move, lie flat on the floor and wait for the simulation to end. The rubber will protect you from the electricity as long as you remain still. Of course, that means your team loses that point. Everything clear?"

We all nod. I bounce on my injured knee, testing the weight. It twinges a little, but I bandaged it up like Dr. Perez showed me, and it's helping a lot.

Dr. Eze smiles down at us, her dark eyes shining with excitement. "All ready?"

She doesn't wait for us to answer as she adjusts a few knobs.

A disembodied voice starts counting down from ten overhead as we all assemble at the starting line. I'm on a team with Domino, Journey, and a few other people I know. Those I don't are easily identifiable by the purple bands we all wear around our biceps.

Rook ended up on the other team, wearing the same bands in green.

The simulation spans the size of several city blocks, and the far wall recedes into darkness, where a large digital scoreboard hangs.

The numbers continue counting down. *3 . . . 2 . . . 1 . . .*

A horn blares, signaling the start of the game, and everyone spins into action. It's slow at first, with everyone taking a moment to assess the corners and angles, the blind spots, the potential paths through the maze. A deep rumbling overhead precedes the start of the first few purple flickers dancing across the ceiling.

I watch several gather into a bright knot just as the first bolt of Spark forms and strikes the center of the room, erupting into a plasma arc before winking out. We're all still safely deep in our ends, so it feels more like a warning strike than anything sinister.

That's when I notice someone running.

Domino is taking advantage of everyone's surprise as she pumps her arms and legs, covering a stretch of open area with her head down.

"There!" someone from the green team shouts, but she's already disappeared into a large pipe by the time they realize what's happened. I cheer quietly for her as I look for an opening of my own. With the green team distracted by Domino's escape, I make a break for it, weaving through a maze of tall towers. The rubber mats absorb the sound of my footsteps somewhat but not entirely.

"This way!" another person shouts. "Get her!"

I swerve as I catch sight of someone between two buildings off to my right. I duck and slide into a rubberized "concrete" tunnel wide enough to barely shimmy my way through. Quickly, I drag myself to the far end to emerge at the edge of a plaza. Checking to ensure the coast is clear, I sprint across and hide behind another building.

A second burst of Spark splits from the ceiling, and I brace myself. It strikes somewhere off to my right, and someone screams as two more successive bolts strike through the simulation.

One hits to the left, and another hits the building across from me.

I barely have time to register the blast before an explosion sends chunks of the buildings flying. I cover my head with my arms and start running. It isn't real—the buildings are made of the same rubberized material, but they look heavy enough to knock someone down.

Something sharp slams into my back, and I go stumbling, barely catching myself before I face-plant on the floor. Instead, I crash into the side of a building, breathing heavily as sweat gathers at my nape.

The scoreboard at the far end blares, and I cheer inwardly as my team wins a point. Someone made it. I attempt to gauge how far I've come and estimate I'm about a third of the way down the field. How did someone reach the end so fast? I hope it was Domino.

After three deep breaths, I forge ahead, snaking past buildings and other obstacles, keeping my eyes and ears peeled for movement.

It grows quiet as people pause to lie in wait.

More rumbles shake underfoot, and another few blasts shatter the silence.

Nothing hits close to where I stand, so I take a calculated risk and run.

I leap over some rubble, checking behind me until I round a corner and stop. Three people from the green team wait for me at the end of a plaza, hunched and ready.

I quickly assess my potential exits. I can't run past them—they'll catch me for sure. An alley opens to my left, and to my right is a dead end.

"We're coming for you," snarls a giant guy with a thick neck and dinner-plate hands. He approaches with two more Fiama members, and I hang a left for the alley.

But they aren't naive. They take off through another exit leading from the plaza, and it quickly becomes obvious they're trying to herd me into another dead end.

I veer left, doubling back the way I came, passing through a ruined section of the simulation and spotting a body lying face down on the floor. I wince and almost stop to check on them, but a team of medics is already approaching.

So I continue running, twisting left and right, attempting to lose myself inside a tight maze of buildings.

"You're surrounded!" the big guy chasing me shouts. "Come out, little girl!"

I spin around and around, trying to figure out where each person is standing. I have several exit options, but if I choose wrong, it'll lead me straight into their arms. As I shuffle to my left, I glimpse the profile of one of my hunters through a narrow opening.

Loping away in the opposite direction, I keep close to the buildings, staying as light on my feet as possible. Good thing I have a lot of practice moving silently through our apartment at home, lest I incur my father's temper.

I spot another person through a different crack and conclude that they're spread evenly apart. So I hedge my bets and pick a path just to the right of whoever I last saw. When I think the coast is clear, I run. I pass another building, and someone jumps out at me.

Damn, it's the same huge guy. I swerve as he reaches out, his fingertips barely brushing my arm. He's big, yes, but that makes him kind of slow, and that's my advantage.

I keep running as all three green team members begin to chase me, hot on my heels.

"Get back here!" someone shouts.

Why do people say that? Does he think I'll just stop and let him have me?

I keep my head down, dodging around the fallen rocks and debris. I turn into another open area and curse. I need cover. I barrel across, but the guy is right behind me, and I can sense him closing the distance.

I barely register the rumble before it strikes. A bolt drops from the ceiling just as I cross the plaza, and it hits me. I know it immediately. My body seizes as the plasma arc swallows me in its boundary, a bright sizzle of pain ricocheting down my limbs.

I gasp and stumble when suddenly, someone grabs me and shoves me into a dark corner. I don't have the presence of mind to scream, but a moment later, I realize it's Rook.

"Put them out," he's saying as he smacks my arms and legs.

"What are you—" I protest, but he's too busy dousing my sparks.

My next words die in my throat as he continues frantically tapping my head, my stomach, and even my cheeks.

He knows.

He *knows*.

When he's finished, he stops and presses a hand to the wall behind me, his shoulders heaving with his breaths.

His gaze slowly meets mine as I gape open-mouthed.

A tiny spark of purple winks in his hair, and I reach up to pinch it as his eyes track my movements.

He knows.

And *he's* immune to Spark, too.

Several things coalesce in my thoughts. That shadow I saw the night I escaped the city. The way Rook found me on the train right after. A part of me was *sure* it was him.

My heart is racing in my chest as a hundred different emotions hit me at once.

We both regard each other with a sort of reserved, guarded awe.

I become increasingly aware of the tightness of the space and how close he is to me. His thighs press against my hips, and his chest brushes mine. Each point of contact becomes a live wire, bright and hot and dangerous.

He's still breathing heavily as he leans in, his expression full of curiosity and a high degree of assessment. "Be more careful," he growls. He's so close, I feel the ghost of his breath against my lips.

My chin tips up, and suddenly, our mouths hover an inch apart. Just like the night he rescued me on the train, I get the strangest thought that he's planning to kiss me, but I don't move, afraid of looking like a fool again.

It's madness that I desperately want it.

A buzzer dings at the far end, reminding me that the game is still on.

We both pause. Did anyone see what just happened?

They haven't stopped us, so maybe the moment went unnoticed.

With my hands pressed to his chest, I shove him back. It takes him by surprise, and he stumbles. Something I sense is hard for anyone to do to him.

We exchange another look heavy with a thousand things neither of us can say. Not here, surrounded by our teammates. By Henry and Dr. Eze. By that monster clad in the color of dried blood, holding a stunner, looking for any excuse to kill us on the spot. Or worse.

So I take off, weaving through the wreckage of the arena.

Someone shouts off in the distance, spotting me, but my feet grow wings as I glide over the debris in my path.

He *knows*.

I think of the Spark winking in his hair like a signal far in the distance.

He knows, and he's like me.

I'm not alone.

He's a monster, too.

I slam into the far wall, scoring a point for my team just as the end-game buzzer sounds.

Breathing heavily, I scan the arena, looking for Rook.

What happens now?

I don't think he can turn me in to the Extinguishers because it would draw too much attention to himself.

He's a Solitude *and* a Keeper—he'd be dead before the sun rose tomorrow.

My gaze slides to Lieutenant Dire standing on the platform overlooking the arena. His gaze isn't on me, and I let out a long, shaky breath. I think we got away with it.

Rook emerges from between two buildings and saunters closer, his eyes narrowing as he scans me from head to toe. It's another assessing look, like he's trying to peel me apart to study the clockwork of my bones.

But there's also something like relief visible in the set of his shoulders.

I think.

All I know is that suddenly, everything has changed.

38

Rook avoids me after our encounter in the simulation. Only part of me is surprised.

He refuses to make eye contact even in biology class, where we're forced to sit at the same table. He responds only in one-word grunts, and it isn't that different from our first day, but I hate that he won't look at me. And I hate that I even care. It shouldn't bother me this much.

When I close my eyes, I can't stop seeing his perfect face as he leaned over me, his lips parted softly, inviting me in like a bad decision I really want to make. I'd never admit it out loud, but I've fallen asleep to that image every night since.

But that's secondary to the more pressing issue.

We have to talk about this.

I refuse to ignore the fact that I'm in the presence of another Keeper.

Even if he won't acknowledge me, I already feel less alone than I have in my entire life.

I'm not the only one. Someone else is like me and trying to hide it.

We could be . . . what? A team? Confidants? Friends?

Probably not, but something.

We have to be *something*.

While Rook avoids me, I avoid Knox.

I show up late to the cafeteria and scarf down my meals before he even has a chance to notice I'm there. Cadet training occupies most of my time, and with my move to Aria's dorm wing, I've become nearly inaccessible.

I might be a social pariah, but I accomplished the two things I wanted, at least.

Unfortunately, it's all overshadowed by my parents, who have continued with their silent treatment, and it's slowly eating me from the inside. Maybe it was naive to think I wouldn't lose them, too. Still, I cling to the hope that our estrangement is only temporary. There has to be a way to make this right.

I'm heading for the gym after classes when someone grabs my arm and spins me around.

Knox stands before me with wild eyes, his hair disheveled, his brow furrowed with what I interpret as worry and frustration. He doesn't look great, and the smallest flare of guilt burns in my chest.

"Poet," he says. "Stop avoiding me."

I huff out a breath through my nose and step back, trying to put some distance between us.

"I don't want to talk about it."

"We *have* to talk about it."

He's so uncharacteristically earnest that I find myself nodding.

"My mom said you called her."

I sigh and tug on my ponytail. "Yeah. My mom is icing me out. And my dad . . ."

"That's what I want to talk to you about," Knox says. "I've spoken with Grady and my dad about you and this whole thing."

My spine stiffens. Of course they've been talking about me.

"Can we go somewhere to talk?" Knox asks. He says it gently, and it occurs to me that I *do* owe him a conversation. Some kind of closure on this chapter of our lives. But I'm also not sure I'm ready for that. Now or maybe ever. I'd prefer it if we could just pretend the last few years never happened.

"I have to get to the gym. I'm already late for training." I thumb behind me, but I realize that was the wrong thing to say because his eyes narrow.

"Training. You're still going through with the cadet program."

Not this again.

"Is that why you haven't been in class? I thought you were avoiding me."

"Well . . ." I wince, unwilling to finish the thought. It's been a bit of both.

"After everything you've done, you still want to join the Storm Guard." His lips press hard enough to go bloodless. "Poet, you're walking the thinnest line here. I'm trying to help you. You have to stop."

I shuffle back as he advances a step. "Absolutely not. I'm not dropping out."

Knox sighs and runs a hand through his hair before he begins pacing.

"Why do you care?" I add. "Just marry Winter instead and forget about me. It's what you want."

That stops Knox in his tracks. "Winter?"

"Yeah. I'm pledging to Aria. You need to marry someone from Fiama."

He shakes his head. "No. Winter . . . What? Who gave you that idea?"

"My father said . . ."

He holds up his hands. "No, this is what I wanted to talk to you about." A group of people appears at the end of the hall and passes us, casting sly looks in our direction.

Knox sighs and reaches for my hand. "Can we not do this out here?"

I check the time and nod before he pulls me into a classroom. I'll be late, but I don't think I can avoid this any longer.

He closes the door and spins around to face me.

"Both our fathers are willing to take you back if you publicly denounce Aria and say you made a mistake," Knox says. "We can still have everything we planned. I know you had a . . . moment or something but, Poet, you belong with Fiama. You know that. I know that. Skies, *everyone* knows that, and they're willing to overlook this little tantrum. We can put it behind us, and everything can return to normal."

While Knox speaks, my entire body goes numb, my fingers and toes tingling. I don't know why he's clinging to this . . . to *us* so tightly, but I need to shut it down.

"Listen," Knox says, coming closer. He takes my hand and gently places it over his heart, the warmth of his skin seeping through his T-shirt. It's the most intimate touch we've experienced in a long time, but I feel nothing. If anything, it repulses me. "If I can convince Grady to let you continue cadet training, you'll do this, okay? I guess you won't let it go. I know you miss Raine, but—"

"This isn't about Raine," I say, my hand closing into a fist. "This is what *I* want. What I've always wanted."

Knox exhales a sharp breath. "Okay, fine. I get it. You want to be a Breaker. If I can get your dad to agree, will you do what they ask?"

It's a tidy solution. Denouncing Aria costs me nothing. They haven't

earned my loyalty yet. I want my family back, even if they're less than perfect. Maybe this is the answer.

"What happens after we graduate?" I ask, and Knox blinks.

"What do you mean?"

"I mean, I spend three years training, and then what? Will you 'let' me
join the Guard? Or do I join the other Society wives like you all expect?"

His gaze shifts. It's obvious he hasn't thought that far.

"We can discuss that when the time comes," he answers.

"No. That isn't good enough."

"Poet, be reasonable. I can't be the scion of Fiama while my wife is risk-
ing her life on a Storm Tower every night. That isn't the life meant for you."

My momentary flare of hope deflates.

"That's what I thought," I say. "I'm pledging to Aria, Knox. I will become
a Storm Breaker, and I will have the life I want."

"What about your family?" he asks, his voice rising. "What about your
position? Your friends! What about us?"

"*Us?* Are you kidding me? There is no 'us'!"

"Poet—"

"No. How *dare* you suggest that we are anything when you walk around
giving attention to every girl who crosses your path? You've humiliated me
so many times, I've lost count. I'm a laughingstock!"

I can feel the tears welling, but I refuse to cry in front of Knox ever again.
I refuse to give him that power over me anymore. Besides, I've had enough
of this conversation. I heft my bag onto my shoulder and brush past him.

"Poet—"

I spin around. "I am not pledging to Fiama. I am not marrying you. This
is over. Tell my father if he wants to have a discussion about this, then he's
welcome to actually speak to me himself."

I wrench the door open with so much force that I almost fall over.

"Wait, please—" Knox says, and I stop to look at him.

"I loved you once," I whisper. "I thought we'd be happy together. I
wanted all of this for us, too, but you've broken my heart too many times."

Knox doesn't answer as I leave the room and close the door behind
me . . . and on us.

Forever.

39

I stomp toward the gym, inhaling a deep, shuddering breath.

I cannot *believe* Knox had the nerve to think there was anything left between us.

What am I most angry about?

My father talking *about* me instead of *to* me?

Knox assuming I would just do what I'm told?

Thinking he could placate me by allowing me to continue my training with the intention of ripping it all away once we graduate?

This is *exactly* why I chose myself over them.

In spite of everything, I know I'm doing the right thing.

I suddenly can't wait to start this afternoon's training.

We're sparring today, and kicking someone's ass seems like the perfect cure for this pent-up rage burning through my veins.

When I enter the gym, I scurry to change into my workout attire before heading to the large sparring mats at the far end of the room. Four different pairs are currently fighting in their respective corners, all reflected a thousand times by floor-to-ceiling mirrors covering three walls.

I spot Domino in a headlock with someone from House Asale, both sweating with exertion.

On the far side of the room, Rook is sparring with a big guy from Tera. I think his name is Ritsu. They're both wearing sleeveless black shirts and shorts, and it's hard not to be distracted by all the smooth, flexing muscle Rook currently has on display.

I study his tattoos that I've admired more times than I care to admit. The thin topographical lines curve over every dip and valley of his muscles. I note where they disappear under his shirt and wonder, not for the first time, where they start and end. Do they stretch across his back? Flex along his chest? Maybe dip in the hollow of his spine?

Suddenly, I'm very warm, and I wipe my forehead with the back of my hand.

Ritsu tosses Rook to the mat with a heavy *thud*, pinning him down.

They're almost matched in size and strength as they twist and turn, but Rook manages to knock him off. They go tumbling in a ball of limbs, and I can't seem to tear my eyes away from the fiery intensity in Rook's eyes.

But he isn't angry, just determined. Beautiful in the way he moves with lethal grace.

"Poet," comes a voice to my left, causing me to practically jump.

Henry's wearing a half-cocked smile as he glances between me and the guy I was practically drooling over. He's kind enough not to draw attention to it. "Ready for some sparring? I'll be teaching you a few new moves today."

I think of my conversation with Knox and slap my fist into my palm. "I'm ready. Let's do this."

Over the next hour, I follow Henry's lead through a series of drills and maneuvers designed to improve my skills at hand-to-hand combat. I empty my mind and lose myself in the dance as my pulse races and sweat beads on my temples. This is exactly what I needed.

My bandaged knee is faring better, so I feel confident dancing side to side, bouncing on the balls of my feet.

Throughout my training, I remain aware of Rook on the near side of the room as he spars with various partners. His trainer, Brooklyn, runs him through numerous drills, shouting out a string of instructions.

Once or twice, our gazes hook ever so briefly before he looks away. Probably because I can't stop staring. Henry notices it more than once but still doesn't call me out, even if I catch his knowing smirk. The thing is, I'm not staring at Rook because he looks ridiculously good in his tight top and shorts, his hair disheveled and a sheen of sweat highlighting the curves of his rounded shoulders.

Okay, that's not the *only* reason.

He's a Spark Keeper. I've never met another Keeper. Has he? How can he *not* want to talk about this? It suddenly occurs to me that Keepers might be a common thing out in the Wastes and I'm not remarkable to him at all. An uncomfortable ache works its way through my chest at that thought.

But then I catch his brief glance, loaded with *something*, and I'm sure that can't be true. I think he wants to talk about it, but maybe he's not ready. He has every reason to be scared that someone might find out. He must understand that I'd never turn him in.

"Okay!" Brooklyn shouts from the corner, shocking me out of my spiraling thoughts. "Time for some more one-on-ones!"

She starts pointing to various people around the room. Domino is paired up with an Asale girl, and Brooklyn points to me before pointing to Rook.

"You two over here," she says, gesturing to a spot on the floor at her feet.

I open my mouth and hesitate. A piece of hair hangs in Rook's face, and he tucks it back, almost like he's opening himself up for a challenge.

"Let's go!" Brooklyn says with a sharp clap. "We haven't got all day."

I nod and then quickly cross the room, stopping a few feet away from Rook.

He hunches over as his face spreads into a wicked grin. "Think you can handle me? I won't go easy just because you're a Society princess."

"I'm not scared of *you*," I retort, earning me another cocky smile. It's partly true.

He rushes for me, but I'm ready. My training first started with Raine's rudimentary lessons in our apartment when I was less than ten years old, and the last few months have taught me plenty more ways to protect myself, even against a much bigger opponent. I brace for impact, and when he's close, I drop and roll, kicking out and swiping my foot behind his knees.

Rook lands flat on his back, and I'm on him, my thighs straddling his chest, knees pinning his elbows to the floor.

"Now who's the princess?" I ask with a smirk.

"Sit a little higher and you'll be a queen," he taunts, and it takes me a moment to process his meaning. I gasp with indignation as his big hands wrap around my thighs, and then he lifts me up like I weigh nothing and tosses me down.

The wind gusts from my lungs, but I have enough presence of mind to roll away as he tries to pounce. He misses as I tumble over my shoulders and then leap up onto my feet in a crouch.

"Ha!" I shout in triumph as we begin circling, light on the balls of our feet.

"Why have you been avoiding me?" I demand under my breath, taking advantage of the fact that he can't run away from me now.

"I'm not." He feints and tries to get in a jab to my side. I drop my elbow, but he's too fast, and I yelp as he scores the hit.

"Don't lie to me. We need to talk about this."

"Talk about what?"

We continue circling, moving in and out.

"You *know* what," I say, lowering my voice even more. I don't think anyone would have a clue what we're discussing, but it's best to be safe.

"I have nothing to say," he answers.

"Rook!" I snap, and then we both blink. I think that's the first time I've ever said his name out loud. He rolls his shoulders and cocks his head, inhaling a long breath.

"No, you're trouble," he says. "Chaos follows you everywhere. I don't want any part of that."

That feels a little unfair, but I brush it off because I need him to talk to me. Maybe he *does* have a bit of a point.

"Please," I beg, almost desperate now.

His jaw hardens, uncertainty flashing over his expression. "Fine. If you can pin me for three seconds, we can *talk*," he says, biting out the last word. I huff a piece of hair from my eye. "And if you can't, then you leave me the fuck alone."

I consider the offer. He's almost twice my size, and I've watched him enough to know he's adept at fighting. Whatever they do in the Wastes taught him a few things about survival.

But I can hold my own. Plus, he's not really giving me a choice.

"Fine. Deal."

The words are barely out of my mouth before he attacks. His arms wrap around my midsection, and we both go tumbling. That's when I realize he was just humoring me before. I don't stand a fucking chance.

I try to wriggle out from under him, squirming and bucking, but he holds me in place, his body wedged between my thighs. Finally, he grabs my wrists and pins them above my head, his lithe body stretching over mine. It's annoying but also kind of hot. Fuck.

"No fair," I say.

"What's not fair?"

"You're . . . You . . ."

He lifts an eyebrow. "Are so much better at this?"

"You tricked me," I hiss, trying to sit up, but he keeps me trapped on the floor.

"I did nothing of the sort—you assumed. Just like you always do."

"We need to talk about this!"

I glance to the side to see if anyone's noticed that we've stopped. Thankfully, everyone's attention is on someone across the room who's lying on the floor, blood oozing from his nose.

Rook squeezes my wrists tighter, pulling my attention back.

I go still, fully taking in the intimacy of our position. His warm body between my thighs. His hard stomach against mine. His breath skates over my exposed collarbone, pulling up goose bumps that I really hope he doesn't notice. The last thing I need is for him to know how he affects me. I'll have no leverage left at all.

"A storm is coming," he says in a low voice, and I nod because I feel it, too.

"You followed me that day."

He exhales softly. His breath touches my mouth, and I lick my lips as his gaze zeroes in.

"I wasn't sure if you saw me."

"I wasn't, either, but then you were there on the train and . . ."

"Right," he says. "I need . . ." He looks up to ensure no one is watching us. Then he shakes his head and shoves off me, kneeling between my legs. I sit up, missing the crush of his body against mine.

"So do I," I say. He needs to absorb a cloud burst. He's probably been struggling within these contained walls, too. The hit I received in the simulation only took the edge off. It wasn't enough. "You don't have to do it alone. We can go back to the edge of the city."

He's looking down with his hands on his thighs. It takes a moment before he glances up. "Sneak out?" he asks, and I nod. "What did I say? *Trouble*."

I narrow my eyes, not sure I like what he's implying.

Then he sighs and gives me a skeptical look. I sense his shell is cracking;

he just needs a little push. A whistle blows, signaling the end of training. Everyone breaks into happy conversation as they head for the changing rooms.

"Tonight," I say to Rook. "Please."

A muscle in his jaw twitches before he stands up.

"Fine," he answers, and then he's gone.

40

Rook agrees to meet me later that night at one of the back entrances of the school that leads into the tunnels.

He claims it's never guarded, and I don't ask how he knows that.

When I arrive, he's already waiting, leaning against the wall with his arms casually folded in that signature way I've come to know. For a moment, he doesn't notice me as he stares into nothing. I wonder what he's thinking about as I study the slope of his nose, the angle of his cheekbones, that glint of the silver bar piercing his eyebrow.

How his perfect mouth tilts at the corners like he's recalling a fond memory.

He's wearing his Amery-issued leather jacket, which conforms to his thick arms and shoulders. Skies, he looks good.

I sigh inwardly, shaking the thought away because that's hardly useful right now.

When he notices me, he straightens and drops his arms. I wonder if I imagine the hint of a blush on his cheeks, then wonder even more what he was thinking about.

Did he leave a girlfriend behind in the Wastes? Does he miss her?

And why does the thought of some nameless stranger burn like acid in my chest?

"Found another good place to stand?" I ask, and he snorts a laugh that echoes against the stone. He looks so shocked that I cover my mouth and giggle.

"Yeah, Trouble," he says a moment later, an almost playful look in his eyes. "It *was* a great place to stand."

I fold my arms and cock my hip. "Oh, I'm so glad you found a new nickname. Tired of calling me a Society princess?"

He winks. "I think this might suit you better."

I roll my eyes as he gestures toward the hole at his feet and the ladder leading down. I peer into it and wrinkle my nose.

"Scared?" he asks in a taunting way that kind of makes me want to punch him in the throat. So much for my admiration.

"I don't love the tunnels," I admit.

"Of course. No Society princess wants to be seen—"

"It's not that," I snap. "Stop assuming you know everything about me. And please stop calling me that. I'm not . . . That isn't who I am anymore."

He raises his hands in a gesture of surrender. "Okay. I'm sorry."

I huff and grab the ladder before climbing down and landing in a crouch on the ground below. It's a cramped spot, dimly lit, and I swallow the shiver of apprehension already clinging to my skin.

Rook drops next to me a moment later and stops to stare at me for a second. He opens his mouth, and I think he's about to say something before he turns and gestures for me to follow.

With my hand pressed to the wall, I attempt to keep up with his long, confident strides, but the floor is uneven, and I can't see very well. I do my best to pick over the rocks littering the floor as I lag farther and farther behind. I'm tempted to reach for my phone light, but I don't want Rook thinking I'm even less capable than he already believes.

Finally, he looks back. I can barely make him out in the dim light, and I wait for whatever scathing words are coming my way. But he says nothing. He waits for me to catch up, then tempers his pace until we reach our destination.

Another ladder deposits us near the entrance of a train station.

"Can we skip the train?" I ask, my voice a whisper. The images from that night still plague my dreams. If I was nervous on the train before, now I'm scared I might descend into full-blown panic. I'm not sure I can handle him judging me again, but he nods.

"Of course."

We head up the stairs and into the fresh air. I inhale deeply and shake out my hair, relieved to escape the cloying heaviness of the underground. The city is alive for the evening, as people traverse the sidewalks beneath the gathering clouds, a tang of worry hanging in the atmosphere. It'll soon be time to hurry home. Hide from the storm. Hope they survive till morning.

I often wonder what it was like during the Warming Age before the storms shifted. I imagine people sitting by open windows and enjoying the sound of the rain. Did they listen to the pitter-patter against the roof as it lulled them to sleep?

No one sleeps during the storms now.

We pass down a busy street lined with restaurants. Large windows are thrown open to the evening air, where people are beginning to clear out. We find a dock and step onto a passenger ferry with a wide platform and perimeter guardrail, accommodating a few dozen people. We head to a corner, where Rook leans his elbows on the railing, peering out at the city as the boat drifts down the canal.

"Is it because of that scar on your cheek?" Rook asks. His arm brushes against mine, releasing a flurry of butterflies in my stomach. "That's why you don't like going underground?"

"Yeah," I say, surprised he noticed it. "Something like that."

He studies me carefully, something nameless passing over his expression. "I'm sorry. I shouldn't have assumed."

I nod, and we travel in companionable silence through New Manhattan. Most of the original buildings were destroyed during the wars and turmoil of the Warming Age. There are photos and images, and people have tried to re-create some of what once stood here, as though trying to capture past glories. Despite all their mistakes, there's also a sense of loss from a time when the world was so much bigger and more diverse. When a hundred different countries and cultures and languages existed together, even if it wasn't always in perfect harmony.

We pass a busy square where music plays and hundreds of people mill about a night market, strings of lights dangling overhead. Vendors are beginning to close up shop as people quickly gather what they need. We pass more restaurants and nightclubs, music pulsing, lights flashing, filled with people who presumably like to live closer to the edge of danger.

I've always been fascinated with the power of collective positivity. That even in the face of constant danger, this city finds a way to laugh. Maybe it's just denial. A refusal to acknowledge that, while we've found a way to exist in a world that's always trying to kill us, surely we'll lose to nature eventually.

The clouds gather above, the rumble of thunder booming far in the distance.

As the ferry putters down the main canal, the streets empty. Lights flicker across the buildings, some of them going dark.

The boat docks at the last stop, and Rook and I hop off before turning to walk the rest of the way. Once we enter the ruins on the city's edge, I ask, "Have you been out here before?"

"Not here," he says. "I didn't know of this exit until I followed you that day."

"Why *did* you follow me?"

He pauses up ahead and looks back. "No reason." Then he turns and continues down a narrow alley.

"Wow, great answer." Apparently, my sarcasm doesn't warrant a response. We keep walking, and he stops to wait for me as I climb over a fallen beam.

"But you've been going somewhere else?" I ask.

"I have a few different spots," he answers. "I know the outskirts well."

Right, of course he does.

"How far away is your . . . home?" I ask, not sure why I choke on the final word. I'm intensely curious about his life.

"You don't have to say it like that," he replies dryly. "I do *have* a home. It's probably not that different from yours. Four walls and windows and everything. Kind of. Probably not as fancy, I suppose."

Skies, why am I constantly sticking my foot in my mouth?

"I'm sorry," I say. "I shouldn't . . . I feel so . . . Never mind what I said. You should assume all kinds of bad things about me. I only know what we've been told, but I can already see—"

I cut myself off. I was about to say something I shouldn't. Something I'm not supposed to say.

"See what?" he asks, clearly goading me further.

"That maybe not everything I've been told is . . . totally accurate."

He cocks his head.

"Well, some of it is," he says as we keep walking side by side. "We *do* eat our babies when there isn't enough food. It's a shame because they don't provide much meat, but it's tender and juicy at least. Goes nicely with the blood of virgins. The cafeteria has been a real change of pace. And before Amery, I hadn't had a proper bath in years. Also, that thing you hear about us sacrificing the hearts of our elders to some gods in the sky is true. It's much messier than you think, but it *is* effective."

He reaches the end of his monologue, and that's definitely the most I've ever heard him speak without taking a breath. I don't even care if he's mocking me; it's just nice to hear him talk.

"Okay, point taken," I answer. "I'm a complete and utter fool and an unbearable snob for believing any of that."

He smirks as we reach the end of the wreckage, checking to see if the coast is clear. The clouds tumble overhead, and I realize I've been so absorbed in talking to Rook that I barely noticed the itching under my skin.

"What's it like for you?" I ask. "When the storms come?"

He peers up at the clouds and then at the Storm Towers looming in the distance.

"It feels like I'm coming out of my skin," he answers. "Like I want to peel it off and offer up my insides to the sky."

His words tear a jagged hole in the fabric of my reality because I understand exactly what he means. For the first time in my life, there's someone else I can share this with.

He takes a few steps closer to the edge of a hollowed-out building and then glances back. "Ready?"

I nod, and we head for the high rock wall and the tunnel cut through it. I'm looking back and don't realize he's stopped.

I stumble as I crash into him. He steadies me with a firm hand, his fingers wrapping around my waist. His touch burns through my coat, and a short exhale blasts past my lips.

We both go still.

"You?" he asks, quickly withdrawing his hand. "How does it make you feel?"

"Something like that, too," I reply.

His gaze lifts to mine, and despite his claim that he didn't want to talk about this, I get the sense that maybe he needs me as much as I need him right now.

We start moving again, emerging on the far side of the barrier and heading to the low stone sitting in the center. "Sometimes I wonder if someone left these here," I say. "Some other Keeper who needed this spot, too."

Rook glances around and then at me before he turns to the sky. We stand side by side, watching the small lilac bursts flashing in the distance.

We lean against the rocks, and Rook pulls something out of his pocket. It's a tarnished metal circle with a lid, and he flips it open to reveal a glass face with a spinning dial underneath.

"What's that?" I ask.

"A compass," he answers. "You use it to tell what direction is north."

He holds it out to show me, and I watch as it spins and then settles, pointing toward the Wastes. I remember that he has something similar tattooed on his arm.

"Is that how you got here?" I ask, and he nods.

"Partly, yeah." He points to the sky, and I look up. "Also using the stars."

"The stars?"

"It's how they navigated the earth during the Warming Age before they had the right technology. And they used these."

He holds up the compass and snaps it shut. "My dad got it off a scavenger a long time ago and gave it to me when he realized I was interested in stuff like this."

"Stuff like this?" I ask. "You have those tattoos, too. They look like maps."

He nods. "I've always been fascinated with . . . adventure, I guess you'd call it. With the places beyond that we lost."

"Is that why you came here?"

He glances at me and then looks away. "In part." He points to the sky. "You can't see it because of the clouds, but if you look that way, you'd find the North Star, and there you'd find Ursa Major and Minor."

"What are those?"

"Constellations. Basically, clusters of stars that ancient people believed were the manifestation of gods living in the sky."

I blink up at the clouds. "Like pictures?"

"Not quite. They're more abstract than that."

"Do you have a favorite?"

He seems to consider the question. "Maybe Andromeda. Lately, I've become more interested in it."

"Why?"

He shrugs and shakes his head. "I guess it reminds me of someone."

I think again of some beautiful girl he left behind as sharp pins fill my stomach.

"That's a pretty name. What does it look like?"

"I'll show you a picture sometime."

"Okay," I say as I follow the direction of his distant stare, wondering what's on his mind.

I feel small and insignificant when I stand under the sky like this. It stretches so far, and I again think of all those worlds that once existed. The countries and cities and billions of people who once crowded this planet. I wonder if it'll ever be like that again.

"My home is comfortable," Rook says, picking up the conversation from before like we never left it. "My parents are the best. My dad is my hero, and my brothers and sister are little pains in the ass, but I love them all."

I wait, sensing he has more to say.

"But it hasn't always been an easy life." He waves a hand at the sky. "We've had to do what we must to survive."

I sense something he can't bring himself to say buried in that statement.

"I'm so sorry," I say again. "I shouldn't have assumed—"

He shakes his head. "I understand what you're told about us, and why would you know any different?"

I sigh, yet again feeling like a complete ass. "You're letting me—all of us—off too easily with that."

He shoots me a dark look, softened by reflections of purple in the darkness of his pupils.

"We're your enemy, Poet. Don't forget that. My people would come into this city and take everything if they could. One day, they might."

There's no threat in his words, just a statement of fact. This is what we've always been told. I blink because that's the first time he's ever said my name, and I like how it sounds coming from his mouth.

But it also brings with it the reminder of who and what he is.

Of who we both are, and that we're standing on opposite ends of a chasm.

Another flash in the distance draws both our attention.

"Who was Raine?" he asks, so softly I almost don't hear it.

"How did—"

"That guy—he said something when you were arguing in the hall."

"Knox."

"Whatever," Rook says. "I don't give a shit what his name is. He's a fucking asshole."

I laugh because he really is.

"My older brother, Raine. He was a Breaker," I say. "A group of Solitudes tried to sneak into the city via his Storm Tower, the Guard was overwhelmed, and . . . He was killed in the fight."

I blow out a breath of a thousand shards stitched together. "I miss him every day."

Rook is silent, and then he asks, "How old was he?"

"Twenty-two. Way too young."

"I'm sorry," he says after a minute. "There's too much needless death in this place."

My gaze jumps to his because this, too, is bordering on something he shouldn't be giving voice to, especially now that he's pledging to Aria.

He will be one of us soon.

But then I say, "Yeah. Maybe."

Another bright flash draws us to the horizon as the storm moves closer, the clouds swelling and fighting for space. Glowing points of light grow larger, spreading out.

"It's coming," I whisper, and I feel him nod.

"Do you know anyone else . . . like us?" I ask.

"No," he says. "Not quite like us."

I stare at him. I remember the first day he arrived, when I caught that deep flash of purple in the midnight of his hair. I thought it was just the light, but now I realize . . .

"Is your hair natural?" I ask.

He huffs out a short breath. "It is."

I offer him a smile. "Mine too."

I press my lips together and then ask, "Do you think it's because we're . . ." I trail off, barely able to acknowledge it. Once I do, it's real. There will be no taking it back.

"Maybe."

After a pause, I voice a question I've always wanted to ask someone but never could. "So why aren't they searching for us?"

He shakes his head. "I'm not sure. Maybe it isn't a common enough trait for them to know about?"

"You think?"

"I really don't know."

We stare at each other. My pulse gallops, and I marvel at the mystery of Rook, but maybe he's starting to feel a little familiar.

He breaks eye contact first, and again, we fall into silence as the clouds swirl and purple flashes illuminate the sky.

I tip my face up as the wind tosses my hair and wait for the storm to draw closer.

More flashes and more rumbles as the breeze picks up.

Without really meaning to, I move closer to Rook. He does the same until we're touching, shoulder to shoulder.

I feel the brush of his hand against mine. I look up, meeting his gaze as he stares down at me. "I never thought I'd find someone else . . . like this," I say. "A monster. A danger. A . . . curse."

"Is that what you think you are?" he asks, tipping his head.

"Aren't I?"

"You didn't choose this, Poet Graves."

"No, but I could turn myself in."

He blinks and shakes his head, as if coming to some kind of conclusion, but he doesn't say anything else.

"I thought I'd always be alone," I add. The words are out of my mouth before I can stop them. It's too much. It's too open and vulnerable. The storm is working its way under my skin, making me reckless.

His mouth presses together, the corners tipping up in what might almost be a smile.

Then he does something I wasn't expecting.

He lifts his hand and holds it out, palm side up.

"What will happen?" I ask. "If we're touching?"

He shrugs. "I'm not sure, but I've always wondered. I only know what it feels like when I'm alone."

"Like you're being torn up from the inside?"

"Yes. Until it changes. Until it becomes . . . bliss."

I smile, knowing what he means. "I crave it sometimes. Even though it hurts."

"I do, too."

Slowly, I slide my hand into his. His warm fingers close around mine.

The wind is cold and the air is crisp, but I'm suddenly several degrees warmer. He licks his lips, and I'm again thinking about what it would be like to kiss him.

Maybe he's thinking it, too, because he leans in as my heart pounds in my throat.

A blast has us both snapping apart as a burst of Spark hits the ground about thirty feet away. A plasma arc swells from the earth, crackling with amethyst energy. We both watch as it slowly dissipates, and the clouds flash and burn through the dark, endless sky.

More Spark hits the earth, and then I sense the moment I'm about to be hit. A pulsing stroke breaks from the clouds, hurtling toward us. It hits me, and I squeeze Rook's hand as I brace myself for the impact.

But it's different. There's no bone-ripping agony. Instead, there is only the euphoria. That endless cotton-candy feeling when I'm hovering above the world, waves of golden light melting through my limbs.

My lips part as I gasp, and I watch Rook from the corner of my eye. He's in shock. I can tell he's feeling the same. That this is different. We're holding hands, and it doesn't hurt. What does it mean?

It might be the most perfect moment of my life.

Slowly, he turns to look at me as we're engulfed inside the swell of the plasma arc. I don't know how to explain it. I don't think I could put it into words if I tried.

The arc reaches its pinnacle, cracking with energy, before it winks out.

Rook's body shimmers with a net of sparks, glowing in his hair, on his clothes, even on the tips of his eyelashes. We're still holding hands, clinging like we'll fall through the earth if either one of us lets go.

A moment later, we're left in relative darkness.

The sky continues to flash, but the storm is already moving away.

"What just happened?" I whisper.

41

A buzz of anticipation hums in the air on the morning of the pledging ceremony. At least for everyone else. I'm carrying around a leaden weight, dragging me through poisoned water. I still haven't heard anything from my parents, but my father *will* be here.

It's part of the swearing in, where the scion welcomes you into your House. Today, I'll meet Surreal Beaufort face-to-face, and I can't even begin to imagine how she'll react to my presence.

We've been given the day off from classes, but I can't relax in my room. First off, I'm not welcome by two of three of my roommates, and of course, I can't stop thinking about my mother.

I put on my workout gear and text her again, asking about their plans for tonight, but I'm met with the same stony wall of silence. I scroll up our lengthy, one-sided conversation as a single tear slips down my cheek.

I swipe it away and head for the gym, finding it mostly empty, save for Henry in the corner.

"Hi," I say as I make my way over. He looks up.

"Poet, how are you?"

"Okay."

I sink down on the bench across from him. We haven't had much time to talk over the last few months. We're always surrounded by people, and all the things I want to say are too intimate with an audience. "I hope this isn't too personal, but can I ask how you've been since . . ."

He lifts his dark brows. "Since Raine?"

I sigh. "Yes?"

He sets the weight he's holding by his feet and clasps his hands. "I was pretty broken up for a long time, but I'm healing. I don't know if the hurt ever disappears, and I miss him every day, but I feel almost normal again."

I give him a half smile. "I'm happy to hear that. Are you dating?"

He laughs and shakes his head. "To the point, I see."

"Raine would want you to be happy."

"I think you're right." He smiles and nods. "I am dating. Nothing serious yet, but maybe I'll meet someone soon."

"I'm glad," I say. "And if you do meet someone special, don't stop yourself from feeling it, okay? He wouldn't want that."

Henry gives me a scrutinizing look. "When did you grow up, little Poet? Get so wise?"

I bark out a laugh as I stand up and rack some plates on the end of a barbell.

"I assure you I'm nothing but a complete mess who cobbles together an articulate thought on occasion."

He chuckles at that. "You've gotten yourself into some trouble . . ."

"Yeah." I nod. "Not sure you should even be talking to me."

He shakes his head. "Storm Guard takes precedence over Society. Out there, we're all brothers and sisters, no matter where we come from."

I cock my head and place both hands on my hips. "Is that really true?"

He shrugs. "Sometimes."

I laugh and then straddle the bench.

"What did your parents say?" he asks.

"Nothing. They aren't speaking to me at all."

His expression presses inward. He rubs the back of his neck and blows a breath. "I'm . . . I can't really say I'm surprised."

"No, I suppose I can't, either, but I hoped—"

Henry watches me. "Do they know you've joined cadet training? Something tells me they wouldn't approve?"

I sigh, my shoulders turning down. "You're right—they don't approve, but they also won't acknowledge me."

I think about my life in a distant future where I might be a mother myself. I don't think I could ever abandon my own child, no matter the circumstances.

But maybe I'm being naive and don't really know or understand anything.

Knox might have told my father about the Storm Guard, but he also seemed convinced I'd drop out, so maybe not.

"How is life in Aria treating you so far?" Henry asks, and I raise my hands in a gesture of defeat.

"Oh, they just love having me around."

He smirks and shakes his head. "Well, if you have trouble with anyone, come to me. I know we haven't talked much, or at all, and that's my fault. I was just hurt and—"

"I get it," I say. "You don't have to explain yourself."

"Well, I think of you as a little sister, too."

"Even though I defected?"

He grins. "Especially then. Raine would have been proud of you," he says as he sits up.

"You think?" I ask, something lifting in my spirit knowing that.

Henry nods. "Absolutely." Then he leans in closer. "You're . . . safe?" he asks carefully. I sense something else he isn't asking, but I can't understand what that might be.

My confusion must be written on my face because he adds, "Your brother . . ." He shakes his head. "He would be happy to see you standing up for yourself. Just be careful, okay? Try not to draw any more attention."

I snort out a dry laugh. "That's the plan. But trouble seems to find me, no matter what I do." I think of when Rook told me the same thing and laugh to myself.

Henry's answer is a searching look. "Like I said, I'm here if you need anything."

I give him a smile, and then we both resume our workouts in companionable silence.

42

Trinity arrives at my dorm room that evening. We're both wearing our dress uniforms as expected for the pledging ceremony. Her silver ribbon has been replaced with one in dark red to signal her recruitment to the E-squad. I avoid looking at it too closely.

Mine is purple, telling everyone I'm a cadet.

Telling my *father* that I'm a cadet.

"How are you feeling?" I ask as she drops onto my bed.

"Nervous. You?"

"Same. Have you talked to your parents?"

Trinity shakes her head. "No, and I've stopped trying. I knew this was inevitable. I understand it."

I frown. "Do you, though?"

I kind of expect this behavior from *my* parents. But the Robinses? I thought they were different. They've always been so kind and understanding, the parents we could run to when we got ourselves into a scrape. The ones who'd speak on our behalf when we needed an adult in our corner.

But I guess they aren't different at all. How could they be? A bit of childhood mischief isn't the same as going against your House, I suppose. Everything they have hinges on their compliance with Society. If they acknowledged Trinity, would they lose everything? They have another child to worry about.

Trinity gives me a sad look. "What else should I do?"

I hate that answer, but I have to concede she's right. A moment later, Domino comes out of the bathroom, also dressed for tonight.

"Hey," I say. "Ready to head down?"

She nods as she exchanges a tight smile with Trinity.

Neither has said anything to me, but I don't sense much warmth between them. I'm not sure if Trinity is being a snob and Domino is picking up on that, but I brush past it because I have too many other things to worry about right now.

The Robinses aren't expected at the ceremony, but I don't have that luxury.

The stalemate with my father is about to end, whether either one of us wants it to or not.

• • •

The pledging ceremony is a splashy affair with fancy food, cocktails, and entertainment. The parents get all dressed up to show off their kids and whatever meaningless assets they've accumulated since the last Society fete. It's Friday, and we have no curfew, so it'll be a late night for everyone. In fact, the celebration will continue through the weekend.

Journey meets us outside her door with a big smile.

"Hey!" She waves. "Who's excited?"

Her enthusiasm chafes my already frayed nerves.

"Actually, you look a little green, Poet," she says, peering at me. "You okay? You're not going to throw up, are you? Should we get a bucket?"

I watch Domino lay a hand on Journey's arm and give her a meaningful look.

"Ohhhh," Journey says, smacking her forehead. "Riiiiight. You've got some family baggage to deal with, I guess, hey? Were your parents mad or something? What did they say? Are you in trouble now? What's the deal when someone like you changes Houses?"

She's talking so fast that my temples throb.

"I don't think Poet wants to talk about it," Domino says, and I toss her a grateful look.

"Yeah, yeah," Journey says, miming the action of shutting her lips with a zipper and tossing the key. I rub my neck and will my stomach to settle, because she isn't wrong.

Before tonight is over, I might actually throw up.

We enter Amery's massive ballroom with high mirrored ceilings, ornately tiled floors, and crystal chandeliers. Waiters dressed in black vests and ties circle the room, balancing canapés and flutes of sparkling wine. Many of the school's parents have arrived, dripping with jewels and dressed in their finery. I can smell their expensive perfume from the doorway.

Domino and Journey hesitate a step behind Trinity and me, and I realize this is completely new territory for them. We've been to a million of these parties, and I can't imagine what it must be like to see this with their fresh eyes.

I notice some of Trinity's new friends waving her over, including the scary girl, Ruby. "I should go say hi," Trinity says. "I'll see you soon."

She doesn't wait for a response before she walks away. I stare at her for a few seconds, slightly put out by her abrupt departure. Shaking it off, I turn to Domino. "Are your parents coming?"

She nods as she bites her lip in a nervous gesture. "Yeah, but they're going to feel so awkward. Everyone's so fancy."

As if on cue, I hear someone call her name. A couple rushes over and hugs Domino. Her mom looks just like her, with her brown skin and shiny black hair, and she frames Domino's face in her hands before kissing each cheek. Domino told me the Parsonses run a successful hardware store and repair shop, and that's how they were able to afford Amery's tuition.

"I'm so proud of you," Mrs. Parsons whispers, tears forming in her eyes. "Have I said how proud I am?"

"Ma." Domino huffs, extracting herself from her mother's hold and playfully batting her hands away. "Only about a thousand times."

"Well, I'm just so proud! Journey!" she says, turning to her. "I saw your parents on our way in."

"Mom, Dad, this is my friend Poet Graves," Domino says. "We're in the same dorm room and in cadet training together."

The Parsonses' gazes then fall on me, and their eyes widen.

"Hi," I say. "It's nice to meet you both."

"It's nice to meet you, too," Domino's father says, holding out his hand and shaking mine. "You'll be pledging with my daughter?"

He asks the question with a hint of hesitation, suggesting news of my defection has reached *everyone*.

"Yeah," I say. "I am."

"Poet pissed off all of Fiama!" Journey says excitedly, with absolutely no self-awareness. "But I think that's kind of badass."

The second statement slightly softens the first.

Thankfully, I'm saved from more of Journey's observations when she shouts, "Mom!" practically in my ear. The two families come together, talking excitedly, and I take the opportunity to extricate myself.

The room is filling up as more people arrive, and I swerve around several groups, some of whom are familiar. The ones I don't recognize are obviously parents from the other Houses.

I search through the crowd for a friendly face, wondering if that even exists in this room.

I round a group of people, my breath catching when I spy Rook standing near the wall, holding a glass. It's the first time I've seen him in his dress uniform, and the effect is . . . something else.

The fitted jacket stretches over his chest and shoulders and then tapers at his waist in a way that makes it look like the fabric is worshipping him. Thanks to all our training, he's already put on more muscle, which both leans him out and makes him appear stronger.

Those solid thighs encased in fitted pants and his tall leather boots *do* something to me. His hair hangs half up, half down, with the top part tied back in a knot. Maybe he senses my attention because his gaze finds me in the crowd, causing liquid warmth to flutter in my stomach.

Since the night we snuck out of the city, we've settled into a sort of polite truce. It isn't exactly friendly, but it's a little less prickly. I've managed not to say anything entirely ridiculous for at least a few days. Despite everything, he's the only one who understands what I'm going through. It's not only nice but a complete breath of relief to be able to share my secret with someone.

And though he's always guarded in our interactions, I think he feels the same.

Neither one of us could explain what happened that night when we held hands and weathered the storm. When, instead of pain, we both felt lighter than air. All I know is I hope we get the chance to do it again.

His mouth presses together, and the corners tip up in the barest fraction of acknowledgment before his tactile gaze wanders over me with a look I feel like a physical touch.

"Poet," comes a voice to my left, breaking my connection with Rook.

Knox.

He's also dressed up for tonight, and though he looks nice, it's nothing like Rook. I admonish myself for the thought. I shouldn't be thinking that about the only person in this room who's even more of a pariah than I am.

Knox notices Rook, and they glare at each other. Knox has managed to stay out of Rook's way as far as I'm aware, and I hope that's the end of their little bro spat.

"I fucking hate that guy," Knox says in a low voice. "He'll get what's coming to him soon enough."

Or maybe not.

Knox looks down at me, his stare bright with accusation. "Right?"

I shake my head. "He's just minding his own business," I say, hoping that's noncommittal enough.

"Was he minding his own business when he nearly choked me to death? When he punched me?"

"*You* started it," I remind him.

"You're defending him? That . . . that . . ." He cuts off, likely unable to come up with an appropriate insult. "Solitudes killed Raine." He hisses the words, like Rook must be shunned because of what someone *else* did.

"Knox, what do you want?" I've truly had enough of this conversation.

He inhales a deep breath, I guess deciding it's not worth making a scene about Rook.

"There's still time to change your mind," he says. "Your father—"

"Is he here?" I peer through the dense crowd, but I can't see much over everyone's heads.

"Yes, he asked me to come talk to you."

I'm already walking away.

"Poet!" Knox calls, but I don't look back as I search for my parents. I take a turn around the room, and then finally, I spot them talking to a couple who lives a floor below us. Their son is in a few of my classes.

They're deep in conversation, cocktails perched in their hands, and I stop, struck by the sight. Seeing them makes me realize how much I've missed my mom.

My dad looks handsome but tired in an impeccable black suit, and my mother wears a sparkling red dress that sweeps to the floor. My throat knots, and I'd give anything to be that little kid who could run over and take comfort in the safety of her arms.

But I'm no longer a child, and I made a decision I knew would tear my family apart.

I don't realize my feet are moving until I'm standing beside them. They don't notice me, but I can feel a hundred pairs of eyes tracking our movements.

Without even saying a word, I'm making a scene.

"Mom, Dad," I say, my voice cracking.

Knox catches up and appears at my side.

"Sorry, Grady," Knox says, "I tried to talk to her."

Grady? Right to his *face*? Since when does he— It doesn't matter.

"If my father has something to say, he can say it to me," I spit. The other couple takes a small step back, not for privacy but to give us more space for this little bit of theater.

"I have nothing to say to you," my father starts, his green eyes flashing and his voice chipped with ice. "You made your choice. I have no children left."

The words are uttered with such final certainty that my heart hammers in my chest.

"That's it?" I whisper. "You're just writing me off? I'm your daughter."

My father's gaze tracks over me, his attention pausing on the purple ribbon around my waist, his mouth pressing into a bloodless line.

"Mom?" I ask as she stands silently, clutching my father's arm. She shakes her head as my father shoves her behind him.

"I warned you about what would happen," he says. "I *cannot* have a child pledge to Aria."

"You *could*," I answer. I can feel tears coating my cheeks. I didn't even realize I was crying. "It's your own stubbornness that's getting in the way. What difference does it really make?"

His glare hardens. "If it makes no difference, pledge to Fiama."

We've gathered an audience, and this might be the most humiliating moment of my life.

"I *wanted* to pledge to Fiama," I answer. "But you drove me to this. You won't let me join the Storm Guard, and I never wanted to marry Knox."

A few gasps circle around the room. I'm making everything worse with every word I say. My father tips his head and studies me, really *looks* at me for maybe the first time in my life.

"Knox is why you did this?"

"I tried to tell you," I say. "You refused to listen. You never even *asked*."

"You won't make this my fault, Poet."

He says it with such vehemence that it punches me in the gut. I glance at my mother peering over my father's shoulder.

"Don't look at her," he says to me. "You won't find an ally there."

I swallow the growing knot in my throat.

"Poet, just pledge to Fiama," Knox says. "This can all be over. You can continue cadet training, and when the time comes, we'll discuss your role as a Breaker, okay?"

Didn't he hear what I just said about marrying him?

However, I acknowledge that if I truly want to make things right, this is the perfect solution.

I look up at Knox. His expression is full of something earnest, but the thought of going back to him makes my stomach turn. They expected me to fight to become one of them, but they won't fight for me at all.

In fact, the moment I stepped out of line, they wrote me off like I never mattered.

Until now, I guess I never truly understood that my worth to them was found in my compliance. Not my presence.

"No," I say to him, then turn to my father. "I won't pledge to Fiama. If you want to cut me out of your life, then so be it. But *you* chose this, not me. You won't make this my fault, either."

I blink back my tears and exchange a look with my mother before I meet my father's eyes again. His jaw clenches, and the look he gives me unzips something down my spine. Like my insides are falling out, but they aren't viscid and warm; they're hard as bricks.

A testament to the girl, the *woman*, I was forced to become.

Neither one of us blinks. Neither one of us will be the first to crack.

I get my stubbornness from him, and maybe that's always been to our detriment.

I don't know if we can ever recover from this.

But the moment is over.

So, I turn on my heel and storm away.

43

I pass through the ballroom in a blur, a hundred pairs of judgmental eyes following me like a barrage of arrows.

I can't believe my family is just . . . gone. Did they ever love me? Did they ever care?

Tears cloud my eyes, and I scrub at them as I march through the doors and into the hall. I'm weaving in and out, barely aware of my surroundings.

Suddenly, someone reaches for my hand and tugs me into a darkened alcove.

"What the—" I say, cutting off when I realize it's Rook. He's regarding me carefully, concern in his expression.

"What are you doing?" I ask, blinking up at him.

"I was by the door when you left," he answers, releasing me from his hold. "That was . . ."

"Humiliating," I finish, dropping my face in my hands. He shuffles back a step, giving me space.

"Only for your parents," he says. "Fuck, your people are cold. You call us animals, but we'd *never* treat our own family like that."

I exhale a shaky breath and lean on the wall, my head thunking against it as I blink back a round of fresh tears. "I can't believe they just . . . dismissed me like that. I thought they loved me . . ."

My eyes squeeze closed as I picture the look on my mother's face before I walked away. That distant pinch of worry I know so well. The relics of her specific brand of love that I'll never know again.

"Of course you thought that," Rook answers vehemently, as if he's seething on my behalf. "They're your mom and dad. They're supposed to love you no matter what."

I snort a derisive laugh.

"I kind of can't believe I'm asking this," Rook says, and the uncertainty in his voice makes me look over. He rubs the back of his head and stuffs a hand into his pocket. "Do you need a . . . hug? Or something?"

I bark out a laugh at the absurdity of *Rook* trying to comfort me.

What a pathetic sight I must be.

But I also find myself nodding. "I haven't had a good hug in a while."

He hesitates, like he regrets asking, and then suddenly, he's in front of me, engulfing our tight corner with his scent and the distinct way he fills out his jacket so perfectly.

Slowly, he reaches out, and the air around me condenses as he gently takes me in his arms. We're both a bit stiff and awkward at first, like we're doing something illicit or have simply forgotten how to move inside the flesh of our own bodies.

A part of me, a big part, wants to fall against him, but I'm not sure he'd welcome that.

It's just a hug between friends.

Sort of.

His arms tighten a little, bringing me closer.

Finally, I allow myself to relax into him. He's warm and solid, and our planes and curves seem to line up with an intentional sort of harmony.

It's nice, and it feels safe.

It *shouldn't* feel safe to hug a Solitude, but for some reason, it does.

The longer we stand together, softening into the moment, the more I become aware of his physical presence.

He smells good. Fresh like Amery's standard-issue soap, layered with something that speaks to the wildness of the Wastes. Wind and open skies and the stars he loves so much.

I find myself tipping forward, my nose burying in his throat, my eyes closing as I inhale a deep, forbidden breath. A pained sort of sigh escapes my mouth, and he hugs me closer. Our bodies are touching everywhere as his hand glides to my nape, and he tips my face up.

Suddenly, this doesn't feel *friendly* anymore.

He licks his top lip, first one corner and then the other. A moment later, he's reciprocating, head dipping so his nose buries into the spot behind my ear.

I exhale in soft, breathless pants as my heart rate accelerates and my temperature climbs.

"Fuck," he whispers. "You drive me to the edge."

The words are ragged and frayed, brimming with frustration.

I don't know if he means "to the edge," suggesting that I annoy him, or if he means it with the same desire pounding in my blood.

The look he's giving me tells me it's maybe a bit of both.

Like he can't believe what he's doing, but he's also powerless to stop himself.

"Rook?" What am I asking? I want to know what happens next. Why did he follow me? Why are we standing here with nothing but atoms vibrating between us?

Suddenly, my throat is dry, and I lick my lips, too. His gaze catches on the tip of my tongue, and I think he might be wondering all the same things.

I've only kissed a handful of boys other than Knox. Small pecks under shadows. A make-out session or two amid the blaring music and free-flowing alcohol of a Society party. Nothing that meant anything.

I haven't *been* with anyone but Knox, and the fact that he's the only real knowledge I have of the male body feels like a tragic hole in the foundations of my education.

Rook's hazel eyes glitter in the dim light of the alcove, and I become vaguely aware of the distant sounds of the party. Maybe they've forgotten all about me already. Except they won't.

What *I* want is to forget, even for a moment.

Maybe Rook senses it. Maybe he understands how much I need this connection.

"I don't understand it," he says.

"What?"

"You are not what I expected, Poet Graves. Spoiled Fiama royalty who has no idea just how good she has it. You and your smooth hair and your perfect skin and your rich-girl voice."

"I don't have a rich-girl voice," I say, indignant.

"Yes, you do. And it pisses me off how fucking much I want to kiss you."

My breath hitches as my hand fists in the lapel of his jacket, while boiling heat torches up the length of my spine.

"Then do it," I say, trying to make it sound like a challenge. The words are barely out of my mouth when his lips slam into mine. I surge up onto my tiptoes as his hand slides to my lower back and he yanks me closer.

Our lips meet in a warm slide, and my soft gasp has him pulling back for the briefest second before he kisses me again. It's slow at first, unhurried, an exploration of textures and the softness of our lips. His tongue finds me waiting, shifting the moment into something else. I moan. This feels nothing like any kiss I've ever known. He licks into my mouth as we grow more frantic. His hands cup the sides of my face, and he tips my head back as he dives in to *devour* me.

We crush together, my body pinned between the wall and his strong arms and chest and legs. Warmth flutters in my stomach and behind my ribs as his hands slide over my shoulders and down my sides, where they settle on my hips.

"Fuck," he breathes as he pulls away to catch his breath. "We shouldn't do this."

My hands grip his jacket again. "Why not?"

He doesn't answer before he's on me again, his mouth against mine, fingers digging into the soft flesh at my waist. I grip his arms, my hands curling around tensed biceps and then sliding up into the soft curls at his nape.

"Poet! Where are you?"

A voice blasts through the moment, tearing us apart. Rook steps away, his back hitting the opposite wall as he drags his hand along the corner of his mouth. Fire burns in his gaze as he stares at me. We both breathe heavily, our chests rising and falling.

"Poet?" comes the voice again as Domino appears around the corner. "I was worried about you. They're about to start the ceremony."

That's when she notices Rook. Her gaze jumps between us before a knowing smile curves on her lips. I take in Rook's mussed hair and the bright, wild look in his eyes. Only a fool couldn't put two and two together.

"Sorry to interrupt," she says with a smirk. "But they need you both."

"You didn't interrupt anything. We were just talking," I say like a big, huge liar while I attempt to straighten myself out. "We're coming."

Domino places a hand on her cocked hip, clearly not buying my shit.

"Okay, but don't dawdle. Scion Beaufort is almost ready, and she doesn't look like a lady who waits for anyone."

I exhale on a sharp, almost delirious laugh. "We'll be right behind you."

Domino gives me a careful look, ensuring that she's read the situation correctly and that I don't need her help.

"I'm good, I promise," I assure her.

She nods and returns to the ballroom before I find the courage to meet Rook's gaze.

"We should probably . . ." I point in the direction Domino went.

"Yeah. You go. I'm coming."

There's enough dismissal in his tone that I push myself from the wall, trying not to take it personally.

As I leave, I glance over my shoulder to find Rook with his head tipped back and his eyes closed, wearing a pained look that suggests he just made a very big mistake.

44

I reenter the ballroom in a cloud of uncertainty to find it emptying of students, each being directed toward the exit for their respective ceremonies. The parents leave with drinks in hand, passing through a set of doors at the far end, where they'll wait for their kids until the pledging is over.

I'm pointed toward the left, where I hover on the edges of the Aria crowd. My lips burn with the memory of Rook's kiss. My knees have become jelly.

"Where have you been?" Trinity asks, walking over and taking my hand. "I heard what happened with your parents. Well . . . everyone heard. Are you okay?"

"Not really."

She squeezes my hand and gives me a sympathetic look.

While we wait, I search for Rook, but before I can find him, I'm whisked through a door and into another room, this one smaller and a bit darker but just as grand. A modest, elevated platform sits in the center, illuminated by a spotlight. Our group comprises about fifty people, and we're instructed to form a wide circle around the perimeter.

Once we're arranged, we all fall into silence by some kind of tacit agreement. I find myself standing between Trinity and a girl who keeps glancing at me and then quickly looking away. I hold in a sigh, wondering if this will always be my reality.

Hopefully, everyone will soon grow used to me and forget that I don't belong here.

Of course, I just caused another scene. No matter what Rook said, I've been humiliated by my parents' very public rejection.

I scan the room, finding him on the far side of the circle. I spot Domino about a quarter of the way around and catch her eye. She gives me a little wave just as another door opens.

Surreal Beaufort is as impressive as her name suggests. She's shorter than I expected, but she gives the impression of being taller with her straight spine, her shoulders thrown back, and her chin tipped up.

Her dark, white-streaked hair is sleek and shiny, cropped into a perfect blunt bob. She wears a three-piece black suit with a waistcoat that flares out from her hips, short black leather boots with impossibly high heels, and carries a long black cane that thunks along the floor as she walks.

Slowly, she approaches, and the circle shuffles apart to allow her through. I wonder what's happening in the Fiama room. Does my father make this kind of dramatic entrance, too? It doesn't seem like his style.

I shake my head and try to put him out of my thoughts.

My father, House Fiama, and everything they do is no longer my concern.

Scion Beaufort takes her time examining our group. She stalks the inside perimeter of our circle and tips her chin to those she must recognize. A few times, she reaches out to squeeze someone's hand. When she arrives at Domino, she pauses and assesses her up and down.

"We have cogs joining our ranks," Scion Beaufort says, her voice echoing around the room via a small microphone pinned to her lapel. "How . . . *delightful.*" Her tone is cool but polite, yet I don't think anyone misses her buried subtext.

"Yes, ma'am," Domino says, dropping her head and dipping a little at the knee. "Thank you for welcoming us."

Scion Beaufort's smile borders on simpering. "Well, I really didn't have much choice."

Domino blinks at the insult, and it takes every ounce of my willpower not to speak out on her behalf. I need to remember I'm no one here.

Scion Beaufort continues her examination of her new pledges, and my neck grows hot with nerves and anticipation.

If she singled out Domino, what will she do with the two of us who switched Houses?

Slowly, she makes her way closer, and her eyes pass completely over both

Trinity and me as she saunters down the line. I exhale the breath trapped in my chest, relieved she isn't planning to draw attention to our presence.

At least not yet.

She finishes the circle, briefly stopping at the far end, where it's difficult to make her out in the dim light. But something tells me she's arrived at Rook's standing place, thanks to several nervous shuffles.

"A Solitude," she says softly, confirming my hunch. "Remarkable. Absolutely remarkable." She steps back as if to admire him. Or more likely to judge.

"I'll be curious to see how you manage outside the Wastes."

In Rook's case, she doesn't sound disgusted.

She almost sounds amused, perhaps even delighted by his presence. It sends a trickle of uneasiness spreading across my scalp.

Finally, Scion Beaufort makes her way to the room's center, where she ascends the platform one slow step at a time. Her heels and her cane thump in alternate rhythms along with the wild, erratic beating of my pulse.

"It's so very good to see some of you," she says, her voice booming over us. "I've watched many of you grow into the young adults you've become. I know you'll do me well in continuing a proud Aria tradition through your schooling and once you graduate and represent our Society in the world."

She waxes on for another moment about Aria's mandate and their duty to ensure the sustainability and health of our population. Then she spends another minute extolling the virtues and achievements of the Extinguishers and their duty to protect infected Keepers from becoming a danger to themselves and to us.

I shift nervously from foot to foot, my gaze slipping to Trinity's profile, and I have to wonder why, if they're so great, they needed to persuade Trinity to join them?

Finally, Scion Beaufort finishes her talk, and one by one, our names are called to approach and pledge our loyalty to our House. It drags on forever as each person takes their turn, bowing before her and reciting their oath before they leave the room.

I stand there for more than an hour, eventually becoming aware that she has arranged it so that I'll be the last person to pledge. Despite the lengthiness of the entire spectacle, it feels like time passes much too quickly before it's just Scion Beaufort and me left in the room.

Is she planning to kill me and dispose of my body right here and now?

She turns around and crooks a finger.

I stare at her, momentarily paralyzed.

"Come. I won't bite," she says, though I'm almost sure that isn't true.

Still, I compel my feet to move. My boots click on the ceramic tiles as I approach and stand at the bottom of the steps. I square my posture and lift my chin while she regards me with all the warmth of an approaching iceberg.

"You've made quite the spectacle of my House, Poet Graves," she says. "And of yours."

"Fiama is no longer my House," I say, and her gaze narrows.

"Why?" she asks.

I swallow the iron knot in my throat.

"I didn't feel that I belonged in Fiama any longer," I reply, figuring that's the sort of answer she's looking for. I doubt she wants to hear about my personal goals and drama.

"You didn't want to kill a criminal," she says with a tut. "How very . . . *noble*."

Her head tosses back, and she laughs. "That's all very well and good," she continues. "But you understand that House Aria is also tasked with a duty? That we hunt down the infected and ensure they are dealt with? That they are one of our greatest threats?"

Slowly, I nod.

Obviously, I know this. I've always known this, but I had no other choice.

"Can you do it? Protect your city?"

"That's all I've ever wanted to do," I answer, and *this* is the truth.

"As a Storm Guard," she says. "That's a very different thing."

I nod. "I will do what it takes."

The words turn to ash in my mouth, but I understand this is also what she needs to hear.

Scion Beaufort takes a slow step and then another, stopping just above me. She reaches out and presses a sharp-tipped nail under my chin.

"Your father is furious with me," she says. "Yet his anger is misplaced."

"He's furious with me, too," I reply, and she nods.

"Your presence in Aria causes nothing but problems for *me*, do you understand that? You've started a war that I had nothing to do with, and I don't take kindly to that."

I try to nod, though I can't move, thanks to her finger keeping my head in place.

"I'm sorry. That wasn't my intention."

She makes a tsking sound. "I'll be keeping an eye on you," she adds. "I don't trust whatever's happening here. Your father and you just put on a very nice show, and I can't help but think that was for *my* benefit."

She leans in close enough that I feel the warmth of her breath on my cheeks. It makes my skin crawl, and I try not to flinch away.

"If you put a toe out of line, you're done. Do you understand? If I get the slightest *breath* of your betrayal, I won't hesitate to take you out, Poet Graves. You are no longer under your father's protection, and every member of my House will be given orders to report anything suspicious directly to me.

"And if they should decide to take matters into their own hands, I will look the other way. Is that clear?"

She pulls up and gives me a hard look.

"Yes," I say, forcing the word through a leaden tongue.

"Yes, *what*?"

"Yes, Scion Beaufort."

Finally, she lets go and backs up, all without taking her eyes off me.

"Then welcome to House Aria, Poet Graves. It'll be a miracle if you last until morning."

45

I find the ballroom mostly empty. Everyone is gathered in the adjoining room, where I can hear the sounds of laughter and mingling. I'm trembling and nauseous and I want to lie down, but I'm also coursing with rivers of pent-up energy.

"Poet!" Someone calls my name, and I turn to find Domino approaching. "Everything okay?"

"Yeah," I say. "I guess. What are you doing here?"

"I wanted to make sure you were all right. I was waiting for you to come out."

"You were?" I ask. "Why would you do that?"

Her brows pinch together in confusion. "Because I was worried about you. Did the scion give you a hard time?"

I offer her a dry smile, grateful for her thoughtfulness. Maybe I'm not as alone as I think. "Just a few open threats. No big deal."

She offers me a sympathetic look. "I'm sorry. Things will calm down once everyone gets used to you."

I return her smile. "That's my hope." I look around the room and then move a little closer. "About what you saw earlier. With Rook?"

At that, her eyes sparkle. "Yes? You looked pretty cozy." She gently hip checks me and wiggles her shoulders, giving me a suggestive look. "Tell me everything." She raises a hand. "Only if you want, of course."

I exhale a long breath, running my hands through my hair. "I'm not sure how much there is to tell. I think it was just the heat of the moment or something. I was upset about my parents, and he stopped me. I was emotional; we got carried away. It was nothing."

"Oh," she says, her expression falling a little. "Well, maybe it'll be something later. He's very cute."

I snort. "He's way more than cute."

Domino giggles and covers her mouth. "I didn't want to say. He's actually fucking gorgeous."

I bark out a laugh and groan. "You don't have to tell me. He's also a very bad idea."

"That hasn't stopped you yet," she says. I look at her as she widens her eyes. "Sorry, I didn't mean—"

I laugh again and shake my head. I love that she feels comfortable enough to tease me. I hope it means we're becoming friends. "No, you're absolutely right." I lean in closer. "Could you not tell anyone? I think he'd prefer it that way. He's kind of private."

"Of course," she says. "I would never. Someone else might have seen you, though. You weren't exactly hidden from view."

I run a hand down my face. "Right. Well, with any luck."

My gaze bounces to the other room, where everyone is mingling. "What are you doing now? Are your parents still here?"

"No, they just left. I'm heading to the after-party ferry now. It's leaving soon. You coming?"

I *could* go and hide. Remove myself from everyone's scrutiny.

It's tempting, but I also don't want to be alone.

"Are my parents still here? Did you see them?" I ask.

"I think they are," she says. "We could go the long way around to the dock. We don't have to pass through."

I heave out a grateful breath. "That would be perfect."

Domino links her arm with mine as something warm settles in my chest. I might have lost everything tonight, but maybe I'm gaining something new.

We skirt through the quiet halls of the school while Domino fills me in on her crush, a guy she's hoping to dance with tonight. My shoulders loosen as we walk. Maybe this isn't so bad. Perhaps there's a light at the end of all my questionable choices.

We exit through one of the doors and make our way around the school, arriving at the arched entrance curving over the canal. Instead of the little gondola we used on the first day of school, a multi-decked ferry stands bobbing in the water, constructed of gold metal molded into filigrees and decorated with hundreds of flowers. Dozens of people already fill each level. The railings and pillars are strung with glowing white lights, and the strains of music float into the sky.

This will be fun, I decide. I don't want to hide. I want to embrace this new reality.

The last few months have been tense, and I want to start enjoying my time at Amery. This is what I wanted for so long. I'm finally free of Knox, and I *kissed* Rook. I still can't believe it. The feel of his lips on mine burns into my skin, and even if he regrets it and it never happens again, I'll carry that memory for a very long time.

But I really, really hope it happens again.

"C'mon," Domino says, tugging on my arm. We cross the gangway and hop on board.

"There you are!" Journey exclaims, approaching with a cocktail in her hand. "You found Poet!"

"Hi," I say, bracing myself for whatever slew of questions she's about to hurl my way.

"Let's get you to the bar," she says with a wink. "Something tells me you could use a drink."

I exhale a shaky breath before she starts leading us to the far side of the main deck. There we find a bar draped in sparkly purple velvet. With glasses in hand, we look for a place to sit and find a wooden bench curving along the bow.

A dance floor sits off to our left, already packed with people who've cast off their dress coats, tossing them all into a pile. I sip on my cocktail, happy to observe for now. I try not to search for Rook, but something tells me this wouldn't really be his scene anyway. He's probably off brooding somewhere and looking very good while doing it.

"So," Journey says, turning to me. "How did that go? Did the scion lay into you? Threaten you? That was quite the scene with your parents. What's it like having all your family drama out there for everyone to see? Does your dad always get that vein in his temple when he's mad? That was kind of scary—"

"Journey," Domino says, cutting her off. "Enough. Leave her alone."

"Oh!" Journey covers her mouth. "I was doing it again, wasn't I?"

"You were," Domino says, while I smile politely.

A moment later, a bullhorn sounds, and everyone belts out a loud cheer. The boat shudders and then starts pulling away from the dock. More cheers as the music pumps, and I turn to watch the ferry gently glide into the center of the canal.

We float through the city, down the main waterway, which is wide enough to accommodate dozens of boats. Many of the buildings have been constructed to mimic the same great city that the gondolas and canals were based on. Beautiful carved marble, colorful facades, and ornate gilded window frames all glow in the evening light.

From here, I can see hundreds of people walking along the shore as they head out for dinner and dancing or wherever their evening takes them. It's a mostly clear night with only a few clouds in the sky, so everyone can relax without the fear of a storm.

I spot Trinity through the crowd, and she waves.

"Excuse me for a second," I tell Domino and Journey before I head toward her. A press of bodies surrounds us as we throw our arms around each other and hug tightly.

"You're here," Trinity says. "What happened with Scion Beaufort?"

I shake my head, recalling how Domino waited for me. "She just wanted to remind me that she's keeping an eye on me and I'm not to be trusted."

Trinity gives me a sympathetic look. "I'm sorry."

"It's fine," I say. "We did it, Trin. We've pledged, and I get to be a Storm Guard and you—" My words cut off. She's joined the E-squad, and the awkward truth sits on my tongue like a barb.

"And you're still Society," I finish, somewhat weakly.

If she notices my hesitation, she doesn't show it. She breaks into a grin and hugs me again.

"What about you?" I ask. "Everything good?"

"Yeah. The scion barely noticed *me*, but what else is new, right?" she answers, a tightness in her tone.

A second later, someone snags Trinity around the waist and lifts her up, spinning her around. A guy who I've seen with her before. One of the E-squad. He's cute with sandy-blond hair and slightly rounded cheeks.

"I missed you, baby," he says, kissing her, his hand sliding over her waist and down to her butt before he squeezes it. Trinity shrieks as she playfully shoves him in the chest.

"Poet," she says to me. "This is Jared."

She leans against him, petting his stomach, as he throws an arm around her shoulders.

"The famous Poet Graves," he says, holding out his hand. "I've heard a lot about you."

I wish I could say the same. Trinity presses her cheek to his chest, peering up at him with a dreamy look. Now she's *dating* one of these guys?

"It's nice to meet you," I say, shaking his hand, hoping my distaste doesn't show.

He then grips Trinity by the back of her neck and tips her face up. "Can I get you a drink?"

She names a cocktail, and he nods, giving her another kiss before he walks off.

"Who's that?" I ask. "You're dating someone from E-squad?"

Trinity tucks a strand of hair behind her ear. "We've been getting to know each other," she says. "He's funny, and Skies—" She cuts off, leans in closer. "Well, he's nothing like Edward was in bed. He's so . . . *hungry*."

Despite myself, I snort and cover my mouth, and we both giggle.

"So that's it? You're done with Edward?"

Trinity shrugs. "I loved Edward, but we can't be together anymore. He has his mom to look after, and if he stayed with me, it would cause too many problems."

I suppose she does have a point.

"I don't think he'd care. He's been pretty miserable without you."

She waves a hand. "He'll get over me soon enough."

"I guess," I say, wondering if I know who this person is anymore. "So, you're still sure about this E-squad thing? I'm worried about you. They're not—"

Jared returns with Trinity's drink, and I stop talking. He passes it to her and slides his hand to her lower back. "Sorry to interrupt, but Ruby wants to see all of us."

"About what?" Trinity asks, taking a sip from her glass.

"Not sure, but she said we should meet at the far end of the boat."

"Sure," she says, turning to me. "Sorry. I gotta go. Let's dance later?"

"Of course," I say, and I watch as Jared hustles her through the crowd, disappearing from my sight. I don't like this. I thought I could talk her out of E-squad, but she's only becoming more and more ingrained.

I promise myself to talk to her more seriously tomorrow, then go searching for Domino, who's now dancing with the guy she told me about earlier: Calloway, another Society-born Storm Guard cadet who also pledged to Aria tonight. They're moving together, his big hands on her hips and her arms looped around his neck. He's a few inches taller than Domino, with broad shoulders, russet skin, and natural hair, shaved on the sides and curly on top.

She spots me and grins. I return it, then find a seat, content to watch everyone having fun. A few people are getting drunker. Someone climbs onto the roof of the boat, a guy from House Tera whose name I don't know. He rips off his shirt, swinging it overhead and shouting as everyone raises their glasses and cheers.

It's fun, and it's light; no one is paying me any attention, and maybe this could be my future. People are far more concerned with their own shit anyway.

As Domino said, everyone will eventually get used to this new reality.

Until then, I'll do my best to blend in.

I sit back, sip my drink, and watch the sky, my heart lighter than it's been in a while.

That's when someone screams.

46

The music cuts off as everyone stops and turns toward the sound. I hadn't even realized the boat had stopped moving. We're now floating in the middle of the canal, bobbing several feet from the shore. The dim sounds of the city continue in the distance, oblivious to what's going on.

What *is* going on?

I stand up on the bench, trying to see over everyone's heads. I catch the flash of lights from the water coming off a small red boat that appears to be the reason we've stopped.

My heart drops to my feet.

Whispers float through the crush of people.

Extinguishers.

The crowd slowly parts, revealing two men and two women dressed in bloodred uniforms. Their boots echo against the wooden deck as they approach the dance floor, and I sway, suddenly lightheaded.

I have just enough presence of mind to search my surroundings for an escape route.

But they're coming for me.

I've always known they'd come.

I should hide. I should run. Jump into the water and swim as fast as I can. But I'm trapped. They'll just follow. They won't let me go.

It's so quiet that all I hear is the lapping of water against the ferry. The rush of the breeze snaking through the crowd. The sound of my doom drawing closer. The Extinguishers stop and unholster the stunners strapped to their backs. Shrieks and screams fill the air as everyone shuffles aside.

"Out of the way," one utters. His voice is low, but it shoots through the crowd like an arrow. The shuffling continues as everyone tries to find somewhere to go. But the boat is packed and the space is limited, so apart from throwing themselves in the water, there isn't much they can do.

The Extinguisher in front stops and looks back, conferring with the woman behind him.

They break apart and scan the crowd. I watch as he leans down to speak with a student. I can't hear what they're saying, but the student goes wide-eyed and points toward the corner where I'm standing.

I stop breathing entirely.

My palms sweat, and my heart melts between my ribs.

I knew this moment was inevitable.

I could only escape for so long.

Again, the lead Extinguisher turns to say something to the woman walking alongside him, and then they're shoving through the crowd.

More scrambling. More shuffling as everyone compacts themselves together.

But I'm rooted to the spot. Unable to move or blink.

I turn to ash, burned down by the lies I've been clinging to since I was seven years old.

Maybe it was finally time. Maybe this is better. I didn't have the courage to turn myself over, so they've done me a favor and saved everyone from me.

The Extinguishers draw nearer. Heavy footsteps ricochet across the planks.

They stop a few feet away as my vision smears, turning white, then black, then red.

"Lacey Turner," someone says. "You're coming with us."

Gasps. Soft murmurs. Everyone turned to stone.

Someone starts screaming.

It takes me a few seconds to process it. To repeat the name in my head.

Lacey Turner.

She's hunched against the wall, crying as she's surrounded by four monsters wearing the color of dried blood.

I still can't quite put it all together. I feel like I'm watching this moment from the clouds.

They aren't here for me.

They're here for *Lacey.*

They take her by the arms, and she's still screaming.

Her knees collapsing as she begs for her life.

"Pick her up!" the head Extinguisher says. "Get her out of here!"

Lacey thrashes and kicks. "No!" she screams. "No! Stop! Don't take me!"

She fights so hard, they nearly lose their grip.

I want to help her. I want to make them stop. But I can't. I know I can't.

My hands curl into fists, pressed to my stomach. I'm a coward. I'm no better than any of them. But I can't undo this.

An Extinguisher bends down and hauls Lacey over his shoulder.

Her resistance is valiant. A last gasp against the inescapable. Some people would give up in defeat. I think to myself that when my time comes, that's how I want to go out. Fighting with a fury to crack the world in half.

My breath stutters as they carry her away.

They take her back to their boat and crowd around her before Lacey suddenly goes quiet.

The silence hangs in the air.

She's lifted off a shoulder, her body limp. Her expression slack. She's laid on the ground, her golden hair spread around her like a tragic heroine in a painting from the old world.

The boat's engine stutters to life, and then it putters away, taking Lacey with them.

No one moves until they're out of sight.

47

Over the next few weeks, I withdraw into myself. I relive the terror of that night over and over. They were so close, and I froze. I hate myself for everything I failed to do.

We aren't told anything about Lacey, either. For all intents, she is gone and never existed.

I've seen Winter crying during mealtimes, her eyes bloodshot, her cheeks pink. Knox trying to comfort her, his face pale and drawn. I sense the shifting mood in House Fiama. They aren't supposed to mourn her, but she was their friend, and no one deserves this fate.

Questions nag my thoughts. Was Lacey really infected? Was there a sign I missed?

I think of her blond hair with its dyed lilac tips. I know they weren't natural. I've watched them fade before she had them redone. Did *she* even know what she was? Were we both living scared for our lives, none the wiser to each other's secrets?

There's no one to ask for more information. Even if someone knew, it would draw too much attention.

My inward spiral isn't helped by the fact that it's obvious Scion Beaufort passed on the message that I'm not to be trusted or treated with an ounce of human kindness.

Everywhere I turn, I'm met with hostile looks, underhanded barbs, and muttered threats. I feel like I can't breathe without someone reminding me that I'm no better than the dirt crusted on their shoe.

I no longer belong with Fiama, but I certainly don't belong with Aria.

I tell myself this will pass. They'll get tired of tormenting me eventually.

I shrink further into myself and draw as little attention as possible. Truly, the only bright spot in my week is time spent in the gym and my simple workouts with Henry as we chat about everything in his life.

Thankfully, cadet training and school keep me mostly too busy to think very much.

Except at night, when I lie awake, imagining that they'd come for me on that boat instead.

Trinity is busy with her E-squad. I've seen her only a handful of times since that night, and she was gleeful about Lacey's capture. Convinced we were all better off. She's been lucky to escape the brunt of Aria's ire for switching Houses, but that's because her squad is protecting her. Maybe a part of me understands why she was drawn to them.

Regardless, Scion Beaufort doesn't have it out for her, and Trinity is mostly ignored outside of her group. She's also been busy with the new boyfriend, Jared. I don't think I like him very much.

We're drifting apart. I can feel it. I just don't know how to stop it.

Rook is also avoiding me, and I want to scream with the frustration of it all. I had no choice but to sneak out alone when a storm came last week, and it took everything in me not to hunt him down and beg him to come.

Rumors have been flying about our kiss.

Someone saw us, just like Domino warned.

He said we shouldn't have done it, and he's making it incredibly obvious that he thinks it was a mistake, so I need to respect that.

The only other bright side is that I've also seen very little of Knox. Nothing more than a glance in the cafeteria during meals, and despite the way I've fucked everything up, at least I accomplished this.

He can marry Winter, and I honestly hope they're happy together.

I also take comfort in knowing I won't be invited to the wedding.

It's late when I return from the outskirts another week later, and things take a turn for the worse. The storm is powerful tonight, the wind fierce, and the closed waterways forced me to take the train back to Amery. Now it continues to rage, exploding across the sky.

When I enter my room, it's too dark to see much, but something makes the hairs on my neck stand up. I scan the shadows, blinking and trying to make out the indistinct shapes. Is someone there?

"Where have you been?" comes a voice from the dark, and my shoulders tense.

This is exactly what I don't need right now. "Who's there?"

"I asked where you've been," the voice repeats.

"I was in the library studying," I say, using my already-planned excuse while slumping my heavy backpack on the floor to punctuate my point.

"Pretty late to be studying," a different voice says off to my left.

"Yeah, I'm behind," I answer as I take a step back.

A light flares, revealing six people forming a half circle, including my two roommates. I recognize Brick and a few other members of Aria.

"What's going on?" I ask, trying to temper the shake in my voice.

"Scion Beaufort wants us to keep an eye on you," someone answers. A girl with spiky lilac hair. "And we've taken notice of your so-called 'late-night study sessions.'"

"I'm busy with cadet training," I say, hating that I feel the need to defend myself. "I have a lot of homework to catch up on. That's all."

"No one else seems to have that problem," Silla, my roommate, says. "They're all tucked cozy in their beds."

I wonder where Domino went. Did they do something to her? She's one of the only people in my life still speaking to me, and a wave of protective-ness burns in my chest.

But what if she knew they were planning to ambush me?

I shake away the thought. She wouldn't do that to me. She's too good. And if she did clear out to protect herself, I can't blame her for that.

"Just leave me alone," I say, lifting my chin. "I haven't done anything to you."

"Haven't you?" asks Cece with an ugly sneer on her face. "We don't trust you. You don't belong here."

"By whose criteria? Some made-up rule someone decided hundreds of years ago? Does this *really* matter?" I ask. "I'll stay out of your way, and you stay out of mine. I promise I'm not here to spy on Aria."

I'm met with a few blinks, perhaps a few light bulbs turning on, but the biased structure of our environment isn't their primary concern right now.

"Get out of our room," Silla says. "Permanently. You're fouling up the entire place." She waves a hand under her nose. "It smells rotten."

"Then where am I supposed to sleep?"

Honestly, I'd prefer to leave, but I also have nowhere else to go.

She saunters closer and folds her arms. "That's not my fucking concern."

Fear and anger twist knots in my chest. I *should* just leave. Sleeping in a random hallway would be better than this. A stone floor. A bed of nails.

"Get out or we'll *make* you get out," Silla says, and it's obvious she means it.

I back up another few steps. "Fine." I can't take on six people alone. Maybe I'll appeal to Stevie, though I know she can't do anything to help. I reach for my bag, but they close in around me.

They have no intention of allowing me to walk out of here without a scratch.

"I'm leaving," I promise. "I won't come back."

From the corner of my eye, I notice someone lift an arm, a flash of brown fuzz catching my attention. The blood drains from my limbs along with a soft, panicked breath at the sight of Brick clutching Teddy in his massive grip.

He grins as a snide chorus of laughter circles through my attackers.

Silla advances, placing herself directly in my path, invading my space. "Aw, the widdle Fiama princess had to bring her widdle teddy bear to school," she says in a baby voice that definitely isn't cute. "How *adorable*."

"Give me that," I say.

The words spill from my lips of their own accord, and I'm a fool because I've just revealed my hand.

"Come and get it," Brick taunts, his ugly face spreading into a sneer.

It's a trick. *Obviously* it's a trick, but I reach for this last thread of an old life anyway. I've lost everything in the past few weeks. My friends. My family. My fiancé, even if I didn't want him. I'm even slowly losing my best friend.

Teddy is the only connection left to who I was.

Brick laughs and then tosses it to another guy on the far side of the room. They all join in the game, maneuvering around me until I'm surrounded as they hurl Teddy back and forth.

I should walk out of here. I should go to a teacher—someone who might help. But who? Fiama's professors won't care, and Aria's will feel the same. I think of Henry, but I don't want to bring this burden to him.

But I also can't leave yet. I can't let them do something to Teddy. I understand it isn't logical—he's just an old toy—but I can't let them have him. If I lose this, then I worry I'll never find myself again.

So I stand helplessly, my fists clenching as they make a sport out of taunting me. I spin around and around, trying to keep the bear in my sight. But they pick up their pace, quickly shuffling him among their hands.

Anger boils in my veins, blurring my sight.

The sound of a hideous *riiiip* fills my ears, and I spin around. "No!"

Brick is laughing, and Teddy is now headless, sheared through the neck. My surroundings turn distant and hollow, like I'm falling into a deep hole. Another rip, and I glimpse soft limbs and white cotton spilling to the floor like tumbling snow.

"No," I gasp as horror burns up my throat, and then I'm being shoved. I don't even have the presence of mind to realize they've pushed me past the door.

"Give him to me!" I scream, setting off another round of mocking. Still, they push and shove, and I'm jostled among them as I reach helplessly for Teddy, who's probably lying in a million pieces on the floor.

"I told you to get *out*," Silla says again, and then she shoves me in the chest. I'm weightless. I don't even realize I'm falling until my stomach lifts into my throat and I hit the floor. No, not the floor. *Stairs.* Because I'm rolling, bumping, plunging to the echoing sound of cruel laughter.

A sharp pain bursts in the back of my head, and then everything goes black.

48

My eyes blink open, red haze bleeding across my vision. Someone jostles me, and I groan. Then a pair of arms lifts me up.

With a whimper, I let my head fall against someone's chest.

I know that scent.

Fresh breezes and warm sunshine. Green apples.

I slip in and out of consciousness as I feel him carrying me upstairs, followed by the steady cadence of a long hall. I recognize the sterile smell of the med wing and hear the hiss of the door as it slides open before I'm carefully laid on a bed.

Shadows move in the periphery of my vision. Hands touch me. Someone rips off my coat, my shirt. My arm throbs with its own heart.

A hand circles my wrist, and a ribbon of fire licks up to my elbow.

I moan. I gasp.

Then darkness takes me again.

. . .

When I wake up, dim light is backdropped by the low sounds of beeps and whirs of medical equipment. I groan and touch my head with a wince.

On my other wrist is a thick bandage. I lift it up and blink, trying to remember everything that happened. They shoved me down the stairs. They told me to leave, ripped Teddy apart, and then tried to kill me . . .

A movement catches my eye, and I look over to see Rook sitting on the floor, leaning against another bed. He's peering up at me with his wrists draped over his knees. I have to blink several more times to make sense of what I'm seeing.

The pieces of Teddy lie between his feet, and he holds a needle and thread dangling in one of his large hands. He's already reattached one of Teddy's arms and closed a rip in his back.

"You're sewing him back up?" I whisper before instantly breaking into sobs.

My tears surface, flowing freely as I curl into a ball and cry hard enough to turn my rib cage inside out. Suddenly, Rook is there, his arms wrapping around me as he settles onto the bed, and I cry into his chest.

I cling to his shirt, and I just . . . let go. My throat is sore, and my lungs ache, but I can't seem to make the tears stop. Distantly, I become aware of Dr. Perez in the room, but she keeps her distance while Rook holds me without a word.

Eventually, I succumb to a set of quiet sniffles and hiccups. I pull away to notice the dark stain on Rook's shirt.

"Sorry," I say, and he huffs out a small laugh.

"It's okay," he answers in a gentle way that nearly has me on the verge of crying again.

I try to smooth away the stain as if that will do anything, but after a moment, it seems more like I'm feeling him up. Mortified, I snatch my hand away, and he laughs.

It's a genuine laugh. Bright and clear.

Not couched in derision or sarcasm. I like that sound. I like it way too much.

My fingertips remember his touch, burning like I've held them to a candle.

The moment ends, but I catch that single moment of joy in his eyes, and it flips my whole world around.

He's always beautiful, but this is something else.

Dr. Perez appears before me. "How are you feeling?" she asks as Rook detangles himself from my hold, clearing his throat as if embarrassed to be caught in this show of tenderness.

The doctor checks the bump on my head and offers me a few more painkillers for my throbbing wrist. Rook returns to his spot on the floor, resuming his work piecing Teddy back together. I watch in fascination as he nimbly threads the needle and reattaches the bear's leg with neat, even stitches

"Your X-ray shows a bad sprain. Should take about a week or two to heal," she says before her gaze slides to me with a look I can't fully interpret. "You've broken your arm before, though? In a few places?"

She says it carefully, like she's trying to piece something together.

I sense Rook look up, watching our exchange.

Suddenly, I'm self-conscious.

My father. Can she tell what he's done?

"I can see a number of old fractures," she says, perhaps sensing my question, her voice turning to a whisper.

I shake my head. "Right. I'm sort of clumsy."

She meets my eyes. "Should I report this?"

Her question could be about two things.

Technically, the school should punish my attackers, but I can't complain to anyone about this. Scion Beaufort gave the go-ahead to anyone wishing to take matters into their own hands, and Fiama won't do anything to protect me.

As for the other thing, no one will stop my father from doing what he wants.

"No," I say.

She presses her mouth together, clearly displeased with my answer. "You're sure?"

"Yes," I say. "Please just leave it alone."

A pause. "Then you're free to go," she says, though she obviously isn't happy about it. "See me in a few days so I can check on how things are progressing."

"Thank you," I say, sitting up with a wince. She walks away, and I take a moment to settle my nerves. Slowly, I place my feet on the floor and stare between them before looking up.

"You carried me here," I say to Rook.

He nods as he pushes the needle through Teddy's fur and pulls it out the other side.

"Thank you."

He says nothing as he deftly knots the string, using his teeth to cut the remaining thread. Then he tests his handiwork, tugging on Teddy's limbs before he presents me with the repaired toy. Teddy's left arm is a little shorter, and a line of stitches curves up his belly like he's had his appendix removed.

But he's whole.

"And you fixed him," I whisper as Rook stands up. I crush Teddy to my chest and smell his head, inhaling the scent of my childhood and simpler times.

"C'mon," he says. "Let's get out of here."

It's obvious Dr. Perez still doesn't like or trust him, but she doesn't object as he takes my arm and leads me out of the med wing. "I can't go back to my room," I say. "They'll . . . I don't know what they'll do, but I can't sleep there anymore."

"I'm taking you to mine," he answers as my brows pinch together.

He shrugs. "I found an empty room downstairs. I hated sleeping near them, and I have three extra beds. You're welcome to one."

I open my mouth, weighing his proposal. "Well, you hardly ever talk," I say with no small amount of wonder. "So that sounds amazing."

He snorts a small laugh and shakes his head. "I wasn't complaining about the space."

"Do you live up to your name, Rook Athira? Do you prefer solitude?"

He seems to consider that and then answers, "It depends on the company, I guess."

A beat passes. "Fair enough."

We continue walking toward Aria's wing, and instead of taking the stairs up, we head for a different set. Rook holds out his hand, and I hesitate before slipping my fingers into his. They're warm and dry and close around mine, inexplicably offering a safety net. He guides me down the winding steps while I clutch Teddy under my injured arm.

We reach the bottom, and he opens the door to reveal a cozy dorm room, much like the one I just vacated, with a stone floor covered in plush rugs.

"I had no idea there were more rooms down here," I say. Soft evening light filters in through round windows set high into the walls. He even has a fireplace where a few glowing embers smolder in a pile of ash.

"It was a bit dusty," he says. "But I got it cleaned up, and no one has objected to me using it. I think they're just as happy to not have me near them."

He's claimed the bed in the far corner, and suddenly, I wonder if this is such a good idea.

I can't sleep in some strange guy's room. What will people say—

I stop, cutting off that pointless thought.

"If you're worried, I promise you're safe with me," he says. "And what else can they possibly say about you at this point?"

I huff out a sound that's part laugh because not only is he reading my mind, he's absolutely right.

I think about how he defended me against Knox without hesitation, and I believe him when he says I have nothing to fear from his presence.

Maybe these painkillers are addling my brain, or maybe I've just been through a lot this week, but Rook Athira, the Solitude from the Wastes, a group I was taught to fear my entire life, is the one person in this whole school who I'm certain *won't* try to hurt me.

I point to the bed in the opposite corner. "Maybe I'll take this one? I'd like to be close to the fire."

"Good choice," he answers.

I sit down on the edge of the bed and test the mattress, already made up with fresh sheets.

"I can go grab your stuff for you," he adds.

I should refuse. He's already done so much, but I don't think I can face anyone else right now.

"Are you sure?"

"I'm not afraid of them, Trouble," he says, but there's no hint of mocking in the nickname. I almost wonder if I detect a thread of affection, but that's silly.

"Thanks," I whisper, still clutching Teddy. "I . . . You're being nicer to me than I deserve."

I chew on my bottom lip as I watch him fold up a T-shirt and stuff it into a drawer.

"You probably deserve more than you think you do," he says softly before he exhales and runs a hand down his face. I have no idea what's eating at him, but his words twist me up, so I brush past them because I have no idea how to respond.

"Who taught you how to sew him back together?" I ask.

He shrugs as his cheeks turn the barest shade of pink. "We have to patch up a lot of our clothing," he says. "You learn to sew at a young age out in the Wastes."

"I would have no idea how to do that."

He walks over, dropping into a crouch. "I'll be right back. You lie down and take more of the painkillers the doctor gave you."

He pulls my shoes off and eases me back onto the bed. We're eye to eye, and it looks like he wants to say something else, but then he gives his head a little shake and stands up.

Without another word, he strides out of the room. I watch the door close behind him and turn to study my surroundings. It's much quieter than the upper-level dorms. Peaceful.

Rook probably liked it down here alone, and now I've intruded on his silence. I recall what he said about enjoying the right company, and I know I shouldn't wonder or hope that I'm included in that list.

Despite the fireplace, the air is cooler down here, and I'm wearing only the tank top I had on under my jacket. I shiver as goose bumps prick my skin and hug Teddy tighter to my chest.

I wonder how long Rook will be and if I should have gone with him. I hope no one tries to hurt him. But I'm lightheaded from the painkillers, and something tells me he can take care of himself. They don't fear me, but Rook has proven several times already that he doesn't put up with anyone's shit.

I cradle Teddy and my sore arm, lying on the soft pillow. It swaddles my head as I nestle into it, and my eyelids instantly grow heavy.

My phone dings, and I open my eyes again.

It's Domino checking on me. In fact, she's sent me dozens of messages. Apparently, she was with Journey working on a project in her room when everything happened and had no idea what our roommates had planned.

I ask if she's safe with them, but she assures me it will be fine.

I slide back to my messages to see that Trinity hasn't sent me anything. Her friend Brick was there in that room. He helped push me down the stairs. Does she know? Does she care? I'm almost too scared to ask.

I have a text from Edward checking on me. At least he isn't letting our Society divide come between us.

And a few from Silver and Hazel, who've temporarily revived our group chat.

SILVER: *poet, girl. are you ok*

HAZEL: *I heard the Solitude rescued you??*

SILVER: *that's not all he's been doing . . . give us the scoop poe! did you really kiss him?*

I sigh, wondering what took them so long to ask.

ME: *I'm fine, just a sprained wrist.*

And that's all I say, ignoring the question about Rook. It's petty, but not knowing will eat them alive. I click off my phone and toss it on the nightstand while I lie back and stare at the ceiling.

I'm wide awake now. Frustrated and angry. I stand up and start pacing back and forth.

The door opens, and I'm so lost in my thoughts that I jump.

It's Rook carrying an armful of my clothing. He stops when he sees me standing in the middle of the room.

"Miss me?" he asks, and I nod and catch myself before shaking my head as he smirks. Maybe I did miss him a little bit.

I step aside as he enters and dumps the entire lot onto one of the empty beds. He's wearing my backpack over his shoulders, and he slides it off and sets it on the ground.

"It's not everything, but it's all I could carry in one trip. I can get the rest tomorrow, if that works?"

"Of course," I say, suddenly intensely grateful. "Thank you. You didn't have to do all this. I really appreciate your help. I really don't have anyone, and . . ."

"I get it," he says and heads for his corner of the room.

"Sorry. Yeah. I guess you do."

I pick through the pile of clothing and start hanging a few things in the closet. I feel Rook glancing over as he kicks off his boots and lies back on the bed. I gasp in surprise when I see that he's now holding . . . a book.

A *real* book, made from paper with a glossy cover, though it's marred with numerous scratches and dents.

He notices where my attention has gone. "We have a few books out in the Wastes. I brought a couple of my favorites with me."

I drop my face in my hands, feeling like a complete and total asshole.

"And I thought you couldn't read," I say, which earns me a genuine smile. It spreads across his face, a dimple forming in his cheek that does something funny and not wholly unwelcome to my insides.

"Here," he says, holding it out.

I walk over and accept the book with the reverence it's due. I flip through the softened pages as they tickle my fingertips. The cover reveals the title of a fantasy book from the Warming Age that was once very popular. It's the same one the architect modeled Amery Academy after.

"You believe in elves?" I ask, scanning the page I've landed on. "Trees that talk?"

"I think we proved the supernatural doesn't really exist," he says, almost mournfully. "But I think it's still fun to dream."

"Yeah," I say. "I agree."

I close the book and hand it back, but he waves me off. "You should read it."

Something hopeful lingers in his expression. Like he really wants me to say yes.

"You'd let me borrow it?" I ask, holding his gaze. "Are you sure? This is so precious."

"Why not?" he says. "They once believed books were meant to be shared, and it's a great story. I think you'll like it."

"Thank you," I say, bringing it to my nose and inhaling deeply. I imagine I can taste its words and thoughts between the pages. "I know I keep saying it, but you have no idea how grateful I am for everything."

"Sure," he says as he opens his drawer, selects another book, and settles back with it. I don't recognize the title, but I get the feeling he's uncomfortable with my gratitude, so I leave him to it as I put away the rest of my things.

When I'm done, I grab a pair of pajamas and head to the bathroom to slide into shorts and a tank top. Then I exit to find Rook also dressed for sleep . . . though "dressed" might be too strong a word. He's changed into a pair of soft black pants and nothing else.

He's stretched on his bed, ankles crossed, with his book balanced on his chest. I stand momentarily paralyzed by the curve of his biceps and the swell of his shoulder. His fingers tap against his flat stomach, and it's the first time I've had the chance to really appreciate the tattoos covering his arms. Sinuous lines of rivers and jagged mountains spread over his skin like a map to lost treasure.

Sensing my attention, he glances over, and I quickly look away, my cheeks heating. I scurry to the other side of the room and slip under the covers, shivering as my skin hits the cool sheets.

"Let me put on a log," Rook says into the dark. "Sorry."

"It's fine," I say as he crosses the room and throws some wood on the fire. He pokes it a few times, blowing on the embers before the flames crackle to life.

"If you get cold at night, just shout," he says. "I can put more on."

I nod as our eyes meet, orange flames dancing in the forest-deep pools of his irises.

It's on the tip of my tongue to say thank you again, but I don't think he wants that. Something tells me he likes to be needed. To be useful.

Finally, he turns away and returns to his bed.

We both fall silent, and I tuck my hands under my cheek, watching him read.

Between the painkillers and the events of the last few days, I feel like I could sleep forever.

"Good night, Rook," I mumble as my eyelids grow heavy, hastened by the warm fire and the soft rustles from across the room.

"Night, Trouble," are the last words I hear before I'm gone.

49

My dreams are plagued with a string of nightmares.

I see my parents with empty black eyes, looming over me.

Brick and Silla with claws and sharp teeth, lumbering on stiff legs as flesh rots off their faces.

I fall, tumbling through nothing until I land on hard stone, my body shattering into pieces.

Trinity turns away to reveal another face on the back of her head.

Lacey screams.

Domino is bent and broken.

Teddy ripped to shreds.

The static sounds of fabric tearing and the heavy thump of cotton.

I bolt awake, covered in cold sweat, wincing at the throb in my wrist.

It's early, with only dusky morning light filtering through the small windows. The sky is quieter down here, less insistent on being noticed. Likely another reason Rook chose this spot.

It takes me a moment to realize the shower is running, and his bed is empty. I stare at the bathroom door, totally *not* imagining what he looks like with water running over the dips and grooves of his chest and abs. I don't give a second thought to the thin wall separating us.

I catch myself, mortified at my behavior, and settle back, picking up my phone for a distraction. Every morning, I reach for it with the tiniest flicker of hope that my mother has decided to break our stalemate, and every morning, I find myself disappointed.

There's still nothing from Trinity, so I swallow my frustration and fire off a message, asking if she wants to meet up later.

Then I type a note to my mother, telling her about my injury. My finger hovers over the send button, and I'm worried I won't be able to handle the disappointment if she doesn't respond.

Could she truly be so indifferent to everything I'm going through?

Does she care that I'm no longer safe in these walls?

Then I wonder if she's even getting these at all. It would be just like my father to confiscate her device. He's done it to control her before. I'm not sure if knowing that makes me more or less depressed.

There's another message from Silver and Hazel's group chat. Far more direct this time.

SILVER: *everyone knows you kissed him and everyone is talking about it*

It feels vaguely threatening rather than her usual playful tone, and I'm not sure what to make of it. What's her point? I've broken every other rule, so what's another?

I'm not embarrassed that I kissed him.

I liked it.

I kind of want to do it again.

Not kind of.

But I also don't want everyone knowing about it and gossiping.

It was a private moment.

The shower stops, and my breath hitches as the door opens to a cloud of steam. And Rook.

Wearing nothing but a towel slung over his hips.

Skies, he's magnificent.

I can't help but stare at his wet chest, the planes of his stomach, and a trail of dark hair that disappears under the towel. My imagination is good, but reality is even better. He uses another towel to rough up his wet hair, his forearm and biceps flexing, sending liquid heat dripping from my navel.

I touch my bottom lip, thinking of our kiss.

His gaze jumps to mine, and there's no use pretending I wasn't staring.

"Sorry," I say, looking down. Eventually, I glance back up to find him watching me, the barest curve teasing the corner of his mouth.

"Nothing to be sorry for."

That answer makes me smile in spite of everything, and I hold up my phone.

"Everyone knows," I say. "About . . . the kiss."

We haven't given it voice, and it almost feels forbidden to say out loud.

He approaches, and I catch a whiff of his clean scent as he leans down to peer at my screen—a droplet slides off the tip of his hair and lands on my hand. I don't wipe it away. I'm officially pathetic.

"That girl is something," he says, straightening up and returning to his side of the room. As he turns around, I notice he has another tattoo on his lower back. Lines joined by tiny stars. I think they might be the constellations he told me about.

"Do you know her?"

"We've met," he says dryly but doesn't elaborate.

"I guess someone saw us that night."

"Would Domino have said something?"

"No, she wouldn't do that." I chew my bottom lip. "You didn't tell anyone, did you?"

"Why would I tell anyone?"

I frown. "Wait. Which syllable were you emphasizing?"

He blinks. "What?"

"Which syllable did you emphasize? The 'why' would suggest you wouldn't tell, the 'tell' would suggest you *want* to keep it a secret, or the 'anyone' would suggest maybe you regret it."

He offers me a bemused look. "I think you're making my head hurt."

I huff.

"That girl is your friend?" He gestures to my phone, talking about Silver.

"Yes. No. She *was* my friend . . ."

"I don't think she's your friend now," he says. "I only met her because she was asking about you and me . . . and the kiss. And, well, nothing she said was very nice."

Something deflates in my chest. I knew it, but hearing it confirmed hurts.

"Everyone's been really hard on you about this whole switching Houses thing," he says.

"I hadn't noticed," I reply with an eye roll, earning me a small laugh.

"Why does this matter so much? Trinity—the other one who switched? Why don't they care about her?"

I press my lips together, and he arches a brow.

"You'll hate this answer," I say.

"You don't know what I'll hate."

"Because I am . . . important." I wince, shamed by the sound of it. "Or rather, my position *was* important. I was supposed to marry Knox to help secure my father's position and keep our House stable. When I switched to Aria, I threatened all that . . ."

I trail off.

"I can't believe they wanted you to *marry* that dickhead."

"Yeah," I say.

"You're right," he says. "I do hate that answer."

But there's no real heat in his words, only a hint of defeat.

"That's a lot to put on you," he adds.

He rakes a hand through his wet hair, while I note the bunching and flexing of his arms and chest as he moves, and it's very distracting.

"I guess," I say.

"I'm sorry," he says. "I bet you don't deserve any of that."

I scoff. "Don't I?"

He tips his head with a sympathetic look. I glance at the towel still around his waist and throw off my blanket before I say something about that drop of water meandering down his chest.

"I'll take a shower," I say. "You can finish dressing."

He nods as I dig through my closet and pull out a few things, clutching them to my chest.

"Are *we* going to talk about it?" I ask as he arches a brow.

"Talk about what?"

"You know what."

Gripping the towel at his hip, he approaches until he's standing right in front of me. His free hand slips under my hair and cups the back of my neck.

"What do you want to say about it?" he asks as he tips my face up.

"I . . . liked it," I say in a rush, earning me a warm chuckle.

"Did you?"

I nod as my cheeks heat, wondering what possessed me to say that.

"I liked it, too," he says, easing the tangled emotions in my chest. "And for whatever it's worth, I don't regret it."

"Oh," I answer as warmth melts through my limbs. "Okay."

He smiles slowly. "I think a storm is coming. Should we go out tonight?"

"Yes," I say. "I need it."

"Same." He leans in closer, his soft breath dusting my lips. I want to kiss him again. I think he might be considering it, too.

"Go get yourself ready," he says a moment later. "Or you'll be late for class."

He straightens up, but the look in his eyes tells me this isn't a dismissal but rather a . . . *let's wait and see.*

Almost reluctantly, his hand slips away, and I disappear into the bathroom with my heart beating hard and my limbs trembling, remembering every moment of his touch.

When I emerge twenty minutes later, Rook is gone. I cross over to my bed and spend a moment straightening up. Teddy lies tangled in the sheets, and as I reach for him, I notice a piece of paper tucked under his arm.

I'm so surprised that I stare at it before I slide it out. Rook left me a note. It's clear he ripped a corner from one of his books, and I'm so shocked I'm having trouble comprehending it. He tore a page just to leave me a message?

Had to see Brooklyn about my training plan, but I'll meet you at the tunnel exit after class. The room code is 3452. — R

His writing flows elegantly across the scrap in whirls and loops with a practiced hand.

Most of us have little use for handwriting. We use our screens for everything, and while we're offered some lessons with a stylus when we're young, signing anything beyond our names isn't much of a priority.

But I cherish these words and how he delivered them, even if they don't say much. Maybe they do. Maybe they're revealing something between the lines. I fold it back up and slide the paper under my phone case to keep it close.

It feels silly, but also kind of right.

After I've made my bed, I consider hiding Teddy in a drawer but decide maybe it isn't necessary.

Rook has now played witness to more of my secrets than anyone at Amery besides Trinity.

Instead, I tuck my bear against the pillow where he can sit and wait for me to return.

I stare about the quiet room, hovering on the verge of content.

It says something that after almost five months at Amery, the only place I've felt I could be myself is with the one person I wasn't ever supposed to trust.

With a deep breath, I head out to my first class, unsure whether I'm more anxious about seeing everyone again . . . or meeting up with Rook tonight.

50

I'm buzzing with anticipation when I arrive to meet Rook that evening. It's Friday night, and we're permitted to leave Amery for a few hours. They even gave us a few days off from training, and my tired body is dreaming of a soft bed, comfort food, and the crackle of a roaring fire.

Almost the entire student body is heading to Sogno for dancing and drinks. I spent years eagerly looking forward to parties with my friends, but none of that seems to matter right now.

When I round the corner, Rook is already waiting. He looks gorgeous and casual, his head tipped against the wall, foot pressed against it, and hands stuffed into his pockets.

When he hears me coming, he looks over, a flare of brightness entering his eyes.

"Hi," I say, suddenly a bit shy.

"Hey. How was your day?" His voice is low, a half smile on his face.

"It was fine. I was mostly looking forward to this."

The admission makes my cheeks heat. Why do I have no filter around him? Something about Rook invites it. I just want to be honest with him. He's free of judgment or expectation.

He gestures to the ladder. "Me too, Trouble."

I inhale a deep breath and climb down, entering the dimly lit space.

Rook follows a few seconds later. "You're all tense. Is it me? Or the tunnels?"

"It's not you," I say quickly, my cheeks warming again.

Wow, Poet, could you be any more transparent?

He smirks and takes a few steps before looking back.

"It's all this stone," I say. "It feels like I'm being crushed."

His mouth flattens as he meets my gaze, then reaches out a hand and holds it there. I look down at his fingers and the edges of his tattoo peeking from under his shirt.

Slowly, I reach for his hand, and his warm fingers close around mine.

He tips his head. "Better?" he asks, and I nod.

"Better."

Much better.

He tugs me gently, and we make our way down the tunnel, with Rook warning me about uneven bits of the terrain. I keep one hand on the wall, the other firmly gripped in his.

"Watch this spot here," he says. "There's a bit of a dip."

He looks back to check on me, and his eyes narrow as he peers past my shoulder.

I turn around, but all I see are shadows stretching in the direction we came.

"I thought . . . I saw something," he says. "Did you hear anything?"

We both hold completely still, and I *do* hear something. A rhythmic sound that could be footsteps or any number of things: the drip of water or the crack of stone.

"Must've imagined it," he says. "Let's keep going."

We board the train and head out, passing through the rubble of the old city. During the journey, I can't shake the sensation that we're being watched. It isn't until we're concealed behind the rock wall that I finally relax.

I inhale a deep pull of fresh air as the breeze tosses my hair. The storm is brewing, the clouds tumbling, gathering in the spot buzzing behind my heart.

"We have some time," Rook says, and I nod as we both settle onto the center rock and stare at the horizon.

"What's up with the claustrophobia?" Rook asks with one knee tucked up under his arm. "Does it have something to do with what Dr. Perez saw in your X-rays?"

I exhale a deep breath and fold my arms tightly across my chest.

Rook touches my elbow gently. "You don't need to do that," he says. "Sorry, I shouldn't have pried."

"It's okay. It's already a very poorly kept secret. My father . . . has a temper. I've spent a lot of time hiding in closets."

Rook exhales a knife-sharp breath. "That same asshole who came to the pledging ceremony?"

"The one and only." I hold my breath, wondering how Rook will react.

He scoffs and tosses a pebble onto the ground, where it lands with a soft click. "We spend our lives being told how civilized you all are—how the Societies represent the height of human existence—but you're all fucking animals, too."

My gaze flashes to his, and he shakes his head. "Sorry. I shouldn't have said that."

"No," I say, reaching over and laying a hand on his wrist. I notice him twitch, but he doesn't pull away. "You're right. If that's what you're taught, then they're wrong."

He selects another pebble, throws it up, and catches it.

"Why did you choose Aria for your pledge?" I ask.

He shrugs. "Honestly, it hardly mattered to me. It seemed like the one I'd have the best chance of succeeding in."

That makes sense. He definitely has that whole "fit" thing going on.

"You move and fight like you already knew what you were doing when you got here," I say.

"Yeah," he agrees, but that word is so weighted with a million sides that I can't begin to understand what he's thinking.

"What did they make you do during your initiation?"

I know I'm not supposed to ask, but I can't seem to help myself.

His jaw hardens before he answers. "They ensured I would start becoming one of you."

When it doesn't seem like he wants to elaborate, I don't push it. It's none of my business, and he must have his reasons for pledging.

"Why are you here?" I ask with that thought in mind. "Why did you come to Amery?"

He looks at me and then turns toward the sky. "For my family. For my people. For a chance to give them more."

His *people*. More and more, I wonder about his life.

"But you won't ever see them again?" I ask. "Don't you have to give them up when you enroll at Amery?"

He shrugs. "I know that's their rule, but I have every intention of finding a way around it."

He says it so matter-of-factly that I believe he'll manage it.

"They're lucky to have you," I say.

"I'm lucky to have them."

I give him a smile. "That must be nice."

Then we both turn toward the sky, where the first flashing cloud bursts are visible in the distance. I scratch the back of my neck and my arms, and I notice the way Rook twitches. He's pulled out his compass and is flipping the lid open and closed. I think it's an anxious habit.

"At least I don't have to do this alone anymore," I say.

He stops flipping the compass. "Yeah."

"You've really never found any other Keepers in the Wastes?"

He hesitates for a moment and then blinks. "No, I haven't."

I get the strangest sense he isn't being truthful. I don't blame him for this, either—he's probably protecting someone he loves. Maybe one of his siblings is also a Keeper.

"And you really don't know what happened last time? When we touched?"

"I don't know. I didn't think that was even possible."

This time, I do believe him.

"Is there anyone who might know?" I consider Dr. Eze and her research. I'm still sure she knows more than she let on.

Rook shrugs. "Possibly. I think The Shield knows more about Keepers than they claim."

Slowly, I nod. That makes sense.

As the storm draws closer, we sit side by side in comfortable silence. I like that I never feel the need to fill the pauses between our words. Rook likes the quiet as much as I do.

I inhale, taking in the scent of the storm. That crisp, electric taste fizzes on my tongue.

"What's your favorite part?" he asks.

"That feeling of being totally alive," I answer without hesitating. "Like I could crush a boulder or kick over a building or tear down the sky."

He smiles, the corner of his mouth lifting. "I like how it almost feels like I'm touching the universe," he says. "Or even something beyond it. I know they once believed in gods, and I swear when that energy courses through my veins, it feels like some higher power is out there working its magic."

I nod. "Yeah, I get what you mean."

He looks over, and our eyes meet. The moment becomes a spark. The ignition of fire that might burn us to dust.

"Do you have other family?" he asks, and I nod.

"My grandparents," I say. "On my mother's side. They aren't talking to me, either."

"Are you close?"

"Not really. We have dinner every few months, and they ask some polite questions about school and my friends, and that's about it. They send something nice for my birthday."

I shrug like it doesn't matter, but it does.

I think about Trinity and the Robinses and how she had two sets of grandparents, aunts, and uncles who were all extensions of her immediate family. But in the end, she's lost them all, too.

"My mom has a sister, and my cousin Anan is in the third year," I say. "We see them sometimes. My dad had a sister, but she died before I was born. She fell in love with a Solitude."

I whisper the words as Rook shoots me a look, his brows climbing.

"Really?"

I nod. "It almost ruined their family. She got pregnant and then . . . he killed her. My parents took the baby in. Raine. So technically, he was my cousin, but he was my brother in every way that mattered."

"I'm so sorry," Rook says. "That must have been hard for everyone." He exhales a wry laugh. "I can see why you hate me, I guess."

"That isn't true. I don't hate you."

He offers me a skeptical look.

"I don't anymore," I say, picking at a loose thread on the cuff of my shirt. "I never *hated* you. I just didn't trust you, but I didn't know you. I judged you based on things other people said."

He blinks, and I sigh and shake my head. "Plus, you're right. My family is so . . . divided. So *loveless*. I sound so fucking pathetic."

I look away, unable to face Rook's expression, worried about what I'll find.

A warm hand lands on mine and curls around my fingers. "You're not pathetic. You aren't responsible for any of that."

I huff out a breath as a gust of wind tugs his hair, blowing strands across his cheek.

I want to reach up and tuck them back.

"I think a lot of people must see a girl who has it all," he says softly. "But they don't see the real you."

His words cut close to the truth, and it's a relief to have someone understand me.

"Something like that," I say. "But I don't want to complain. I grew up with everything I could have ever wanted. I'm not a . . ."

"Solitude," he says. "You can say it."

"Sorry." I rub my face with my hand. "Old habits."

"Do you really think we're all so poorly off?" he asks gently. "Are you still convinced you have it better in the Houses?"

"No," I answer immediately. "Not anymore."

His mouth presses together as a cloud burst explodes overhead. Energy strikes the earth, swelling into a plasma arc swirling with amethyst sparks. Rook hops off the rock and holds out his hand. I slide my fingers into his, and we take a few steps deeper into the open plain.

"You have every right to hate me," I say. "For everything. For who I am. For what I represent. It's all true. All the ugly, horrible parts."

"I don't hate you," he says softly.

"Not anymore, you mean?"

He smirks but doesn't reply.

"Can I ask you a question?" he starts a moment later.

"Sure." And I mean it. I want to tell him anything. Everything.

"Do you ever feel like you can . . . control it? The Spark?"

I exhale a soft breath. "I'm not sure. Do you?"

He shrugs and turns back to the sky. "Maybe."

"What do you think that means?"

"I have no idea," he says. "But it must mean something."

His expression is inscrutable, and I wonder if he's keeping something else from me.

The wind is picking up, and more flashes light up the horizon. Rook's hand squeezes mine tighter as a knot of emotion swells in my throat. I shouldn't feel so connected to him. The story about Raine and his birth mother should be a reminder, but I'm not afraid. It feels like we'd be different. But I'm probably getting ahead of myself.

"Hold on to me?" he asks. "Last time . . ."

"Yes," I say. "I want to do it again."

Bursts of ultraviolet light illuminate the clouds like puffs of powder smoke. Out here in the open, I feel even closer to it, like I might become one with the sky.

My mouth parts as a cloud explodes and jagged streaks of Spark spear toward us.

It knows we're here and we're waiting.

I brace myself for the onslaught. For the agony before the calm, not sure if the last time was a fluke.

We're struck. I gasp as the light sizzles through me, burning in my limbs and bones, but not with the same shredding force I know. Rook's hand squeezes mine, and it's like the combination of our touch concentrates the power, filtering it *through* me instead of into me. Every cell in my body fizzes and pops, coming to life.

Laughter bubbles up my throat. A heightened euphoria that twists and bends in on itself, and I don't just feel the burst of plasma and crackling sparks around us.

I feel *everything*.

The sky and the stars and the distant planets spinning in the heavens.

I am vapor and breath.

Churning earth and rushing water.

I open my mouth, scream into the wind, and just let everything *go*.

A twist of emotion. Of sorrow. Of losing my best friend. My family.

Walking away from everything I've ever known.

I chose a different path, and now I'll have to find a new way to exist.

Maybe that starts today.

I look over at Rook, who's watching me with a grin on his face. Skies, he has a beautiful smile. It's not even the physical perfection; it's the way he smiles with his entire body, like he *understands* joy.

I wonder if everything I've ever believed is wrong.

Purple sparks dance through his hair and clothing. I reach out to grab one between my fingers, but he pulls me toward him, his arm banding around my waist.

My heart races as he breathes against my mouth.

"Rook," I whisper.

And then he kisses me, and I forget everything else.

51

His hands slip into my hair as he holds my head and tips it back. Purple sparks fizzle in the spaces around our skin, buzzing in the air, almost like they sense this thing swelling between us.

I try not to examine it too closely. I lose myself in the moment. In the warmth in my limbs and the heat in my stomach as our tongues slide together. He moans into my mouth, flattening himself against me, his hips guiding mine against the cold stone at my back and the feverish blanket of his body.

His hands slide lower, curving over my rib cage and my hips, while I slip my hands up the back of his shirt, exploring velvet skin stretched over valleys of bone and muscle.

He leans in to suck on the curve of my throat, and I tip my head, inviting him in. A small gasp escapes my lips when his leg presses between my thighs. He grabs my hips, fingers digging into flesh, generating a desperate sort of friction.

My stomach swirls, molten ribbons spiraling out as his fingers slip under my top, the fire of his fingertips pulling up gooseflesh over my skin.

We move together, hips churning and bodies flush. The swirl of my hips meets the breadth of his thigh, the heaviness beneath my navel tightening. I light up. I burn down. I become liquid.

It takes only a minute before I burst apart with a breathy moan, deep and bottomless like the shadowy reaches of some unnamed universe. I cling to him, and he devours me as the wind howls and amethyst light explodes across the sky. He sighs into the curve of my throat, collapsing against me, caging me between his arms, drowning me in his scent.

We come up for air, our gazes meeting in a hazy darkness illuminated by the storm. His expression is bright with fire and want. Brimming with a thousand words. Slowly, he peppers kisses to my shoulders and throat and finally meets my mouth before pulling away.

Another flash of Spark sears across the landscape, and we both look up as a few drops of rain begin to fall.

"We should get back," he says, pushing off me and taking my hand. "Before anyone notices we're gone."

I nod, though even that feels uncertain. Rook literally knocked the wind out of me, and I'm having a hard time catching my breath. He leans in, cupping my neck and consuming me again, fast and hard.

One last kiss stolen under an amethyst sky.

"We really need to go." He pulls me more insistently.

Then we head back, stumbling onto the subway like our limbs have given up. We find a spot near the window before the train hurtles us back to the heart of the city.

We're about halfway home when it stops at a busy station, passengers filtering in and out. To my right sits a market, still bustling with life despite the waning hour. I've always maintained a tepid fascination with the vast variety of wares available underground, though I haven't explored the markets much.

My gaze snags on a Hollow sitting against a pillar. It takes me a moment to process her face. It's the same woman I recognized months ago. The one who reminded me of my former nanny.

I lean closer, squinting through the glass. She takes a sip from a water bottle in her hand before wiping her mouth in a gesture that is so *familiar*.

She looks over, and our eyes meet with another flicker of recognition.

Suddenly, I'm moving. "Poet?" Rook asks. "Where are you going?"

I shove off the train, sensing Rook behind me as I push through the crowd. I lose sight of the woman as I'm jostled left and right, but I keep fighting against the tide.

After we emerge, I locate the pillar, but the woman is gone. I spin around and around, finding only a nondescript sea of people in every direction I look.

"Poet?" Rook asks. "What's going on?"

I shake my head. "I don't know. I thought I saw someone I recognize."

"Who?" he asks.

I exhale a breath, suddenly feeling silly. "I'm not sure," I say, understanding how unbelievable that sounds, but he doesn't press the matter.

"Okay," he says. "Do you want to keep looking?"

I take another glance at our surroundings and decide I imagined the entire thing. "No. We should get back."

"You're sure."

"Yeah, I was mistaken."

He nods reluctantly and leads me back to the platform, where we wait for the next train to arrive. We return to our room without being spotted and take turns changing in the bathroom. When Rook comes out, he's wearing only his pajama bottoms.

My cheeks flush as I think about our night. I have a feeling that's going to happen a lot.

He must be harboring similar thoughts because he gives me a warm look that sends shivers down my spine.

"Everything okay?" he asks, probably wondering why I'm just standing in the middle of the room.

"I was wondering . . ." I fiddle with the hem of my tank top. "If you wanted to sleep next to me tonight?"

Again, I can't fathom what possessed me to say that.

He smiles slowly as he approaches and places a finger under my chin. He searches my face, and I can't determine what I read in his expression. Does he regret what we did? Am I being too much?

"Never mind," I say, pulling away. "That was silly."

"No," he says, reaching down to lace my fingers with his. "It's not silly. It's just . . . I don't want to make any assumptions about what this is between us, but there are some things you should know about me before we get any closer."

My brows draw together. "Okay," I say. "So tell me. I want to know everything about you."

"Do you really?" he asks, something pointed in the question. "Because once you know, you can't unlearn certain things."

"This is very cryptic," I say as anger twists in my stomach and I release his hand. "If you don't want to 'get closer,' you don't have to make stuff up just to scare me."

"I'm *not*," he answers with so much sincerity that I find myself believing him. "You and I come from different worlds, Poet."

"I know that," I say, blinking up at him. "You think I don't know that?"

"There are so many things you don't understand about the Wastes, and I've had to do some things I'm not proud of to survive. I worry once you know, you won't look at me the way you are now."

"Whatever it is, I'll understand," I insist. "I would never judge someone for surviving."

He nods, though I'm not sure he's convinced.

"You can tell me," I say.

"Not yet," he answers. "But I *do* want to get closer."

"Even though I'm trouble?"

He smirks, leaning in, his big hand sliding into the curve of my lower back. "Even then. Your bed or mine?"

"Doesn't matter," I say with a shrug, trying for casual and failing. Taking my hand, he tugs me toward my corner and drops down onto my mattress. He scoots back, and then I slide in beside him.

He folds me into the circle of his arms, and I trace a tiny scar on his chest. I think about what he just said, wondering what he's endured living in a world so different from mine.

I want to find a way to earn his trust so he'll let me in and share all his secrets, no matter how ugly they are.

"Okay?" he asks, and I nod, snuggling into him.

"It's been so long since . . ." I swallow my words. I was about to say it's been so long since I felt connected to anyone, but I barely know Rook, and I can't say that out loud.

Still, I haven't experienced any real sort of affection outside of Trinity in a long time, and lying in Rooks's arms cracks open a fissure in my heart. Maybe it's the way he's been so kind, even though I don't deserve it. Maybe I'm desperate for any sort of acceptance.

Maybe he understands what I'm not saying, because his arms tighten around me before he kisses the top of my head and mumbles, "Get some sleep, Poet."

52

When my eyes peel open the following morning, the first thing I see is Rook, his hair tousled, his face soft. He lies on his back with one arm under me and a hand on his chest. My duvet hugs his hips, giving me an unobstructed view of his upper body, and I do my best not to linger. It works a little bit.

If anyone knew we'd slept in the same bed, they'd no doubt say the most awful things, but I'm having trouble caring. I also slept better than I have in months. Sunlight filters into the room, suggesting it's a rare sunny day and that we must've slept late. It's warm and cozy, and I really don't want to move, but my bladder has other ideas.

Carefully, I extricate myself from Rook's hold, trying not to wake him. When I come out of the bathroom a few minutes later, he's sitting on the edge of the bed with his elbows on his knees. He looks up, his gaze lingering over me in my sleep shorts and top. My cheeks heat at his perusal, but I have no desire to cover myself up.

"Good morning," he says, his voice raw and husky. "How did you sleep?"

"Really well," I say, and he smiles before he stands. He approaches, and I wonder if he'll kiss me. Skies, his lips are all I'll ever be able to think about again.

"Done in there?" he asks, pointing behind me.

"Yeah, of course," I say, moving out of the way.

"How's your arm feeling?" he asks as he brushes past, and I look down at the wrappings on my wrist. I circle it carefully.

"Better, I think."

He nods and then closes the door, leaving me on the other side. The water turns on, and I realize I'm loitering outside the bathroom like a weirdo. So I retrieve my phone, almost dropping it when I see a notification from my mother. My hands shake as I click over to my messages.

MOM: *Poet, please tell me these rumors about you and that . . . person aren't true.*

MOM: *I didn't think your father could be any angrier.*

MOM: *But it's like you're trying to destroy him.*

MOM: *You will cease all contact with this Solitude, or there will be consequences.*

MOM: *You KNOW what that monster did to your aunt.*

MOM: *What would Raine say?*

And that's it.

Nothing about what's happened. Nothing about the fact that someone threw me down a flight of stairs. Nothing asking after my well-being at all. Just this.

A scolding. An order.

From someone who abandoned me weeks ago.

I squeeze the device in my hand, anger swirling in my chest. Before I know what I'm doing, I'm calling her.

It rings, and I will her face to appear on the screen.

Of course, she doesn't answer. This wasn't an offer of communication. This was damage control. Another attempt to dominate every aspect of my life, even knowing they've washed their hands of me. How dare she use Raine to guilt me into ceasing contact with Rook?

"Everything okay?" Rook asks, pulling me out of a spiral. My phone is still ringing, the tinny sound filling the quiet room. I hit disconnect and shake my head.

"Just my mom," I say. "She finally contacted me."

"Yeah?" he asks, something hopeful lifting in his voice. He doesn't like my parents and thinks they're terrible people, but he understands why my relationship with them is important.

"Not to reconcile," I say, withholding the true contents of the message because I refuse to hurt Rook's feelings any further. "Just reminding me how disappointed they are."

His shoulders drop. "Oh. I'm sorry."

"It's okay. I don't know why I keep expecting something different."

Then I turn around and pretend to busy myself with my tablet because I can't bear to find any sort of pity in his eyes. A drawer opens and closes, and a soft rustle signals him dressing.

"Poet?" he asks, somewhat tentatively.

"Yes," I say, turning around.

"I've been thinking about last night. Remember in the tunnel, I thought I saw someone?"

"Yeah?"

"I'm just worried . . . What if someone was following us? They could find out where we're going . . ."

"Right," I say. "That would be bad. Do you really think you saw someone?"

"I can't be one hundred percent sure, but I think we need to be careful. With what happened to Lacey . . ."

"It was terrifying," I agree.

"To that end, we should probably avoid being seen together," he says. His tone is neutral, and his expression gives nothing away. Is this really a precaution, or is he trying to distance himself? We shared something in the heat of the moment last night, but here in the cold light of day, he is still a Solitude, and I'm still Society. We don't fit. We don't belong together.

"You think so?" I ask.

"I think we draw a lot of attention, especially when we're together."

"Yeah," I say, realizing that I might be drawing the eyes of the Extinguishers straight to *him*. "It's safer for you."

"Right." He nods. "For you, too, Poet."

I don't want to agree with him. But my mother's texts sit in my thoughts, reminding me this is probably for the best.

"Right," I echo. "Of course."

He stands from the bed, and I realize he's wearing a T-shirt and shorts.

"Where are you going?"

"To the gym."

"But we have the day off."

He sighs and rakes a hand through his hair, ruffling it to annoying perfection. "Yeah, I need to work off some . . . energy."

"Oh, right. Well, I'll see you later?" I can't keep the hopeful tone out of my voice. If we're distancing from each other, I should probably find somewhere else to sleep.

But I don't know where, and more importantly, I don't really want to.

His expression doesn't convey pity, but it definitely closes down any invitation to further communication. Okay, hint taken. I'm a danger to him and myself if we keep drawing attention to ourselves.

"Have a good workout," I say, and he nods before he leaves the room, closing the door behind him. I stare at it for a minute, mourning the brief bit of happiness I experienced last night.

I thought I'd made a new friend, but he, too, has walked away, leaving me on my own.

53

Rook remains true to his word, and over the next couple of weeks, we barely speak. He returns to our room late, often when I'm already asleep, and is gone when I wake up. I wonder where he spends all his time.

We eat on opposite sides of the cafeteria, where he sits alone, and I join Domino and Journey. For once, I'm thankful for Journey's stream of observations because I don't have to come up with anything to say.

Trinity and I exchange hellos as we pass each other, but that proposed hangout never materializes. She's still spending time with Brick, despite knowing what he did to me. It hurts, but I push it away, determined not to let it bother me.

My wrist heals, the bandages are removed, and I return to my full training routine. My fellow Aria members still aren't friendly, but they seem to have embraced begrudging tolerance.

And maybe what Henry claimed about Storm Guard loyalty before Society is partly true, as a few other cadets begin to soften, ever so slightly, toward me. One can only hold a pointless grudge—and I'm convinced it's entirely pointless—for so long while spending countless hours sweating, fighting, and growing in one another's company.

The artificial lines erected between us hold no real weight when held under scrutiny. It's not everything I hope for yet, but it feels like a future with Aria is possible.

Another week later, Domino, Journey, and I arrive to find out we're heading on a field trip to the Tempestade, where we'll witness Breakers in training and join in some of their drills. Everyone chatters excitedly until a chorus of pinging chimes draws everyone's attention to their devices.

An emergency news bulletin has arrived announcing that a dozen people were found murdered in the square outside the Citadel this morning. We all look up, staring in the direction of where it happened. Just steps away from where we stand.

The bulletin goes on to describe the bodies as violently disfigured and dismembered, and I cover my mouth as bile churns in the back of my throat. Our excited talk turns to horrified whispers as Henry and our other trainers confer in low voices. The article isn't naming suspects yet, but it assures us that The Shield is investigating the matter thoroughly. Everyone is asked to remain vigilant for any suspicious activity related to these deaths.

"Cadets!" Henry shouts over our heads. "I understand this is troubling news, but I think it's best we remain focused on our usual routine. If anything, this impresses upon us the need to ensure you're trained to the highest standard."

Everyone nods as we slowly shuffle out the doors, passing the plaza where lines of bright yellow tape have cordoned off the area. Several members of The Shield's Circle Guard move among lumps covered in white sheets.

The bodies.

I come to a stop, unable to tear my eyes away, imagining the horrors underneath.

A hand rests on the small of my back. "Don't look," Rook says in a low voice, and it's silly that I'm relieved he's talking to me at all. This is a horrible reason to break our silence. "Just keep walking."

I nod as I allow him to steer me toward a set of sliding glass doors, admitting us to a sprawling marble lobby decorated with golden-framed mirrors, creamy white statues, and a massive fresco painted on the ceiling. The entrance closes behind us, muffling the din of the city. The only sounds are the low murmurs of my classmates and the occasional squeak of footsteps in the distance.

A sharp rap of someone approaching draws us toward Dr. Eze, who's carrying her trusty tablet under her arm. She's also accompanied by another woman with auburn hair pulled into a tight bun. Her white skin is tinged pink, and her green eyes scan us without emotion.

"I'd like to introduce you to Dr. Cummings," Dr. Eze says cheerfully. "She's the lead scientist in charge of electromagnetism here at the Tempestade. Her job is to create the most realistic version of Spark bursts for training, and she's been instrumental in the project to capture actual galvanic energy to be used in our simulations."

Dr. Cummings gives us a curt nod. "I thought you'd like to witness a real simulation today," she says. "And get a look at our training facilities. They're quite good at the academy, but there's no comparison with the real thing."

We're told a few more tidbits about what to expect, and then we're escorted through the Tempestade. First, we pass a lab where several Breakers are in the middle of electrodesensitization training. "Even after years in the Storm Guard, our members must continually maintain their resistance to the electricity they're subjected to almost daily. One problem we've been trying to solve for a long time is the regression that occurs when the body is no longer exposed to therapy. Though it slowly adapts to the foreign intrusion, it quickly returns to its natural state."

We continue walking, passing through the gym, where dozens of extremely fit people are lifting what seem like impossible weights. Finally, we pass a set of wide steel doors with about half a dozen keypads along each side.

"What's that?" someone asks, and Dr. Cummings pauses.

"That is where the Extinguishers bring potential Spark Keepers for testing and sequestering," she says. "Beyond those doors are some of the most dangerous people in New Manhattan."

"Are we going in?" a guy asks, his voice filled with hope, while several people side-eye him with incredulous looks.

Dr. Cummings's expression is withering. "Absolutely not. That area is highly classified and secured. Permanently above your pay grade."

My palms begin to sweat as I stare at the door, and my gaze meets Rook's. We've still never found out what happened to Lacey Turner. Rumors persist about her disappearance, but for all intents, she was simply erased from existence. Winter seems to have moved on, or maybe she's just putting on a brave face. We aren't supposed to mourn the loss of the infected, and her grief would only have been tolerated for so long.

Rook runs a hand through his hair, probably having similar thoughts, and exhales a long breath before we're once again on the move.

Over the next hour, we're shown the sleeping quarters, the cafeteria, and the other common areas where Storm Guards can relax when off duty, stirring up the excitement of everything I've been wishing for. The Storm Guard. *This* is why I chose Aria.

We finally enter another giant lobby decorated much like the first, with soaring pillars stretching overhead, a massive trickling fountain, and a set of heavy iron gates at the far end.

Dr. Cummings turns to address us. "This is the entrance to The Shield's information and security wing," she says. "Intelligence about the city, communications, and the movement of outside threats are all sent here to be analyzed and discussed with our leaders. They spend much of their time here, meeting with House scions and working with their teams to neutralize possible attacks."

"Do they know what happened with the people who died last night?" someone asks, raising a hand.

Dr. Cummings shakes her head. "The matter is still under investigation. More than likely, it was either an internal threat or someone breached our perimeter and Solitudes entered the city."

"I heard it was someone infected," another person says. "The bodies were all torn up."

My stomach drops as everyone shifts uncomfortably where they stand.

It's been a long time since there was a public incident involving a feral Keeper. This is bad. It'll put everyone on alert.

Dr. Cummings arches a brow, her mouth pinching into a frown. "It's possible. Keeper murders are very specific, and the bodies will be closely examined for evidence."

Her answer tightens the knot in my chest.

Another set of sliding glass doors opens, admitting to the lobby an older man with dark-brown skin and gray hair. I recognize him as another scion: House Asale. He's been to some of my parents' parties.

He tosses us a quick nod, then approaches a security scanner, swipes a red key card across the panel, and the gates swing open. He enters and disappears around a corner.

Dr. Cummings orders us to keep walking, and we finish the tour to find ourselves inside a glass booth overlooking a simulation room. It's at least three times the size of the one we have at Amery, accurately mimicking a smaller version of New Manhattan. Standing in a circle at one end are about a dozen Storm Guards wearing their black tactical gear and goggles. Instead of their usual shiny purple harnesses, they're wearing fitted purple vests that mold to their chiseled forms.

"We're about to witness a demonstration," Dr. Cummings says. "We've been experimenting with a new material that helps neutralize storm charges. Lab tests have been promising, but we've yet to try it out in the field. Our Guards are wearing the prototypes, and we've gathered some of the energy from last night's storm to use."

Dr. Cummings turns a few knobs and pushes some buttons on the console stretching before us. A timer starts counting toward the simulation, and the Guards spring into action.

"Their goal is to rescue the group in the middle," Dr. Cummings says, gesturing to a screen off to our right. The camera reveals three Hollows, all huddled together in the center of the arena.

Immediately, that same nauseous feeling twists in my gut.

The Storm Breakers are on the move, darting in between buildings and obstacles.

They flow like water, dodging a blitz of strikes raining from above. Their pace is much faster, movements more aggressive. They're mesmerizing to watch, almost like dancers. I feel Rook move beside me as he studies the Breakers weaving in and out.

"Where did you come up with the design?" Rook asks Dr. Cummings. "For the vests and for collecting the charge?"

She blinks, clearly taken aback. "You're the Solitude," she says. It isn't a question, but there's plenty of heavy implication in her tone. Rook doesn't answer, simply stares at her, all confidence and self-assurance. How does he do that?

"Through many iterations and years of testing," she finally says. "General Sol helped develop the earliest prototypes. They were useless at first, but over time, we managed to perfect them to what you see before you."

Almost as if the energy hears her, one of the Guards is struck, and we all gasp as she flies through the air and a plasma arc flares around her before fading away. It takes me a moment to realize the Breaker hasn't been blitzed. I watch in fascination as she glitters with the remnants of purple Spark, which must be an effect of the vest. Then she rolls over onto her back, staring up at the ceiling. She doesn't move, but she isn't dead, and she definitely isn't a husk of ash.

It's becoming clearer to me that while I thought I'd be relatively safe training to be a Breaker, their technology is advancing at a rate that could put me at a greater risk. I wonder how often they've started training with real Spark instead of the simulated version we use at school. I might need a plan if I continue on this path . . . or I might need to give this dream up.

The thought sits heavy in my chest.

Dr. Cummings flicks on a microphone and orders the medical team to remove her, but she wears a pleased smile. "This is very good," she says almost to herself.

"So everyone could have one?" Rook asks. "No one would have to fear the storms again?"

Dr. Cummings shrugs. "Perhaps in time, but they're incredibly costly to make and require materials that are difficult to obtain. The priority will be Breakers and other people of importance first."

She returns to the simulation, and again, I'm struck by how the Breakers move so seamlessly over the terrain. It takes about a quarter of an hour for two of them to near the center of the arena. I find myself gripped by the scene as my gaze darts between the Breakers and the huddling Hollows on the screen.

Spark hasn't breached their circle yet, but a charge spears down and hits the ground a foot away, exploding up, leaving behind a charred ring. The Hollows' mouths open in a scream before they leap for cover. That's when a Breaker emerges between the buildings, shouting orders for them to run.

Dr. Cummings leans forward and reaches for a knob, cranking up the barrage of bursts. More jagged bolts fall from the ceiling, gathering into a potent strike. It hits the Breaker and then the Hollows. Everyone flies several feet.

I squeak out a shocked gasp as we all wait with our hearts in our throats.

It takes a minute for the dust to clear, revealing a coughing Breaker clutching his chest and three blitzed Hollows.

The Breaker struggles to his feet, hacking, struggling to breathe. But he's alive.

The Hollows, however . . .

They're nothing but ash and smoke, their bodies charred to husks.

I cover my mouth, horrified.

"Excellent," Dr. Cummings says with a definitive nod. "Excellent."

54

Once Dr. Cummings ends the simulation, we're invited to the arena floor, where we walk around, exploring its nooks and crannies. The Breakers answer some questions about what it's like to work on the Storm Towers, and then we do a series of drills.

But I can't focus or concentrate. I can't stop seeing the blitzed Hollows, nor the easy cruelty with which they were treated.

Dr. Eze pulls me aside. "Are you okay, Poet?" she asks, and I shake my head.

"I'm not feeling well," I say. It's not a complete lie, but I'm almost positive she isn't taking my answer the way I intended.

"Why don't you just have a seat, then?" she says, steering me to a quiet corner. "We're almost done here anyway." She sits me down and then crouches before me. "I've been meaning to talk to you," she says. "I'd like for you to come to my lab for some extra testing."

My head snaps up. "Why?"

She shakes her head. "Just some anomalies I noticed. I'd like to check things again."

"Anomalies?"

Does she know about me? Can she tell what I am?

Her smile softens before she glances left and right, but we're alone. "Don't worry, Poet. You're safe with me." She winks and pats my hand, and my brow furrows because I think she's trying to tell me something.

Before I can ask, she stands and walks away. I watch her before I lean forward and stare at the floor between my feet. By the time we leave, I've managed to pull myself together at least on the outside, but inside, I'm a twisted knot of confused emotions.

"You all right?" Domino asks, looping her arm through mine while Journey walks on my other side.

"Yeah, just dizzy," I say. I look for signs they feel the same. I see it in the tightness around their mouths and the blank look in their eyes. But I understand none of us are *supposed* to feel this way. By the tenets of New Manhattan, those people should have been honored to give up their lives for this worthy exercise.

Even Journey is quiet, which tells me a lot.

"Hey, we were planning to go to Sogno tonight," Domino eventually says. "You should come."

"I don't know," I say. Apart from avoiding everyone, I'm not sure I'm in the mood. Besides, I was still hoping I'd go with Trinity. But she also hasn't been answering my texts or requests to meet up, so maybe I'm feeling a little defiant.

"Come on," Domino says. "We can dance, have a few drinks, loosen up."

She gives me a meaningful look. We can try to forget what we just saw. Maybe she's right and it's exactly what I need.

"Maybe," I say, and she does a happy bounce.

"Say yes," she insists, and I look over at Journey, who nods.

"Fine, that sounds fun."

"Yay!" Domino says, and we start walking a bit faster, our moods already lighter.

"I just wish I had something new to wear," Journey says as we enter the school, gesturing down at herself. "I've worn the same outfit three times now."

"Oh, I can help you with that," I say, dragging them down a hall and toward my room.

. . .

A few hours later, it looks like a sparkle bomb exploded on the floor. Shiny fabrics lie everywhere in haphazard piles, and I think Domino and Journey tried on every single outfit I own before they both settled on something for Sogno. We've had such a good time that I'm even more thankful the vandals who destroyed my room were focused on my uniforms, not my fun clothes.

Journey opted for a cute pink satin dress with thin straps and a skirt that skims the tops of her thighs. She's currently seated on one of the empty beds, doing her makeup.

Domino chose a burgundy sequined dress that falls to her knees with a long slit up to her hip. The neckline plunges low, nearly to her navel, and she's tied up her hair in a high knot to show off the back, which is draped with gold chains.

"You look stunning," I say, handing over a pair of gold stilettos that should fit her. "Try it with these."

She steps into the shoes and does a little twirl in the mirror. "We can't thank you enough," she says, admiring her butt before she bursts into giggles.

"It's no problem. Seriously, any time. My closet is yours."

"You're going to regret saying that," Journey promises from across the room, where she's lining her lips in hot pink. I grin.

I hop up from the bed before heading into the bathroom to change. Despite everything, I feel lighter than I have in a while. I *should* go out and have some fun. Everything's been so heavy for the past six months, and this is what I need.

I exit the bathroom to a cloud of powder and perfume and Journey and Domino laughing. I watch the scene for a moment with a kind of wistful longing. These aren't the friends I expected to find, but I appreciate them more than they know.

I sit down next to Journey and start applying my makeup when the door opens, and Rook enters. He freezes as he takes in the mess, his gaze sliding over discarded heaps of clothing. We were sure to leave his corner of the room completely untouched.

"Hi," I say, sitting up straighter.

His eyes widen. "Hey," he says. "I didn't know. I thought . . ."

"We're leaving," I say. "You can have the room to yourself. Right, girls?"

"Yup," Domino says with an eager nod, snapping her compact shut. "We're all done. Sorry about the mess."

She grabs the evening bag she borrowed and gestures for Journey to follow.

"I'll meet you upstairs in a minute," I say, and they nod before closing the door. I immediately bend down and start gathering my clothes into armfuls.

"I'm sorry," I say. "I'll clean this up."

"Poet," Rook says. His voice comes out raspy, and it makes me look over. "It's fine. You're allowed to exist in this space."

My shoulders drop, throat knotting at the fierce sincerity in his tone. "Okay. I'll finish it tomorrow, if that's all right?"

"It's definitely all right."

I drop the pile on one of the empty beds, and I hear his breath hitch. I turn to find him watching me with his jaw a little slack.

I'm wearing a sleeveless, sparkly black romper with shorts that stop right below my butt. My hair is tied into a ponytail to expose the opening that plunges to my lower back. The outfit is completed with tall black boots, some gold hoops, and a bit of makeup.

"You look . . ." he says, rubbing his chin. "Fuck, you look amazing."

The compliment warms me from the inside out, making my stomach dip.

"You could come with us?" I ask, trying to keep the hope out of my voice. I miss talking to him. I miss being in his presence.

He shakes his head. "No thanks."

"You sure? You'd be welcome. It'll be fun."

He pauses, his gaze tracing over the line of my exposed thigh up past my hips and shoulders encased in glittering black velvet. A breath expels from his chest that feels like an earthquake.

He seems to consider my request. Pick it up, examine it, and then . . . he discards it with another shake of his head. "I don't think so, but thank you."

"Okay," I say, trying not to wear my disappointment like a neon sign.

"Maybe we could hit the gym tomorrow?" he asks, and I return a tentative smile. It's not much, but it's a tiny little glimmer of hope. But maybe he's just being nice.

"I'd love that."

"Okay, see you tomorrow. Have fun tonight."

"Thanks." I cross the room and find my purse, stuffing it with my lipstick and a few other items. The entire time, I *think* I can feel him trying not to watch me. If I bend over to give him an extra-good view of my butt in these shorty shorts, then it's totally an accident.

I stand up and peer over my shoulder. He flinches and looks away.

He was definitely staring. My triumph knows no bounds.

"Sorry," he mumbles and rubs his face.

"See you later," I say with a wave.

"Have fun," he says again.

I close the door behind me and lean against it, grinning so hard, my cheeks ache.

55

I hop off our gondola where it's stopped outside Sogno with Domino and Journey in tow. Music pumps from the building, and dozens of people mill around, waiting for friends, talking, and downing sips from passed-around bottles before they head inside.

The building rises three stories, with large rectangular windows fronted by wide sweeping balconies filled with dancing people. The white marble exterior is ornately carved with flowers, vines, and leaves, while lights flash inside, illuminating the night with bursts of transparent color.

We run up to the bouncer, who gives us a once-over before waving us in.

The decor evokes the sensation of dreaming, with sleek white floors, walls, and fluffy white clouds suspended from the ceiling. People wearing white underwear and translucent gossamer scraps sport feathered wings and weave through the crowd with crystal drink trays propped on their hands.

At the far end of the room is a giant mirror, bordered by more carved marble and covered in dozens of glass shelves, holding a hundred different types of jewel-toned liquors. The long crystal bar stretches across the room, where a line of muscled, half-naked men mix drinks.

Domino squeezes my arm and squeals with delight; her excitement is infectious. This is exactly what I needed—no more hiding and moping in my room. The point of going to Amery was to enjoy being young before the responsibilities of adulthood weighed us down.

"Drinks first!" Journey announces, taking my hand and dragging me into the crowd. Domino grasps my other side, and we weave through the gaps, approaching the bar. A cute bartender spies us and winks as he approaches.

"What will it be, ladies?" he asks, flashing us a bright grin.

"Something yummy!" Journey announces, and he nods before he begins picking up various bottles and dumping ingredients into a golden shaker. We all enjoy the view of his shirtless torso as his muscles bunch and contract while he moves.

When he's done, he pours three pale pink cocktails into cut glass tumblers and garnishes each with a puff of cotton candy. "A Sweet Dream," he says, passing the drinks over.

We toast and take a sip. It's sweet and light, and I can already tell I could drink a lot of these before I feel the effects. But I don't care. I'm tired of being responsible and worried about everything, and I want to let go for one night.

"Time to dance!" I shout, and we head for the floor, where we lose ourselves in the sea of people. Over the next hour, we spend our time singing to the music and swaying with the crowd.

At some point, I spot Knox with Jackson and Sal, along with Winter and some other members of their friend group. Knox and I haven't spoken in months, not since the night of the pledging ceremony, when my parents publicly dropped me from their lives.

He stands with an elbow on the bar, drinking a beer, a scowl on his face. Winter is next to him, looking uncertain and obviously trying to draw him into conversation. He scans the crowd, and I feel the moment he spots me. Our eyes meet, and it's like I've just been shoved against a hard corner.

Suddenly, I don't feel very well.

"I'm going to the bathroom," I shout to Domino, who nods. Then I turn in the opposite direction of Knox, weaving toward a hallway. I enter the bathroom to a haze of perfume and conversation, where a dozen girls sit on the plush settees while touching up their makeup and hair.

I head to a sink and inspect my face before wetting a towel and pressing it to my reddened cheeks. Then I find an empty spot and sit, trying to shake off the remnants of Knox's presence. I hate that he affects me at all. I want to be free of this. Don a cloak of indifference and shield myself from every moment of hurt he caused.

Maybe someday I'll get there.

When I've stopped shaking and cooled down a few degrees, I decide the night is young and Knox isn't ruining my fun.

Unfortunately, when I open the door, he's waiting in the hall.

I wordlessly study him as he unfolds himself from where he's leaning.

"Hey, can we talk?" he asks, gesturing to a room with low tables and couches. When I hesitate, he adds, "Just for a minute. Please."

I don't want to go anywhere with him, but if I don't, he'll probably just bother me until I agree. So I nod and follow him into the quieter space. The floor vibrates with thumping music, but we can talk without having to shout.

We find a table and settle side by side on a white couch that runs along the wall. A waitress appears, and I order another drink, because something tells me I'll need one for this conversation. In fact, I consider ordering two.

When she leaves, I turn to study Knox's profile. He's staring at the room with one arm slung over the bench and his jaw tight.

"So?" I ask, hoping to get this over with. "What's up?"

He glances at me. "How are you doing?"

I shrug and shake my head. "I'm okay. It's been rough, but I'm managing."

His eyes flick over me before he returns to surveying the room.

"Knox, is there something you want? I really need to get back to my friends."

"Your friends?" he asks. "Do you have friends in Aria?"

His tone isn't pointed but rather curious, yet I bristle at the question regardless. "I do."

"Cogs," he says, somewhat dismissively.

"Aria Society members," I say. "They've pledged. They're one of us now."

He sighs and slouches on the couch, his hips sliding forward. "Whatever."

Again, he remains silent, and this is starting to become annoying. The waitress arrives with our drinks, and I pick mine up and take a sip. "Okay, well, if that's it, then I'm gonna get going."

"Do you miss me?" he asks suddenly. "Do you miss what we had at all?"

The question stops me in my tracks. I study his face. He can't be serious. But he holds still, clearly waiting for an answer. "What did we have, Knox? An agreement on paper? Me as your little trophy wife while you fucked around?"

His face darkens. "I . . ."

"Why did you do it?" I ask. "Why did you insist on humiliating me?"

"I don't know," he answers as a wounded look passes over his face. "I don't know why I did it."

It's such a painfully inadequate answer, but I think he's telling the truth in his own pathetic way. He doesn't understand himself, either.

"Okay, well, as long as you have no idea why you decided to hurt me over and over. No, I don't miss you or what we had. We didn't have anything to miss."

Again, I try to leave, but he stops me, wrapping a hand around my wrist. His touch is like oil, coating me in sludge. "Touch me again, and I'll scream," I say. Quickly, he releases me. "What's going on? Winter not living up to your expectations?"

"I don't want Winter," he says. "I never wanted Winter."

I scoff. "Not to marry, you mean. But to fuck while you were engaged to me. Then you wanted her, right?"

He has the grace to look guilty, at least.

"I'm sorry," he says. "I fucked everything up. It was all so much pressure."

"What pressure?"

"My dad's expectations of me. The way he assumes I'll be just like him, but I'm not like him at all." He shakes his head. "Fuck. I don't even know what I'm saying." Then he adds, "He's replacing me."

"What?" I ask.

"Your dad found someone else to groom as the future scion of Fiama. And my dad agreed it's for the best. Said after everything that happened with us, I haven't proven my character or some bullshit like that."

"What about their alliance?"

"Still intact," Knox says. "They're stronger than ever. It just no longer has anything to do with me."

"Oh," I say.

He looks away, staring at a distant spot. I sigh and shake my head.

"I understand he expected a lot from you," I say. "My dad expected a lot from me, too."

Knox looks over, studying me. "I know."

"None of it gave you the right to treat me that way."

"I know that, too," he says, then adds, "I think I did it because I never would have been good enough for you, Poet."

He sits forward, sighing in obvious frustration. I'm stunned, frozen in my seat as I wait for him to continue. "I loved . . . I love you. I always have, but you're so damn perfect. You think I didn't know you could do better than me? The only reason you were stuck with me was because of our fathers, and I was just . . ."

He trails off, and I have no idea how to react.

"You were just what?"

He shrugs, though the movement feels forced. "Just a consolation prize, I guess. You had to settle."

"And?" I ask. "You decided to treat me like shit for that?"

"I know it's fucked up, but I thought I'd keep the upper hand. That I could convince you I was too good for you instead."

I exhale a breath of disbelief. "Oh, that's great, Knox."

"It didn't work," he says, somewhat miserably, and I take a long drink from my glass, hoping the alcohol will burn away this memory forever. I'll need a swimming pool full of this shit at this rate. "You're still too good for me, but I *still* love you, Poet, and I can't help but wonder if there's any way you can forgive me."

I take another pull of my cocktail and wipe my mouth with the back of my hand, smearing it with pink lipstick. "You're absolutely right. I am too good for you." I stand up, clutching my glass. "You have no idea what love actually is, Knox. And I can't believe you have the *nerve* to sit there and ask for forgiveness after everything you put me through."

He holds up his hands. "Please, what can I—"

I don't let him finish, merely upend the rest of my drink onto his head. He jumps as ice, booze, and sticky strawberry juice drip down his face. "What the hell, Poet?"

"There is nothing you can do," I say through clenched teeth. "Not one single thing you could ever say or do to make up for how much you've hurt me."

I glare as he wipes his face, taking one last look before I turn and walk away.

Entering the dance floor, I press a hand to my chest, willing my racing heart to settle. Domino spots me, and I shake it off. I don't want to talk about it, so I plaster a smile on my face.

I hold up a finger, telling her I'll be there in a moment, then head for the bar, where I order some water before joining my friends and losing myself in the lights and noise for the next several hours.

56

Throughout the night, Domino, Journey, and I alternate between dancing together as a group and with more than one cute face.

Domino is getting cozier with Calloway, the guy she's been crushing on for a while, and Journey has been spending more time than not dancing with a girl from House Tera whose name I don't know yet.

Eventually, I start dancing next to a guy from Aria who's also a Storm Guard cadet. Riley is tall with wide shoulders and a tapered waist. Dark-brown hair curls around his ears and is streaked with pops of lilac at his temples.

He's handsome, and I'm sure those adorable dimples and that easy smile melt the knees of plenty of others. Not me, though. I'm here for the music and the freedom.

The good news is that the pounding, thumping music has the intended effect of taking my mind off what happened at the Tempestade and the conversation with Knox. I haven't seen him since, and I hope that means he left and, more importantly, took the hint never to bother me again.

I don't believe that he really loved me. I think he loved the idea of what we could have been. The scion of Fiama and his docile wife attending parties and reveling in the perks of our positions.

Even if Knox had been faithful. Even if I still felt anything for him, I would never have wanted any of that.

I'm spinning and moving my hips, but I'm also lost in my thoughts.

"You okay?" Riley asks, leaning down to shout in my ear.

"Sure, but why are you talking to me?" I ask, raising my voice. "You're supposed to shun me, remember?"

He gives me a warm smile and shouts back, "I happen to think you're kind of cute."

I snort. It's not a very dignified sound.

"And that's enough?" I ask.

He shrugs and then grins. "It's a start."

I giggle. Then throw my head back and laugh. It's definitely not that funny. It might even be a little bit offensive, but everything is hilarious right now. Pouring that drink on Knox set something free. A heavy weight I've been carrying over my head.

I smile and twirl, hands raised, again and again until I get a little dizzy. I stumble, and Riley reaches for me, trying to help, but he misses, and my ankle bends.

Suddenly, I'm on the floor, but I'm still laughing.

"You all right?" Riley asks, bending down and holding out a hand.

Suddenly, a different pair of hands shoves into my armpits from behind and lifts me like I weigh nothing. I look past my shoulder and peer up to find Rook's green-and-gold eyes.

"Hi," I whisper, completely thrown off by his arrival as something sparkly fizzes in my chest. What is he doing here?

I flip myself around so I'm pressed against him with his hands loosely on my hips.

Lifting my fingers, I rub the stubble on Rook's jaw, making sure he's real and not a figment of my imagination.

"Hey." I hear Riley over my head. "We were dancing."

"So you're the one who let her fall?" he demands. He sounds kind of angry. It's sort of hot.

"She tripped!"

Riley must say something else because Rook growls. It vibrates through my chest and does something funny to my stomach. His arms tighten around me, and I nuzzle into him, warm and safe.

"Get out of here," I hear him say to Riley, and he must clear out because suddenly Rook is peering down at me, and it's like we're the only two people left in the room.

"We weren't really dancing," I say. "Now that I think about it, I was wishing I was dancing with someone else."

"Yeah? Who?"

The look he's giving me tells me he knows it was him.

But I don't give him the satisfaction of answering.

"Why are you here?" I ask, and he shakes his head.

"Honestly? I have no idea." He tucks a piece of loose hair behind my ear. "The room was lonely without you."

My face stretches into a smile as my heart grows heavy with the weight of some emotion I can't name.

"So, dance with me," I say.

"I'm not really a dancer," he answers, uncertainty crossing over his expression.

"I don't believe that for a moment. Not with the way you move on the sparring mats."

The corner of his mouth kicks up.

I take his hands and give him a little shake. "Come on! I know you want to."

"How much have you had to drink?" he asks. "You just fell."

"You're so responsible," I coo. "I just got dizzy, that's all. I've had one drink." I pause. "And a sip," I add, thinking of the cocktail I dumped on Knox's head. "I promise I'm fine."

I start moving, swiveling my hips as he watches me with a hungry look in his eyes. Slowly, I turn around, my arms lifted, and then his hands close around my waist.

But I catch his wrists. "Wait, you didn't want to be seen with me, right? You were worried about attracting *attention*."

His jaw hardens, and his gaze flicks across the room before he looks back at me. "I *did* say that."

"Hmm, too bad," I say, then I turn to walk away. A moment later, I feel him behind me as he wraps an arm around my midsection.

"I changed my mind," he whispers in my ear.

"So, you do dance?"

"For you, I'll make an exception."

My face spreads into a wide grin as I spin and throw my arms around his neck.

"What did I tell you?" he says, still whispering into my ear, his warm breath pulling up shivers across my skin. "Nothing but trouble."

I laugh and then lean against him as we move together.

"But we *should* get another drink!" I shout over the music, and he nods before following me to the bar.

With cocktails in hand, we return to dancing, our hips circling together as we lose ourselves in the music and the lights. I know Rook was worried, but everyone is too lost in their own fun, and no one is paying us any attention.

One song ends and another begins, this one pulsing with low, long beats that bring to mind heaving breaths and stolen moments in the dark.

Rook's eyes blaze, green and gold melting together as he snakes a hand behind my head and drags me closer. Our mouths hover inches apart.

"I'm going to kiss you," he says, then waits for me to nod before he presses his mouth to mine, his lips hot, his tongue searching. My limbs are soft, and my heart flutters wildly in my chest. He's warm and hard, and his scent is addictive.

We dance for what feels like hours, his hands on my hips, sliding up my back, his mouth on mine. We drink. We laugh. And I want it to last forever.

The beat slows, dragging us once again together as my head tips against his chest. We've both had several drinks, and I'm starting to feel a little woozy.

I can sense his body soften, curling against me, easing into our warm cocoon.

"I'm sorry I'm a bit of a mess," I say. A dizzy spell hits, and I canter to the left. But Rook catches me before I have a chance to go far.

"You're beautiful," he answers, burrowing a line of sunshine through my chest. My hands grip his biceps as my eyes flutter, and I hum a happy tune. *This* is what I needed. This was what I wanted tonight.

With my cheek pressed to Rook's shoulder, my eyes slowly open, and then I catch a glimpse of Trinity standing at the edge of the crowd. She's with her E-squad, and she's watching us, her gaze darting between Rook and me, her lip curled in distaste.

My head snaps up.

She came here without me.

And her obvious judgment twists through my chest.

Suddenly, I don't want to be here anymore.

"I need to go," I say.

"What?" Rook asks as I push off him and start shoving through the crowd.

"Poet?" Trinity asks as I stumble past. "Where are you going?"

The dancing, intoxicated mass presses in around me as I jostle my way through.

"Move!" I shout before bursting through the edge and stumbling out the door to a blast of cold night air. I grab a railing for balance, inhaling deeply.

I make it to the bottom of the steps, nearly tumbling in my haste.

"Poet, what's wrong?" Rook asks as he catches up.

I exhale a soft breath as my forehead tips against his chest.

He doesn't say anything as I breathe against him, waiting for my pulse to slow. His arms slide around me, and I sag, seeking comfort in his strength. Suddenly, I'm exhausted.

"I think you've had enough. We should get you home."

I nod. "I need to tell Dom and Journey."

I feel him maneuver me toward the building. He presses me to the wall and speaks to the bouncer. "Watch her for a moment, will you?"

Then he's gone for what feels like only a second before he leads me to a waiting gondola. He helps me into the boat before the driver pushes off.

"Sit," he says, and I shiver as I wrap my arms around myself. A moment later, he drapes his jacket over my shoulders, and I shrug into the leather, still warm from his body. His arm comes next, and I lean into him as we float through the city.

I peer up at the net of stars hanging in an unusually clear sky.

"Can you see Andromeda?" I ask him. "You said it's your favorite, right?"

I get a half smile, and he points out the cluster of stars that apparently make up the constellation. They blur before my eyes, and I can't make out much of anything, but I appreciate him sharing this with me anyway. I rest my head on his shoulder as my eyes open and close.

"She just abandoned me," I whisper after a moment. "I thought we were best friends. Why? All so she can hang out with those monsters?"

His hand lands on my knee, giving it a reassuring squeeze.

"I'm not sure," he says. "Sometimes people grow apart."

I shake my head against his shoulder. "She's one of them, Rook. Even if she wanted me around, how can I get past that?"

"I don't know," he answers, and we both float silently for a moment.

"Did you have fun tonight?" he asks.

I offer him a smile. "Of course. I did with Dom and Journey. And then you showed up."

Something passes over his expression, and I swear his cheeks turn a little pink.

"I had fun, too," he says.

I blink up at him. "When did you arrive?"

He shrugs. "Right before I found you."

"Hmm," I say as I snuggle in closer and we drift through the quiet city, bathed in a glow of lights. "I'm glad you came. Even if I'm trouble."

He chuckles softly, his lips pressing to the top of my head.

We reach Amery, and he helps me out of the boat and down to our room. After he closes the door, he sits me on the bed and kneels, taking off my boots.

"This is nice," I say dreamily as he peers up.

"I'm glad you think so, because you're going to feel like hell tomorrow."

I giggle because even though he's right, his serious tone is making me laugh. I'm rewarded with a ghost of a smile as he tugs down on my boot's zipper.

When he's finished, he places his hands on the bed on either side of my hips. "Are you really okay?" he asks. "I saw that asshole talking to you."

"Riley? Was that his name? He wasn't so bad."

"No. Your . . . former betrothed."

"Oh." I tip my head and cup his cheek with my hand. "Aw, are you jealous? You sounded so mad just there. Even more than usual, I mean."

His eyes darken. "I'm not jealous."

He stands up and tugs the covers back before laying me down and lifting my legs.

"Stay with me," I say, reaching up.

He leans over me, studying my face.

"You should sleep," he says. "You're a little wasted."

"I really am," I agree. This time, he actually laughs. "I love it when you laugh," I say, again touching his face. "It's so rare. Like precious jewels or something. You have such a great smile."

"So do you, Trouble." He leans over and presses his lips to my forehead, and my eyes slide closed again. I'm so tired that I'm drifting away.

"I wanted to get drunk," I mumble.

"Why?"

"Because of what they did. To the Hollows. I wanted to forget, but I can't forget."

"The simulation," he says. My hair rustles against the pillow as I nod.

"Why do they do it? Why be so cruel? What's the point? What does it prove?"

My words drift off, and Rook is silent for so long that I think he won't answer.

Or maybe I've fallen asleep.

Then I feel his lips against my forehead. Softly, he says, "I think sometimes... the cruelty is the only point."

57

The next day is rough.

I'm not sure how long I sleep before my crusted eyes peel open, and I immediately bolt for the toilet. When I return, I notice someone has left me a glass of water and a bottle of painkillers on the nightstand. My gaze travels to Rook sleeping peacefully in his bed, one arm thrown up over his head and the other resting on his bare stomach.

I attempt to piece together the events of last night, but I'm almost positive I'm still drunk. Skies, going out to party seemed like such a great idea twelve hours ago.

I take some pills and drink the entire glass of water before I disappear under my blanket. For the rest of the morning, I alternate between my bed and kneeling on the bathroom floor, wishing I could die.

Around midday, Rook arrives with some plain toast, fruit, and coffee. I sit up and accept the mug, taking a long sip. It instantly makes me feel more human.

"Thank you," I moan. "Why are *you* so perky? You were drinking, too."

"Clearly, I can handle it better," he answers with a wink.

"Well, you've been way too good to me this morning."

"Stop that," he says somewhat tersely as he pulls up my desk chair and sits. "You needed to blow off some steam. We've all been there. You deserve to be cared for."

His voice softens at the end, and his earnestness is so sincere that I almost believe him.

"I appreciate it," I say.

He nods and rests his elbows on his knees. "Now that you're feeling better, there's something you need to see."

"What?" He hands me his phone, open to a news bulletin.

"There were more murders last night."

I scan the article. Two dozen people this time, found in the middle of a market square.

"They're saying it was a Spark Keeper?" I ask. "I thought it was Solitudes?"

"Yeah." He presses his mouth together. "But the bodies resemble those who died at the hands of Keepers. There's no reason Solitudes would kill with such reckless violence. Only a tortured mind would be capable of such brutality."

I scan the article. Scion Beaufort is quoted as saying Extinguisher patrols will be doubled as they ramp up their efforts to root out more of the infected in light of these deaths.

"What's this?" I ask, noting where she hints that they also have a new tool at their disposal. "What is she talking about?"

His gaze holds mine. "I have no idea, but it doesn't sound good."

"It sounds dangerous," I answer, handing the phone back and exhaling a sound of frustration. "Are we monsters, Rook? Should we be turning ourselves in? What if we kill someone?"

He considers me. "Do you think you're a monster, Poet? Do you think I am?"

I exhale a sharp breath. "That's all I've ever been told," I say. "That I'm a danger. A problem to be dealt with."

He says nothing, giving me space to continue.

"But they lied about you."

His brow arches, and he sits straighter.

"Maybe they lied about this, too." I read the article again. "They should be *helping* people like us, not hunting us down."

"I know," he answers, and I look up. It feels like there's something else he isn't saying, but we're both silent for a moment.

"Do you ever *feel* like you're losing your mind?" I ask carefully.

He inhales and considers the question. "Sometimes after I've touched Spark, my mind feels stretched. Porous. Like it's not fully intact, but just for a little while."

"Same," I say.

"But the last two times, when we were together, it didn't happen. Something was different."

I nod because it's been the same for me. He gives me a look I can't interpret. All I know is I'm scared.

Skies, I'm so tired of being scared all the time.

Fuck the Extinguishers. Fuck The Shield for doing this to us.

"We need to be careful," Rook says. "If they suspect either of us . . ."

Our eyes meet. If either one of us is caught, we're dead.

"Could your father protect you? He's a powerful man."

I shake my head. "He doesn't want anything to do with me, and even if he did, I'm not sure he wouldn't be the first in line to turn me in. His loyalty has always been to The Shield."

Rook is silent, and I glance up to find him glaring at a spot on the floor with a dark expression. He mumbles something under his breath that I can't quite make out, but it sounds scathing. He runs a hand through his hair with a prolonged sigh.

Then he holds out his hand and pulls me toward him. "How are you feeling now?"

I shrug. "Exactly like you might expect. Thank you again for taking care of me last night."

His face spreads into a grin. "I think I like seeing you messy."

I exhale a sound of indignation. "I was perfectly composed." He chuckles, and I lean into him. "I liked it when you yelled at Riley for letting me trip. Why were you so mad?" His expression turns contrite as I fold my arms and cock my hip, giving him a smug look. "It wasn't really his fault."

"I had to be mad at someone," he answers like he's still kind of angry about it.

I smirk and take a step closer. "And just how long were you at Sogno anyway, given that you saw Knox and me talking?"

He faux scratches his head. "I . . . uh . . ."

Now I'm right in front of him, peering up. "What were you really doing there? Do I remember you saying that our room felt empty? Or did I imagine that?"

He cocks his head, trying to contain a smile. "You must've imagined it. I just wanted to see what all the fuss was about."

"And what did you think?"

His heated gaze scans me up and down. "I think the view was excellent. One person in particular."

"Oh yeah? And who might that be?"

He licks his lips as his gaze dips to my chest and stomach and thighs. "Someone in this little black number that made me fucking *wild* as she danced the night away."

I tap my chin. "Hmm, she sounds interesting."

He smirks. "Oh, you have *no* idea."

"Does she have a rich-girl voice?" I ask with a tip of my head.

That earns me a wicked smile. "She does. She smells rich, too."

"So that's the only reason you came?"

He shrugs. "Among other things."

"And making sure I got home safely?"

"Someone had to do it."

I huff out a small laugh. "You called me beautiful," I whisper. He moves closer, his hand sliding to my nape before he tips my head back.

"Because you are."

"Then why have you been avoiding me?" I unfold my arms so he's flush against me, and I grip his biceps for balance.

"You know why."

"You're worried about us."

"Not me. You. I was only worried about you."

"Why?" I ask as he lowers his head, pausing an inch from my mouth.

"I don't know," he answers. "I'm not supposed to worry about you, yet . . ."

He stops, and the air around us condenses, sealing us in this moment.

"Maybe I came because I wanted to kiss you again," he says softly. "Maybe it made me a little reckless."

"I liked it when you kissed me." My voice is breathless, stretched thin by his confession.

"Yeah?"

"Yes. Do you want to do it again?" I offer, and then he leans in and seals his lips over mine. I exhale into his mouth as his hand wraps around my waist, and he yanks me closer.

We moan as our tongues slide together, and his touch slides lower, smoothing over the curve of my butt and then down my thigh as he hitches my leg over his hip.

I'm light as air as he lifts me up and then lowers us onto his bed before he stretches over the top of me.

"Rook," I gasp as he wedges himself between my thighs, and he sucks on the curve of my throat before his mouth travels over my collarbone and then back to my mouth, where he consumes me with his kiss.

We lie together, our bodies moving, our hips insistent, and I *feel* what this is doing to him in the hardness pressing against me. After a minute, he pulls away, his eyes bright and his cheeks flushed.

"Poet," he says in a rough voice as he hovers over me, his hands planted on either side of my head. "I wasn't expecting this. I didn't think I'd feel anything at Amery."

I smile up and tuck a piece of his hair back before my fingers dance across his lips.

"Feel what, Rook?"

"Like . . . I want to question everything I've ever known."

I sense something important in that statement. In the wild, churning heat in his eyes. I've never been in love, but I've always wanted it. It's too soon for those kinds of sentiments—I know that. But I can't help but acknowledge this bubbling in my chest, churning to the surface.

"Me too," I answer, because I didn't expect it, either. Because over the last few months, I've also looked into the shadowy, hazy eyes of truth and wondered if it has been ringing false all along.

"Whatever happens, I'll protect you, Poet."

"But you think I'm trouble," I say, and he smiles.

"Nothing but."

Then I don't get the chance to answer, because he closes the distance, and we're kissing again.

58

It's two weeks later when we find ourselves back in the Central Park Tree Farm for our year-end cadet training exam. Dressed in our tactical gear, we huddle together in the cool morning breeze.

My gaze catches Rook's, who stands relaxed on the edge of the crowd. While we've limited our public appearances, we've been spending a lot of time alone in our room together. Sometimes, he reads to me from one of his books. The series I'm loving best is about a girl who's forced to compete in a government-sanctioned death match alongside a bunch of other kids, only to discover they're all being manipulated. I can't get enough of her strength and resilience, and how she'd do anything for the people she loves.

Sometimes, we just sit quietly, staring at the fire, and more often than not, we do a lot of kissing and touching and yearning. I can't stop blushing at random moments, thinking of his hands and mouth. We haven't taken it any further yet, though I desperately hope we do.

Rook doesn't talk much about his past in terms of other girls, except to tell me he's had a few casual relationships and wants to take things slow between us. I know there are things in his past holding him back, but I don't want to pry where he doesn't want me. I hope I can earn his trust enough to share the stories he's reluctant to reveal.

I've been fine with it, but I'm also crawling out of my skin.

I want to wipe every memory of Knox from my body, and something tells me Rook could do that in a single night.

"Good morning, cadets!" Henry's voice booms over our heads. He stands in his full Storm Guard gear along with about a dozen other fully trained Breakers, everyone wearing their tactical pants and tank tops, layered with shiny purple harnesses. "I'm happy to see so many of the same faces we welcomed during our first week of training months ago. You've all worked hard and been tested to your limits, and today, you'll demonstrate where all that effort has paid off."

He gestures around us. "Central Park is approximately two and a half miles from end to end, and nestled within the trees, you'll find an obstacle course that includes ropes, swings, bridges, and more. The path is marked, so you'll follow it through to the other side. Of course, it won't be that easy."

He looks up, and the same net I remember from my Society test winks into focus as the purple crisscrossing pattern buzzes overhead. "You'll also need to avoid this. The grid must discharge occasionally to release buildup. That means it can strike at random intervals throughout the park. So, keep your focus and your eyes and ears peeled. You'll receive only a second of warning."

Domino links her elbow with mine, leaning against me. I don't think she even realizes she's doing it as she joins everyone staring at the flickering net overhead. I lay a hand on her arm, and she looks at me, almost as if she's surprised I'm there. I try to offer her a reassuring smile. We've made it this far. We're so close.

"The cadets from each Society with the three fastest times will automatically be granted entry into the second-year program," Henry says now, eliciting an excited chorus of chatter around the circle. "The rest of you will be evaluated based on your training and tests throughout the past year.

"You'll begin with staggered starts in alphabetical order. The only rules are that you cannot touch anyone else or the trees. You must stick to the course and cannot deviate more than six feet beyond it."

He scans our line. "Everything clear?" We all nod, and then his expression shifts. "Before we begin, we have one other item we must deal with."

A rustle comes from behind us, and I nearly squeak at the sight of four Extinguishers emerging from the trees with Lieutenant Dire among them. Behind them come several E-squad recruits, including Trinity. I haven't spoken to her in weeks, haven't even *seen* her since that night I ran away from her in Sogno. Our gazes meet, and guilt flashes over her expression.

"As many of you are aware," Henry continues, "numerous deaths within New Manhattan have been attributed to the presence of the infected in the last few weeks."

I shift on my feet, still clinging to Domino. In fact, there have been two more incidents since the night at Sogno, and we've been subjected to more Extinguisher presence than ever.

"House Aria has been developing a new tool to help root out infected Keepers, and we've been asked to let them test it on all of you today."

Henry's expression makes it clear what he thinks of this request.

The Extinguishers pass through our line and turn to face us, while the E-squad spreads around them. Lieutenant Dire steps forward and holds up a small device with a screen. "It's very simple," he says in a rough voice. "We'll be drawing a small sample of your blood to be scanned by the meter. It tests for the presence of the infection. We've performed some trials on several test groups, and the results have been nearly perfect so far."

He smiles, though there is no warmth in it. "Please form three lines, and we'll get started."

My heart was already racing, but now it's pounding so hard that I feel like I'm underwater. What are Rook and I going to do?

But it's already too late. An Extinguisher has approached Rook with the device. He grabs Rook's wrist and presses a knob at the top to the tip of Rook's finger. Rook winces, and my breath stops as I wait for impending disaster.

Everyone falls silent as we watch. They're all horrified; I can tell by the tension in the air. And they don't even know how much danger he's in. The device whirs and beeps a few times, and then a green light flashes on the screen.

"Clear," the Extinguisher announces, and I exhale the heavy breath lodged in my chest.

Rook's gaze meets mine, and he blinks. I'm not sure what just happened, but I nearly collapse in relief.

The Extinguishers continue, while I wait in anticipation. Just because Rook passed doesn't mean I'll have the same result. I hold my breath as Lieutenant Dire gestures with a crooked finger for me to approach.

My knees have locked, but I force myself toward him and hold out my hand. He presses the device to my finger, and I feel the prick as the needle pierces my skin. I concentrate on breathing, trying not to faint. Thinking noninfected thoughts.

A few seconds pass as Dire looks at the screen, and then . . . it flashes green. I nearly laugh with relief.

I shuffle back, catching sight of Trinity, noticing a strange look pass over her face.

Our eyes meet, and she gives me a small, uncertain smile. I nod, then find my place next to Domino until everyone has been tested. Thankfully, everyone passes with a green light. I don't think I could bear to watch another person taken away.

Henry stands before us again. "With that done, we can begin," he says, eyeing up the Extinguishers with barely veiled distaste. I'm not sure if they notice. He pulls out the tablet tucked under his arm and taps the screen. "Rook Athira, you're up first!"

We're all arranged in a line, with Rook at the head. I wish I could tell him good luck. As Henry checks us all off, the other Storm Guards disperse into the trees to keep an eye on us during the exam.

I wait for the Extinguishers to leave, but instead, they follow the Breakers into the trees along with their student recruits. I watch Trinity disappear into the bush, angry that they're staying to observe. They already tested us. This is just to assert their dominance and scare us. They're nothing but a bunch of bullies.

I look up at the net of Spark buzzing overhead.

Now I'll have to be extra careful out there.

I watch the back of Rook's head from where I find myself about halfway down the line. He looks over his shoulder and winks, giving me a cocky smile. He must also be feeling the stress of the Extinguishers' presence, but he's hiding it well. Or maybe he's just that confident. I take comfort in it, allowing his self-assurance to seep into my watery nerves. If he can be brave, then so can I.

I put the rest out of my mind. Qualifying for second year is my first priority.

Next, I search for Domino closer to the end of the line. We nod to each other, firming up our resolve.

Henry sets a timer on his watch and signals to Rook.

"You'll go every two minutes on the minute!" Henry shouts, and then he counts Rook into the course.

"Three, two, one . . ."

He's off. Rook disappears into the trees at a full clip, the rustle of leaves signaling his flight until the forest goes silent except for our soft breaths and the sound of the wind.

"Next!" Henry shouts, and the line shuffles forward. "All good?" he asks when I reach the front.

I nod with a sharp dip of my chin. "I'm ready."

He claps a hand on my shoulder. "Raine would be so proud of you," he says, and I wish that didn't make me want to cry. "Ready!" he shouts. "Set! Go!"

And then I'm off.

I race through the trees, following the markers down a narrow, shaded path. My first stop is a tower a few handspans wide, adorned with metal rungs. I climb up, one hand over the other, to reach a rope attached to a beam running across a wide space.

I can't help but think of my Society test, when two innocent people were nearly killed in these very trees. I wonder what ever became of them and hope they're safe.

But I need to focus.

I empty my mind of all thoughts but me and the obstacles in my path. I grab the rope and swing, kicking my feet out and landing on the far platform with plenty of room. The act has the effect of clearing my mind and shifting me into focus. I push the Extinguishers and my House test, and even Rook, from my thoughts.

Next, I reach a set of rings hanging from a rope dangling high above the ground. I grab the first and then swing down and begin the arduous task of lurching across. It's hard work, but it's also not as daunting as I thought. It's my first chance to marvel at how strong I've become over the past few months.

Still, as I reach the three-quarter mark, my shoulders scream and my arms ache. If I fall, I probably wouldn't die, but I would likely break an ankle, which I guess is kind of the point. I notice someone lurking in the bushes under the trees: a woman with tanned skin and a long red braid, woven with plum-colored strands. Her shiny purple harness tells me it's one of the Breakers keeping an eye on us.

Again, I clear the next platform to reach another climbing pole.

When I reach the bottom, the route feeds me through a tight path, bordered by dense bushes, before I come upon a small corner of a lake with a balance beam stretching across it. The net above my head buzzes, and somewhere off to my right, the first burst of Spark strikes.

It spears down, and I listen for the sound of anything to suggest someone was hit. When nothing happens, I breathe out a sigh of relief, mostly worried about Domino, Journey, and Rook.

I hop onto the beam and, with my arms out, lightly step across, maintaining my balance. It's surprisingly simple given everything, and I hop down, running to the next pole, which finds me at another ladder leading into the trees.

My confidence wanes when I spy the obstacle before me.

A long, narrow platform stretches ahead with less than a few feet of space between the planks and the electricity net hovering above it. The goal is clearly to shimmy across without breaching the barrier. I wonder if anyone has been blitzed, but I don't notice any charred bodies nearby. Hopefully, that's a good sign.

I drop down on my hands and knees and then realize my ponytail will cause an issue. I yank it out and quickly braid it tightly so it hangs down over my shoulder. Then I flatten myself to my stomach. There is only a hairbreadth of distance between me and the Spark waiting to expose my lies.

Fuck, this is going to be tight. Slowly, using my fingertips, I drag myself forward, focusing on keeping my stomach and hips pressed to the surface. I lay my head down as my cheek scrapes along the wooden plank.

With my hands stretched out in front of me, I scoot forward and then slowly inch my way across, using the toes of my boots for leverage. The sun is rising over the park, burning through the morning clouds. A bead of sweat slides down my temple as I stop to rest. The low drone of the net buzzes in my ears like a siren's song luring me to jagged rocks.

The sound intensifies, the frequency pitching up. I whimper, sure it's a sign that the net is about to discharge. What if it decides this would be a good spot? A strike hits in the distance, and someone screams. I yelp and twitch, trying not to jump and touch the net.

A moment later, everything goes silent, save the low drone of Spark.

I don't dare lift my head to check my progress, but I gauge that I'm about halfway across. Another reach of my fingertips and I drag myself farther with a series of heavy grunts and pants.

I anchor my toe into the wood and wince as my palm snags on a splinter. Something else catches near my eye, and I resist the urge to brush it away, blinking rapidly through my watering vision.

Bit by bit, I inch my way across until I'm almost at the end.

When I have just a foot or two left, I collapse onto the wood to catch my breath, praying this is the hardest part of the course. Probably not.

When I'm ready, I lurch another few inches just as the buzzing intensifies again. I don't know why, but some instinct tells me it's coming for me.

With every ounce of strength I can summon, I drag myself through to the end, jumping up as I clear the net. A blast of energy strikes the very spot I was lying, catching my foot.

I don't scream. Instead, I launch myself behind a tree and stamp out the sparks climbing up my leg, hitting and swatting myself until they're doused.

That's when I notice a movement in the bushes.

A dark shape shifting and then retreating.

A flash of red hair.

I think.

I hold still, hoping I just imagined it.

My muscles seize, my heart pounding up my throat.

Was someone there? An Extinguisher?

Or the Breaker I saw earlier?

Did they see?

59

I stand still for several more seconds, focused on the same spot. Maybe waiting for the Extinguishers to burst through the trees.

When I see no other movement, I tell myself it was nothing. I hope.

I don't have time to dwell on it.

I climb down the pole and then wind along another path, twisting and turning, before I happen upon another lake with a bridge running across.

A blast of Spark has already severed it about a third of the way down, where the planks smoke with embers. I'll have no option but to jump. Thanks to the adrenaline coursing through my veins, I barely feel a thing as I stomp across the bridge and then leap, landing on the other side before running again.

I become dimly aware of a telltale flicker overhead. It's too far to hear the increased buzzing, but premonition tells me the net is preparing to release again. I pick up my pace just as a bright line peels off the net and strikes the bridge almost directly in front of me.

I scream, trying to dodge it. The only thing I accomplish is losing my balance, going over the edge, and plunging into the lake as icy water fills my mouth, my nose, my boots.

Fuck. Fuck. Fuck.

I kick and flail, bursting through the surface, grabbing onto a piece of debris. As I catch my breath, I start floating away. The bridge smolders and smokes, tiny flames licking at the edges.

It takes me a moment to remember that if I go off course, I'll be disqualified. I don't know where the boundary ends, but I'm not taking any chances.

I kick against the water, my boots heavy and dragging, but I can't take them off. I still need them to complete the exam.

The bridge continues to smolder where the energy hit, so I maneuver away. I consider floating to the far shore, but not only would that take longer, I don't know if that's against the rules. It's too big a risk.

I grab on to the edge of the bridge, but with no handrails, there's nothing to use for leverage but the slippery planks. I heave a waterlogged leg over the edge, followed by the other, eventually rolling onto my back.

The net above me flickers, almost like it's laughing.

Or I really am losing my mind. Nevertheless, some part of me registers that if I remain still too long, I'm a sitting target.

With a groan, I roll over onto my hands and knees and then force myself up. The same ankle that I twisted a few months ago throbs as I take a step. I must have reinjured it. Pushing past the pain, I lope to the end of the bridge, then dive into the trees once again.

For a short while, the path continues, skirting around a fountain that's been smashed apart. I quickly scurry past, reasoning that I'll be safer from Spark within the trees.

Up ahead, the forest parts to reveal an open field. At the far end, I spot several people shouting and clapping, and I choke out a sob of relief.

But that relief is short-lived when I spot several Extinguishers waiting with the finishers.

I think back to the moment I was hit.

Did I see a person? Did they see me?

I can't get that flash of *someone* out of my mind.

I slow down as everyone cheers. Rook is watching me with a line between his brows. He can tell something is wrong, but I can't warn him.

I limp toward the finish line, focused solely on Rook's worried face.

If I'm about to be taken, I want this to be the last thing I see.

I pass over the line to a chorus of cheers, holding my breath.

But nothing happens. The Extinguishers are talking among themselves while the E-squad is busy horsing around. Rook embraces me, and I squeeze him back, pressing my face to his chest.

I don't care who sees us anymore.

"Are you okay?" he whispers, framing my face with his hands.

"I don't know. I have to tell you something after." He gives me a quizzical look, but I shake my head imperceptibly. "Later."

Not only is there the question of whether someone saw me or not, but there's the added puzzle of us both fooling the Extinguishers' new contraption.

Something isn't adding up.

We both face the finish line and wait for everyone else to arrive. When Domino and Journey both cross, we give each other hugs and high fives, and I even get some congratulations from my former Fiama and new House Aria colleagues.

Storm Guard over Society. That's what Henry promised.

We *are* becoming a team, slowly but surely, and I try to muster excitement, but my stomach is churning. I notice the same Breaker I spotted during the course, her bright red hair glowing in the sunlight. I try to catch her eye, but she doesn't look my way.

"Cadets!" Henry shouts after everyone finishes. "Well done! Every single one of you made it. It's been years since the Storm Guard had a full class complete the course."

Everyone else cheers at that, and he grins, giving us a moment to savor this victory.

When we've all quieted, he holds up his tablet. "And for our winners."

Everyone shares nervous glances around the circle. I have no idea how my time stacked up. I wasn't the fastest, but it's clear from everyone's haggard state that I wasn't the only one who struggled today. One girl's hair is still smoking, a few people are soaking wet, and others nurse bruised knees and elbows.

He goes on to name the top three rankings from Fiama, Asale, and Tera. There's a lot of cheering and back slapping. Smiles and congratulations.

"And finally, Aria," he says. "In third place with thirty-one minutes and forty-three seconds . . . we have Poet Graves!"

I'm so shocked that I don't register my name at first, but Domino and Journey are both hugging me. Everyone else joins in as Henry gestures me up to the front. I approach, and he grins as he holds out his hand.

"I knew you had the Graves' Storm Guard gene in you," he says with a wink. Then he peers at me. "Are you okay?"

"Sure," I say, still conscious of the Extinguishers intruding on our celebration.

"Okay, well done," Henry says, gesturing for me to stand to the side as he consults his tablet again.

"In second place with a time of twenty-nine minutes and twelve seconds, we have . . . Domino Parsons!"

Domino shrieks, and I shriek, too, as she runs over and tosses her arms around my neck.

"Ahhh!" I shout, lifting her and spinning her in a circle while she screams. "You're amazing."

When I set her down, Henry shakes her hand and offers some praise before consulting his tablet again.

"And in first place, with an Amery record–breaking time of twenty-five minutes and fourteen seconds, we have Rook Athira!"

A chorus of cheers goes up, and Rook blinks, slowly unfolding his arms before he shakes his head and saunters over. His posture is casual and collected, but I can read his shock in the set of his shoulders. I think I'm learning to understand his body's cues.

He cocks a half smile as Henry vigorously shakes his hand.

"Well done," he says. "I've never seen someone run like that." He slaps Rook on the shoulder and then the back, and Henry looks like he's about to burst with pride. It's not lost on me that three of Society's outcasts were the fastest. I have no idea how I managed to do that.

But for now, everyone is happy for us.

"Not only have you all won yourself a place in second-year training," Henry says, "but you'll be honored at the graduation ball by The Shield themselves with a special token of your achievement."

While everyone celebrates, I summon a smile for the others' sakes and try to look happy about it.

After all, I just scored a spot in second-year training.

This is what I've always wanted.

As another round of congratulations ensues, I shift on my feet, uncomfortably aware that someone saw me. The longer I sit with the thought, the more I'm sure of it.

I scan our surroundings, searching for a clue.

A hand lands on my shoulder, and I jump, only to find Trinity smiling at me. Her red hair is pulled back into a high knot, and her gray eyes are searching.

"Well done," she says. "And congratulations."

"Thanks," I say. "How have you been?"

"Good." She pauses before she draws me into a long hug. "I'm proud of you."

Then she pulls back, studies my face with a tight smile, turns around, and walks away.

60

Later that night, Rook and I sit by the fire in our room, trying to make sense of everything that happened.

"Why didn't their device work on us?" I ask. "Was it defective, or was it just us?"

"I don't think it was defective," Rook answers, reading something on his phone. We've tossed some pillows on the floor, and he's leaning against one with his arm tucked under his head. The orange light reflects off his nose and cheeks, highlighting the crown of his dark hair. "This says they've already caught numerous people by using them. I think they work."

I huff out a breath, tucking my knees up under me. "Unless they're lying," I say. "Trying to make it look like they're doing something."

"That's possible," he says. "But something tells me they aren't."

"We're different," I say. "I'm sure of it. Something about us is different. Right?"

He glances at me and then looks away, staring at the fire.

"What?" I ask. "There's something you haven't been saying."

Rook sighs and sits up, pulling a knee toward his chest.

"I wasn't entirely truthful with you when I said I'd never met another Keeper," he starts. "They're pretty common in the Wastes."

I'm not all that surprised to hear this. "Why did you lie about it?"

He shakes his head. "Because I wasn't sure that I could trust you yet. But I don't think I'm the same as the other Keepers. I thought I was the only one, but then I met you." I study him, waiting for him to continue. "Part of the reason I came to New Manhattan was to find out why I'm different. I don't think I am a Keeper, at least not in the way it's always been defined.

And I don't think you are, either. The truth is, I told you I'd never touched another Keeper during a storm, but I have. It had no effect. What happened with us—that was new."

"So, what are we?" I whisper.

He shakes his head. "I'm not sure."

"Why do you want to know? Other than the obvious?"

He rubs his jaw. "I've always wondered if I might be protected from the madness."

I stare at him, weighing the implications of that. "And you think The Shield knows what you are? That you exist?"

"Possibly."

"If they knew, wouldn't they tell us?" I ask.

He shrugs. "They might have something to gain from our ignorance."

"Like what?"

Again, he shakes his head. "I'm not sure."

"But you have a hunch."

He sighs and straightens his legs before running his hands down his face. "I can't say for sure, but I think there's at least one other person like us."

I frown. "Who?"

"General Sol."

The air gusts from my chest, like I've been kicked. "General Sol. You think she isn't really a Keeper?"

"Doesn't it stand to reason? Why is she the only one who hasn't succumbed to the . . . infection?"

"Because she's trained against it," I argue. "She learned how to . . ." I trail off as Rook watches me, waiting for me to put it together. "And this might be another lie."

He tips his head. "Very possibly."

My breath comes out in a shaky, frustrated huff.

"It's only a hunch," he says. "But I want to find out. I just don't know how." He sighs. "It was a fool's hope, really. I've spent months trying to learn more about the Tempestade's research, but it's locked within The Shield's computers, which I could never hope to access. I thought joining the Storm Guard might make it easier, but that was naive. I'd have to move much higher up their ranks, which will take years."

We both fall silent, listening to the crackle of the burning logs.

"Do you think if we could prove to the world that we're something else, it might protect us from the Extinguishers?"

"It might," he says.

"And you really think it's possible we're immune to the infection."

"I'm surer of it every day. But we need proof. No one would believe us otherwise."

"And The Shield could be concealing this information."

"Someone must know, and that seems the most likely place to start."

I consider everything he's saying. I've lived in fear for most of my life. Hating what I am. Hating myself for not being brave enough to turn myself in.

But what if I only *seem* like the thing they all fear? What if I could escape this curse?

"Anyway," Rook says. "I have no clue how to access The Shield's computers, so it's likely impossible."

"The Shield's computers. That's what we need?"

"Yes, but . . ."

I jump up and head for the door.

"Where are you going?" Rook asks.

"I'll be back soon. I have an idea."

. . .

The first thing I do is text Edward. We've been messaging, while I've been checking on him a few times a week to ensure he's okay. I feel terrible that we haven't spent more time together. He was Trinity's boyfriend, but we were friends, too. I don't think Trinity was obligated to stay with him if she was no longer interested, but I also think she owed him more than cutting him off without a second thought.

Or maybe I'm just bitter about the way she abandoned me, too.

I find him sitting in a quiet corner of the cafeteria with his shoulders hunched as he picks at his food. He still looks terrible—thin and tired and pale—and I sit down across from him as he peers up.

"Hey," he says sullenly, stirring his noodles with a listless motion.

"Hi," I answer. "How are you doing?"

He shrugs and slurps down a spoonful. "How does it look like I'm doing?"

"I'm sorry," I say. "You deserved better than this."

With a sigh, he plants his elbows on the table. "Have you talked to her?"

"Not much," I say. "Honestly, we've really drifted apart. She's busy with her new friends."

"I don't understand what got into her."

"People change, I guess."

"I wish . . ." He trails off and stabs a cherry tomato with his fork with such force that it goes flying off the plate. It barely misses my shoulder, sailing past and landing on the floor.

"I miss her," he says so softly that I barely hear it.

I slide my hand across the table, just within his reach. "I miss her, too."

"Is she seeing someone else?"

I swallow the thick knot in my throat. I know this answer will hurt. "She might be."

He drops his head into his hands, and I give him a moment to collect himself. I watch a few people enter and leave the room, some of them tossing glances in our direction. I'm sitting on the Fiama side of the hall, and it's likely only a matter of time before someone makes it an issue.

"How are your classes going?" I ask. "You're not skipping school because of this?"

His jaw tightens. "So what if I am?"

"Edward, Trin wouldn't want you to screw up your future because of her."

He shrugs as if he doesn't believe that. Then he picks up his fork and aims for another tomato, securing his kill.

"I was," he says, popping it into his mouth. "At the beginning, I was skipping classes, but they called my mom, and she tore me a new one." He winces. "Skies, sometimes I forget how loud she can yell."

I snort because the image of Mrs. Chu's furious face feels so . . . normal.

"She can be terrifying," I agree, earning me a small laugh.

He tips his head and peers at me. "You're doing okay?" he asks carefully.

I shrug. "As good as I can be."

"How's cadet training?"

"It's pretty good," I say honestly, and he offers me a tentative smile.

"I'm glad. I've always considered you my friend, too." He shoves another forkful of noodles into his mouth. "So why did you want to talk to me?"

I inhale a deep breath. I need him to trust me, given the scant details I can offer. "There's something I need. Some information."

"What kind of information?"

"The confidential kind that can probably only be found in The Shield's computers."

He frowns at me. "Are you in trouble, Poe?"

"Maybe. Sort of? Possibly yes."

His brows draw together. "I'm going to need more than that."

I check to make sure we're completely alone, then lean in. "I need some information about the Tempestade's research and what they have on Spark Keepers." My voice drops with each word until I'm mouthing them by the end.

Edward's eyebrows shoot up, his rolling gaze swinging around the room.

"Don't say anything," I plead. "I'm begging you."

I don't *think* he'd turn me in.

"Poet," he hisses.

"I know, I'm asking for the world, but this is important. I wouldn't ask otherwise."

Edward assesses me, his shoulders relaxing after a moment. "Even if I agreed, I can't hack into those computers. It would be a suicide mission. We'd have to do it remotely, and I don't have the equipment I'd need to cover our tracks."

His words are full of skepticism, but I can tell he's already thinking about the possibilities. The challenge. Edward has always loved a puzzle, after all.

"Could you get the equipment?"

"Possibly, but it would be difficult. It's not something you can just walk into a store and buy. I'd have to piece together various parts, probably build the entire thing myself. And all that would raise a lot of questions. Ones I'm assuming you don't want to answer."

His look is pointed as I huff out a breath of frustration. "There has to be a way."

"If I could access them from *inside* the Citadel," he muses, twirling his pasta and taking another bite, "then I could find out anything in those computers."

"Inside?" I ask. "As in, break into The Shield's security wing?"

He chews thoughtfully. "I didn't say *break in*, but it's interesting that's where your mind went first."

I frown. "How else would we do it? Ask nicely?"

He levels his fork at me. "You have a point." Another twirl of spaghetti finds its way into his mouth as I cycle through a million ideas.

I recall the House Asale scion with his key card accessing the communications wing.

Would I dare ask my father?

No, I couldn't.

I'd have to steal it.

Interesting how quickly my mind went there, too.

"What's that look?" Edward asks, chewing and circling the tines of his fork at my face. "You're planning something."

"What if we *could* break in?" I ask. "Forget the logistics of it. What if I could get us in there? Would you do it? *Could* you do it?"

"Why, Poe? I could be arrested. You would be, too."

"I know," I whisper. "But I'm in trouble. Someone I care about . . . someone I *love* is in trouble. If we don't find what we're looking for, then I'm scared of what our futures hold."

He studies me with his dark gaze, something flitting across his face. "You're the only person who's given a shit about me since Trin and I broke up," he says. "No one else has checked up on me or asked how I'm doing."

"Oh," I say, confused by the shift in conversation. "I'm sorry."

He shakes his head and wipes his mouth on a napkin. "No, I mean, I appreciate it. I'm grateful that you didn't forget me, too."

"We're friends," I say.

"Will you tell me what specifically I'm looking for?"

"I think we should wait until we're inside. Just in case."

He nods as if that's the answer he expected. Then he sets his fork down before wiping his hands. He looks around the room, his gaze sliding over the other students, eyes darkening. I peer over my shoulder, noticing that Trinity has entered with her new friends. Another recruit has his arm around her shoulders—not the one I met on the boat, a new guy—and it's obvious by their body language that they're more than casual acquaintances.

I turn around to look at Edward, his brow lowered as he works his jaw. I have no idea what to say.

His gaze meets mine.

He shakes his head, and I think he's about to get up and walk out, but something shifts in his expression.

Uncertainty morphs into determination. Like he just came to some kind of conclusion.

Then he levels me with a look.

"Fuck it. If you can get us in, and this information exists, I'll find out whatever you want."

61

"**Y**ou want to do *what?*" Rook asks after I return to our room a little while later. He's sitting on his bed, staring at me like I've grown another head.

"I want to steal my father's access card and break into The Shield's office."

I say it calmly, but only because I spent an hour walking around repeating it to myself until I could do so without wanting to throw up.

"Poet," Rook says, a warning in his tone. "That's an incredibly dangerous idea."

I twirl a lock of hair and place a hand on my hip. "I know, but you must admit, it has some merit."

He snorts a laugh and shakes his head. "I suppose it does, but even with a key card, anyone who sees us will know we don't belong there."

"You're right," I say. "So we use a distraction."

"A distraction?"

I pace away, crossing the room and then back. While trying to convince myself this isn't the worst idea I've ever had, I also considered some logistics that just might make it work.

"The graduation masquerade is coming up in a week," I say, and Rook arches a brow.

"And?"

"And it's a huge party," I say. "All the Houses will be there. The Shield. The scions attend. Their families. All the important players come to 'welcome the future of Society.'"

"Okay?"

"And it takes all kinds of resources to pull off. The whole city celebrates in its own way, meaning an increased need for security, so the Citadel operates with only a skeleton staff."

Rook sits up straighter, paying closer attention. "I didn't know any of that."

"Most people don't," I say. "They keep it quiet, but I've overheard my dad talking about it many times. There are always concerns about riots or Solitude attacks that night. Even with everyone on duty, they have only so many resources to draw on. And if there's a storm that night, the Patrol is stretched even further."

Rook stands up and crosses the room, stopping before me. "This still seems risky, Poet."

"It does," I answer. "But I need to know what I am, and that's what you came here to find. We need to understand why they'd keep this from us."

His nostrils flare, and he inhales a slow breath. "All of that is true."

"With more and more deaths, they'll keep looking harder. They won't ask questions if they discover us. We have to get ahead of it. This is the first time since I was a kid that I can see a future for myself that doesn't end with me in the Extinguishers' clutches."

He places his hands on his hips and blows out a sigh. "And Edward is really going to help?"

"Apparently."

"Why?"

"Because he's my friend, and I think he understands I'm in trouble even if I can't tell him everything. Besides, I think he's miserable, and this gives him something to focus on."

I tell him what happened in the cafeteria before Edward agreed.

"So, maybe he feels like he has nothing left to lose," Rook says.

"Maybe that," I agree.

He shakes his head. "When are we breaking into your parents'?"

"We? I don't want you to get caught."

He leans down, the tip of his nose brushing mine. "Yes, *we*. Did you think I was letting you do this alone?"

"If you get caught, you'll be in huge trouble," I say.

"Like I asked, when are we going?"

I hesitate for only a second before I answer, "They always go to dinner with their supper club on the third Saturday of the month."

"So tomorrow night."

I nod. "Enough time to get the key card before the masquerade."

"Do you have any idea where it might be?"

"My father's study would be my best guess."

"What if he takes it with him?"

I shake my head. "Honestly, I don't know—I'm winging it here. Let's hope he doesn't. Otherwise, we'll have a few days to figure out a different plan."

"Okay."

I reach up and cup his face in my hands. "You're sure about this?"

His expression turns serious, cementing us to this moment. Maybe to each other, but those are thoughts I'm too afraid to entertain.

"I promised I would protect you, Poet Graves, and I meant every word of it."

62

The next night, Rook and I enter the main floor of Fiama Society Tower A through the service entrance. I've snuck in and out of this building enough times to know how to do it without being spotted by the doorman who sits at the front.

Cyril is also eighty-seven years old and tends to sleep on the night shift. Even without using the back entrance, slinking past him isn't much of a challenge. But the job seems to offer him purpose, and the Fiama Towers are safe from thieves, with every floor equipped with state-of-the-art security systems.

A would-be troublemaker wouldn't get far.

We both decided to dress in regular clothing on the off chance that we're spotted. I can pretend I'm returning to my parents' apartment to pick up something I need for school.

I'm wearing jeans and a pink crop top, while Rook is wearing his signature denim and black T-shirt with cowboy boots. As we wait for the elevator, I can't help but admire the way the worn denim hugs his thighs and hips.

"What is it?" he asks, arching a brow, obviously reading my mind and fishing for a compliment.

I shrug. "Nothing special."

He smirks as the doors slide open, and we ride up to the penthouse.

"They're gone for sure?" he asks, watching the glowing numbers climb.

"Cara confirmed they were heading out at seven tonight, so the coast should be clear."

"Who's Cara?"

"Our housekeeper."

He looks at me, pausing momentarily before he watches the numbers again. I hate how many differences come between us, highlighted by these constant reminders of how divided our worlds are.

"She has the night off," I say quietly. "So she won't be around."

"I'm not blaming you for having a housekeeper," he says.

"I know you're not."

"It's just . . ." He runs a hand through his hair. "When it's just you and me, I forget who you are and who I am and that none of this makes any sense."

I cross the space and lean against him, so we're pressed to the wall. His hands land on my hips, warm fingers digging into the exposed skin of my midriff. "I don't care about any of that."

"You say that, but you're used to a certain life and I—" He pauses, a sigh heaving from his chest. "I have no idea what's in store for me."

I offer him a curious look. "You'll finish at Amery and become a Storm Guard," I say. "You'll have all the privileges of Society. Our differences won't matter then."

He doesn't reply, his mouth pressing together before the elevator glides to a stop and the doors open with a soft *ping*.

We enter the living room, lit only with a few dim lamps, as Rook exhales a low, impressed whistle. "This is quite an apartment." There's no judgment in his tone, only interest and a bit of awe.

He walks over to one of the floor-to-ceiling windows overlooking the city before stuffing his hands into his pockets. "And this view. I think I could stand here every day. Almost feels like I could see home from here."

Home. He says it so warmly and with such longing that I don't know if I've ever really understood how much he misses it until now.

"How far is it?" I ask, approaching. We stand side by side, watching the city lights as he hesitates. A glance at his profile reveals his distant stare, like he isn't sure how to answer me. Or maybe doesn't want to.

"Far," is all he says, and when it's obvious that's all he's saying, I turn toward my father's study.

"We should keep moving," I add.

A green lamp on the desk offers enough light to maneuver through the room. I open a few drawers and pick through the contents, careful not to disturb anything too much.

Rook enters and slowly circles the space, peering at the shelves and art and furniture with acute interest.

Suddenly, I feel self-conscious with him standing in the circle of my advantages. We've worked so hard to break down the barriers between us. Watching him examine the opulence I grew up in is wiping away those carefully erased lines.

I open another drawer to reveal a row of shiny cards tucked into neat little slots.

"Here," I whisper, and he walks over.

"Which one is it?"

I shake my head and begin removing them one by one, holding them up to the light. Some are obviously used for various payments, and others are different types of identification.

"These are spare apartment keys," I say before stuffing them into their slots and revealing a few red cards emblazoned with the House Fiama logo. "This must be for his office."

I sift through the others until I come upon a plain silver square without markings or emblems. I hold it up, examining it under the light. "You think?"

"If I wanted to create a key for a highly classified security office, I'd probably make it as nondescript as possible," Rook answers.

I nod, but something about it doesn't feel right. I distinctly remember the flash of red in the scion of Asale's hand.

"Or disguise it to look like something else," I say, picking up the House Fiama cards.

I flip them over and study them under the lamplight, comparing them for any clues.

"This one," I say, revealing a card with no writing on the back. I tilt it toward the light, catching a holographic flash of The Shield's logo, cleverly hidden unless you're looking for it.

"Okay," Rook says with a skeptical brow. "If you're sure."

"I'm not, but let's hope my hunch is right."

I replace everything in the drawer and tuck the key card into my back pocket. "Let's get out of here."

We enter the living room again, and Rook stops. "Can I see your room?"

"Why?"

"I'm curious. I want to see what makes Poet Graves tick."

I glance at the door, worried about how long we've lingered.

"Just for a second," he says, and I lead him down the hallway and open the door.

Light from the city illuminates the surfaces, shadowing the dim corners.

"It's . . ." I try to find an explanation for why it looks like a child's bedroom. "I never got around to redecorating."

He smirks as he stuffs his hands in his pockets and glances around the space. "It's strangely you."

"What? Pretentious? Ridiculous and immature? Overly complicated?"

He huffs out a small laugh and then turns to face me, running a finger along my hairline and down the curve of my jaw. "No, warm and safe. Beautiful and special." He pauses. "Concealing layers of emotion underneath."

I give him a half smile. "I'm sure you're lying, but I'll take it."

He breaks into a beautiful smile that inexplicably makes my heart hurt. I hate how tenuous this all feels. Like we're both glass left to sit on a window ledge on a windy day.

"It's strange having you here," I confess. "I didn't think I'd ever see this place again. It feels like I've compartmentalized my life into before Fiama and after Fiama, and this apartment lives in the before, where I think it'll probably stay forever."

He tips his head. "And I'm after?"

"You are. You're a part of my real life now. The one where I stood up for myself and finally started being true to who I want to be."

Pride flashes in his eyes as he takes my hand, kissing my fingers. "Thank you for showing me this piece of you. We should probably go."

I nod, and the lights flip on, casting us into a harsh, accusing glare. We both spin around to find someone standing in the doorway.

"Mom," I gasp.

63

"**W**hat are you doing here?" she asks, blinking. Her hair is tied up in her sleep bonnet, and she's wearing her robe and nightgown, everything made of lustrous silk in bright colors.

I yank my hand from Rook's, whipping it behind my back. "I thought you were out for dinner. Isn't it your supper club night?"

Her mouth flattens. I basically just admitted I was avoiding her.

"I wasn't feeling well, so your father went without me. I woke up and heard voices." She presses a hand to her chest. "You scared me half to death. What are you doing here?"

I open my mouth to answer as her gaze slides to Rook, judgment written into every line of her moisturized face.

"Is this . . . the Solitude? You brought him *here*? To our *home*?" Her eyes widen. "Wait, are you in trouble? Is he forcing you to do something?"

She steps away, backing out of the room. "I'll call the Patrol."

"Mom, no!" I say, moving closer with my hands out like I'm trying to calm a wild animal. "I brought him here. He's not doing anything wrong."

She grips the doorframe, looking between us before glancing at our hands, which she definitely saw us holding. "Why are you with *him*?"

"His name is Rook."

"I don't *care* what his name is," she spits. "I ordered you to stay away from him. Didn't you get my message?"

"Your message?" I ask, unable to believe my ears. "Your *message*? I don't know, Mom, maybe I missed it while sending you hundreds of messages you didn't bother answering!"

"What did you expect?" she cries. "What do you want me to do?"

"I want you to act like my mother!"

She shakes her head and lays a hand on her throat. Tears form in her eyes, and I squint because it's then that I notice the faintest hint of bruising on her skin.

"What did he do?" I ask, my voice dropping low. "Did he hurt you?"

I'm moving closer now, my mother backing into the hall.

"What did you expect him to do, Poet? Did you think all your little stunts would go unpunished? He couldn't reach you, so he opted for the closest thing. If he found out I'd been talking to you—"

My shoulders drop, sharp needles exploding in my stomach. She took the brunt of his wrath for me. "I'm sorry," I whisper. "I'm so sorry. I didn't mean—"

"I know you didn't," she says firmly. "I know this was not the intended outcome when you set out on all this." She waves a hand up and down. "But you need to understand that you have ruined everything. Your father had to scramble to find a successor, and Trey and Molly are no longer speaking to us. They're trying to establish their own pick as scion while your father's power slips away."

As she lays out the entire picture for me, nausea creeps up my throat. Knox told me everything was okay, but that was weeks ago, and things have clearly progressed. I knew choosing Aria would have consequences, but I never really understood how far my actions would spread.

We both fall silent before my mother asks, "Poet, what are you doing here? If your father had been home . . ." Her gaze darts to Rook. "You would both be in more trouble than you can possibly imagine."

"I needed something," I say, picking up the lie I'd already prepared. "A sweater I forgot."

"You came back here for a sweater?"

I nod. "I needed it."

She eyes me with a wary look, and I'm pretty sure she knows I'm lying, but she doesn't press it.

Her gaze slides over me. "Fine, did you get what you needed?"

"Yeah."

"Then you should both go."

She steps aside and waits. I share a glance with Rook and gesture him toward the hall.

"You go ahead," I say. He nods and then walks up to my mother, stops, and looks her up and down. He's made no secret of how little he respects my parents, but he stares at the bruise on my mother's throat, and I note the contrast of his softening eyes and the tightness around his mouth.

"If a man ever laid a hand on your daughter, I'd kill him," he says, and my mother blinks, her mouth falling open. No one has ever spoken to her like that. Rook cocks his head. "I still might."

She stares up at him, her lower lip trembling, before Rook turns and heads down the hall.

"Mom," I say. "I would have told you I was coming, but—"

Slowly, she turns to look at me. "But I wasn't answering your messages. I understand."

I stand before her, my mouth opening and closing. I have so many things to say, but they sit in a tight knot lodged at the base of my spine, impossible to unravel.

"You should go," she says.

"That's it?" I ask. "We're just finished forever?"

Finally, she meets my eyes. "I don't know what you want me to say, Poet. You made a choice, and now we must all live with that."

I'm about to tell her I'm sorry again, but I understand there's no point. All the apologies in the world won't change the facts.

My heart splinters into pieces as I look at her, maybe for the last time.

"Okay." I'm turning to leave when she calls after me.

"How's the cadet program?" she asks. "Is it everything you hoped it would be?"

I exhale a shaky breath. "Yeah, Mom. It's amazing. I made it to second year. I had the third-fastest time in our final exam."

She nods, a hint of pride straightening her shoulders. "Of course you did. I had no doubt about that."

I hesitate again, sensing Rook standing by the door, waiting for me, witnessing this pain and ugliness between me and the one person in the world whose job it was to protect me.

Her gaze lands on my throat and the mask dangling from the chain around my neck. She reaches out and snags it between her fingers.

"Do you know why I got you this?" she says.

I shake my head. "I always assumed it was a metaphor. Something for me to hide behind."

"No," she says, her forehead crumpling. "It was a reminder to never be like me. I'm the one who hid, but you were always so brave. So determined. And look at you now. Your own person, making your own decisions."

She sighs and releases her hold, her hand dropping at her side.

"I'm sorry," she says. "If we'd listened to you, then maybe—"

She shakes her head, and I rush to throw my arms around her, hugging her tightly. She returns my embrace as we both start crying.

"I love you, Mom," I say, pulling away. "Dad made it really hard, but I want you to know that I *do* love you."

She reaches out and cups my cheek, closing her eyes as a tear slips from the corner. "You have no idea just how much I love you, my baby girl. I'll regret every day we're apart. I'm not sure if you believe that, but it's true."

"Maybe this isn't goodbye forever," I say. "Maybe just for now."

"Maybe," she says. "Now go. Please. I don't want him to see you."

Her gaze moves past me to Rook, and I can't quite interpret what I see in her face. Perhaps a begrudging respect. Maybe a bit of relief.

"Take care of yourself," she says to me. "And hold on to anyone willing to fight for you, my girl."

My throat is too tight to speak, so I turn away.

Rook and I enter the elevator and ride down in silence, the glowing numbers reversing their course as we make the descent. We reach the bottom and slip out the service entrance and into the brightly lit streets.

It's several minutes before Rook asks, "Are you okay?"

I exhale a shaky breath. It feels like I've left my body, floating through the clouds, frothing over the sky. "I don't know."

He accepts that answer because he understands it.

"Thank you," I say. "For defending me. No one's ever done that before."

He peers over with what I can only describe as a scrutinizing look. "I already told you, I'm here to protect you, no matter what."

64

We decide to ride the train back to Amery. Rook sits silently, perhaps sensing I don't want to talk. I'm grateful for his steady presence and how he stood up to my mom.

When he said those words, I felt something loosen. Knox would never have chosen me over my father. I would have spent the rest of my life living in fear.

My only regret—and one I will live with for the rest of my life—is that I had to leave my mom behind. At least for now. Maybe I can find a way to help her, too, though divorces are rare in Society. She'd be left with nothing. Once I'm a Storm Guard, I'll receive a salary. Maybe then I can take care of her. It won't be the life she's used to, but I don't know if I'd call her current existence living at all.

My pulse thunders against my ribs, making it hard to breathe.

The train stops at one of the city's central stations, and suddenly I feel like I'm being buried under stone. "I changed my mind about the train," I say. "I want to get out."

"Sure," Rook says, already standing. He grabs my hand, and we exit the platform, taking the stairs up to ground level. We enter the station with its soaring ceilings and shiny marble floors, packed with at least a hundred different vendors selling wares. They include not only Hollows and their ubiquitous cabbage stew and scavengers with their rows of foraged goods, but also artisans and even some food stands, the tantalizing aromas valiantly trying to cancel out the sour smell of cabbage.

The twinkling strands draping across the ceiling glow with soft light, illuminating the entire bustling scene. A string quartet in the center plays soft music, backdropping hundreds of conversations. A few swaying couples dance in the middle of the room, adding to the dreamlike vibe.

"I haven't been here in a while," I say as my racing heart slows. "I forgot how magical it is at night."

"Do you want something to eat?" Rook asks, gesturing to a stand selling colorful desserts. Next to it is a cart offering paper boats filled with crisp fries and topped with your pick of creamy sauces.

"No. I'm not hungry, but I'll come with you."

"Okay, because I'm always hungry," he says, and yeah, with all the exercise we get, he probably needs thousands of calories a day to maintain all that muscle. We approach the fry truck, and he orders a large doused in spicy ketchup with swirls of mayo and topped with crispy onions. He grabs two forks, and we head over to a bench before he hands one to me.

He digs in while I sample a few bites, surprised by how much some greasy food settles my stomach.

"I know I already said thank you," I start. "But I really do appreciate how you stood up to my mom."

He pops a fry into his mouth. "What can I say? Parents always love me."

I snort out a laugh, then start giggling hysterically. "I can't believe I just broke into my own apartment to tell my mom I needed a *sweater*."

"Did you even grab a sweater?" he asks, pretending to check behind me.

"No!" I shout, and we both start laughing. It releases the swelling pressure compressing my ribs. "She knew it, too."

"Do you think she'll say anything to your dad?"

"I don't think so."

My head tips against Rook's shoulder as he nearly polishes off the fries, offering me the last bite with a raised eyebrow.

"You go ahead," I say, and he swallows it down before tossing our garbage into a nearby container. His hand settles loosely on my thigh while I hang on to his arm and we watch the passersby. The chatter swells, the dancers twirl, and if the desire for a life of peace and stillness were an image stirred into motion, this would be it.

"Wanna dance?" Rook asks, and I find myself nodding immediately.

"I thought you didn't dance," I say, dropping my voice, trying to mimic his stern words from the night at Sogno.

He chuckles. "You're the exception, remember?"

I grin as he draws me up, and we wrap our arms around each other before we start to sway. I rest my cheek against his chest as he gently spins us in a circle. After everything I've done and all the pain I've caused, I don't know if I deserve peace, but I can't help wanting it anyway.

The soft strains of music harmonize against the cadence of voices, almost like a lullaby.

That's when I notice someone watching me through the crowd.

I blink and then blink again.

It's the same familiar Hollow I've seen from the train more than once.

"Hey," I say and lift my head.

She turns and starts running, and I'm after her before I can think. I chase her through the station, under an archway, and down a flight of stairs.

"Wait!" I shout. "Please wait!"

She spirals down a staircase that levels off into the tunnels.

"Please! Stop running!" I shout. "Who are you?"

She looks back and then stumbles, allowing me to catch up. I snag her by the elbow and push her against the wall.

"Are you following me?"

She shakes her head and tries to yank her arm from my grip. "No, please. I'm not going to hurt you. Just tell me who you are."

Finally, she stops fighting and sags against the wall, her chest heaving with ragged breaths. She had a head start, but I'm in much better shape. I hear footsteps behind me, and I know it must be Rook, but he hangs back, giving me space.

"You look so much like my old nanny," I whisper. "But you can't be her."

The woman's eyes shift left and right, hunting for an escape.

"I'm Greta," she says finally. Wearily. "I'm her daughter."

I frown. "She didn't have any children, and you're older than me. She *didn't* have kids," I insist, as if my certainty will make it true.

"Seven years older than you," Greta says. "She didn't tell anyone about me."

My thoughts grind to a stop. "Why?"

Greta offers me a withering glare now that she's caught her breath. For some reason, she already hates me. "Take your hands off me, and I'll answer your questions."

"You won't run?"

She shakes her head, and I loosen my grip, ensuring I'm close enough to stop her from bolting again. "Start talking," I say. "Why did she hide you?"

Greta smooths down the front of her tunic.

"Because of what I am," she says plainly, but I understand the uncomfortable shift in her eyes.

"A Keeper," I guess, searching her face, but her hair is light brown, without any hints of purple.

So not exactly like me, but always living in fear regardless.

Greta nods. "She spent every day in the home of one of The Shield's most loyal families. The last thing she wanted to do was draw attention to my existence."

"You mean she spent every day with Raine and me and then went home to you?"

"I barely saw my mother," Greta answers with a defiant lift of her chin.

I shake my head. "Is that why she left? To spend time with you?"

Greta searches my face, bemusement creasing her brow. "You really don't know?"

"Know what?"

"She didn't leave. Your father had her killed."

My stomach drops through my feet. "Why would he do that?"

"I know what you are, too, Poet Graves," she sneers.

I exhale a sharp breath and take a step back. "Did your mother tell you? She was the only one who knew."

Greta scoffs, and what I clocked as mere dislike clearly runs much deeper than that.

She *loathes* me. I took her mother from her, but I'm still not sure why.

"She *wasn't* the only one who knew. Do you really think you could hide that from your father?"

I shake my head, trying to piece it all together.

"Your brother, too, of course," Greta adds, triumphant. She's enjoying this slow reveal of my life peeling apart.

At that, I look up. "Raine? He was a Keeper, too?"

Greta shakes her head with a cruel laugh. "They didn't tell you anything, did they?"

"My *father* knows what I am?" I ask, my mind spinning with a thousand disparate thoughts.

Greta folds her arms, her expression softening, maybe pitying me for how clueless I've been. "He does. And he went to great lengths to protect your secret, leaving me with nothing. Without a mother, I had no one to take care of me. I almost died."

"I'm sorry," I say, hoping she understands how much I mean it. "I'm sorry you lost your mother because of me. Because of us."

And Raine. Why did he never say anything? He was a Keeper, too? Does it run in family lines? Were we bonded by blood in ways I couldn't begin to imagine?

"Does my mother know?"

Greta shakes her head. "I don't know."

She peers past my shoulder, and I look back at Rook, still keeping his distance.

I turn to Greta again, but she's already started running, disappearing down the tunnel, swallowed by the shadows.

"Wait!" I call. "Let me help you!"

She ignores me, and I don't try to follow. Maybe she'll find me when she's ready.

A moment later, Rook approaches and carefully takes my hand.

"Who was that?"

"Someone I knew. Or I mean, someone who was connected to someone I knew."

"Are you okay?"

I blow out a breath and rub my forehead as a sharp pain shoots across my scalp.

"I think I need to lie down."

"Let's go," he says, taking my hand and leading me back to Amery.

I'm grateful when Rook doesn't ask me any more questions.

I'm not sure I can offer up this shame for him to witness.

Greta lost everything because of me. She grew up without a mother.

And my father . . . Every time I think he can't get any crueler, he surprises me in the worst possible way.

I guess we've both had our secrets to keep.

65

With just a few days until the graduation masquerade, the school descends into a flurry of final exams and event preparation.

I spend half my time with Domino and Journey, shopping for dresses and planning our night, and the other half designing the break-in with Rook and Edward.

Our little "project" seems to have invigorated Edward. He's animated again, coming up with ideas and theories, downloading maps, and scoping possible entrances and exits. He even paid a visit to Trinity's parents and swiped a key card from Mr. Robins so we can access his office and, more importantly, his computers, once we get inside.

Throughout it all, I try to be normal. I try not to let that encounter with Greta in the tunnels throw me off. Raine was a Keeper, and now he's gone. He left me and never confessed. I'm desperate to ask my mother what she knows, but I can't put it into a text that could be monitored by The Shield.

She'll be at the masquerade, and I'm hoping I can talk to her then.

I also haven't shared what Greta told me with Rook. I'm not sure what's holding me back. I'm ashamed of what happened. It feels like some of this was my fault.

I do plan to ask Edward if he can look for information about Raine's death once he hacks the government computers. I need to know if there's more to the story than we've been told.

I also don't tell Rook that my father *might* know I'm a Keeper. Maybe Greta was mistaken? Maybe it was something she told herself to villainize him. Whatever the case, I'm not ready to discuss it yet—with anyone.

It's the night before the party, and I'm tossing and turning. Dreaming of long tunnels and shadows snatching me from darkened corners. My mother's face and a string of bruises on her neck. Rook being thrown off cliffs and high towers.

Then someone is gently shaking me awake.

"Poet." Rook's deep voice slices through the dark. "Wake up."

My eyes pop open, and I stare up at him, disoriented, breathing heavily.

"You were calling out," he says.

I sink back into the pillow and brush a piece of hair from my forehead. "Nightmares."

He drops down to the side of my bed. "You okay?"

"Just anxious about tomorrow, I think."

He takes my hand and holds it close to his chest. "Makes sense."

"Will you lie with me?" I ask, and he nods.

"Of course."

He climbs over me and settles on the far side against the wall.

"The storm isn't helping," I whisper. A bright flash illuminates the window, a soft amethyst glow highlighting the contours of his face and reflecting in the piercing in his brow. We haven't had an opportunity to visit the outskirts with everything going on, and the incessant itching is starting to get to me.

"I know," he whispers back. "We'll head out as soon as this is over."

We. He says it so casually, but I think this is what we're becoming.

We. Us.

It's at that moment that I feel connected to him by more than just the touch of our hands and the brush of our knees. We are bound by this secret that draws a line between us despite every difference and every barrier. An understanding forged from the need to spend a lifetime hiding in the light. Maybe if we're successful tomorrow, we won't have to hide anymore.

I smile and reach out to touch his cheek before resting my hand on his chest, the rapid thump of his heart vibrating up my arm. He closes his eyes and exhales softly, his fingers trailing against my stomach. I turn ever so slightly toward him.

Thanks to final exams and plotting our break-in, we haven't had much time alone. I bury my nose in the curve of his throat and inhale deeply with a gentle whimper.

"What are you doing?" he asks with what sounds like barely restrained control.

I peer up. "I've missed you."

"I've been right across the room."

"It isn't close enough."

His hazel eyes shine in a flash of purple, and a smirk curls on his lips as we shift until we're pressed together, our mouths hovering an inch apart.

Slowly, he lowers his head and kisses me, his warm lips fusing with mine. His fingers twist in the fabric of my tank top while our thighs and knees tangle together. Slowly, his hand slides higher, trailing up my stomach, where his fingertips brush the bottom of my breasts.

"Rook," I moan. "I want . . ." I can't seem to articulate my thoughts.

"What do you want, Poet?" he asks. "Tell me."

"I want you. All of you."

He makes a pained sort of sound as his hand travels back down my stomach and teases the edge of my sleep shorts.

"I want to touch you," he whispers. "I want to touch you so badly it hurts. Sometimes it's all I can think about."

"Yes," I say. "Please."

His mouth closes over mine, and his hand slides lower, dipping past my waistband, gently finding the place where I need him. I gasp into his mouth as his warm fingers play over me, making my hips writhe.

"You're so fucking beautiful," he moans against my lips. "Strong and brilliant. I just . . . I just wasn't expecting this. *You.* I wasn't expecting you."

"Rook," I gasp, clinging to his shoulders while his fingers tease out ribbons of satin heat.

He smiles against the curve of my throat, his hand moving between my thighs, bringing me to the edge before he kisses me again, and then I burst in a glittering shower of sparks. I moan against him as he continues teasing and touching, leaving me breathless and limp under the warmth of his body.

Slowly, he slides his hand away as we kiss again. My fingers trail over his stomach, the planes of muscle and dusting of hair. I drift lower, running a fingertip over the waist of his pants.

"Poe," he gasps when I shift lower, feeling his hardness pressing against the fabric, and he exhales with a soft whimper.

"I want to touch you, too," I whisper.

"Skies, please, Poet. I'm losing my mind."

My hand returns to his stomach and then slips lower, down past his waistband, where I find him hot, heavy, wanting. My fingers wrap around him before I slowly, carefully slide my hand down. His hips thrust, and I grip him tighter while he urges me on.

"Like that," he rasps. "Yes. More."

More. I want so much more.

A minute later, I feel him release with a shuddering moan.

Eventually, he pulls me up and touches his forehead to mine. We stay like that for a long minute, not moving, just breathing, just existing together. I'm not sure how many perfect moments we're afforded during a life, but this feels like it might be one of mine.

"We should get some sleep; we have a big day ahead of us," he says before he grins. "Tomorrow, when this is all over, I want to celebrate with you. All night. Until the sun comes up and neither of us can walk straight."

I giggle and return his smile.

Then, I reach up to kiss him and whisper into the amethyst shadows, "I can't wait."

66

Amery buzzes with news of another attack near the school the following morning. Another Keeper. The culprits have already been arrested, and the knowledge does nothing to settle the constant worry forming a knot in my stomach.

The Extinguishers have been seen everywhere. Roaming supermarkets and public events. Walking through the city. I consider asking Rook if we should call off our whole mission and wait for a less precarious moment to do this, but they're closing in on us, and we're running out of time.

When Rook and I woke this morning, we were still tangled together, and I can't stop thinking about how he made me feel last night, nor his promise to "celebrate" once we've accomplished our task.

My cheeks heat as I absentmindedly stir my soup at the table in the cafeteria where I'm sitting with Domino and Journey.

"Hello?" Domino snaps her fingers under my nose. "Earth to Poet?"

I look up, and both of my friends give me knowing looks.

"Do you have something to share with the class?" Domino asks, folding her arms. "Perhaps something about a gorgeous outcast from the Wastes?"

I can't even pretend to hide it as a grin stretches across my face, and we all break into giggles. I shake my head and continue stirring my soup as they beg for details. A normal, everyday interaction like this is exactly what I needed to settle the anxious churning in my gut.

"Stop it!" I laugh. "I'm not telling you anything."

"Just tell me he's a good kisser," Domino says. "He looks like he's a good kisser."

"He's a very good kisser," I say with another grin that I'm helpless to contain, and they high-five each other. They needle me a while longer, while I offer up a few details without invading Rook's privacy. It's nice to feel like they're genuinely happy for me and aren't just digging for gossip.

"So, we're getting ready for the party in your room?" Domino asks.

"Of course. Go grab your things, and I'll meet you there."

"Perfect," Domino says before they both leave.

After they're gone, I try eating a few more bites of soup before I give up and head back to my room to find Rook pulling on a black velvet jacket embroidered with black detailing at the cuffs and down the front. He's wearing fitted black pants and a tailored white button-up shirt with black boots.

"Hi," I say, closing the door behind me and admiring how everything molds to the curves of his arms and legs. "You're dressed already?"

He shrugs on the coat and buttons it up before spreading his arms and staring down at himself.

"How do I look?" He peers up at me with an uncharacteristically vulnerable expression.

"You look really good," I say a little breathlessly. "Like . . . wow."

He assesses himself again. "You think? I've never worn anything like this in my life."

"Well, it suits you," I say, leaning in the doorway and taking my time scanning him from head to toe, very obviously checking him out.

"Keep looking at me like that, Trouble, and—" he growls.

I meet his eyes. "And what?" I challenge.

He huffs out a short laugh. "And you're going to be the death of me, aren't you?"

I smile and drop my arms, crossing the room and stretching up onto my tiptoes to peck him on the lips. He cups my elbows with his hands.

"Thank you for all your help," I say. "With the planning. For just being there for me the last few months. I blew up my whole life, and yet, I can't help but think you've made that one of the best decisions ever."

He offers me a half smile. "Poet, you have no idea how important this time has been to me. I—" He stops, inhales sharply, wavers about something in the flash of his eyes. "Tomorrow, I want to talk about a few things, okay? Stuff about my life, and more about why I'm here. There are some things you should know about me that I wasn't sure I could share, but I think . . . I think I can trust you."

"You can," I reply immediately. "With anything. I want to know all your secrets, Rook. The dark ones and the happy ones. I want to know *you*."

He searches my face. "I want you to know me, too, Poet Graves." After another moment, he adds, "I'm going to meet with Edward to go over the details one more time. I'll see you at the party?"

"I'll be there," I say. "I'll be the one with the dress."

He leans in to kiss me, then picks up the black velvet mask from the bed, tying it over his face. I don't know how it manages to make him look even more devastating, but I struggle to breathe around the sparkling thing fizzing in my chest. He looks dangerous and mysterious, just like that day when he first arrived and upended all our worlds.

We stare at each other for another second before he takes my hand and presses his lips to the back. "I'll see you soon."

Then he leaves the room while I wait for Domino and Journey to arrive.

An hour later, we're all dressed for the ball. Domino opted for a bright red dress with a strapless bodice and a skirt made of swooping layers of satin. Her ornate mask is decorated with bits of red and gold lace and beading. Journey chose a sequined black dress with hot pink lining that peeks through a high slit up the side and a sleek mask of pink leather.

My dress is soft and flowing, with a cascade of purple roses traveling over my shoulder and a skirt of white and amethyst layers of sheer silk. It's absolutely beautiful and one of the prettiest dresses I've ever owned.

My purple half mask ties with a white ribbon, accented with white lace and beading.

"You look almost like an Empire Storm," Domino remarks as I check myself in the mirror. I smile before I walk over and give her a hug.

"I'm so glad you came to Amery." I look at Journey. "Both of you. This year has been so much better with you two in it."

Journey scoots off the bed, and we all hug.

"Next year is gonna rock!" Journey says, and I have to laugh at her enthusiasm.

"It really is."

As long as I can stop the Extinguishers from hitting the target on my back.

While I put on the finishing touches of my makeup, I can't help but think of Trinity. We should have been doing this together. Instead, we haven't spoken in what feels like forever.

A blast of wind rattles the windows, and I turn to look outside.

"Weather's getting rough," Domino says, a worried groove forming between her brows, but the storm will also serve as the distraction we need tonight.

My cadet boots lie in the corner, and I walk over to stuff my feet inside. I do have a set of pretty purple heels, but they don't seem practical for the break-in.

"Boots?" Journey asks.

"I did something to my ankle in the gym yesterday," I say, tying them up and throwing my skirt over the toes. "See? You can't even tell."

Journey gives me a skeptical look and shrugs as another gust of wind tosses a blast of raindrops at the windows.

"Ugh, we're going to get wet," Domino says. "It's starting to rain."

"Bring a jacket," I say, opting for cropped, fitted black leather. "It's a quick walk across the plaza."

"My hair," Journey whimpers as she fluffs it up in the mirror.

"I have one with a hood you can use," I say, opening my closet and handing it over.

Once we're all suitably covered, we head upstairs to find dozens of other students joining the flow, everyone dressed in their best. An electric sense of excitement hangs in the air, and despite the nervous pit in my stomach, I find myself swept up in everyone's enthusiasm. We scurry across the plaza, clinging to our skirts that toss in the wind before entering the lobby of the Citadel.

Servers dressed in black-and-white suits bearing golden platters with flutes of sparkling wine greet us as they direct us toward the ballroom. The hall is magnificently decorated with giant drooping boughs of greenery, covered in colorful bursts of flowers and tall golden candelabras, each fitted with dripping candles.

The ballroom is resplendent with its gilded, frescoed ceilings and walls. The hardwood floors gleam in the flicker of candlelight and the thousands of rows of string lights draped across the ceiling.

Domino gasps and clings to my arm as we take it all in. It's positively magical. "Some days I wake up and can't believe I'm here," she says. "A Society party."

"Let's ditch these jackets," Journey says, shaking off a shower of rain-drops. "And then I want one of those cocktails."

We're moving toward the coat check line when I spot Edward standing in the corner. "I'll be right back," I say, waving at Domino and Journey before weaving through the crowd.

"Hey," I say, coming up to Edward. "Are we all set?"

He's dressed for the ball in a suit similar to Rook's but with a more disheveled air, thanks to his undone jacket and the open top buttons of his shirt.

"I'm ready," he says with a lopsided grin that seems at odds with the moment. "Everything's good to go."

"You're sure?"

"Don't worry—I've got this handled."

He doesn't seem nervous at all. In fact, he seems eager.

"Okay, thank you. I know this has been a lot of work."

"I like working with Rook," he says. "He's different from what I thought he'd be."

"Yeah," I say. "I know the feeling."

"What's with you two?" Edward asks. "You've gotten pretty close, it seems."

It's my turn to smile. "I think so?"

"Do you like him?" I shrug, trying to make it look casual, but Edward grins. "Well, he's obsessed with you."

My forehead furrows. "He is?"

"Definitely. I can tell. I'm happy for you. You deserve someone special, Poe."

I exhale a soft breath. "Thank you," I whisper. "Before I forget, there's another thing I'm hoping we can find out. I learned something about Raine recently, and I need you to see if there are any more details about his death."

"Raine?" he says, his eyes widening. "What happened to him?"

"I'm not sure, but I need to find out."

"What do you mean by that? He died in a Solitude attack."

"I know, but it might not be that simple."

He studies my face, trying to read what I can't and won't share.

"Okay," he says. "I'm trusting you."

"You're the best, Edward. I'd love to see you more. Maybe we can grab coffee sometimes?"

Losing Trinity has been extremely hard, and if I examine myself more closely, I realize how I let myself get distracted by everything else in my life. It's made the pain of losing her a bit softer, without all the same rough edges. Edward has been sitting with only this piece of him she carved out.

"I'd like that," he answers before we're interrupted by a voice booming over the loudspeaker.

"Ladies and gentlemen!" I turn toward a stage at the room's far end, where a man stands holding a microphone. "Welcome to New Manhattan's annual graduation masquerade! It's my pleasure to welcome all four of our esteemed Houses to participate in this most honored of traditions." The man pauses for a round of applause before gesturing to his left. "I'd like to welcome The Shield to the stage!"

Another chorus of thunderous clapping breaks out as Chancellor Marks, General Sol, and Chancellor Orsen all emerge from a door along with a contingent of their Circle Guard. General Sol bounds up the stage, formidable in a purple velvet suit with curve-hugging pants and a jacket that flares elegantly at the waist. Her silver boots are polished to a high shine, and her hair is pulled back into a high knot with the tail draping over a shoulder.

Chancellors Marks and Orsen both wear dark suits, crisp white shirts, and shiny black shoes.

General Sol accepts the microphone and bows.

"Welcome!" she says to the room. "We are honored to join you at the end of another school year, when New Manhattan's brightest and best come together to celebrate our successes."

More applause as several new people join The Shield on the stage, including an elegant couple dripping with jewels and confidence: Scion Beaufort with her stunning wife.

They greet the leaders with air kisses and handshakes as another pair ascends.

I knew they'd be here.

Obviously, they were expected to attend.

But seeing them in the flesh becomes a sharp kick to the stomach.

My parents.

67

I immediately start drifting toward the stage, drawn in by the gravitational pull of my mother and father. Mom looks regal in a dress not dissimilar to mine, adorned with purple roses and black sparkling lace. My father's hair is neatly slicked, a perfect complement to his dark, elegant suit.

My throat hurts, and my heart pumps painfully in my chest as I stare at them. I miss my mom so much. The key card I stole burns a hole in my pocket, and I wonder if my father has noticed its absence. Maybe he has multiples and this was a backup.

General Sol is saying something, but I can't hear it over the blood rushing through my ears. I become aware of Rook and Domino appearing at my sides, prepared to take the stage due to their finishing times in our final test, but I only have eyes for my parents.

My father knows what I am. He killed someone to protect me, leaving Greta without a mother. It was wrong and heinous, and though I'm not surprised he'd do it, I *am* surprised he'd do it for me. He lied to The Shield for the sake of his children. Why?

I didn't think he had that in him.

As if feeling my eyes on him, my father looks over, and our gazes catch.

A shadow passes across his expression, his lips pressing together. I don't know what I read there. Regret? Sadness? Maybe I'm just seeing what I want.

"Please welcome to the stage Poet Graves!"

When I hear my name, the world around me shrinks, noise spilling into my ears like I'm emerging from under a layer of dirt.

"What?" I ask no one in particular.

"Go on," Rook whispers in my ear. His hand rests on my lower back. "You're being called up."

Right. I'm being honored for winning third place during the cadet exam. I nod, and then I start walking. The room has gone strangely quiet as I place a boot on the step, trying to gather myself. My knees have become spring twigs, thin and delicate, likely to bend under my weight.

Slowly, I climb the stairs to notice three other groups of students are already waiting—evaluation winners from the other Houses. They eye me with suspicion as I approach the general, who waits in the middle of the stage. She watches me with an assessing look, as though she can sense something is off.

I stop in front of her, and she holds out her hand. Somehow, I manage to reach out and shake it. Can she feel the clamminess of my palm? She grips my hand tightly, her expression wholly focused.

She warned me about defecting from Fiama.

"Congratulations," she says. "Despite your rather dramatic year, it seems you've managed to end on a high note."

A swell of nervous laughter travels through the room at my expense.

"Yes," I say weakly. "Thank you."

The general eyes me for another moment before dismissing me and moving on to announcing Domino and then Rook. I take my place in front of the Beauforts, placing me right next to my parents, and I can't help looking over my shoulder.

They play their parts well, as I should have known they would, keeping their eyes forward as they stare out at the room and offer congratulations to the three House Fiama evaluation winners. It all happens as if I'm in a dream, like I'm moving through sludge.

The general talks about something, but I hear none of it.

When applause erupts and everyone begins moving off the stage, I assume we must be finished. I start walking and bump into someone. My mother turns around and looks down. I've stepped on the train of her dress, and we both stare at the toe of my boot peeking from the edge of my skirt.

"Poet?" she asks. "Why are you wearing that jacket over your lovely dress?"

It's exactly the kind of thing she'd say, and for a moment, it feels so *normal* that I want to cry. I grip her elbow, squeezing it.

"Did you know, too?" I ask in a low, desperate whisper.

"What are you—" She tries to wrench her arm away, but I grip her tighter.

"Did you know?" I demand again. "Did you *both* know?"

"Poet," my father interrupts sharply, wrapping his big hand around my wrist. "Let go of your mother."

"Dad," I whisper, searching for any sign he still loves me.

He pauses, contrition flashing in his eyes, before he glances past me. His gaze lands on Chancellor Marks, whose head is tipped in curiosity. My dad's expression shutters, and he yanks my mother out of my grip, breaking my heart all over again.

A commotion at the back of the room has them both turning away. The crowd has parted, revealing an Extinguisher with his stunner gripped in his hands and his feet spread. "Bring her out!" he demands.

A group of people moves at the back of the crowd. A moment later, Lieutenant Dire appears with Trinity's elbow in his grip while she stumbles behind him. They stop, and he pulls her toward him, pressing her back to his chest and banding a thick arm around her throat.

"Which one?" he demands, and Trinity peers up at him with frightened eyes.

It's then my heart begins to pound as her gaze finds the front of the room.

Everything coalesces. Calcifies into clarity and the certainty that I was right.

That flash of red hair during my final cadet exam.

The hug she gave me before she walked away.

Not the Breaker. But my best friend.

The years we've spent together, when she had to know there was *something* different about me.

I take a step, moving slowly.

Trinity is crying. Sobbing. Shaking her head.

"Which one!" Dire demands again. "Who did you see?"

He squeezes his arm, and Trinity gags.

"I won't ask again," he snarls.

Everything slows down.

"Poet," Trinity chokes out. "Poet Graves."

A collective gasp circles around the room. My entire body goes numb.

They're coming toward me. Extinguishers holding their stunners.

Burgundy uniforms.

The color of dried blood.

I can't seem to move. Can't put these pieces together. How could Trinity do this?

That's when the sirens start.

Red flashes filter through the windows, painting everyone in bloody light. The Circle Guard closes in, surrounding The Shield as the entire room erupts in panic and dozens more Guards stream through the doors.

The wailing continues, blaring out over the city in warning.

A Blood Storm is coming.

68

I'm shoved left and right as the Guards close in. The room swirls with panic, shutting off the path between the Extinguishers and me.

I snap out of stasis. I have to run.

I search around me, but every familiar face is gone. I hop up and down, looking for Rook, Domino, my parents, but I can't find anyone in the surrounding crush. It doesn't matter. I need to get away.

I spot the general walking toward me, while Chancellors Marks and Orsen are enclosed by their Guards, no doubt headed for their personal fireproof shelters. Everyone will be running for cover inside one of the city's many communal sanctuaries.

I consider my options. They know what I am, and they'll be hunting for me now. More than ever, I need to expose the truth and prove I'm not what they think.

Stick to the plan, I decide, hoping Edward and Rook do the same. With any luck, everyone will be too busy with the storm to worry about me right now. I pick up my long skirt and pound down the stairs, shoving among the crowd flowing out of the room as red lights flash through the windows and sirens wail, nearly shattering my eardrums.

I grunt and push, dragged by the tide of bodies until we spill outside before everyone scatters. The sky is on fire, red clouds bleeding across the horizon, flashing with crimson points of light.

Blood Storm cloud bursts don't explode with galvanic energy.

It's much, much worse.

They hurtle balls of fire toward the earth, burning down huge sections of the city and killing everything in their path.

A shiver runs along my spine. I've only ever seen one in my lifetime, when I was a little girl. I remember the screams tearing through the night sky as the city erupted with fiery explosions.

I spot dozens of Patrols in their dark uniforms already flooding the plaza, trying to snuff out flames and protect the Citadel.

Thankfully, it seems that I've been forgotten in the chaos, and I make my way to the back, where I planned to meet up with Rook and Edward.

When I arrive, I find Edward already pacing with a large pack strapped to his back. He stops when he sees me. His gaze is searching as he scans me from head to toe, probably wondering about a lot of things I could never tell him.

"Is it true?" he asks. "Is this why you need to break in? You're a . . . Keeper?"

I nod, panic swelling up my throat. "I'm sorry. I should have told you. I—"

He shakes his head. "Poet, it's fine. I think I understand, but . . . I hate to ask this. Am I safe with you?"

"Yes," I gasp in a rush. "I'm fine. I promise."

"Okay," he replies, zero judgment in his eyes. "How could Trinity do that to you?"

"I don't know," I whisper.

"Skies," he says. "She's never been the person I thought she was, has she?"

Edward presses his mouth together as a cloud explodes overhead. A blazing comet hurtles toward the plaza, sending up a shower of fiery stones and debris. A blast of heat burning my cheeks, Edward and I step back, seeking shelter in the recess of the door's alcove.

"Where's Rook?" I ask, checking my phone, hoping that he's messaged me. Nothing. Did he get caught in the crowd? I try calling, but there's no answer.

"Poet, if we're doing this, we have to do it now," Edward says. "We look even more suspicious loitering out here."

"You're still with me?"

"Yes, let's do this."

"We have to wait for Rook." I peer across the plaza, hoping he'll appear.

"You can't stand out here any longer. They'll be looking for you."

Reluctantly, I follow Edward into the lobby and approach the gates leading to The Shield's security wing. I pull out my father's stolen key card and hold it against the magnetic panel with my breath held. It beeps, then the lock clicks.

Edward shoves the gates open as I stand paralyzed with indecision.

"Come on!" he says. "We can't wait for him."

A planter sits next to the gates, and I shove the key into the soil, ensuring it's covered with a thin layer of dirt.

"What kind of plant is this?" I ask.

"What?" Edward asks, practically bouncing on his feet.

"What is this?" I ask again.

"Fuck, I don't know! A ficus?"

"Okay," I say and text the word "ficus" to Rook, hoping he understands my cryptic clue.

"Poet," Edward hisses, and I follow him inside. We enter a small area with a bank of elevators blessedly free of Guards or personnel.

At least this part of my plan worked.

"Let's go," Edward says, punching the button. An elevator to the far left immediately slides open with a soft ding that sounds more like a cannon shot.

Inside, he presses another button for the thirty-second floor to access Mr. Robins's office. While we make the ascent, I explain everything to Edward about what I'm looking for. To his credit, he doesn't freak out. Just takes it all in stride.

After he taps our second stolen key card on the panel, we enter a spacious room with hardwood floors overlaid with rugs, two love seats, and a sofa arranged in the center.

Everything glows with red shadows reflected through massive floor-to-ceiling windows. I watch the tumbling storm clouds bleeding across the sky as fiery scarlet orbs plunge toward the earth. I've never witnessed a Blood Storm up close, and there's something mesmerizing about its casual, violent destruction.

Edward wastes no time, crossing the room and passing through a set of double doors that reveals a large U-shaped desk topped with a bank of computers. Behind that, a wall of screens reveals various parts of the building.

Edward studies the screens for a moment, and I check my phone, praying Rook has replied. I send him another message with the word "office."

Edward has pulled up to the desk and settled into Mr. Robins's big leather chair, already typing a million miles a minute on one of the numerous backlit keyboards. The room is completely silent but for the distant, muffled wails of the Blood Storm sirens and the rapid click of his fingers.

I can't sit still, so I pace back and forth, checking my phone every few seconds for a reply from Rook.

"Can you stop?" Edward asks. "You're making me anxious."

"Sorry," I mumble and return to the sitting area, giving him space to work.

Another wall of monitors covers one side of the room, and I walk over to ensure we've gone undetected. A screen reveals the immediate hallway outside, perfect for keeping an eye out for any unwanted visitors.

I study each monitor, noting a few Guards stationed at various points, but almost everyone has left to deal with the storm.

A figure catches my attention, moving down a hallway, opening and closing doors. I can't be sure at first, and my eyes must be deceiving me, because I'd swear it was Rook. I move in closer, but there's no mistaking it now. I'd recognize that easy gait and that flop of hair anywhere.

What is he doing? The number in the corner of the screen tells me he isn't anywhere near the thirty-second floor. In fact, he's somewhere lower, in something called Sub Basement B.

He's holding something in his hand that looks like a key card, but not the same bright red one I left for him inside the flowerpot. I search the bank of screens and find the door where Edward and I entered, noting the pile of soil now lying at the foot of the planter.

Quickly, I search for Rook, a pit of dread solidifying in my stomach.

I tap out another message.

I text the word "in," suggesting Edward has accessed the computers.

For a second, I think it's nothing—just a hitch in his stride, the way people pause when they remember something small and unimportant.

Then he pulls his phone from his pocket.

My breath stutters. I lean closer to the screen, as if distance is the problem, as if I could somehow make him feel me watching.

He looks at the screen. His thumb stills.

I know that look. I've seen it a hundred times—the faint narrowing of his eyes, the way his mouth becomes unreadable when he's thinking. When he's deciding.

My chest tightens, sharp and sudden, like something inside me has been grabbed and twisted.

He doesn't type.

He locks the screen and slips the phone back into his pocket.

Just like that.

My hand flutters up, pressing flat against my chest. I welcome it. Anything to anchor me here, in this moment, where I'm watching the man I trusted choose something else.

Rook turns back to his search, checking doors and locks. Focused. Intent.

Whatever he's looking for matters more than I do.

The thought lands softly, almost gently. Maybe that's what makes it so unbearable.

I swallow, but my throat feels sealed shut. My ribs ache, like they're being pulled inward, like my body is trying to protect something that's already broken.

I realize, distantly, that I don't actually know anything about Rook Athira. Not really.

I know the version of him that arrived from the Wastes with a cocky smile and a confidence sharp enough to cut through my defenses. I know the way he looks at me when he thinks I'm not paying attention. The way he kisses like he means it.

But standing here, watching him ignore me, I understand how little of that was ever mine.

Rook Athira.

I don't even know if that's his name.

He came from nowhere. No past. No history.

And apparently, a future I'm not part of.

As he continues searching rooms, descending another floor, it's obvious he's on a mission. One he had planned all along.

Slowly, I watch his progress. I search the screens, wondering if I can see what's inside the rooms, but they reveal nothing, only the hallways. I consider sending him another message, but I don't know if I can stomach watching him ignore it again.

He knows where I am, so what is he doing? What is Rook planning?

Are Edward and I in danger?

"Poet!" Edward hisses from the other room. "Come see this."

I stare at the screen for another moment before I stumble toward Edward. "Any luck?"

"I'm still working on accessing the research files, but I found this."

My gaze pings to where he sits typing on a keyboard, his cheeks contoured by the white glow of the screen on one side and the swirling crimson clouds on the other.

He then points to the TV screens at my back.

The wall lights up with a low-res black-and-white video playing a scene, multiplied a dozen times. I tiptoe over and peer at the closest.

It takes only a moment to understand it's a video feed from one of the Storm Towers that surround the city. My mouth parts when I spot Raine fighting hand-to-hand with a Solitude.

There are dozens more. Breakers and Solitudes are all locked in a violent skirmish. But I can't take my eyes off my brother. I reach out to touch him, wincing when a shock of static snaps at my fingertip.

Despite his obvious distress, I can't help but cherish this glimpse. I miss him so much.

More Solitudes swarm into the scene, carrying makeshift weapons, outnumbering the Guards.

And then I see *him*.

Rook.

A few years younger. Slimmer. Less muscle. His hair a bit shorter, but I have no doubt it's him. He's busy fighting with a Breaker, and now I understand why he was already so good on the sparring mat. Why he beat us all in the cadet examination with ease.

Rook Athira was never who he claimed.

I can't decide where to look.

My gaze pings between Rook and my brother. He was there that night. He was *there* the night Raine died.

The sky flashes in grayscale cloud bursts as the fighting continues.

I move closer, my nose almost pressed to the curved glass, my chest heaving with the fiery residue of Rook's lies.

Spark explodes from the heavens, forming several plasma arcs, blitzing half the scene. There's no sound in the recording, but I imagine their screams. More people enter and exit from the sides. I can barely discern what's happening through a flowing rush of bodies.

Then Raine is hit.

A bolt of Spark strikes as he's knocked off his feet by a Solitude.

But they both come out of the plasma arc unscathed. Another Keeper. Raine goes flying, landing on the ground, sparks dancing across his hair and clothing.

It takes me a moment to realize the Solitudes have fled, leaving only a circle of Breakers behind. I watch a Guard stand up and walk over to Raine, where he stares down at my brother's limp body still glittering with Spark.

They know what he is.

The Guard looks up and starts shouting something.

I wish I could reach into the screen and put myself in this moment.

What happens next?

Raine's chest rises and falls as the wind tosses his hair.

Nothing happens for several minutes as the Guard stands over Raine with a stun gun pointed at my brother's head. I slowly piece together what must be happening.

They've called for the Extinguishers to collect Raine.

My stomach churns, fear curdling in my gut.

A moment later, the Guard straightens, his posture erect as he salutes someone off camera.

A person enters the frame, but it's not who I expect.

General Sol approaches on sure steps, standing over Raine's body.

She toes his boot as he shifts, his eyelids fluttering.

Not dead, just passed out.

"Raine," I whisper, touching the screen.

The general gestures to someone, and then two of her Circle Guards appear. One approaches the Guard who was standing watch over Raine and blasts him in the stomach, killing him instantly. I gasp and cover my mouth as the general reaches down and snuffs out the sparks clinging to my brother's body.

When she's finished, she nods, and her Guards take him by the wrists and ankles before they carry him away. The general stares at the spot where he was lying and then looks at the sky and the rolling clouds flashing with light.

A moment later, she also walks away.

The feed cuts off, and I stare at the blank screen, trying to comprehend everything I just witnessed.

My head is spinning, a wave of dizziness making me stumble into the wall. I lean one hand against it, letting it hold me up as my legs threaten to give out. My brother wasn't dead. The Solitudes didn't take his body.

The general knew what he was, and *she* took him. Why didn't she call the Extinguishers?

It was never the Solitudes.

And Rook . . .

Rook, who lied about his intentions tonight, was there the night my brother was taken.

That's when the office door bursts open and a Circle Guard enters, pointing his stunner at us.

"Get your hands up!" he shouts.

69

Edward and I both spin around.

"Hands up where I can see them!" the Guard repeats, training his stun gun on me. "Who are you, and what are you doing here?"

I stagger on my feet as he aims his weapon at Edward, who slowly lifts his hands off the keyboard.

His gaze flicks to me.

He saw everything, too. He also knows what Raine was.

"Who are you?" the Guard asks again.

I don't know how to answer his question. Who *am* I? An hour ago, I was Poet Graves. Storm Guard cadet who thought she was figuring out her life.

And now? I have no fucking clue.

The Guard reaches for the comms pinned to his uniform to call for backup. The only way out of here is through the door he's currently blocking.

"Attention, Circle Guard," he says. "I have two break-in suspects on thirty-two in quadrant five."

Edward is side-eyeing his monitor, where the video of Raine has looped back to the beginning. With a quick glance in my direction, he lunges for the keyboard, striking a key before the screen goes dark, wiping away the evidence of our investigation. I hope.

"I said don't move!" the Guard shouts as he fires his stunner. A bolt of light strikes Edward in the chest. He goes flying, crashing into the bank of computers and slumping to the floor in a shower of glass and sparks.

I scream. At least I think I do. *Someone* is screaming, and my throat is raw. I dive for Edward, but the Guard shouts again, "Don't move!"

I stop, raising my hands as I stare helplessly at Edward. At least he wasn't blitzed. Blood trickles down his temple, but he's still breathing.

The Guard approaches on careful steps, his weapon pointed at my chest.

"Who are you, girl? Why are you here?" he asks with a snarl.

I back up, hitting the window until he's almost on me.

Then something knocks him from behind, and he trips forward. I manage to sidestep out of the way as he crashes into the window.

Rook tackles him to the ground, using his element of surprise. The Guard grunts and kicks, while Rook throws several punches. I think of the video I just saw and the way Rook fought the Breakers with such ease and skill. It becomes obvious as they roll together across the floor that, despite his competence on the sparring mats, he was always holding himself back.

They continue tussling, and I can't decide what I should do. Run? I don't want to leave Edward, but I'm also not sure if I'm safe with Rook.

He cocks his arm and delivers a blow to the Guard's cheek. The man cries out, and I hear the crack of bone before Rook snatches his stun gun and scrambles up, blasting the Guard in the chest.

He didn't even blink.

I stare at Rook, surer than ever that I have absolutely no idea who he really is.

"Are you okay?" he asks, looking up. Despite the fight, he's barely winded at all.

Am I *okay*?

"Did he hurt you?"

"No," I say. "I'm fine."

Physically, at least.

"What's wrong?" he asks, because I haven't moved. I'm just staring at him, trying to organize my thoughts.

"You were there that night," I say. "When Raine was attacked."

He blinks, something passing behind his eyes.

I want him to deny it. Tell me I was mistaken. That the video was fake, or he has an evil twin brother, or something.

"I was planning to tell you," he says, knocking the breath from my chest. "I was going to tell you everything."

"Everything?"

Obviously, there's more to say. I think about Rook searching those hallways. This is about so much more than my brother and that night. He didn't *just* come here to find out more about what he is.

"Poet, we have to get out of here before they come for us. They know what you are now. I promise that I'll tell you everything, but not here."

I shake my head. "I don't know who *you* are."

He approaches, the stunner still gripped in his hand and his palm flattened to his heart. "I'm still me—I swear to you. There are some things I couldn't share, but I promise you have nothing to fear from me."

I open my mouth and close it. "We can't leave Edward."

Rook glances at his unconscious form. "They aren't after him. They're after you."

"Me?" My mind is having trouble catching up. It's all clouded and foggy, swimming through mud.

"The Extinguishers are coming for you, and they won't ask questions, Poet. They'll shoot before they listen to a word you have to say. Please. I'm begging you," Rook pleads. "Just come and I'll tell you everything as soon as we're safe."

Slowly, I nod as he takes my hand. I'm numb. I barely feel it as he tugs me away, glass crunching under my feet as we cross Mr. Robins's office and enter the hallway. I look back at Edward's slumped form, praying he'll be all right, but Rook is pulling me away.

"Stop!" someone shouts from the far end of the hall. Two more Guards materialize, and Rook spins, shoving me back. He fires the stunner, two blasts in quick succession, striking each Guard before they have a chance to react.

"Run!" he orders, pulling me by the hand in the opposite direction.

More Guards appear.

"This way!" Rook shouts as we barrel into a stairwell.

Footsteps pound from below, and the blast from a stun gun fires up.

"Climb!" Rook says. I'm too dazed to resist. I follow him up and up, spiraling higher and higher until we reach the top floor. The sounds of the chase are growing closer as we emerge onto the roof of the building, where the wind gusts and red clouds churn across the sky.

Rook is moving behind me, using something to barricade the door. I see none of it. Feel nothing as I drift toward the edge to take in the city burning below. Flames flicker in the dark, where hundreds of Patrols direct the people of New Manhattan toward safety while others attempt to control the blazes.

I look out across the scarlet sky and to the Wastes—a black blot in the distance.

"Poet!" Rook shouts. "We have to jump!"

He points to the far side of the roof where the top of Amery sways a few feet away. No, not a few. Several. Close enough to potentially clear the jump, but it isn't guaranteed. I remember this. My initiation. I remember thinking it didn't seem that far. Now I think I must have been delirious.

A flash of red light illuminates the net I landed on far below.

"They're coming for us!" Rook shouts, taking me by the shoulders, trying to wake me up. "They know what you are, Poet. Who I am! If they catch us, we're dead. Do you understand me?" He shakes me gently, rustling me like a dried-out husk. "Poet, snap out of it. I'm sorry I didn't tell you everything, but I need you to snap out of it."

He cups my face in his hands, and then he kisses me.

That does the trick.

I shove him back and slap him across the face.

"You lied to me!" I scream.

"I did," he says. "But I had to."

I shake my head, taking a step away.

The wind tosses my hair and my dress, the fabric billowing around me in a cloud of creamy lilac.

"Please believe I never meant you any harm," he says. "I swear to you, I never intended to hurt you, but we *have* to get out of here."

The door to the roof is shuddering under the weight of the Guards.

It won't hold much longer.

Rook reaches out his hand. "Please. Jump with me," he says.

I don't think I have a choice. They know what I am, and I'm already dead. I nod and reach for him, my limbs scooped dry.

"I'll go first and catch you," he says. "Okay?" He thrusts the stunner into my hands.

"Shoot if they break through. Don't hesitate."

Then he's off. He races for the edge and leaps, suspended in the air, his arms and legs windmilling.

I hold my breath.

3 . . . 2 . . . 1 . . .

Until he lands safely in a crouch.

"Poet!" he screams. "Your turn!"

The door to the roof bursts open, half a dozen Guards spilling out.

I don't think. I run. I toss the stunner to the side, and then I barrel at full tilt, my boots slapping concrete and my skirt twisting around my ankles.

I focus on Rook, who stands with his hands out, ready to catch me.

I'm here to protect you, no matter what.

He lied to me, but I still believe this.

So I run.

The edge of the building draws closer, and I will myself not to chicken out.

I'm dead if they catch me.

I think of the Guards carrying away Raine's body.

What happened to him? What did the general do?

Maybe I'm worse than dead if I end up in their hands.

I pick up speed, my arms pumping, and then . . .

I leap.

70

My arms and legs churn through nothing as my stomach drops out through my feet. The wind rushes in my ears as a massive cloud erupts overhead, like I'm leaping straight into its bloody, beating heart.

Then I'm falling.

Rook snags me around the wrist, and I drop, my shoulder wrenching as I come to a sudden, jarring stop. The world spins below me as I scream and kick, fighting for solid ground.

"Poet!" Rook is screaming. "Stop kicking!"

He shouts and shouts until I finally register his pleas.

"Look at me," he says. "Don't look down."

I tip my head up and stare into his eyes.

Those green-and-gold eyes that told me I was beautiful and special, that he felt something for me. I see it there in the shadowed depths, but then I remember him searching through those subterranean levels. I remember seeing him the night Raine was taken from me.

"Help me," he says, gripping my arm with his other hand, muscles straining with the effort of carrying my weight. "Use your feet! Poet, please. You have to help me."

I do as he orders, slamming my boots into the side of the building to anchor myself as he drags me up, my skin burning where he's gripping me tight enough to bruise.

"One, two, three!" he counts, and then, with a final heave, I go tumbling up the side.

I crash into him, and we roll across the rooftop.

"Stop! By order of The Shield. Stop!" a voice shouts through the sounds of wind and fire. Rook jumps up, taking me with him, and tugs me behind an air-conditioning vent.

I peer around the corner to find several Circle Guards surrounding the rooftop. I have only a moment to wonder where the Extinguishers are.

"We need to keep going," Rook says. "Are you with me?"

I'm hesitating, unsure how to answer, when another figure appears through the stairwell door.

General Sol.

Her hair tosses in the breeze as she begins shouting orders to go after us but to bring us back alive.

"This way," Rook says, dragging me toward a door. The same one I exited during my first Aria test. He yanks on the handle, but it doesn't give.

"Shit. It's locked!" Rook scans the roof. "Off the building. We've done it before." He pauses. "Poet?"

I nod. "Okay," I say. I'm with him for now, at least until we can hide.

"Stop them!" someone shouts. I look over to see one of the Guards backing up. A ping from a stunner blazes past us, barely missing my arm.

Rook reaches out and takes my hand.

I look over at him as the wind tosses his hair.

He's so beautiful it makes my throat ache.

"Count of three?" he asks.

I nod. What choice do I have?

"One, two, three."

Then we're running for the edge. We leap, and then we're falling.

The descent catches my skirt so that it billows around me in ripples of purple and white. It tugs at my hair as my stomach lifts into my throat. We tip, turning face-first as the ground races up toward us.

My fingers slip from Rook's as we near the net, and then . . .

SLAM.

I land with a bounce, then fly up, my legs and arms kicking on the rebound.

After another few bounces, I come to a stop.

"Poet!" Rook shouts. "Get off!"

He's already on the ground with a knife in his hand, sawing at one corner of the rope. I scramble off, my dress tangling around me as I land beside him and retrieve the knife from my boot.

If I squint, I can just make out two figures standing on the roof.

They jump, plummeting toward us.

"Faster!" Rook says, sawing harder.

The Guards tumble as we slice through the rope. Seconds feel like hours, and they're nearly at the bottom when the strands give, splitting apart and dropping one side of the net.

The Guards must notice because they start screaming.

Rook takes my hand and wrenches me away.

"Don't watch," he orders, and then we're running. A second later, I hear the thuds, the gruesome splats. A telltale crack and a slap of the Guards hitting the pavement. I heave and will myself not to throw up.

More scarlet streaks flash across the sky as we skirt the edges of the buildings and arrive at the plaza between the Citadel and Amery. The entire space is engulfed in flames, while dozens of Patrols try to put them out.

We hide around a corner and peer out.

"They're distracted," Rook says. He turns to me and cups my shoulders. "I need you to pack a bag."

"What?"

"We're leaving."

I shake my head. "I'm not going anywhere with you."

"Poet, The Shield knows about you. They'll find you, and they'll do unspeakable things to keep you quiet."

"What are you talking about?"

"I don't have time to explain everything—"

CRASH.

The corner of the building smashes apart. We both duck under a hailstorm of brick and cement to find a group of Guards running toward us.

"This way!" Rook shouts, and then we barrel across the plaza. It's a sight of chaos, and we lose ourselves in the mess, bursting through the doors of Amery.

The hall is empty, eerily quiet but for the muffled sounds of confusion bleeding in from outside. We won't have long before the Guards find us.

Rook cocks his head, and we turn left, heading down a deserted hallway. I'm still having trouble arranging my thoughts into coherence as our soft footfalls echo in the silence.

"Here," Rook whispers. "I think this hall leads toward our room."

Our room.

The place where Rook made me feel safe when Amery became a viper's den.

Where he read to me. Where we kissed. Where he . . .

I shake my head, even as my cheeks heat at the memory.

Maybe all of that was a lie, too.

We round a corner, keeping close to the walls. I keep seeing Raine's body. Rook running onto that screen. Trinity giving me up to the Extinguishers. The moment when she uttered my name.

My mind is liquid, melting through my pores. There's too much to process.

I wonder where she is and if I'll ever get the chance to confront her.

A door slams in the distance, and we both stop, our eyes meeting as we wait in stillness. When nothing else happens, we proceed down the hall, turning another corner.

Everyone has hidden away, seeking shelter from the storm. We've been lucky so far—if you count any of this as luck—but we shouldn't remain exposed for too much longer.

I peer down at my feet, covered by the now-dusty edges of my skirt, wondering where my parents went. Did they get to safety?

I watch Rook's back as we snake through the corridors. I have at least a thousand questions for him, but now isn't the time. Am I really thinking of leaving with him? Where would we go? To his home? Through the Wastes?

If I don't, then what will happen to me? Everyone knows what I am now thanks to Trinity. Even if The Shield didn't already know the truth, I broke into their headquarters, and they would find me. I'd be questioned, and it wouldn't take long to reveal everything.

"Almost there," Rook says softly as we round another corner and enter a wide hall.

We're deep enough inside the building that I can't hear anything happening outside.

Rook stops suddenly, his hand reaching out to block me. I stop, wondering what's set him off. Then I hear it. Footsteps. Several sets.

We tense up as someone rounds the corner.

Rook appears ready to bolt, and I'm about to follow when I see who it is.

"Knox?" I ask as he appears with Jackson, Sal, and several other guys I recognize from House Fiama.

"We've been looking for you." Knox sneers. He approaches on casual steps, his fingers tucked into his belt loops like a complete jackass. "I always knew you were a *freak*, Poet."

Despite everything, I roll my eyes. "We really don't have time for this," I say. "Get out of the way."

But they close in, surrounding us, forming a wall of losers. Knox stands at the head of the circle between Jackson and Sal. "I don't think so. You're a Keeper, and the Extinguishers want you. Finally, that Robins was good for *something*."

"Knox, stop this!"

He folds his arms. "You're always so fucking eager to run from me, aren't you?"

I inhale a deep breath, searching for patience.

But he has that look in his eyes—the one with the mean streak he loves to indulge.

"Jackson, please," I say, appealing to a more reasonable source. "Tell him to stop. Just let us go. You don't have to do this."

Jackson's eyebrows jump as he looks between Knox and me.

"He's not helping you," Knox says as he pushes Jackson to the side and then strides up to Rook. "This is finally my chance for retribution." He stops, his chest puffing out. Unfortunately for him, Rook has several inches on him and does a spectacular job of looking down at Knox like he's a steaming pile of shit.

Knox doesn't actually care that I'm a Keeper. He cares that I rejected him and that Rook humiliated him so many times. This is all about his ego.

"Is there something I can help you with?" Rook asks.

Knox places his hands on Rook's chest and shoves, but Rook doesn't budge. His feet remain firmly planted like he's been nailed to the stones.

"You can apologize for laying your hands on me," Knox snarls.

Rook snorts. "Yeah, I'm not doing that."

Knox shoves him again, but Rook is a mountain.

"Knox!" I say, trying to slide between them. "Stop this right now!"

I'm increasingly aware of how long we've been standing still. The Extinguishers could be right around the corner. "Move out of our way."

Knox's circle has tightened, cinching us like a noose.

He cracks his knuckles, and I am desperate to end this pathetic B-rate show of fragile male ego.

"No," he answers, and then he lunges.

Suddenly, Rook is swarmed, and someone grabs me from behind, wrenching my arms behind my back. I'm dragged away as the rest move in on Rook.

"Let go of me," I grunt as I struggle against my captor's hold, trying to kick or headbutt or do something to release myself.

"Poet," my captor says, and I realize it's Jackson.

"Jacks, let me go. This isn't you."

I look up at him, and something like contrition flashes over his expression. He shakes his head. "Sorry," he mumbles, unable to look me in the eyes.

By now, Rook has been shoved against a wall, each arm pinned by two of the other guys. Knox approaches and makes a fist, punching Rook in the stomach so hard that he jerks. Rook groans as his head droops.

"Stop it!" I shout, struggling against the iron of Jackson's hold. "You jackasses! Stop it!"

"He humiliated me!" Knox shouts. "You fucking scat! You think you're so special. So fucking full of yourself!"

"Leave him alone!" I scream, jerking my shoulders, my wrists. "You're hurting him."

"And you," Knox says, glaring at me. "Is *this* why you rejected me? So you could spread your legs for this *animal*?"

Knox delivers a second punch to the stomach and then a hook to the jaw. Rook's head snaps back, hitting the wall with an alarming crack.

I scream. I'm furious with Rook, but I also can't bear to see him hurt.

"Jackson, let go!" I shout.

I've always liked Jackson, but he has far too much misplaced loyalty when it comes to his friend. Months ago, he could have easily overpowered me, but they've all clearly forgotten what Rook and I are capable of.

I don't want to hurt Jackson, but he's leaving me no choice.

It's at that moment that several things happen at once.

Rook looks up. His nose is bleeding, but a smile spreads over his face.

"What are you grinning about, asshole?" Knox sneers as Rook wrenches his arm from Sal's grip. His fist connects with Knox's jaw, and he goes flying.

At the same moment, I stamp on Jackson's foot, hard enough to crunch a toe. He howls, his grip loosening, allowing me to spin around and aim a right hook for his jaw. I connect with his cheek, and he goes stumbling against the wall.

Rook has freed himself now, and the entire scene becomes a flurry of limbs and shouts as he fights them off one by one. He's outnumbered, but it's clear they don't stand a chance.

Another pair of hands seizes me from behind, but I'm ready. I grab his wrist and yank, flipping him over my shoulder and onto his back. Sal lands with a thud and a groan, and though I want to kick him in the ribs as hard as I can, I resist.

These guys were sort of my friends once. They're just a little misguided.

"Poet, what the fuck!" he howls. "Where did you learn how to do that?"

"Please," I scoff. "What do you think I've been doing for the last months of cadet training?"

Jackson helps Sal up and they stumble to their feet, both facing toward me with their stances spread. While Rook continues fighting off the rest, I have the barest moment to glance at Knox, whose face is now covered in blood from a broken nose and what appears to be a few missing teeth.

"Don't do this," I say to Jackson and Sal. "You can't really want to hurt me. I know you're both better than this."

They are. I have to believe that. They've never been vindictive.

I see the hesitation in their eyes.

"Please. We have to get out of here. Please help us."

Their gazes slide together, checking in with each other, but I don't get a chance to find out what they'd do because a moment later, more shouts draw our attention to a trio of Extinguishers rounding the corner.

"Everyone stop!" one of them demands as Rook punches an attacker in the face. He goes flying, and my and Rook's gazes meet. We *have* to get the fuck out of here.

That's when Jackson rushes past me.

He barrels into one of the Extinguishers, knocking him over, raining punches as the other two try to draw him off.

Sal goes next.

He shoves the Extinguisher off Jackson, pinning him to the floor, and it becomes a silent signal. Suddenly, everyone switches sides, and more fighting breaks out as several Guards appear. It becomes chaos.

Shots are fired, exploding against the ceiling.

Rook grabs my hand, and we shove through the mess, just as even more Guards appear at the far end.

"Let's go," he says, pulling me harder as we stumble in the opposite direction.

"There!" someone shouts. "Stop them!"

We keep running, bootsteps echoing against marble.

A body slams into me, and I go flying again. Someone is on top of me. Knox. One hand grips my throat, and the other is lifted, the glint of steel reflecting off the dim corridor lights.

"I lost everything because of you!" he roars, and the blade flashes as he swings.

The scream tears out of me on instinct—sharp, panicked, familiar.

This is how it always goes.

The shouting.

The blame.

The moment where I'm supposed to shrink and make it stop.

My father's voice echoes in my head.

Knox's layered right on top of it.

Look what you made me do.

The blade is coming for me.

I have time—just a heartbeat—to understand something.

I am so fucking *tired*.

Tired of swallowing the pain and calling it peace.

Tired of being the reasonable one.

Tired of bleeding quietly so other people don't have to feel uncomfortable.

I'm not about to die.

Not like this.

Not for *him*.

The fear burns out of me, replaced by something hot and steady and absolute. Every hand that ever grabbed me too hard. Every time I was told to smile. To endure. To be grateful.

I make a fist.

And for the first time in my life, I don't pull the punch.

My knuckles connect with his already broken nose, and the impact reverberates up my arm like thunder.

Knox howls as he's launched backward, slamming into the wall with a sickening crack.

I scurry to my feet and stand there shaking—not from fear.

From relief.

I look over to find Rook close by, wearing a proud smile on his face. "Good girl."

I don't say anything—I'm not sure I even can—but can't help the matching smile curving one corner of my mouth.

Knox is groaning, crumpled in a heap, the bloody knife lying on the floor. Rook's expression turns into a mask of rage. He grabs Knox by the collar, pulling him up.

"You would never have been good enough for her, dickhead."

Then he strikes, his fist connecting with Knox's other cheek.

Knox howls before he drops to the floor with a thud.

Rook shakes out his hand as he steps away. "Fuck, that felt good."

He turns back to me, his gaze darting over my shoulder before he shouts, "Poet! Run!"

He grips my hand as we stumble together, trying to find our balance.

We make it a few feet, and I cry out as pain bursts in my left side.

Suddenly, my legs and arms stop working.

My body freezes, and I begin to fall.

71

"P oet!" Rook shouts, catching me just before I crash to the floor. A
moment later, he's hauling me onto his shoulder, and then he's running. I bounce against him, my stomach digging painfully into bone.

Why can't I *move*?

I can hear and think and see, but my bones have been sucked out, leaving
me as limp as Teddy.

I want to do something, but all I can manage is a helpless whimper as
Rook finally reaches the staircase leading to our room and pounds down the
steps.

He bursts into our dorm room and lays me on the bed.

"You're awake," he says, his brow furrowing, his breathing labored.
"Their stunners must work differently on us."

He doesn't wait to figure out what it means before disappearing from
my view. I hear him moving around the room, and it becomes obvious he's
packing a bag. I hear the rustle of clothing. The crackle of paper.

He moves to my side and appears above me again. I blink uselessly at
him, trying to make my tongue cooperate, but it just comes out as a groan.

"Poet, I need you to trust me. We have to get out of here." He watches
me. "Please blink three times and tell me you understand."

Indecision wars in my gut. I know he's right, but he's been deceiving me.
I wish I could speak. I need to know when he realized he was there the night
Raine was taken.

Did he lie to my face?

The rest I can understand, I think. But *not* Raine.

Rook was there . . . Meaning he was at least partly responsible when I lost one of the most important people in my life. My stomach lurches, but I can't curl into myself because I can't fucking *move*. I wonder what would happen if I threw up.

"The Shield is lying to all of you," Rook says. It's not the answer I wanted, but at least it's something. "And if they get ahold of you, then you will wish for death. Do you understand me? You don't know what they're capable of."

He drops to his knees and takes my limp hand. "Please, they're coming. We don't have much time."

I inhale a sharp breath and . . . I blink.

Once. Twice. Three times.

"Thank you," Rook breathes, kissing my fingers before he's up again. I hear him shuffling through my drawers and closet, stuffing more items into a bag. I don't know what he's taking, but I suppose it doesn't matter much.

"I'll keep you safe, Poet." He says it like it's an oath. I want so desperately to believe it.

He's still talking, but I can't follow what he's saying as my thoughts pile up on top of one another, draining together like grains of sand.

He tosses a few more things into the bags and zips them up before hoisting them on his shoulders. How is he planning to carry all that and me? His movements are stiff and jerky as he approaches. That's when I realize he's bleeding.

A bloom of red spreads across his white shirt, revealed by his open jacket.

I make a strangled sound in my throat. What happened?

It's then that I remember the blood on Knox's knife.

He hurt Rook.

I'll *kill* Knox.

I want to ask if Rook is okay, but I can't. How bad is it?

I watch as he strips off his shirt and quickly wraps a thick bandage around his midsection. Then he finds a clean gray shirt and tugs it over his head before pulling on his jacket.

He scoops me off the bed. I dangle from his elbows like a newborn kitten as he kicks open the door, pausing to listen. When everything seems quiet, he hauls me against him, and then we're leaving.

"I hope this will wear off soon," he says.

He sounds almost panicked. Nothing like the coolly composed man I've come to know over the last several months. Is he worried about *me*? Himself?

Or something I can't even begin to imagine? Why doesn't he just leave me behind?

He took a knife for me.

Instead of turning back up the stairs, he heads deeper into the building.

"We're going through the tunnels," he says, anticipating the question I can't ask. "There's a secret entrance that leads into the Wastes."

What?

"They'll spot us if we try to leave over land," he says, still talking. "We're too exposed out there."

If I thought I had questions a minute ago, now they come rushing at me like water through a shattered dam. I whimper, frustrated that I can't voice a single one.

"Don't worry," he says, breathing heavily. "I don't think they know where we went."

No. I want to scream. *Tell me what's going on.*

Rook grunts as we turn another corner, arriving at the entrance we've used before to access the tunnels. He sets me on the ground and drops the bags to the bottom, where they land with heavy thumps.

He places his hands on his knees, assessing me. "I'm not sure how to do this."

Just as he finishes the thought, he's hauling me up and approaching the ladder. Anchoring me to his front with one arm around my waist, he uses his other, jumping between the rungs to lower us. I hear his pained grunts. See the wince in his features. He's badly hurt, while I flop in his arms and hate how useless I am.

Rook groans as he bears his weight and mine, his forehead shiny with perspiration. I'm not sure I've actually seen him break a sweat before.

What a strange thing to notice.

Maybe I *am* losing my mind.

Somehow, we make it to the bottom, where he again sets me on the ground and wastes no time closing the hatch, then slinging the packs over his shoulders. A moment later, we're delving deeper into the tunnels, lit only by the occasional dim light.

If the power goes out, we won't be able to see anything at all.

A few minutes later, I curse my prescient thoughts because the lights flicker, and we're plunged into the darkest black.

"Shit," Rook hisses as he nearly stumbles.

I wonder if this is a real outage or if they've purposely cut us off.

"I'm going to set you down again, okay?" he asks.

I blink, but I don't think he can see it. Nevertheless, he gently places me on the ground, leaning me against a wall. A light flares a moment later, courtesy of his phone. He uses one of the backpack straps to attach it to his shoulder.

Then he picks me up with a wince, and we continue through the tunnels lit only by a small circle. The darkness presses in on us, and my breathing turns shallow as I imagine us buried alive.

"It's okay, Trouble," Rook says softly. "I'm getting us out of here. Not too far to go."

I want to nod. I want to hug him, but also punch him, because I'm so confused and turned around. I want him to keep talking. He said he'd tell me everything, but he grunts and strains against the weight of our packs, his injury, and my limp body. He needs to focus on getting us to safety.

But where is that? And is *safe* even a possibility?

The Wastes. He said he's taking me to the Wastes. My mind screams with the possibilities of what that means.

We keep walking, and I'm not sure how long it takes, but everything feels like it's taking too long.

Rook is sweating, his arms trembling beneath me, his breathing labored as he presses forward. He's always seemed so formidable, so unshakable, but Rook is only human, too.

He stops every few minutes to ensure we aren't being followed. The path behind us remains quiet, but I don't trust it. I'm not sure I can trust anything ever again.

That's when I notice I can finally wiggle the tips of my fingers. I whimper, trying to signal that the stunner's effects are wearing off. He looks down at me, and I blink and blink.

"What is it?" he asks. I groan again, wiggling my fingers and then my whole hand.

Relief softens his features. "Thank fuck," he says. "I was worried . . ." He shakes his head. "It doesn't matter. You'll be okay soon."

He says it firmly, like he's trying to convince himself, and I frown, my eyebrows drawing together. It's instinctual but also like stretching sore, unused muscles because I can *move* again.

"Almost there," he reassures me as he walks.

The sawing sound of his breath echoes against the walls, and I'm not sure if I imagine his pace slowing. I estimate another ten or fifteen minutes before Rook stops and places me back on the ground. He moans as he drops our packs and stands up to stretch his back and shoulders. Sweat drips down his temples and his throat, soaking the tips of his hair. He must be exhausted. I can't believe he carried me all that way.

He faces the far wall, pressing his hands to the surface as he takes a minute. My limbs are tingling, slowly regaining feeling. I shuffle my leg, sliding it across the ground, and Rook spins at the sound, dropping into a crouch. He's pale, the color leached from his skin, dark circles ringing his eyes.

"How are you feeling?" he asks.

I nod, and despite everything, we both nearly smile, because I *can* fucking nod again.

"We have a little way to go until we reach the exit," Rook says, pointing into the dark. "We'll rest a minute. Hopefully you can walk soon."

He sinks to the floor, leaning against the far wall. His eyes slide closed as his breathing labors. Even from here, I can see that he's shaking. I need to cast off this paralysis. If we have any hope of surviving, I need to walk. He can't possibly carry me another step.

I focus on my useless limbs, willing them to move. My hand clenches into a fist, and I slowly lift my arm, like I'm breaking out of a lacquered shell.

"Rook," I manage to whisper, though it comes out garbled over my frozen tongue.

His eyes snap open. He crosses the tunnel in an instant, fully alert again.

"It's wearing off," he says, taking my hand and kissing my knuckles. "Fuck, I was so worried."

I realize all his assurances were as much for him as myself. We wait a few more minutes as feeling returns to the rest of my body. I'm weak and shaky, but I think I can finally walk.

"We should keep moving," Rook says. "I know you're confused and have a million questions, but we can't do this here." Every word comes out of him like a stone pushed through a wall.

"You need help," I say, gesturing to him where fresh blood has started seeping through his bandages and his shirt.

"I'm fine," he says. "We can't stop here."

He isn't fine, but he's already taking my hand and pulling me up. I grab one of the packs and sling it over my shoulders while he picks up the second one.

"Let's go," he says, taking my hand as we continue winding deeper. Everything is silent except for the sound of our steps and heavy, sawing breaths.

Now that he's no longer carrying me and two bags, Rook seems to have caught a second wind as he urges me to pick up my pace.

"Almost there," he says after we've both been quiet for a while. "Don't stop."

I'm exhausted, my legs and feet aching, my throat parched. But I don't complain. At least I'm not fucking bleeding.

A bang sounds in the distance, and we both stop, our eyes meeting in the low light.

"Did they find us?" I ask.

"Faster," he says. "The exit is here."

He points to what looks like a dead end.

I can tell he's struggling, desperately trying to keep up.

But he's growing paler by the moment.

I wonder how much longer he can hold on.

If he dies . . . I can't even think it.

"This is it," he says, turning toward me. He stretches his fingers out, waiting for me to accept. I meet his eyes before I look back at the darkened tunnel.

"Poet, I won't force you to come with me," he says, reading my mind. "But you aren't safe here anymore."

After a year of uncertainty, I stand at yet another crossroads, forced to make another impossible choice.

Another decision that will alter my life forever.

"Who are you?" I ask, and he shakes his head.

"I'm exactly who I told you, Poet."

"Are you?"

"The essence of me, yes. But there were things I couldn't share. I came here to accomplish something, and I didn't think I could trust anyone at Amery."

"Did you accomplish it? This thing?"

He presses his lips together and shakes his head. "I didn't even come close, but my instructions were to leave the city if anyone found out what I was looking for."

"Instructions from who?"

With every word out of his mouth, I have more and more questions.

"My superiors," he says, and I'm about to ask what *that* means when another bang in the distance draws our attention.

We peer into the darkness and then look at each other.

"We have to leave," he says, still offering me his hand. There's no order in his voice, only a plea. I watch his face, his hazel eyes, understanding that the lines of Rook's truth have blurred. He claims he's exactly who he told me he was, but it's obvious I don't know him at all.

I have only two choices.

I can leave with him and take my chances, or I can stay here and die for good.

"Do you trust me now?" I ask.

I don't know why it matters, but I need to know.

Rook doesn't hesitate. "Yes." He inhales sharply, groaning as a wave of pain consumes him. "And I'm asking you to trust me. At least to get you somewhere safe."

He promised he'd protect me. And maybe I'm the world's greatest fool, but I believed it.

Apparently, I still do, because I find myself nodding.

His hand closes around mine, and he pulls me close.

"You'll come?" he asks, relief written into every line of his expression.

"Yes," I say. It comes out as a breath.

"Thank you," he whispers before he turns away. I'm not sure exactly what he's grateful for, but I follow Rook to the dead end as more noises sound in the distance, closer now. He runs his hands over the surface until he flips a latch. The rock trembles and then begins to slide, revealing a narrow opening and a tunnel leading up.

I'm too shocked to move. A secret entrance into New Manhattan. How did he do this? It probably wasn't Rook but these superiors he just referenced.

"Let's go," he says, returning to take my hand.

But they've found us. The voices echo around the corner, calling for us.

"Come on," he urges, and I walk-stumble with his arm anchoring my still-hesitant steps.

The footsteps and voices grow louder.

They aren't even trying to be stealthy.

They're in the tunnel, and they're coming.

Rook pushes me through the opening, and then he's following. He searches the wall, looking for whatever mechanism closes the door from this side.

"There!" someone shouts. "Stop them!"

Rook is cursing, poking, and pressing stones, his fingers trembling.

"Where is it?" he mutters to himself.

The Guards are coming quickly now, running full tilt. A blast fires, striking the rocks above my head. I cry out as stones tumble over us, but Rook is still searching.

"Poet, get up the path," he orders, but I can't seem to make myself move.

Finally, a click sounds, and the door shudders, slowly dragging closed. The Guards are just steps away, and the one out front lunges, just as the rock slams in his face.

Rook sags against the wall, breathing heavily. "Fuck, that was close."

That's when the rock starts rattling, and debris falls around us. They're doing something on the other side, trying to get to us.

"We need to keep moving," he says, taking my hand. His is cold and clammy. I don't know how he's still walking.

He pushes past me and tugs me up a sloping path.

In the distance, I hear the Guards. They haven't found the switch to open the barrier, but it's only a matter of time. "Nearly there," Rook promises as we pick down the tunnel.

I hear the telltale scrape of rock against stone. They've opened the door. Rook squeezes my hand, walking faster until we're running. Our footsteps echo around us, mixing with the Guards' pursuit in the distance.

We reach another dead end, and Rook fishes out his compass from his pocket. It's covered in blood, but I watch in puzzlement as he notches it into a slot and twists.

A key.

It's a fucking key.

I hear a metallic clink and then a loud snap.

Another slab of rock shudders and grinds open, slowly sliding away.

It takes a few seconds before I feel a cool breeze, and starlight filters around the cracks.

With Rook's hand clasped in mine, I watch in amazement as my world shifts again.

It takes another second for the door to finish opening before I'm standing on the threshold of . . . the Wastes.

72

Rook presses me forward, through the opening, and then I'm standing on the outside of my world with only trees and earth and rocks stretching in every direction.

The storm has cleared. I've never been so . . . free, and yet, the air sticks in my lungs, nearly choking me.

Rook is right behind me, and I spin around to snatch a glimpse of the Guards on the other side. I see Knox. His twisted face. His hair falling in his eyes. What is he doing with them?

They're approaching, shouting at us. Telling us to stop.

Rook flips another switch, and the door begins to close.

The cavern shakes, rocks tumbling down. I realize it's been designed to cave in.

My gaze locks on Knox, and I see so much written on his face.

I wish . . . I don't know what I wish exactly, other than I wish things hadn't turned out the way they did. I wish we could have stayed friends. I wish he hadn't humiliated me. I wish . . . this all could have been easier.

Everything is happening in slow motion but also at light speed as the tunnel shakes, the ceiling falls, and the door closes and then seals shut. A roar punctuates the air, and I know—I just *know* the cavern has started collapsing.

I cover my mouth, stumbling back, tripping over the edges of my tattered skirt and landing in the dirt.

The rumble of stone fills the air, and I will them to run. I know they were after us, but I don't want anyone else to die. There's nothing I can do. Just watch.

It takes about a minute while I try not to picture what's happening.

Then everything goes silent save the crackle of settling stone.

The rush of the wind.

A moment later, it's over.

Stillness surrounds us, giving me a moment to catch up.

"Are they . . ." I ask in a whisper.

Rook is on his hands and knees, his head hanging, one of our bags lying on the parched grass. "I don't know," he grits out.

I crawl over to Rook, shirking off the pack I was wearing. "Knox was there. I saw him."

"I'm sorry," he chokes out. "It was the only way to make sure they couldn't follow."

We both glance at the door, the nondescript wall of rock belying everything that just happened.

That's when I start shaking. My limbs tremble, my heart pounds, and I clutch my chest, my lungs turning to lead.

"Poet," Rook whispers as he collapses onto his back. "Poet, it's okay."

"Where's the city?" I ask. "Where is New Manhattan?"

I feel untethered, unmoored, like I'm coming apart and drifting away into nothing.

The city and its barriers are the only things I've ever known.

"On the other side of the rocks," he assures me. "It's there."

"Will I ever see it again?"

He says nothing for a moment and then finally answers, "Probably not."

It might be the most honest thing he's said to me in a while.

"Are you okay?" I ask, leaning over him. "You're bleeding too much. What do we do? You need help."

"I'm . . . fine," he says. "I just need a minute."

"You're not fine!" I shout. "Did you pack a first aid kit?"

I open the closest bag and start rummaging around inside it.

"Front pocket," Rook says, and I dig around for it.

I snap it open and find a needle and thread.

Then I stare at Rook.

"Do you have *any* idea what you're doing with that?" he asks.

"No," I say primly. "But you fixed my bear, and now I'm fixing *you*."

"*Skies*, I'm fucked," he groans.

Then I crawl over and settle on my knees. I pull up his shirt, revealing his soaked bandages. Using a small pair of scissors from the kit, I cut them away to reveal a long gash up his side.

"That asshole," I say, speaking about Knox. "Shit. I shouldn't speak ill of the dead."

"Nah, I'm sure he's fine. He's like a cockroach," Rook says.

I can't help the snort that bursts out of me. "That's terrible."

"But you laughed."

I shake my head and use some wipes from the kit to clean his wound. He lies still, and this must hurt like hell, yet he doesn't complain.

"Tell me something about yourself," I say. "Something no one knows."

"What?"

"You promised you're exactly who you said you were. So tell me something, Rook, if that's even your real name."

He winces as I finish cleaning the wound, his lips pressing together as he groans.

I shake my head, then unwind the thread and feed it through the needle.

"Sterilize it," Rook says. "Whiskey."

I fish out the tiny bottle from the kit and dip the needle in.

"Drink the rest," I order. "For the pain."

He offers me a skeptical look, but he lets me tip it into his mouth.

Then I inhale a deep breath and study the gash. It's a few inches long, and it's still lightly bleeding.

"A story," I demand. "Now."

"When did you get so bossy?" he asks as I press my fingers to his skin and squeeze the wound together. He groans, his head twisting to the side.

"Stop being a baby," I say, and he almost laughs. "Story time. Start talking."

"Okay," he breathes as I pierce him with the needle. "I was ten years old, and I was afraid of the dark."

"You afraid of something? I don't buy it."

He chuckles, then inhales a sharp breath as I feed the thread through his skin.

"My mom gave me this flashlight," he continues. "She told me it had magic powers."

I smile at the wistfulness in his tone.

"That if I clicked it on and off three times, nothing scary could ever come into my room."

He grunts as I keep sewing, slowly closing the gap.

"My brothers would have mocked me until the end of time if they knew about it," he says. "So it was always our little secret. When she'd kiss me good night, she'd always remind me to click it when I needed it. I kept that thing for years, even when I was a teenager. Before I left home, I'd still use it sometimes."

I swallow thickly as his voice cracks.

Another stitch, and his chest heaves up and down.

"Your mom sounds awesome," I say.

"She's the best."

"You're very lucky."

"I know."

I meet his gaze and offer him a small smile before I study my handi-work. I don't think it looks very good, but at least it's closing the wound. Nevertheless, he's clearly in pain, and I need to keep him distracted.

"You know," I say as I keep working, "now that I'm living in the Wastes, I do have some expectations."

"Oh yeah?" he asks. "Like what?"

"I'm not sleeping in the dirt. And I'm not going more than a day without a bath."

He grimaces as I push the needle in again. "Seems reasonable."

"And I want dinner served on real plates with silverware. Crystal goblets, too."

"I wouldn't expect anything less."

"New clothes. A big closet. Weekly hair appointments."

He groans, inhales a long breath. "Whatever you want, Your Highness."

Finally, I finish up, tying off the knot. Then I cover the wound with a set of fresh bandages. Rook is flushed, his skin hot. I whisper a curse, hoping infection hasn't set in.

I find some painkillers and make him take twice the recommended dos-age as his eyes drift shut.

"Skies, I feel like shit," he says, his voice hoarse.

"You are not fucking dying on me, do you hear?" I say. "You owe me answers, and you're not getting out of this so easily."

"Fuck, you never talked to lover boy like this. Can't a man die in peace?"

He's right. I never really fought back against Knox, did I? I learned the lesson from my father never to resist, and I carried that with me until this very moment.

It's like a light suddenly comes on, bright and clear.

"Knox was never worth fighting for," I say, and Rook looks over, blinking at me. He reaches out, takes my hand.

"Thanks for sewing me up."

"Anytime," I say.

"And I'm not dying. There is no fucking way I'm going down because of that asshole."

I snort out another laugh, and then his pale face breaks into a smile.

"I don't think I can get up, though."

"You need some rest." I look up, noticing nothing around us. Just sparse trees and dead grass. "Are we safe here?"

"Probably for a little while."

I nod and clean up the first aid supplies before finding some crackers and water in one of our bags. I share them with Rook, and I think he might be looking a little better despite the amateur job I did on his stitches. It's the first time since I noticed the blood on his shirt that I allow myself to breathe.

"Lie with me," he says, lifting his arm. "You must be cold."

I shuffle toward him and lay my head on his shoulder as he pulls me against his unwounded side. He presses his nose into my hair and inhales deeply.

"I can't believe we did all that," I say. "Why did you carry me out? You could have just left me there."

He scoffs. "I would never have left you."

"But I'm nothing but trouble."

I feel the rattle of his chest as he laughs softly. "Poet Graves, you are the best kind of trouble I've ever found in my life."

Then I feel his breathing slow as his eyes drift shut. I lift my head to find him asleep, his dark lashes forming shadows across his cheekbones. I study the map of freckles bridging his nose.

Softly, I kiss him on the lips.

I'm still furious with him. He still has things to tell me, but I also don't think I could go on if he died.

After another moment, I lay my head back down and snuggle into him.

I stare at the sky. At the clouds and the stars, and I wonder what comes next. I think of the stories Rook shared with me in our cozy little room. Any place that has books can't be that scary. Right? Especially if we're doing this together.

With a smile on my face, I fall asleep, too.

73

The sound of a click drags me from sleep. My eyes open. The sky is just beginning to lighten, suggesting only an hour or two has passed.

It takes me a moment to realize something is pointed at my face.

Something long, round, and metallic.

I feel Rook shift beneath me, and we slowly sit up.

The sight before me leaves me speechless.

A dozen people stand stretching across the horizon.

Rook groans, and he exhales a leaden breath as they all approach, slowly surrounding us in a wide circle.

They're clearly an organized group. They wear tactical gear, though it's mismatched, like they've had to accumulate various pieces to form a whole. Regardless, they're all physically imposing, armed, and clearly trained for fighting.

I wait for some signal from Rook.

Does he know who they are? Are these the superiors he mentioned?

But what I see isn't reassuring.

His forehead furrows. He knows who they are, but this isn't a happy reunion.

That's when someone else approaches, peeling away from the line.

Dressed in tactical pants, a fitted sleeveless top, and combat boots, she might be the most strikingly beautiful woman I've ever seen. With strong, angled features; lean, muscled limbs; and long brown hair pulled into a tight braid.

"Fuck," Rook says, putting me on alert.

The circle closes in, and the woman stops, spreading her stance and folding her arms across her chest.

Her blue eyes are cold, devoid of emotion, but the faintest cruel smile curls on her lips.

"Rook Athira and"—her gaze skips to me, her nose wrinkling—"whoever *you* are—by order of Commander Fisher Sterling, you are both under arrest."

The End . . . For Now

KEEP READING
FOR BONUS SCENES!

BONUS
CHAPTERS

48

Teddy Bears

—Rook—

'm heading back to my room when the sound of raised voices draws my attention.

"I told you to get *out*," someone says just as I round the corner and spot a group of people at the top of the stairs.

And then a scream.

I'm moving before I understand what's happening. A flash of deep-purple hair. A face I see in my mind a little too often.

It's Poet.

They just shoved her off the staircase. Someone here is about to die.

"What the fuck is going on?" I demand as several pairs of eyes turn to me. I recognize them. Two of Poet's roommates. A couple of those sick fucks in their ugly red Extinguisher shirts.

I spot Brick holding something. A stuffed toy. It's a teddy bear, ripped with the stuffing spilling out. Its leg and an arm lie on the floor. Some instinct tells me it has something to do with Poet. I snatch the bear from Brick, pick up the extra pieces, and then I'm barreling down the stairs to where she lies at the bottom, passed out.

Red. I see nothing but red. I take a split second to calm myself.

She needs me to keep my shit together. I fall to my knees and check her pulse. When I pick up her steady heartbeat, I exhale a sigh of relief. She's just knocked out.

I glare up the stairs to find everyone watching. Some of them look ashamed. Not all of them, though.

"You better get the fuck out of my sight," I say. "Before I hunt each of you down."

A few nod and then start to move, but I ignore them as I gently scoop Poet into my arms. She groans softly as I hug her against me with the pieces of her bear dangling in one of my hands.

Then I'm on the move, headed for the med wing. I need someone to check that she doesn't have a concussion. As we walk, several people stop to gape. They probably assume I'm the one responsible. Sometimes I really hate this place.

Then I look down at Poet cradled in my arms, her head leaning against my chest, and she makes me hate it a little bit less.

All I can think about lately is her. And that kiss. *Fuck*, that kiss shifted something inside me I didn't even know was there. I shake my head. These aren't productive thoughts right now.

When I arrive at the medical center, I bang on the door. It takes only a moment for it to pop open, revealing Dr. Perez. She doesn't like me. The feeling is mutual.

"Her roommates pushed her down the stairs," I say just as she's about to open her mouth. She snaps it shut and then nods.

"Bring her in."

I carry Poet across the room and lay her gently on the bed. Another soft groan as her lashes flutter against her smooth cheeks. Her face is soft like this. Free of the tension she usually wears.

"She passed out," I say to the doctor, who nods again. "I think there might be something wrong with her wrist."

I notice it's swelling and turning a bit purple.

"Please give me some space," the doctor says.

I don't want to move. I want to stay by her side. It's irrational, but the truth is, Poet makes me feel a little irrational.

"Please," the doctor says. "I can't help her otherwise."

Finally, I step back, conceding her point. A few other medics enter the room and set to work, checking her vitals. It's obvious they're capable, and Poet is breathing and groaning, which eases the tight knot in my chest. I hate seeing her in pain, but she's alive.

I step back and realize I'm gripping the stuffed bear so hard that my knuckles are turning white.

Quickly, I scan the room and notice the supply closet. I don't ask for permission before I find some needle and thread, then head to the other side of the room, where I sink to the floor and lean against an empty bed.

I assess the bear's damage.

The head has been nearly torn off, dangling by only a scrap, so I decide to start there. Some of the stuffing has fallen out, leaving him a little mis-shapen. It's probably lying somewhere between Poet's room and the stairs. I need something to fill him back up.

I look around and spot the pillow on the bed. I reach up and snag it, then tear it open.

"Hey!" one of the medics says. "What are you doing?"

"Nothing," I say as I pull out some of the cotton, then toss the pillow back up. "Focus on your patient."

I begin stuffing the bear's head, making sure it's full, while I wait for someone to come over and scold me. From the corner of my eye, I see they've all returned to their work, and I assume they've decided not to make a fuss about it.

Once the head is reattached, I sew up the belly with more stuffing, then start on the leg.

By the time I'm finished, Poet is lying back with a bandage on her wrist, her hair spilling across the pillow. I watch her breathing, her chest rising and falling as she makes the softest sounds.

I shouldn't think about kissing her again at a time like this, but her lips are so pink and perfect. She tasted so good. Like strawberries and the rain. We haven't talked about it—that's my fault—but that moment left me con-fused and also wanting more.

"She should wake up soon," Dr. Perez says. "She has a sprain in her wrist, but it doesn't look like there's anything else to be worried about. I'll give her some medicine for the pain, and she should be okay within a week or so. What happened?"

I tell her what I saw, and she presses her mouth together in obvious disapproval.

"Well, it's a good thing you found her."

I understand this is an offer of peace. An apology for how she treated me the last time I was in here. But she helped Poet, so I'm feeling charitable, and I nod.

"You're sewing him back up?" comes a soft voice a moment later.

I look over at Poet as her big, dark eyes fill with tears. And then she breaks down. Comes apart. I'm on my feet before I know it, sitting on the bed and wrapping her in my arms.

She sobs against me, her lungs rattling and her entire body shaking.

I hold her tighter and give her the space to let go.

Suddenly, I want to be her person. To be the one she can trust. To be the soft place she can land.

And for the first time since I noticed her standing in the hall on the first day I arrived, the thought of that scares me only a little.

54

Rook's Night Out
—Rook—

The door slams, leaving Poet on the other side, and I'm having trouble catching my breath. She looked so fucking delicious in that outfit that it was all I could do not to fall to my knees and agree to anything she asked.

She's disappointed that I didn't come. I saw it in the flash of her eyes, and I *hate* hurting her, but this is better for both of us. I draw too much attention to her. I thought people would get used to my presence eventually, but it's been months, and no one here will let me forget what I am. I suppose I should have expected that.

All I want is for her to be safe. And a part of me understands she'll never truly be safe in this city, not with the way they hunt down people like her. Like *us*.

So I'll do what I can.

But keeping my distance is driving me to the edge.

I start pacing the room, head down, shoulders hunched, feeling like a caged animal.

Stop thinking about her.

I take in the mess Poet, Domino, and Journey left behind. I consider cleaning it up, but I don't know if she'd welcome me touching her things, nor do I know how she likes to organize her stuff. Maybe I can help her tomorrow when she's back.

She can sit there and tell me what to do. I'd welcome it.

I admonish myself because every thought leads me back to her, even when I keep telling myself I should stay away.

Looking for a distraction, I head to my corner, pick out a book, and toss myself onto the bed. I flip it open, but I see none of the words as I turn the pages. It's one of my favorites. I've read it a million times. Love poems from the Warming Age. Neruda.

As soon as I heard Poet's name, I thought of it. I wondered if someone in her life named her that because they also had a soft spot for the lyrical cadence of a poem. Then I saw her father and disavowed myself of that notion.

It apparently was a coincidence, yet it almost seems like fate that she'd come by that name. That her very essence contains the same layers and emotions as a beautifully written sonnet.

A line jumps out at me. One I've read a thousand times about loving someone between shadows. It reminds me of her, too. The way she tries to hide herself in the darkness that surrounds her. Except I've watched her emerge from them for the last several months. Slowly, tentatively, but with confidence.

Along with Poet, I also can't stop thinking about the simulation we watched inside the Tempestade today. Sometimes it's easy to forget how easily lives are disposed of in this place. How people are so readily used to justify the "greater good."

Another page, and I still can't focus.

I check the time. She left about thirty minutes ago. This is going to be the longest night of my life if I don't find some way to occupy myself.

Go to the gym? I'm not in the mood.

Go for a walk? That'll still give me too much space to think.

I keep flipping the pages, but after another ten minutes, I toss it down in frustration.

I sit up, plant my elbows on my knees, and picture her with her hair up and her makeup on as she laughs with her friends. I loved seeing her smile as she let herself go a little. She's always so serious. I love how good Domino and Journey are for her. I know she's had a rough year, but she's better off leaving all those people behind. They never deserved her.

My jaw ticks and my knee bounces while I picture her dancing.

Her hips moving in that cute little outfit she was wearing.

Fuck, I want to kiss her again.

Before I give it too much thought, I'm up.

I grab my jacket, and then I'm on my way to find her.

ACKNOWLEDGMENTS

I'm writing these acknowledgments as I put the finishing touches on *Storm Breaker*, and I'm feeling pretty emotional. When I first started writing, I always assumed I'd publish YA books. I've always loved YA. The sparkle. The excitement. The idea of growing into yourself and finding your place in the world. I'm so happy it was finally time, and I couldn't have found a better home for this book than with Mayhem and Entangled.

With that in mind, my first thank-you has to go to my brilliant editor, Liz Pelletier. Thank you for your time, your knowledge, your keen eye, and your unwavering enthusiasm for Poet and Rook. I have never worked with an editor who pushed me this way. Who just kept taking what I thought was already a pretty good book and making it better and better. I learned so much, and you made me become better, and for that, I will always be grateful.

A huge thank-you always goes to my agent, Lauren Spieller, and her ability to strategize every level of my career with me. I always feel like I'm in such good hands. Plus, I just have a lot of fun whenever we talk.

To LJ Anderson and Elizabeth Wayant for this incredible cover. My jaw dropped the first time I saw it, and I've only grown to love it more and more. I can't even imagine anything else that would encapsulate this story so perfectly. And to Bree Archer, Elizabeth Turner Stokes, and the rest of the wonderful art department.

To Stacy Abrams for your keen copyediting skills (and all the other million and one things you do). You saw things my eyes missed way too many times. Also to Madison Pelletier for all your hilarious and on-point insights.

To the team at Entangled, including but definitely not limited to:

Heather Riccio, Molly Majumder, Meredith Johnson, Melanie Smith, Lindsey Staub, Curtis Svehlak, Hannah Lindsey, Jessica Meigs, Deon McAdoo, Victoria Chew, and everyone who makes the world tick. Thank you for your support, your feedback, and all of your help.

To my UK team, Rebecca Hilsdon, Yasmin Anshoor, and Jessie Beswick at Michael Joseph, for bringing this book across the pond.

To Tina Mars. Yes, she gets a whole paragraph, because this thank-you is long overdue, and I promised. Thank you for all your unwavering support and just for being the best. I'm so glad I met you and that we've become friends, and I cannot wait for the world to read your masterpiece very soon.

To all my writing friends, I don't know what I'd do without any of you. Thank you for being there. For commiserating. For making me laugh. On the days when this writing gig can feel very hard and lonely, you make it all so much fun.

And of course, to my little family who had to put up with a LOT of "I'm working, I'll pay attention to you soon" for this one. I love you all so much. Thank you for being so patient while I've followed my dreams.